The Dark Secrets of Oliveto

The Dark Secrets of Oliveto

By

Stefano A. Giovannoni

ISBN-13: 979-8-218-08879-8

Cover design by Ian Garatt/Zavo Design.

Formatting by William Opperman/Keep the Voice Editing.

I would like to dedicate this book to the following people:

Dana, Gillian, and Trish: At different times of my life, each of you were *my* Sofia – a best friend, a person to share adventures with, and most importantly, someone who accepted me as I am.

To my nonna: you taught me so much and loved me unconditionally. You and your beautiful smile are truly missed, but will never be forgotten.

To my loving mother: without you being the "wind beneath my wings", I don't think my imagination could have taken flight and soared so high. Thank you for your inspiration, love, and support.

To you, my dear reader: thank you for choosing this book to be your next read. May your visit to Oliveto be a magical one; one with many happy returns.

Table of Contents

Chapter 0: The Day Before

It was the tail end of winter in the small town of Oliveto, California, and on this very evening Chiara Scuro-Frantoio was making final preparations for what she knew would be her last night alive.

The early part of her evening had been spent at St. Anthony's speaking with Father Michael. She had visited him in order to share her fears and relay her final wishes; she was even able to persuade him to perform the sacrament of extreme unction, although he was reluctant at first, since to him she appeared a picture of good health despite her sixty-odd years.

It was now a little before eleven o'clock, and the late evening winds began to pick up, blowing any remaining dead leaves and twigs off nearby trees, and causing them to rustle down the street. To a third of the townspeople, the howling strong winds were just a spooky sound which would continue throughout the night and cause many a restless night of tossing and turning. But to the remaining inhabitants of Oliveto, those who were familiar with such strange things, this sound was not only known but dreaded—the wailing of the banshee Orla, signaling that a member of their secret circle would soon die.

Chiara anticipated that she had about an hour left, based on a premonition she had had a few days prior. She had spent the previous day seeing her lawyer in order to make updates to her will, and stopping by the bank to secure some valuables in her safe deposit box.

She knew that nothing could stop this night—it was her destiny. She went into the kitchen and filled a kettle with water. Before bringing it to the stove, she peered out the window and watched as the gusty winds pushed the rainclouds overhead, blocking out the moonlight and darkening the evening sky. She turned and placed the kettle on the burner, ignited the gas, and set it on high. A nice cup of chamomile tea, she thought, would help soothe her nerves, and so she went to get some from a nearby cabinet, but she was out. She decided to check downstairs in the basement where she kept a variety of dried herbs in one of its many storage rooms.

When she reached the basement floor, she paused to listen. She could hear the sound of rain pouring down heavily. The lights suddenly dimmed and then returned to their normal brightness. She continued onward to the storage room where she kept all her herbs and various supplies. She found an old apothecary jar labeled: *Chamaemelum Nobile*, and removed its glass lid. While inhaling the calming herbaceous and apple-like scent of the dried chamomile, she took a small muslin drawstring bag from a nearby drawer and filled it with some of the desiccated flowers.

She replaced the lid and left the room. As she headed back to the stairs, the lights dimmed once again, but this time they went out completely; she was now in complete darkness. A flash of lightning, vivid through the barred basement windows, briefly illuminated her way back to the stairs going up. As her eyes re-adjusted to the darkness, a loud clap of thunder startled her, causing her to drop her muslin bag of chamomile flowers.

Slightly unnerved, she picked up her tea bag and cautiously headed back toward the stairs, feeling her way along the cold cement wall. With a sense of relief, she finally felt the wobbly handrail of the stairs and, gripping it tightly, began her ascent. Midway up the stairs, the light flickered back on. She hurried back to the stove, relieved that she was no longer down in the cold, damp lower level of the house. No sooner did she reach the stove and catch her breath, than the kettle began to whistle oddly, so that she almost confused it with the banshee's howl.

She placed her muslin tea bag into a cup and poured hot water over it. Rain tapped sharply against the kitchen windows. The cold, moist winds pierced the walls of her drafty home, causing her to shiver. She decided to go to her bedroom and retrieve her shawl while her chamomile tea was steeping.

She grabbed a book of matches from a kitchen drawer and headed to her bedroom. When she reached the end of the frescoed hallway, she lit a match. Her room was dark, the only room in the house not wired for electricity. As she slowly walked toward her nightstand, the dim light of the matchstick revealed her beloved antique candelabra. She treasured this special gift, which had been given to her over twenty years ago. She finished lighting the last of the three candles just as the flame of the match was about to burn her fingertips.

Bringing the candelabra with her, she went over to her closet, opened the door, and set the candles on a nearby dresser. By the flickering candlelight, she found the black crocheted shawl which she wrapped around her shoulders. She ventured further into the closet, toward a locked door in the back. She could barely see its silver doorknob. She turned it to make sure it was still locked, and, reassuringly, it was.

Chiara returned to the kitchen with her candelabra in hand and placed it on the large marble island in the center of the room. She retrieved her cup of tea and sat down. Also on the island was a large, leatherbound book which she had been looking through earlier in the evening; the word *Malandanti* was embossed on its cover. She opened the book at its middle as if she were checking something and then immediately closed it with a thump.

She took a deep breath, inhaling the tea's calming fragrance, and then took a few sips. She closed her eyes and reviewed her mental list of things left to do in her final hours. She took another deep breath, removed one candle from the candelabra, and then picked up the heavy book and hid it in a safe location elsewhere in the home.

When that task was done, she returned to the kitchen, restored the candle, and sat back down to finish her tea. She took a sip and thought of her late husband Benito, who had died an early death almost ten years ago to the day; how she wished he were there to protect her now.

Her eyes became heavy, and she dozed off.

The stately grandfather clock in the living room rang the hour, waking Chiara and echoing throughout the house. Eleven o'clock. She had less than an hour left to live. She jumped up from her seat and went to the kitchen sink to wash out her teacup. She dried it and returned it to the cabinet where it had come from. She knew her dutiful daughter Siena would be there tomorrow for her Tuesday afternoon check-ins, and even in her last moments, her sense of pride in keeping a tidy home remained.

Chiara turned off the kitchen light and picked up her candelabra. At the end of the frescoed hallway, she turned off the last light in the house and entered her bedroom. She replaced her candelabra on her nightstand and changed into her nightgown.

She crawled into bed and sat up against the headboard with a few pillows propped behind her back. The sudden sound of croaking frogs alerted her that her time was near. She went through her mental to-do list one more time and realized there was one final task to be completed. She quickly reached over to her nightstand and took out a piece of ivory stationery and a pen. She had been in the habit of writing down her dreams in the morning in order to interpret them later in the day, but she knew she would have no more mornings. She wrote out a brief note to her beloved grandson Nico, folded it, and held it tight in her fist.

The banshee Orla neared the Frantoio family home. Chiara could hear the sound of shattering glass from the basement. This was it. She slid down into her bed and lay there perfectly still, listening intently to the now fervent croaking of the frogs. She looked up at the ceiling and watched the ominous shadows created by the candlelight slither and swirl about. She held on tightly to the note for Nico while gripping her bedcovers in terror.

She tensed up at the sound of the basement door creaking open and then slamming shut. She heard the heavy-footed steps of something coming down the hallway toward her bedroom door.

Frozen in fear, she watched as the doorknob to her bedroom door began to turn. To her mounting horror, the door opened to reveal a dark, menacing figure standing in the threshold. She frantically reached for the candelabra, but the intruder quickly rushed up to her and covered her mouth with a gloved hand. She continued grasping for her candelabra, but her reach wasn’t long enough, and instead it was knocked to the floor during the struggle. One of the three candles immediately went out as it hit the floor, slightly darkening the room, and making the mysterious figure’s face imperceivable.

Her heart began to beat faster as she tried to take in air from what little space the gloved hand hadn’t covered. She watched as her assailant reached into its trench coat and pulled out a large syringe filled with a mysterious, glowing, green fluid.

As the dark figure continued covering Chiara's mouth so she could not scream, it raised the syringe high above her. A strong draft of wind, coming from nowhere, suddenly blew into the room, snuffing out the second candle from the candelabra and leaving the single remaining one flickering over the diabolical event.

Chiara's assailant looked into her terror-filled eyes and swiftly drove the syringe into her chest cavity. As the plunger was depressed, releasing the glowing green liquid into Chiara's body, a loud wail could be heard from within the room as the banshee Orla materialized to signal Chiara's last moments of life. Startled, the masked figure whose ears began to bleed from Orla's lengthy cry, quickly removed the spent syringe, placing it back in its pocket, and covered its ears while fleeing the room.

Chiara looked up at Orla, whose ethereal body now floated above her. She could feel her heartbeat begin to slow; her breathing became shallow. Chiara took advantage of these final moments to perform a selfless act. She mustered her remaining strength and spoke:

On this dark winter night of wind and rain,
My body racked with agony and pain,
In this moment as I draw my last breath,
Hide from Nico this moment of my death.

With that, Chiara exhaled one last time. The banshee let out a final resounding wail to alert the town of Chiara's death. And, as Orla left, her ghost-like form drew the air from the room, causing the last remaining candle to be extinguished.

Chapter 1: Spring Break '87

Hey, Sofia!" Nico abruptly called out while putting down his textbook. "Do you and your brother have any plans for spring break?"

Sofia walked over and stood in the doorway of their adjoining room. She looked over at Nico sitting up on his bed, various study sheets and books scattered before him.

"Paolo is going to Daytona Beach with friends, but I have no plans. I guess I'll work on my psych paper for Professor Cerveau's class," she responded with a tone of disappointment.

"Come home with me to Oliveto! My mother has always wanted to meet you, since I talk more about you than school. Plus, you've never been to California, and I want you to see my hometown—we'll have a blast!"

"Well…" she hesitated before continuing. "OK, let's do it! I'll have plenty of time to work on my psych paper when we return. By the way, have you even started yours?"

"Nah. It doesn't matter if I start now or wait until the last minute. I'll probably still end up with a less than stellar mark from the professor. No matter which class I'm in, or how hard I try, my work always seems to be viewed as mediocre, at best. I've just begun to stop caring."

Nico and Sofia had met during their second year at Yale while both were attending one of their required psychology classes. Nico's chosen major was urban studies, with a minor in psychology, while Sofia decided to major in psychology and minor in theology and religious studies.

They immediately hit it off and became great friends. When Nico heard that the room adjacent to Sofia's at the exclusive Hornsby Manor Boarding House had become available, he seized the opportunity and quickly moved out of the campus dorms. They treated their spacious, mahogany paneled bedrooms as if they were one large room, always keeping the connected door open.

"Anyway, I'll make the flight arrangements and let my mother know to prepare one of the spare bedrooms. We'll leave this Friday!" Nico said with excitement.

At that moment Nico's phone rang. He had an eerie feeling it might be his mother calling.

"Mom?" Nico said into the receiver as he answered.

"Nico, I have some bad news," Nico's mother, Siena, said while trying to hold back her tears. "Your nonna has died."

After a moment of silence, Nico responded, "But how? What happened? No, this can't be true! She seemed in excellent health when I saw her at Christmas."

"I don't know, Nico. She just—I mean, I went over to visit her yesterday around noon, and I found her…she was dead. I'm so sorry. I should've called you sooner. I know how close the two—" Siena said, before being interrupted.

"Something doesn't seem right, mom. Was there an autopsy?"

"The funeral director said he would update us once the results were known—I'm guessing we should have an answer in a few days," Siena replied. "The one thing he was able to tell me is that she appeared to have been dead for about twelve hours."

"So that means she died around midnight?" Nico deduced.

Ignoring Nico's response, she continued, "I'm planning her funeral for this Sunday. Will you be able to fly out?"

"Yes. I was planning to come home this Friday and stay during spring break."

Nico reached over to his nightstand and grabbed a tissue. He quickly blotted a tear that was forming in his right eye and then continued speaking.

"I've invited Sofia to come with me, and I'm grateful that she accepted—it'll be nice to have her by my side for support."

"You're lucky to have such a good friend, and I look forward to finally meeting her. I just wish the circumstances weren't so grim. I'll keep you updated when I know more."

"OK, mom. I love you," Nico said with a shaky voice.

"Love you too, my Nicolino," Siena replied as she hung up the phone.

Having heard most of the conversation, Sofia ran over to Nico. Pushing all the books and papers off his bed, she then joined him and gave him a big hug. Nico began to cry and tried his best to formulate a complete sentence.

"We…were…so close. How did…how did I not know…or feel that this happened?"

In an effort to try and comfort him, Sofia shared some advice, "Back in Calabria when I was young, my nonna would tell us that when you don't sense the moment that someone close to you has died, it is because that person loved you so much that they didn't want you to know and become sad."

Nico was touched by his friend's sage advice. And, as a sense of calm washed over him, he realized that he was no longer crying; Sofia always seemed to know exactly what to do.

"I didn't know you were from Calabria. I knew that we're both Italian, but I thought you were born here in the United States, like me."

"No. Paolo and I were born in Calabria, but we're not actually Italian—it's a wild story. Maybe it will take your mind off things if I tell it to you."

Sofia repositioned herself on Nico's bed to a more comfortable position, and then continued.

"Paolo, as you know, is my fraternal twin. He never really cared much about our past, but I had a thirst for knowledge. So, after countless hours of research, I was able to piece together that we were part of a Romani group that was violently attacked one night while encamped outside of Naples. Apparently earlier that day, one of the other children had found a lost piglet in the forest and brought it back to the camp as a pet. That evening, when the autumn moon was bright, a sounder of angry wild boars invaded our camp, having followed the scent of the lost piglet. They massacred most of our tribe, leaving Paolo and me orphaned at the age of six.

"Other than a few memories of time spent with my nonna, I barely remember much of our youth before then, except that we traveled often, moving from place to place in an old wooden caravan that had the image of a big, half-opened green eye encircled by ivy vines, painted on each side.

"The people you know as our parents adopted us a few months after we were found. They have always taken good care of us and provided us with the best of everything. But I've always felt that we were just accessories to them; like another one of their many flashy items to show off to their friends.

"So, after many years of questioning my adoptive mom about our past and not receiving a response, I cornered her one day in her huge walk-in closet—I was sixteen—and demanded that she tell me about our past. That's when she finally broke her silence."

Sofia paused to take a drink of water from Nico's bedside glass before continuing.

"Apparently, she and my adoptive father had traveled to Italy to celebrate their fifth wedding anniversary. While staying in the southern town of Foggia, they decided to commemorate their anniversary by making a sizable donation to a local abbey—probably to get their name on a building or something just as pretentious. As the abbot was giving them a tour, they noticed me running around a decorative water fountain in the center of the sunlit, cobblestoned courtyard. My brother was splashing water on me each time I would pass by him. My mother said she was smitten with our beautiful, shiny black hair, unblemished olive skin, and soulful, dark brown eyes. She had to have us—yes, 'have' is the word she used. And so, a sizeable donation of one million dollars became the price for the 'mysterious Romani twins from Naples,' as we were many times referred to in local newspapers.

"My new father was never able to say 'no' to my new mother's wishes, and so within days we were off to our new home in the United States. It still amazes—and disappoints—me, as to how money can buy anything and bypass laws. I was just about to ask her how she was able to get us into the U.S., when she turned to a shelf and pushed aside a stack of folded cashmere sweaters, revealing an old, worn cigar box. She handed the mysterious box to me and said that it was left with my brother and me when we were brought to the abbey.

“I opened the box and peered at its contents. It contained four items: something rectangular, wrapped in a deep-red silk cloth; two horn-shaped amulets; and a note. I knew that the amulets were to ward off the ‘malocchio,’ or evil eye, as we say in English, and even though I was drawn to the unknown contents of the wrapped item, it was the note that piqued my curiosity most. I reached for the aged, dirty, parchment-like note and read its contents:

Una risparmiata.
Uno sfregiato.
Prenditi cura di entrambi.
- Endora

“It roughly translated to:

One spared.
One scarred.
Take care of both.
- Endora

“The only thing that I could think of was that I was the one ‘spared’ and Paolo was the one ‘scarred,’ since he has a large scar running across his chest from when the boars attacked our encampment. But as to who Endora was, I am still, to this day, trying to figure that out. Was she a Romani from our group who bravely rescued my brother and me, and brought us to the abbey? Or was she a local that found us after the massacre? I guess I will never truly know.

“Now, back to the cigar box and its remaining contents. I reached for the wrapped item and slowly removed its crimson shroud. It was a very old and heavily worn deck of tarot cards. They seemed to vibrate ever so slightly in my hands, and I felt as if they were signaling to me that they had finally been reunited with their proper owner.

“I looked up at my parent of ten years and gave her a big hug. I knew somewhere inside my being that it must’ve been hard for her, after all these years, to finally answer questions about the past. She began to cry, and I could feel that she was releasing a big burden—that she had been afraid I’d be mad at her or reject her once I knew the truth. Maybe my brother and I weren’t just accessories to her after all? Maybe she did care about us more than I had ever imagined?

"All I had ever wanted was to learn a little more about where we came from and how we got here. Now I finally had some answers. Although, one day I still want to find out more about the mysterious woman named Endora."

"Wow," said Nico, "it's amazing that I never knew any of this. I'm honored that you felt comfortable enough to share your past. And thank you for consoling me—it means a lot. But are you sure you still want to go to California with me? I mean going to a funeral for part of your spring break doesn't seem that exciting."

"Nico, I will always be here to support you. I already said that I'd go, and I never renege on my commitments. Besides, the funeral won't last all week, so you'll have plenty of time to show me around the town," Sofia said enthusiastically.

"Sounds like a plan," Nico said, while trying to hold back a yawn. He began organizing his books and papers that Sofia had pushed off his bed and continued, "Well, I'm exhausted and need to get some sleep. I'll purchase our tickets tomorrow and we can pack after our final classes."

"Good night, Nico." Sofia said, rising from the bed and walking back to her room.

"*Buonanotte*, Sofia."

Chapter 2: Off to Oliveto

A few days passed, and Friday had arrived. Excited for their trip to Oliveto, they both had woken up early to begin packing. Once finished, Sofia rolled her luggage into Nico's room.

"Ah, there you are," Nico greeted as soon as he saw Sofia enter the room. "OK. Suitcases packed—check! Plane tickets—check! Hmm…is there anything else we need to bring with us to the airport?" Nico asked.

"Looks like we are good to go…crap hold on, I knew I was forgetting something," Sofia said and rushed back to her room.

Nico walked over to the threshold of their connecting door to see what the fuss was all about. He noticed Sofia retrieving something from the top drawer of her nightstand. As she turned around, he saw that she was holding something wrapped in a crimson red silk cloth.

"Sofia, is that the deck of tarot cards you told me about last night?"

"Yes," answered Sofia. "I always keep them near me, and I wouldn't feel right if I left them behind."

"Do you even know how to read them?"

"I do! And, with great accuracy," Sofia replied while grinning. "In between classes, I have been giving readings to students in the library. The atmosphere there is perfect, plus it is very quiet, so I can really concentrate and focus."

"Yet another thing I didn't know about you," sighed Nico. "I'm beginning to feel like I've been going through life and missing out on some incredible things."

Sofia removed the cloth from her tarot deck and handed the cards to Nico; he then sat down on her bed, unsure of what would happen next.

"Shuffle the deck and then hand them back to me."

Nico began shuffling the deck; showing off his skills as if he were a professional card dealer from Las Vegas. In the middle of his third shuffle, one of the cards flew into the air and fell onto the dark, hardwood floor.

"Well, there's your card!" Sofia exclaimed while chuckling. "That's that Four of Cups. Upright, it means that you are going through a period of apathy and are ignoring what the universe is trying to show you."

"You're just saying that because that's what I was just whining about," Nico said in disbelief.

Sofia turned back to her nightstand and retrieved a book from the same drawer that housed her tarot deck. She flipped through some of the pages and then turned the book toward Nico and pointed to a section saying, "Look! Even the tarot reference guide says the same thing."

Nico read the description:

"Four of Cups—upright—feeling a sense of apathy or indifference about life; depression; missing out on opportunities; not seeing what the universe is trying to offer you."

"I guess I owe you an apology—you sure do know your stuff, Sofia! That card is pretty spot-on in regard to my current life situation."

"I have a feeling this trip will be a turning point for you. And I don't even need my tarot deck to tell you that," she replied with a sense of hope and certainty.

Sofia gathered her cards, wrapped them back up, and placed them in her purse. They each grabbed their luggage and went to lock up their rooms. Together they walked down the long hallway and descended the grand staircase to the entrance hall. Nico opened the heavy double doors for Sofia. The crisp, spring air invigorated them as it touched their faces; a refreshing change from their musty rooms. Outside, the sun, doing its best to push through the fog that perpetually surrounded the property, provided enough warmth to feel comfortable as they walked down the boxwood-lined pathway.

As they headed toward Sofia's car, she suddenly remembering something. "Dammit! I forgot to water my plants. I'll be really quick. Here's the car key—you can start loading up the car."

"Yes, hurry! I can hear the plants calling out to you. 'Sofia we are thirsty,'" Nico teased in reply.

"Oh, you can hear them, too?" Sofia said with a straight face and then turned back toward the manor.

Nico was confused. *Was Sofia being serious or just joking back?*

He put it out of his mind and brought the luggage to Sofia's well-maintained, black Volkswagen Cabriolet. His two suitcases and carry-on took up all the trunk space, so Sofia's only suitcase was put on the back seat. As he closed the rear passenger door, he turned back toward the manor and was startled by Sofia running up to him, slightly panting.

"Geez you scared me." After composing himself, he continued, "How did I end up with so many items of luggage and yet you only have one suitcase to bring?"

"I guess it's my Romani blood—we're used to traveling and don't need much," Sofia replied with pride in her voice, and a smile on her face. "Oh, by the way, I also stopped by the kitchen and filled up a thermos with coffee—we can drink on the way to the airport."

As they got into the car, Nico let Sofia know how much he appreciated her driving them to the airport. Driving was not something Nico ever relished doing. In fact, he would purposely drive recklessly with his friends in order to scare them into always offering to drive.

After driving eighty miles and having sung along to music from all their favorite New Wave bands, they finally arrived at John F. Kennedy Airport. They checked in their bags and received their boarding passes.

"Dare we get more coffee before we board our flight?" said Sofia with a note of temptation in her voice.

Still amped up from the coffee they had while on the road, Nico replied, "Let's! The worst thing that can happen is that we'll serenade the airplane cabin with our own renditions of popular Duran Duran songs."

They both looked at each other and burst out laughing while walking toward the nearest coffee kiosk.

"Flight 711 for San Francisco International Airport now boarding," announced a disembodied voice from the loudspeaker.

"That's us, Sofia!" Nico blurted out. "And the flight number is a lucky one too. My nonna was born on July 7th and my mother was born on July 11th!"

"Now, finally something about you that I didn't know," Sofia responded in amazement. "Oh, and get this; since your birthday is June 28th, that makes you the third in a line of family members all born under the Cancer sign! This is important stuff. It means you are destined to have special gifts."

"Ah, I don't really believe in all that astrological stuff. I just like the numbers and always make sure to use them when I play the lottery—mostly because they remind me of the two people that I love the most…."

Nico began to tear up as he started to think of his nonna and her recent passing.

Feeling his pain, Sofia changed the subject to distract him and said, "I think they called our section for seating. Let's head to the gate."

They approached the boarding gate and handed their tickets to the gate agent.

"Seat 28D for you sir, and 28E for you miss. Enjoy your flight," the rather perky gate agent told them.

"Thank you," they both replied in synchronized harmony.

Sofia and Nico boarded the plane and quickly located their assigned seats.

"Now, I'm actually excited," Sofia blurted out as she sat down.

"Oh. What do you mean?" Nico replied.

"I love flying on planes; I just dislike the wait time to board them. But, once I'm on the plane and we begin to take off, I find it rather thrilling and almost glamorous."

"Well, enjoy the next six-plus hours of feeling like a super star. I'll let the flight attendant know that we have a genuine Calabrian princess onboard," Nico replied sarcastically and then began to laugh. "Maybe they will move us to first class!"

As the remainder of the passengers finished taking their seats, a rather exotic looking male flight attendant approached Nico and Sofia. His pinned-on name tag read: Lucas.

"Excuse me," he said in a professional tone. "Are you Nico Frantoio and Sofia Saggio?"

Nico looked up and replied, "Yes, we are, Lucas."

"Great. You are actually in the wrong section. Would you please come with me?"

Confused, they grabbed their carry-ons and began to follow the flight attendant.

"Lucas, our tickets show that we were in the right section. What's the mix-up?" Nico asked.

"You've been upgraded to first class—unless you prefer to go back to your previous seats?" Lucas said, flashing a devilish grin.

"Nico, you made this happen by willing it!" Sofia whispered.

"Sofia, this is just another coincidence," Nico whispered back to Sofia.

As they made their way past the first-class curtain, Nico thought more about what Sofia had just said, and asked Lucas, "How did we get upgraded?"

"We received a last-minute call at the gate, shortly after your boarding passes had been given to you. Apparently, someone named Siena Frantoio-Kynigós had you upgraded.

"Ah, yes! My mother. Mystery solved," Nico said and then turned to Sofia. "See Sofia, there's always a rational explanation. Not everything is some secret mystical occurrence."

"That's a very kind—and expensive thing for your mother to have done. You are quite fortunate," Lucas said while taking their pre-flight beverage order.

"I'm craving a Bloody Mary, how about you Sofia?" Nico asked.

"No, I think I'm going to have some red wine, even though I'm sure I'll have my fill of it once we are in the wine country. Lucas, Bloody Mary for him and red wine for me."

"Coming right up!"

A few minutes later Lucas returned with both drinks on a silver tray. He placed them down on their tray tables and then returned to the galley area.

Sofia awkwardly reached for her glass and spilled the wine all over the tray table.

"Oh shit!" she cried out and began grabbing all their cocktail napkins to soak up the spill.

Having heard the commotion, Lucas rushed over with a damp cloth and began to wipe up the mess, while saying, "You know, in Malta where I'm from, that's an omen of good luck."

"In that case, bring over the whole bottle," Sofia replied, trying to be playful.

The plane soon took off and was en route to San Francisco. A few hours into the flight, Nico reclined his chair and began to take a nap. Soon he fell into a deep sleep and began to dream. In it, he was transported to his nonna's house and found himself in one of the hallways of the family home. Ahead was the closed door of his nonna's bedroom. He approached it and slowly turned the doorknob. As he pushed the door open, a breeze of stale air blew past him, as if it were trying to escape the room. Almost everything appeared to be as he remembered it, but something wasn't right. Then he noticed what was out of place. A candelabra that was normally on the nightstand was now on the floor lying on its side.

"Nico wake up. They're serving food," Sofia said, elbowing Nico.

"What? Huh? Oh, how long have I been asleep?"

"About twenty minutes—not long."

"I had the craziest dream. I was at my nonna's house and was drawn to her bedroom. It was as if I was floating down the hallway. I—"

"Excuse me. I am about to serve lunch and would like to know if either of you would care for another beverage." Lucas interrupted.

"Just water for me," replied Nico. "I don't think that Bloody Mary agreed with me."

Sofia turned away from Nico's half-dazed face and responded to Lucas, "I'll have club soda. He should probably have one as well. Maybe the bubbles will help wake him up."

Lucas walked away, and Nico continued, "The dream was so real. I honestly felt like I was there!"

"Dreams can reveal many things. Sometimes it isn't a dream at all—you might have astrally projected."

"You mean left my body?"

"Exactly. You said you felt like you were floating. That is one of the signs of astral projection."

"I guess anything is possible, but I think it was just an odd, alcohol-induced dream. I'm not used to imbibing spirits regularly. Plus, we hadn't had any breakfast—only coffee."

Thankfully, lunch was soon served, and the remainder of the flight went by quickly as they watched the in-flight movie—*Poltergeist.*

About a half hour after the movie ended, the plane made a smooth landing. Nico and Sofia collected their carry-on items and exited the plane, heading to the baggage claim area. They didn't have to wait long as their suitcases were some of the first to slide down the ramp onto the carousel. They loaded their luggage and other items into a rental car and Nico proceeded to drive them to their destination: Oliveto.

Chapter 3: Homecoming

After being on the road for exactly one hour and forty-five minutes, they finally arrived at the home of Nico's mother and stepfather.

They got out of the rental car and stretched their legs. Nico approached the wrought iron entry gate of the impressive Mediterranean-style estate, which dominated the end of the cul-de-sac, and opened it. Ahead was a long stone pathway lined with cypress trees leading to the front door of the home. As they began to walk down the path, Sofia noticed that between each gap of cypress trees, manicured hedges were on either side of them; each hedge was shaped in a geometrical design and filled with colorful flowers, currently in full bloom.

Ah, spring is in the air, Nico thought as he inhaled the fresh air.

As they approached the front door of the house, Nico reached to ring the doorbell but was interrupted as Siena swung open the door.

"Nicolino!" Siena shouted in excitement while reaching to embrace him.

Nico hugged his mother tightly. As he gently began to release his embrace, he said, "Mom, this is Sofia. Sofia, this is my mother Siena."

Sofia nudged Nico out of the way and gave Siena a big hug. "It's so nice to finally meet you," she greeted.

"Likewise," responded Siena. "I hope your flight went well."

"It was quite exciting!" Sofia quickly responded. "This was the first time I've flown first class."

"Yes, thank you," Nico added. "We were both surprised when the flight attendant came to escort us to the front of the plane."

"I'm glad you enjoyed my little surprise," Siena said. "Knowing how sad you were when we last spoke, I thought if I could help make your long flight pleasant in some way, then I should—Anyway, please come inside."

As they entered the palatial home, Nico blurted out, "Mom, do you have the key to nonna's house?"

"Yes, I do. Why?" his mother responded, a bit perplexed.

"I just feel a need to go there. In fact, can we stay there during our visit?"

"Are you sure you want to?"

"I am. Besides, if Sofia and I decide to stay out late, then we won't disturb you and dad when we come home."

"Do whatever you wish, it's your home now—let me get you the key."

Siena walked away and Sofia turned to Nico and said, "Your mother is really nice and quite beautiful—stunning actually. Her light, aqua-colored eyes are mesmerizing. I've never seen anyone with eyes that color."

"My nonna's eyes were the same color. Unfortunately, for some reason I didn't inherit that same coloring. My father—whoever he was—his genes must have influenced my eye color."

"Nico, your eyes are amazing in their own way. I'm always staring at them—green with a starburst of gold around the iris."

"I've never noticed you staring at my eyes," Nico remarked.

"Of course, you wouldn't," Sofia said with a chuckle. "Wait! You don't know who your father is?"

"Shhh! We can talk about that later. Here comes my mother. She doesn't like me talking about it."

Siena approached them with a larger-than-normal iron key. "Here it is. The utilities are still turned on, so you should have all the comforts you need. You just might have to air out the house and fluff up the bedding in the guest bedrooms.

"By the way, your father has made reservations for all of us tonight at Trattoria Moraiolo. Sofia, you like Italian food, don't you?"

"*Certo*!" Sofia replied in agreement. Her stomach began to rumble with hunger at the mere mention of food.

"Great. Meet us there at 6:00 pm. Nico, you remember where it is?"

"Mom, the town isn't *that* big," Nico joked. "It's still on the piazza, right?"

"Yes—same building it's been in for almost a hundred years."

"OK, we'll see you then," Nico replied as he and Sofia began walking back to the car. Then he stopped suddenly and turned back toward Siena and asked, "Oh, is my brother coming, too?"

"No, he'll be staying with a friend for the weekend," Siena replied, "I figured he's still too young to attend a funeral service and burial—I thought it best he avoid it. As it is, he's been having terrible nightmares lately.

"I'm sorry to hear that—poor kid," Nico said, saddened by the news.

Nico and Sofia waved goodbye and continued walking back to the rental car.

Once inside, Sofia asked, "So, your mother refers to your stepfather as your father, and you call him dad, right?"

"Yes. Pétros raised me as if I was his own child. He's been a good father to me all these years, and I've always felt comfortable calling him *dad*, especially since I never knew my biological father. Eventually he and my mother had a child of their own, my half-brother Remus, and much of their attention has been dedicated to him—and rightly so; he's a handful!"

Nico started up the car and continued the conversation, "So, the reason why I didn't want to talk more about my biological father while my mother was close by, is that…well, I heard that she was raped. They say that when she was eighteen years old, she was attacked while walking home from the annual Harvest Carnival. She had taken a shortcut—the townspeople call it Dead Man's Path, since it's between the cemetery and the park. It isn't very well lit, and even in the day it's rather dark and spooky, due to all the trees that block out the sunlight.

"Well, she never came home that night. Fortunately, Santo Servitore, the church deacon, found her during his morning walk. She was lying unconscious on the path; her clothing covered in mud and damp from the morning dew. The police said it looked like there was a struggle and that there were multiple sets of footprints in the mud. To this day, she doesn't remember anything about that night, other than finding out a month or so later that she was pregnant with me. I've always wanted to ask my nonna if she knew more about the incident, but since the topic was of a sensitive nature, I never brought it up. Now, it's too late."

"Oh my God, that's horrible. I feel so bad for your mother—I guess it's a blessing in disguise that she cannot remember that night."

"Not only can she not remember that night, but six months of her life prior to that night is also a blur to her. I guess the trauma must have caused repression of her memories."

"Professor Cerveau could probably get her to remember. Everyone on campus says he is a master at hypnosis."

Interrupting Sofia while driving the car under the *porte-cochere* of his nonna's home, he blurted out, "We're here!"

"Wow that was a short drive. This really *is* a small town."

Nico went to the trunk of the car to retrieve their luggage, while Sofia seemed entranced by the outside of the home, and just stood there staring at it. The house was more modest than that of Nico's mother and stepfather, but it still exuded a unique, old-world charm. Similar to Siena's home, the front was landscaped with cypress trees and formal hedges, but this property also had the addition of three majestic olive trees.

"What kind of olive trees are those, Nico? They look very old," Sofia asked.

"Why Frantoio, of course!" Nico said with pride. "My great-grandfather, Supremo Frantoio, planted them a few years after his arrival from Italy."

Sofia extended her hands and stood there motionless. "Nico, do you feel that? There's a unique energy here—I've never felt anything like it."

"All I feel is *tired* from our long journey," he replied sarcastically. "Let's go inside and get settled."

Chapter 4: Household Exploration

They walked up the aged limestone steps to the front porch. Facing them was a large wooden door, carved with detailed images of olive branches. Each of the branches appeared as if it was growing from the edges of all sides of the door, growing toward an impressive cast iron door knocker in the shape of a raven. The ebony creature sat in a perched position facing the door. Pushing down on its tail would pull back its head until the tail was released, causing its beak to rap upon the door. To the left of the door was an overstuffed mailbox. Mail addressed to *Mrs. Chiara Frantoio* was spilling out onto the porch. Simultaneously, Sofia and Nico bent down to pick up the mail and bumped heads.

"Ouch!" They both exclaimed in unison, and then started laughing.

Nico rose to take the rest of the mail out of the mailbox as Sofia continued to collect the remaining mail on the ground. From the corner of her eye, she noticed a small, raised area in the rather worn doormat. Curious, she lifted it up and found a single bean had been the cause.

"Nico look at this. It looks like a fava bean. What an odd place to find a random bean. I'm sure it didn't get there by the wind, so it must have been placed there on purpose."

"Very odd indeed. But why would anyone put a bean under the doormat?" Nico responded. "Anyway, would you please hold this mail while I get the door?"

"Sure. Of course."

Nico reached into his pocket and pulled out the heavy iron key to the house. It seemed to have similarities to the door handle and lock. Each looked hand-forged with irregularities and slight hammer marks.

"*Toccare ferro*," Sofia said in a perfect Italian accent while pointing to the raven door knocker. "It means 'touch iron.' There is a superstition in Italy that touching iron helps ward off evil spirts and protect against the evil eye. It now makes perfect sense why a door knocker might be made of iron. A guest would have to touch it to announce their presence before being allowed entrance to the house. If there was any potential mal intent, then they might be repelled by the iron."

"My nonna told me that it was a wedding present from her mother. My grandparents added it to the door shortly after they took over the home from my great-grandparents—they'd chosen to downsize into a smaller home located next door. It's one of the many things about this home that hasn't been modernized; probably the only house in town that lacks a doorbell. You either have to use the knocker or jingle the three bells at the back door—they're probably made of iron as well, now that I think of it."

Nico inserted the key into the lock and rotated it counterclockwise two full turns. *Click*. The door was now unlocked. He pushed the heavy door open, and they entered the foyer with their luggage. The air was stale with pungent notes of garlic occasionally assaulting their senses. Everything seemed still.

Suddenly the door *whooshed* shut behind them. Startled, Sofia jumped and grabbed Nico's forearm.

"Before you begin thinking that was something supernatural, I have to let you know that it sometimes happens when a large truck or bus drives by the house. The air movement created by the passing vehicle seems to pull the door with it, causing it to slam shut. There's nothing to be afraid of. That scared me a few times when I was a kid until my nonna explained the science behind it," Nico reassured her.

Nico placed the iron house key on a round stone entry table located in the center of the foyer and arranged the collected mail into a neat pile alongside it. Then, picking up Sofia's luggage, he headed off to his right and led her through the living room and to the home's front bedroom. Opening the closet door, he pulled out a luggage rack, unfolded it, and placed Sofia's luggage on top.

"Thank you, Nico. You're such a gentleman. Someone will be incredibly lucky to have you in their life one day," Sofia stated while looking about the room. Then something caught her eye. "Wow, this is a gorgeous chest!"

Sofia was referring to an antique hand-carved walnut wood chest, situated at the end of the bed. Ornate marquetry work, using maple wood to contrast against the dark walnut, displayed detailed images of various types of flowers.

"That chest was passed down to my nonna by her mother—given to her before she was married. I remember it always residing in this room and how much I was drawn to it. When I would spend the night here as a kid, I would wait until my grandparents were fast asleep and then try to open it. I longed to sneak a peak of its enigmatic contents but could never figure out how to get inside. I even tried pulling it away from the bed, but it was too heavy. Looking at it now, you can see how the weight of it has caused a slight depression in the hardwood floor."

The room needed fresh air. Nico drew the curtains and opened the windows. "Oh, look," he said. Sofia joined him to see for herself. From the south side of the room, the windows revealed a lush garden below, and to the right, hanging terracotta pots with white, trailing geraniums were soaking in the last of the afternoon sun. Below them were more terracotta pots, shaded now, but each filled with vibrant, red geraniums.

"I just love geraniums," Sofia said with delight. "And now I can wake up looking at them!"

"Me too. They remind me of my nonna—she loved them as well," Nico reminisced. "But oddly, as much as she loved geraniums, and as extensive as the garden is, outside this room is the only place on the property where you'll find them.

"Now, you get settled. I'm going to bring my stuff to the back bedroom and unpack."

Nico left Sofia's bedroom and paused to admire the ornate marble fireplace that was the main focus of the living room's north wall. Above the mantel was a large portrait of Supremo Frantoio, one of the town's founders, along with his wife Margherita and their son Benito. Flanked on either side of the portrait were bookcases filled with old, but well-persevered, leather-bound books.

Nico walked back to the foyer and grabbed his luggage. He looked down a short, frescoed hallway that led to what was commonly referred to as the middle bedroom. This had been his nonna's bedroom for many years up until the time of her death. The door was closed.

Deciding to face entering that room later, Nico went down a long gallery hallway to his left. Portraits of family members from various generations lined the Venetian plaster walls. There was even one of himself with the family pet whippet, named Dolce, that was painted shortly before she died. But it was the portrait of his nonna, commissioned after her marriage into the Frantoio family, that caught his attention the most; it faced the door to the back bedroom and was slightly askew. Nico paused and went to reposition its tilted gilt frame. What might be considered a minor or unnoticed detail to most, Nico's eagle eyes would usually spot immediately.

Nonna was such a perfectionist, Nico thought as he corrected the position of the portrait. *She always kept her home immaculate, and nothing was ever out of place.*

He continued to the end of the hallway and opened the door revealing the light-filled, garden level bedroom. The curtains had already been drawn, as if he were expected. As he entered, a strong smell of geraniums filled the room. He felt comforted by this sensory reminder of his nonna's favorite flower and deeply inhaled the green, earthy fragrance. He now felt more relaxed and the tension from the day's travel began to release. *Ahh, this is what a home should be like. A magical place of calm, where one feels secure and all worries from the day seem to melt away.*

"Nico. Nico, where are you?" Sofia's voice echoed from another part of the house.

She had been heading down the frescoed hallway toward the closed door of the middle bedroom, when she heard Nico reply, "Follow my voice. I am down the other hall; the one with all the portraits."

Sofia turned around and the floor let out a loud creak, startling her. She quickly exited the one hallway and began to walk down the other. Slowly passing by the portraits and eyeing each one, she entered the bedroom where she thought Nico's voice had come from.

"There you are. Wow, another great bedroom!" Sofia exclaimed.

"This used to be my grandparent's bedroom before my nonno died. When he died, my nonna moved into the middle bedroom. During the course of my childhood, I had a chance to sleep in each of the bedrooms at one time or another. This bedroom has always been my favorite since it has direct access to the garden. Plus, the sound of trickling water from the fountain would always lull me to sleep."

"I love all of these portraits in the hallway. The one of your nonna is exceptionally beautiful."

"How did you know which one was hers? You've never met her or even seen a picture of her."

"I'm guessing it's the one of the perfectly coiffed, raven-haired woman—the one with a regal posture and surrounded by geraniums."

"Ah yes, the geraniums gave it away."

"I truly admire the medallion around her neck. It's so pretty."

"What medallion?" Nico questioned as they both began to approach the portrait.

"Look, right there," Sofia pointed to the silver medallion that hung just above the subject's cleavage.

"I've viewed this portrait hundreds of times and I've never noticed that necklace. I certainly never saw it worn by my nonna when she was alive."

Looking closer, Sofia began to examine the detailing of the medallion and said, "It looks like there is an image on it. It looks like…hmm…it looks like a large, black bird."

"It's probably a raven since the door knocker is one. Maybe geraniums weren't the only thing my nonna favored."

Nico began to feel anxious. He knew he had to go back to the frescoed hallway and visit the middle bedroom.

"Come with me Sofia. I need to go to my nonna's room, and I don't want to go alone."

They walked back to the entrance of the frescoed hallway. Nico entered and flipped on the light switch illuminating the faux-candle sconces that lined both walls. As they headed down toward the closed door of the middle bedroom, they noticed that the painted images of vines on the walls and ceiling seemed to come to life. The vines appeared to move, ever so slightly, in a serpentine way. Maybe it was the low-wattage lighting of the hallway creating an illusion; or maybe it was Nico's presence? Either way, neither spoke about what they thought they had observed.

Nico reached for the lightly tarnished silver doorknob at the end of the hallway and turned it to open the door. The room was dark; lighting from the hallway seemed to be their only way to view the room. Sofia felt around the walls for a light switch, but there was none. Nico went over to the windows and drew open the curtains, allowing the remaining light of the day to seep into the room and offer more visibility. He noticed a small candelabra lying on its side on the floor and began to recall his vision on the airplane earlier in the day.

"Nico, is there not a light switch for this room?" Sofia asked as she obsessively continued her search for a switch panel.

"No. None. This is the only room in the entire house that has no electrical source. While it is often called the middle bedroom, my nonna used to refer to it as '*la stanza naturale*'—the natural room. She said she wanted to keep one room in the house in its natural state; one room not modernized by today's inventions. And this bedroom became that room.

"I'm sure you can guess that this was my least favorite bedroom to sleep in. It's the smallest of the three bedrooms and has no electricity, heat, or air-conditioning. One has to live like they are in the past and rely on candles for lighting, extra blankets for warmth, or opening the windows during the hot summer months and praying for relief from an occasional breeze."

"Sounds adventurous to me," Sofia said with a note of positivity. "Like camping or living at a time when things were simpler. I think being in this room would elicit feelings of appreciation for all that one has in life outside of this room. A room of self-reflection and minimal distractions."

"Would you like to switch rooms?" Nico chuckled in response.

In reaction to his teasing, Sofia playfully shoved Nico. Caught by surprise, he lost his balance and began to fall toward the nearby nightstand. The palms of his hands braced him as they met the doily-covered marble top of the bedside companion.

"I'm so sorry, Nico. I didn't mean to push so hard."

Nico shrugged and said in reply, "No biggie. The distraction took my mind off of being depressed. Now, would you please hand me that candelabra? I want to put it back on the nightstand where it belongs. My nonna once told me that it dated back to the Renaissance period and had been given to her as a special thank you gift. She would always say that it 'protected her during the night.' I'm guessing because it would light the way if she had to get out of bed. For that or another reason, she considered it one of her most prized possessions."

"It's in impeccable condition and must be worth a fortune." Sofia said as she picked up and examined the detailed, gilt wood candelabra. Three candles, nearly spent, were firmly affixed with the hardened, off-white wax that had dripped down their sides. The triangular base of the candelabra was adorned with three griffons, one on each side, poised at attention with their wings raised. Underneath its base, what appeared to be the letters: *VL*, were neatly carved into the wood.

Sofia handed the candelabra to Nico and, as he began to place it back onto the nightstand, he noticed a small piece of crumpled stationery; its ivory-colored paper seemed to blend in with the coloring of the aged linen doily.

He took the paper and unfolded it. It was a hastily scrawled note written in his nonna's handwriting. It read:

Nico never give up on hope!

Sofia peered over his shoulder and mumbled the written words and then asked Nico, "What does it mean?"

Nico began to recall memories of when he used to visit his nonna's home as a child. His mother would frequently drop him off to spend the night. In the evenings, his nonna would play card games with him, read him stories from old texts, and they would put together jigsaw puzzles; all in an effort to dissuade him from wanting to watch television. She wanted to encourage his imagination and sharpen his intelligence. But the one thing he really enjoyed during his visits occurred in the morning. It was not the delicious lemon ricotta pancakes that she would make him, but instead what came after he finished his plate. Promptly at nine o'clock, she would tell him a riddle. He then had until three o'clock to figure out the answer. After every hour, if he did not correctly guess the answer, he would receive a hint or clue. If he were able to answer the riddle correctly in the allotted time, he could pick one of the little boxes of Torrone from the candy drawer and play with the button jar. While the soft, nougaty goodness of the Torrone was a delicious reward, there was a greater appreciation for having access to the magical button jar. The old, wide-mouthed pickle jar with a dented, rusted lid housed a collection of random buttons that had been added to the jar over a span of sixty years. Nico would reach into the jar and pull out one of the unique buttons. He would then get to tell his nonna a story about the button. Where he thought it came from; whom it might have belonged to; what it may have experienced or seen during its previous time attached to a garment.

"It's a riddle! It just has to be," Nico said with excitement. "But we can work on figuring it out tomorrow. For now, let me show you the garden before the sun finishes setting, and then we can get ready to meet my parents for dinner."

They walked back to Nico's bedroom and exited the French doors onto the courtyard of the well-manicured gardens. The sweet perfume of orange blossoms permeated the air and hummingbirds playfully zoomed about. One paused briefly and hovered inches from Sofia's face, as if it were greeting her, and then flew off. Another flew over to investigate the flurry of activity in the yard and rested on Nico's shoulder. As Nico was turning his head to acknowledge it with a smile, it quickly flew away.

Nico beckoned Sofia to follow him and he began to give her a brief tour of the expansive garden area.

To the right, along the south side of the house, was the vegetable garden. Six raised beds covered most of the area and were separated by pea gravel walkways. A few of the raised beds contained the unharvested remains of various root vegetables from a winter crop; others were prepared for a future spring planting or contained perennial herbs. Directly against the house were climbing roses, which scaled its side, reaching toward the roof. An assortment of sun-loving plants was interspersed amongst the roses and completed this section of the garden.

To the left, was the moon garden. Beautiful specimens of night-blooming fragrant flowers, mostly with silver or variegated leaves to catch the moonlight, dominated this section along the east side of the house.

But straight ahead, at the southeast corner of the property, was Nico's favorite area: the citrus garden. Flanked by the two mature orange trees was the grand fountain that could be heard from Nico's bedroom. Other citrus varieties, lemons, limes, blood oranges, and grapefruits, grew in aged terracotta pots placed strategically to create a barrier, thus preventing access to the furthermost part of this southeastern section.

As they approached, Nico reached over and pulled a ripe blood orange from a nearby tree and began to peel it, allowing the pieces of rind to fall to the ground.

"Mmm, my favorite," he said and bit into it. Sanguine-colored juice began to drip down his chin and onto his hands. "Messy but delicious!"

Sofia was more focused on the garden than Nico's snack.

"There's no way your nonna could have kept this garden so well maintained all by herself. There are so many plants, and everything is so neatly trimmed and shaped—it's picture perfect."

Sofia's curiosity drew her further into the garden to see what might be beyond the potted citrus wall.

"Nico, what's over here?" Sofia asked.

"I'm not really certain. That's the only area of the yard that my nonna would never let me explore. She said it was off-limits."

"I can see why she wouldn't allow you into the area. Look, there's Monkshood, which is also known as Wolfsbane, and that's Mandrake next to the Jimsonweed. Over there is Nightshade growing under the Angel Trumpet. The others I'm not familiar with." Sofia said as she pointed to each plant while naming it.

"Sofia, thank you for the master class in botany. And what, pray tell, is so enlightening about your observation?"

"They're all poisonous. Nico, this is a Poison Garden!"

"Well, I always knew my nonna was a little eccentric—I wonder why she would create such a space?" Nico questioned and then changed the subject. "Anyway, we better get inside and change for dinner or we're going to be late."

As Sofia followed Nico back toward the bedroom entrance, she tripped and fell to the ground with a thud.

"Shit!" she exclaimed.

Nico ran over to Sofia and helped her up from the ground.

"Are you OK?"

"Yes. I guess I wasn't watching my step and stumbled on a rock."

"That wasn't a rock, Sofia," Nico replied while starting to laugh. "That was Stinky."

Sofia looked down and noticed a garden gnome near where she had tripped. The gnome had a blue, conical hat, and a green shirt that was belted over his blue pants. A slight grimace was perceivable through his white facial hair.

"Nico, you know how garden gnomes creep me out—wait, what did you say? Stinky?"

"Yes." Nico replied while continuing to laugh. "When I would stay here as a kid, the family dog would always pee on him. Because of the smell, I named him Stinky."

Sofia looked up and suddenly began to notice other garden gnomes in the yard that she hadn't seen previously. She started to feel uncomfortable.

"I never named the other five gnomes—just this one. I remember always feeling sorry for him because of his constant predicament with the dog, so I'd always make sure to wash him off with the garden hose. I guess I should've given him a nicer name, but heck, I was four or five years old when I named him," Nico continued as they walked back into the house to change for dinner.

Chapter 5: Dinner and a…

Refreshed and ready for dinner, Nico locked up the house and they headed toward their rental car.

"Sofia let's walk! The piazza and restaurant are only a few blocks away—it'll be good exercise for us since we've been sitting most of the day," Nico suggested.

"Sounds good to me," Sofia agreed. "I can't wait to see more of this lovely town, and what better way than by foot."

They began their stroll toward the piazza. Numerous times, as they walked toward the town's center, their small talk was interrupted by a passerby's "good evening" or a cheerful "hello." Oddly, each unprovoked greeting seemed to be directed toward Nico.

After a few blocks, they crossed the street to enter the piazza from its northeastern corner. The worn cobblestone terrain was a noticeable change from the smooth pavement they had been walking on. From the center of the piazza grew an exceptionally large olive tree. Its twisted and gnarled trunk rose up from the ground, expanding into four predominant branches. Each arm-like appendage differed slightly from the others. A small bronze plaque before the regal tree read: *The Oliveto Founders' Tree. Planted in 1887.*

"Nico, I've never seen an olive tree like this before," Sofia said as she stopped to look up at the large tree before her.

"As kids, we were taught that it's the only one of its kind in existence. Each branch produces a different cultivar of olives. That unique tree, along with the wonderful olive oil and excellent wine produced from this region, are just some of the many reasons why this sleepy little town has become a top tourist destination."

"That's truly amazing"—Sofia began tugging on Nico's jacket with excitement—"Nico, promise me we'll come back toward the end of the year so that I can see the tree when it's bearing fruit."

"Of course, we can come back. I can never be away from here too long before I feel as if the town is calling me to return."

Sofia turned her attention away from the mighty tree and began to focus on the various people walking about. This truly appeared to be a melting pot of people.

"The people here seem to be very friendly and diverse," Sofia said. "And I've never seen so many little people in one community—it's wonderful."

A sudden breeze touched their faces, and the smell of patchouli permeated the air. Out of nowhere, a man approached Nico.

"Excuse me," whispered a rather lanky man, dressed in vintage attire; his shirt sleeves rolled up revealing his heavily tattooed arms. "Do you know the time?"

Nico checked his watch and then replied to the man, "Certainly. It is 6:06 p.m."

"*Grazie*, Nico! I will see you soon," said the man as he walked away.

"Nico, do you know him?" Sofia questioned.

With a puzzled look on his face Nico responded, "Not at all. I'm not sure where he even came from—he just appeared. But what I do know is that we are late for dinner and better get moving."

Hurriedly, they continued crossing the piazza and reached its southwestern corner where they waited for the traffic light to signal them that it was safe to cross the street.

While waiting, Sofia surveyed her surroundings. She spied a variety of retail stores and tasting rooms, many of which she wanted to explore during her visit. But then her eye caught something odd, something that seemed out of place. On the corner block, diagonally across the street from her, stood: P. Cadaveri & Sons Mortuary. *What an odd place to have a mortuary*, she thought.

"*Avanti!*" said Nico in an irritated tone. "Let's go Sofia. The light says *WALK*."

"Sorry, I spaced out for a second. I just found it odd that a mortuary would be so close to the main part of town. I guess I was trying to rationalize it and wasn't paying attention."

"Oh, yes—an unpleasant surprise to most and a reminder of our mortality. It's been there for nearly a hundred years. When the town was much smaller, this was the main hub for the people, and so everything was centralized."

A few doors down was their destination: Trattoria Moraiolo. Double wooden doors graced the entrance of this famed establishment where people would drive for miles just to savor a slice of their authentic Neapolitan-style pizza. A row of leaded glass windows to the left of the entry doors provided a distorted view of the restaurant's interior while affording privacy to its diners.

As soon as they opened the door, the pleasing aroma of items being baked in the wood burning oven delighted their senses and caused their stomachs to growl in anticipation.

"Nico! Over here!" Siena called out while waving her right arm in the air.

"Ah there are my parents. Sofia, I hope you've worked up an appetite!"

Nico and Sofia made their way through the sea of red-and-white-checkered tablecloths. As they approached their table, Nico's stepfather stood up to welcome them.

"Hey dad! This is my college roommate and best friend, Sofia."

"Pétros Kynigós. A pleasure to meet you, Sofia. Siena is always telling me about how much Nico talks about you."

A now blushing Sofia replied in a meek tone, "Nice to meet you as well, Dr. Kynigós. I've always been jealous of your son's perfect smile. I guess that's one of the perks of having a dentist as a father—Kynigós, is that of Greek origin?"

"Why yes, it is. My parents immigrated to the U.S. from Crete sometime in the 1930's and had me later on, once their livelihoods were established. And, Sofia, please call me Pétros. No need for titles and formality around family."

A rather exuberant waiter approached the table. "*Ciao ragazzi*! Welcome!" he interrupted. "My name is Matteo—I'll be your waiter this evening. May I start you off with some wine or an appetizer of arancini?"

With a commanding tone, Dr. Kynigós addressed the waiter, "Matteo, a bottle of the Satyr Knoll Zinfandel, an order of arancini, and the antipasto platter. That should get us started while we catch up on life and decide what to order."

"*Subito*!" Matteo responded and darted off.

Nico began speaking with his stepfather and Siena turned to Sofia and asked, "Are you all settled in at Nico's home? You know you can stay with us if the accommodations are not to your liking—that house is rather old and drafty."

Nico's ears perked up at the mention of "Nico's home" and he began to drift away from listening to his stepfather's voice and began focusing more on Siena and Sofia's conversation.

"I'll be fine, Siena, thank you. I'm totally enamored with the house—it has so much character and unique period detailing. I think Nico was only able to show me part of the house before we had to leave for dinner. I can't wait to see the rest of it in the morning."

"Well, our guest room is already made up for you, should you change your mind." Siena responded, slightly disappointed, and then moved on to the topic of the Frantoio home. "That home is very unique. When I lived there as a child, the old timers of this town used to tell me that I lived in the 'house that was never built, but rather born from the earth and alive.' I think that was said because the library's historic records have no blueprints or reference of when the house was actually built, or by whom."

Nico interrupted the dialogue between Siena and Sofia. "Mom, why do you keep referring to nonna's house as my house? That's the second time today."

"Well, your nonna left it to you—it's all yours now. And, although the official reading of the will isn't for a few days, I remember her telling me that she was leaving you the house so that you 'will always have roots in this town.'"

Sofia reached over with her left hand and patted Nico's back while saying, "How fortunate for you, Nico. You haven't even finished college and you're already a homeowner with an actual yard!"

Touched by his nonna's thoughtfulness, his eyes began to water, and then he spoke. "Wow, that was so kind of her—I so love that home. I always feel protected and at peace when I'm there."

Matteo returned to the table with the bottle of Zinfandel, presented it to Dr. Kynigós, and then poured him a sample to taste. Once given the approval, he filled the rest of the glasses and then zoomed off to the kitchen. He quickly came back with the appetizers and placed them in the middle of the table.

After a brief toast and a clinking of their glass, all present at the table took a sip of the delicious vintage.

Sofia put her glass down and continued conversing with Siena. "I was amazed by how many types of plants are in the garden and how well managed it is," Sofia said.

"Yes, so 'amazed' that she wasn't watching her step and tripped," Nico said with laughter as he began to feel the alcohol enter his bloodstream.

"Stinky tripped me—it was all his fault," Sofia replied and started to laugh with Nico.

Looking confused, Pétros inquired, "Who or what is 'Stinky'?"

"He is one of the garden gnomes in the backyard. Come to think of it, they look similar to the ones at the boarding house we live in off-campus—Sofia doesn't like them at all," Nico answered.

"Oh yes, the gnomes," Siena added. "When I was young, your nonna told me that they were given to them as a wedding gift. Some aristocratic couple had traveled all the way from England just to attend their wedding—I forget their names."

Nico whispered to Sofia, "Oh no, be prepared. Here comes one of her long-winded stories."

"Anyway, years later, a party was held for your grandparent's thirteenth wedding anniversary—I guess because the number thirteen is considered lucky by most Italians. The English couple had returned for the celebration, and I had the opportunity to meet one of them. The impeccably dressed wife, whose flawless porcelain complexion was interrupted by her bright carmine lipstick, approached me. I was the only child there and so I sat away from the crowd and was eating a piece of cake. Her gloved hand caressed my cheek as she greeted me by my name. 'Siena how are you getting along with the gnomes?' she said with a grin. 'I hope they are being nice to you.'

"With my mouth full of cake and the most delicious butter cream frosting on my lips, I just looked at her puzzled and…"

Pétros waved his hand in the air, catching Matteo's attention.

Matteo approached the table. "*Scusi, ragazzi*. Would you like to order?"

Again, Nico turned to Sofia and whispered, "Saved by the waiter. My mother would've continued this story into dessert if he hadn't come to the rescue."

Pétros spoke up to order for the table, "Yes. One Margherita pizza, one Truffle and Porcini, and…," turning to Sofia, "… you do like pizza?"

"Love it! Part of my youth was spent in the Campania region of Italy, and I developed a fondness for good pizza," Sofia replied with a smile.

"Wonderful," turning back to Matteo, "we'll also have one of the house special pizzas."

"*Subito signore*!" And Matteo darted off once again to give the kitchen their order.

"Mom, I want to know more about nonna," Nico asked. "When I went to her room, I found a crumpled note on the nightstand. It was a message for me."

"Nico, it was terrible. The day I found her—she had this awful, frozen look of terror on her face. One of her hands was reaching toward the nightstand—the other held a wadded piece of paper clutched tightly to her chest. I guess I was in such shock that day, that when the funeral director and his two sons came to remove the body, I must've unconsciously put your note on the nightstand and forgotten all about it."

Anxious to learn more, Nico continued his questioning, "You must have received the coroner's report by now? Did he say what the cause of death was?"

"The report stated it was SCD—Sudden Cardiac Death. I was told she died quickly."

"It just seems odd. She appeared to be so healthy and active. I mean, anyone at her age who can keep an entire house spotless and still have time to care for a large garden, must be in extreme good health, or has a good housekeeper and gardener."

"To my knowledge, she never had a housekeeper or gardener. Somehow, she managed to do it all on her own after your nonno died. She was always doing something and was very active in the community."

Breaking the rather somber moment, Matteo arrived at the table with three thin-crusted pizzas and placed the food before them.

"*Mangiamo*!" Siena said with gusto in an effort to lighten the mood.

A few minutes later Matteo returned to check on their table. With a grin on his face, he said, "And is the southern-Italian girl enjoying her pizza?"

Caught by surprise, Sofia quickly swallowed her bite in order to respond. "This is the best pizza I have had outside of Naples! What's your secret?"

"*Arrangiarsi*! The art of making something out of almost nothing. We accomplish this with three main ingredients: the best imported 00 flour from the motherland; authentic sun-ripened San Marzano tomatoes; and the special ingredient—*l'acqua*; the water.

"Similar to Mount Vesuvius, but on a smaller scale, the mountain that is a backdrop to our charming town, is actually a dormant volcano; its mineral springs provide the town's drinking water. We use it when making the pizza dough since the pH is perfect and it reacts well with the yeast, leading to a perfect crust."

"That explains it! If only you delivered to Yale University, you'd make millions," Sofia suggested.

After enjoying the delicious dinner, followed by tiramisu and espresso, Nico and Sofia said their goodnights.

"Thank you, Doctor—I mean Pétros," Sofia began to blush again, "and Siena for this wonderful dinner, and making me feel so welcomed."

"We're delighted to have you here," Siena replied. She then turned to Nico and, while pinching his left cheek, continued, "I am glad my Nicolino has such a good friend to be here for him."

"Mom, stop! You're embarrassing me," Nico said in a sarcastic tone.

"You two enjoy the rest of the evening—the night is still young and there's a wonderful moon out tonight. You never know what can happen!"

"I'm going to show Sofia around the piazza so we can hopefully walk-off some calories, and then we'll probably head back to the house."

Pétros put his arm around Siena and replied, "Very good, son. Take good care of her." The two then waved goodbye and began walking to their car.

"Good night," Nico and Sofia replied in unison.

"Sofia, I saw you blushing a few times tonight when my dad spoke to you. Do you have the hots for him?"

"I can't help it—he's quite striking," Sofia replied while giggling.

"I'm just giving you a bad time. Many of the woman in town find him attractive, so you'd have quite the competition. Unfortunately for you, and the others, he's completely devoted to my mother, and she is madly in love with him."

They began their walk around the piazza to browse the variety of stores surrounding it. While heading back in the direction of the mortuary, Sofia stopped at a store window on the corner.

"Schwartzman's Quality Clothing," Sofia read the store name out loud. "We're definitely coming back here during the day—you know me and clothes shopping! And we need to find you some new clothes—you're always wearing the same pair of shorts."

"You're right, I'm totally due for a wardrobe update," Nico replied. "Schwartzman's has always been one of my favorite stores. The owners are genuinely nice and give back to the community, plus all the clothing is made by them."

"Too bad the blinds on the windows are down—you can't see anything inside," Sofia said, slightly disappointed. "You'd think they'd want people walking by in the evening to see their designs to entice them to return the following day."

"I think they change out the mannequins every night. I actually don't recall ever having seen the same displays for longer than a day,"

Nico replied, trying to offer Sofia a plausible reason for the windows being covered.

Continuing their stroll, they crossed the street and approached the mortuary. A large raven abruptly swooped down from the air and startled them as it landed on the building's sign. It looked down at Nico and Sofia and let out an ominous *kraa-kraa*.

A feeling of dread suddenly began to overcome Sofia. Her chest began to tighten as her breathing increased. The raven continued maniacally—*kraa-kraa*—and Sofia could feel her heart beating faster and faster, as she tried to catch her breath.

Nico put his hand on Sofia's back, gently rubbing it in an effort to calm her. "Breathe slowly, Sofia. Take deep breaths. Everything is going to be OK."

The raven continued calling out with an increased tempo. Nico turned with fury and yelled, "Quiet!"

The raven looked at them in silence and then flew away. A sense of calm returned to Sofia and her breathing regained its normal rhythm.

"Nico, I don't know what happened. I've never hyperventilated before. It's such a scary feeling—I don't know what I would've done if you weren't here."

"I'll always be there for you Sofia." Nico embraced her for a minute and then pulled back to look at her. "Hey, let's cross the street and leave this part of the evening behind us. Time for some ice cream from the corner drugstore. My mom would always bring me there for a scoop to cheer me up."

With a sad look on her face, Sofia asked, "Do they have gelato?"

"Of course, they do!"

Sofia's eyes lit up and she began to smile.

They crossed the street and continued their walk along the piazza's west side, passing by Edoardo's Emporium, Pendolino Savings & Loan, D. Grigio Fine Arts, and finally reaching their destination: Doc's Drugstore & Soda Shop.

Holding the door open for Sofia, Nico enthusiastically spoke, "Prepare for the best gelato you've ever tasted!"

Doc's Drugstore & Soda Shop was truly a throwback to the 50's. With its original soda fountain and décor in the front and a complete drugstore in the back, this was a popular stop for people of all ages. Autographed pictures of movie stars who had visited this hotspot, filled the walls behind the counter.

"Ah, still looks the same—so many memories!" Nico said. "My first after-school job was behind that counter making milkshakes for all my friends. Now, another lucky high schooler has the job."

"What would you like, Miss?" said the modern-day soda jerk in a rather flirty tone.

"Miss? Sounds so proper," Sofia began to giggle. Then, spotting his name badge, which read *Tomás*, she continued, "Tomás, I'll have a scoop of chocolate mint gelato in a cannoli cone."

"And for you sir?"

"I'll have the Meyer lemon sorbet in a cup," Nico replied.

"Of all the choices of ice cream and gelato, you choose the sorbet," Sofia joked.

"I was set on having gelato but then I saw that sorbet—you know how much I love anything made from lemons."

"Here you go," said Tomás, as he handed them their desserts. "That will be $6.00."

Nico paid the tab and they both walked outside, deciding to eat while continuing their walk.

Crossing the street to the north side of the piazza, they passed Mystic Tea & Herbs and stopped in front of S. Frantoio & Company Real Estate.

"Nico, is this your family's business?"

"Yeah—the town's first real estate company," Nico responded with pride. "And still in the same building, after almost a century. Just like the other three founding families, who each still have an active business on the piazza: Moraiolo's, where we had dinner; the bank that we passed; and Filippo Ascolano, Esq., the town's top lawyer, which is on the east side of the piazza, between the Hotel Oliveto and our local newspaper."

"The piazza reminds me of a giant Monopoly board and the four founding families are the railroads," Sofia said just before taking a big bite into her cannoli cone.

"Yeah, I never thought of it like that, but you're right," Nico paused for a second to scoop out the last bit of sorbet from his cup. "Sofia, are you up for something impulsive before we head home? It's still early, and I'm still a little buzzed from the drinks at dinner." Nico said with a thrill of excitement in his voice.

"Like what?" Sofia asked.

With a devilish grin, Nico paused briefly to build excitement and then blurted out, "Tattoos!"

"I'm so in—it's the spring equinox after all; a time of change and new beginnings—let's do it!" Sofia said in agreement.

Noticing something from the corner of her eye, she turned away from Nico. To the right of the real estate office was an old, boarded-up building. She pointed up to its partially uncovered, original signage:

The G   n's   aw

"What was here?" Sofia asked.

"Honestly, I don't know. It's been boarded up ever since I was a kid. I am surprised no one has done anything with it after all this time. Come on, let's get to the tattoo shop before they close; it should be around this corner.

"Wait," Sofia said, noticing a knothole in one of the higher placed pieces of lumber covering the building's façade. "Give me a boost. There is a natural peephole in the wood—I want to take a look."

Nico knelt down, locked his fingers together to create a place for Sofia to place her foot, and lifted her up to the knothole.

It took a few seconds for her eye to focus as she pressed against the wood to get a good view of the building's contents. "Incredible!" Sofia exclaimed.

Nico lowered her back down to the ground and asked, "So what's in there? I'll have to admit you've got my curiosity piqued now."

"Well, it was hard to see completely, but with the nearby streetlights beaming through the gaps in the wood I was able to make out that it's a bar. And the odd thing is, since you said it's been boarded up for all these years, it looks like it's been frozen in time. All the tables seem to be in place, a variety of liquor bottles are on the wall behind the bar—nothing appears to have been disturbed."

"Too bad it's not open for business—this is a prime space for a bar," Nico commented. "Come, let's go."

Chapter 6: The Boy with the Griffon Tattoo

Rounding the corner, they could see a faint glow coming from the alleyway ahead. A sign on one of the buildings at the beginning of the alley read: *Vicolo Fato / Fate Alley*. They approached and looked down the narrow walkway, which cut through the center of the block and eventually ended in darkness. A glowing sign ahead was the only source of light.

"I don't remember passing by this alleyway when we walking to dinner," Sofia commented.

"Neither do I," Nico responded. "But at least I think we've found the tattoo shop. That neon arrow must be pointing to the entrance. Let's go."

As they approached, Sofia looked up at the glowing arrow which was about six feet above her. It seemed to somehow dance and move about. She squinted her eyes to get a better focus. "Nico that isn't a neon sign. It looks like...like…like fireflies."

"Wow, you're right!" Nico responded in amazement. "I am not sure how this is even possible. West coast fireflies are rarely seen glowing. And they are just hovering there in formation—nothing is containing them and preventing them from flying away. This is amazing."

They turned away from the awe-inspiring insect display and faced the doorway. A sign on the door read: *Indelible Delights – Your Skin, Our Ink.*

Nico reached to open the door but there was no door handle or knob. He tried pushing the door inward, but it would not budge.

"How are we supposed to get in?" Sofia said in a frustrated tone.

Looking around, Nico spied three tiny bells hanging to the right of the door; their dark color and size made them almost imperceptible to the eye. Not seeing a proper way to ring them, he passed his hand through them. The tintinnabulation of the three bells echoed for a few seconds and then the door clicked open.

"There. We're in!" Nico said and smiled.

They stepped into what appeared to be a waiting area for customers; the faint smell of patchouli revisited their senses once again. A worn Persian rug covered most of the terracotta tiled floor, and the walls were covered with numerous sketches of various tattoo designs. Opposite a comfy looking, yet well-worn leather couch was a counter with an antique cash register. To the left of the counter was a large paisley-patterned floor-length curtain that closed off the room to what they assumed were more rooms beyond it.

Nico closed the door behind them. A light *click* was heard; the door must have locked itself. They walked over to the couch and sat down. A small coffee table had design albums on it. They each picked up an album and started thumbing through for ideas.

"Any idea of what you are going to get?" Nico asked Sofia.

"I'm feeling inspired by the hummingbird that first greeted me in your nonna's backyard. I'm thinking of having it drawn on my inner wrist so that when I hold it up to look at it, it will mimic that first magical moment in the yard as it hovered in front of my face.

"That's a totally rad idea—I like it! For mine, I'm thinking of a griffon on my right bicep. They've always been my favorite mythical creature—wise like an eagle and strong like a lion."

"Kind of like you!" Sofia tried to say somewhat seriously, before busting out into laughter.

"Hello!" spoke a rather waif-like female as she came out from behind the curtain. Her eyes fixed on Nico, as she continued to speak, "Are you here for a tattoo?"

Sofia quickly responded, "*We* both are—this will be our first time."

"Wonderful. My name is Fawn. Let me get my father from the back and we can get started."

Fawn drew back the curtain with her hand and headed back to where she had come from. Nico and Sofia could hear sounds of whispering coming from the unknown back area.

"What do you suppose they are chatting about? I could've sworn I heard your last name mentioned," Sofia asked.

"I don't know. She's been back there for almost five minutes now," Nico said with a tinge of irritation in his voice. "I wonder what the holdup is."

Fawn returned carrying a small serving tray; a teapot and two cups with saucers balanced on top of it. "I made you some herbal tea to help you relax—it's our special blend. First-timers usually benefit from something calming—it helps them acclimate to the sensation of the needle."

Setting the tray down on the coffee table, Fawn poured Nico and Sofia each a cup of the fragrant, loose tea.

Sofia picked up one of the cups and inhaled the herbal aroma. "Chamomile, lavender, lemon balm, and…"—Sofia took another inhale hoping to decipher a possible fourth ingredient—"Passionflower!"

Fawn looked over at Nico and responded, "Wow, she's good! Those are the exact four ingredients."

"She's a total phenom when it comes to herbs and other flora," Nico boasted.

Suddenly, from nowhere, a disembodied male voice chimed in, "Yes, she seems to be quite gifted."

Nico and Sofia looked around to see who had spoken. The curtain once again was drawn back and a man appeared; they gathered he might be Fawn's father. He looked familiar.

Sofia whispered to Nico, "Isn't that the man from the piazza that asked us the time?"

Nico quietly responded, "Yes, that's him. I recognize the tattoos on his arms. I guess he was right when he said: 'I will see you soon.'"

"Nico, my name is Sterling. I'll be creating your tattoo. You've already met my daughter Fawn." He then looked over toward Sofia and continued, "She's an excellent artist and will make sure your desired image is almost life-like. Now finish up your tea and follow us."

Nico and Sofia each took another quick sip and put their cups back on the tray.

"Father, wait," Fawn interrupted and turned to Nico and Sofia. "Are you two up for a quick reading of your tea leaves? I'm still learning and am always grateful for an opportunity to practice."

Sofia's Romani blood was all too familiar with the custom of reading of tea leaves. And, while her primary method of fortune telling was reading tarot cards, she was also well versed at reading tea leaves. She now relished the challenge to see how well Fawn could do and the opportunity to give her a few pointers.

"Sure, let's test your skills," said Sofia with a tone of doubt in her voice.

"OK. With your left hand, take your teacup by the handle and swirl the remaining contents in a counterclockwise direction three times. Then turn the teacup over onto your saucer."

They did as Fawn asked and sat there patiently as she turned over each cup. She peered into Nico's cup first.

"Ah, a lot of symbols! I'll start with your past first. Here, I see an airplane, which means you recently traveled. To the right of the handle, near the lip of the cup in the area representing the present, I see a wheel—this means that change is about to happen in the next twelve to twenty-four hours. Near the wheel, further down in the cup is another symbol—a key! The key represents a need to be cautious and aware in the coming week. I see two more symbols. Adjacent to the key is an ant. This means that an impending trial or test will begin soon. And the final symbol I see…is a tree. This is in the area of the cup representing home and self, which is near the handle. The image of the tree means strength or help is coming—you will either find this at home or from within yourself."

"Awesome! I can't wait to see how the next few days play out," said Nico.

"OK, let's take a look at Sofia's cup. Hmm. Father, come here and take a look at this. I've never seen this before."

"What is it, Fawn?" Sterling responded as he moved closer to peer into Sofia's cup.

"She has the same symbols as Nico! What are the odds of two people having their leaves end up in the same formation?" Fawn exclaimed with amazement.

"Well, what do you think that means?" Sofia asked.

"I don't know," replied Fawn. "In all of the tomes of tasseography that I've studied, there was never mention of what was meant when two people have a duplicate reading."

"It means that he and I will share a similar fate—the journey in the coming week will be one that is shared by us both. I'll have to give you credit though; you did interpret the symbols correctly. Now I'm the one who is impressed!" said Sofia.

"As my father said, you are truly gifted," Fawn said, in awe of Sofia's vast knowledge.

"That's so kind of you to say. I guess there are many things I've retained from my Romani heritage."

"Come. Let me take you back so we can get started. I have so many questions I want to ask you about Romani culture and lore."

Sofia arose from the couch and followed Fawn past the curtain to the back area.

"Nico, shall we get started on your tattoo? Follow me this way," said Sterling.

Nico followed Sterling past the curtain and down a long hallway. Doors on either side lined the hallway. *Very reminiscent of a bordello*, thought Nico. At the end of the hallway, he could see a small kitchenette-like area, two sinks, a tea and coffee area, and a small refrigerator, all framed by cabinetry for storage. As he approached the end of the hallway, he could hear the laughter of Sofia and Fawn; apparently, they were bonding well.

Sterling opened the last door on the right. "Have a seat, Nico, and make yourself comfortable. So, have you decided on a design?"

"Yes, sir. I'd like a griffon on my right bicep. I saw two images in the design books that I was drawn to. One was of the griffon lying on the ground asleep and looking peaceful; the other was of a griffon sitting on its hind legs at attention and with one claw raised. I'll let you decide what you think would look best—for some reason, I feel that I can trust you."

"Very good choice—not only in trusting me, but the image as well," Sterling chuckled. "Take off your shirt so that I can prep the area before I begin."

While Sterling shaved and sterilized the area on Nico's bicep, a gentle tone came from his voice as he said, "My condolences to you and your family. Your grandmother was a wonderful member of this community and has helped many of *our* people."

"Thank you. I appreciate that. I was extremely close to her—she was a wonderful and incredibly wise woman," Nico responded as his eyes began to tear up.

Sterling inserted a sterile needle into the tattoo pen and offered some words of reassurance to Nico, "Just relax now. I'll try to make this as painless as possible."

Nico took a glimpse at the needled device which was about to permanently mark his virgin flesh. It was absolutely captivating; antique gold in color and with various symbols engraved into it.

"Wow, that looks like it could be extremely old, yet appears to be in mint condition. You must really take good care of your equipment."

"It has been in the family for a very, very long time. Now keep still, I'm going to begin," Sterling replied.

Nico braced himself. The buzzing sound grew louder as the tattoo pen approached his bicep. *There's no backing out now*, he thought.

As the shiny, stainless-steel needle began to pierce his skin, he winced ever so slightly. Then, almost immediately, he became accustomed to the stinging, vibrating sensation, and was able to ignore any further discomfort. His mind started to wander off as his body began to relax. Now in a dreamlike state, he saw himself back at his nonna's home, but things were different; he was in the past, in the front bedroom. He was assisting his nonna with making the bed. He intensely watched her fluff up one of the pillows and then tried to duplicate her actions with the other pillow. "Bravo!" she commended him. Then she went to the end of the bed near the antique chest and grabbed the top of the coverlet. Nico grabbed the coverlet from his side of the bed and helped her pull it up and realign it. "Nonna, what is in that old chest? I've never been able to open it." Nico asked. His nonna smiled and said, "Only a lady can open it, but one day, when the time is right, you'll be able to see its contents."

"Nico, are you OK?" Sterling asked, slightly jarring Nico out of his memory. "I'm almost finished, just need to step out and get more ink."

"Oh, yeah, I'm fine. I guess I spaced out for a bit," Nico replied.

Sterling left the room and closed the door behind him. Nico could hear his footsteps walking down the hallway, followed by the sound of running water. *He must be at the end of the hall, in the kitchen area*, Nico thought.

Nico then heard the brief sound of someone crying out. It sounded like a male voice in pain, so it must have been Sterling. *What could have happened?* he thought.

A few moments later Sterling returned to the room carrying a small ceramic cup. He sat down and said to Nico, "OK, let's finish your tattoo."

Nico noticed that Sterling's left wrist was now bandaged. "Did you hurt yourself out there?" Nico asked.

"Oh, I…I scraped my wrist against one of the cabinet doors. It's nothing," Sterling replied. Once again, the tattoo pen resumed its buzzing and Nico felt the now familiar sensation in his arm as Sterling continued his artistry.

After about five minutes, Sterling looked up and said, "There, all done. Some of my finest work!" He quickly cleaned the area and covered the tattoo before Nico could view it. "Let me walk you to the front. I think your friend Sofia is there waiting."

Nico got up and put his shirt back on. He walked to the front with Sterling and saw Sofia and Fawn sitting on the couch talking and laughing, like longtime friends.

"Looks like you two hit it off well," Nico said.

"Actually, we did," replied Sofia. "Surprisingly, we have a lot in common."

"I am so glad to hear that. The three of us should meet up for drinks one night," Nico said and then turned to Sterling and continued, "Sterling, how much do we owe you for the tattoos? I'd like to pay for Sofia's as well as mine."

Sterling smiled and replied, "No charge. Your grandmother has done so much for this community that we are forever in her debt."

Sofia stood up and responded to Sterling's comment. "That's very kind of you. Maybe one day we'll be able to do something nice for you."

"Yes, I'm sure you will," Sterling replied with a grin.

Sofia and Nico waved goodbye and exited the building. Exhausted from their long day, they headed home to get some rest.

Chapter 7: The Morning After

Sofia woke up early but was still exhausted from the events of the previous evening. She fought the urge to go back to sleep and got out of bed. Grabbing her favorite oversized college sweater from her suitcase, she put it on. Barefoot, she decided to explore the rest of the house. She walked through the living room and into the foyer. She had not realized how impressive the room was. This truly was the heart of the house, and all hallways were connected to it. One hallway that she had not noticed before was just to the left of the one that led to Nico's bedroom. She decided she would follow it to see where it led.

This hallway was the shortest of the three in the home. On one side was a large rococo-style mirror, detailed with acanthus leaves. Directly opposite the mirror was a small niche which contained the bust of a male figure. At its base was a small placard with a name: Benito Frantoio. *This must be Nico's nonno*, she thought. Sofia turned to look at herself in the mirror. Her hair was flattened on the side she had slept on. Running her fingers through her wavy hair, in an attempt to add volume back to the one side, she noticed that the reflection of the statue behind her seemed to blink. She quickly turned around; the statue was still stationary. *I must still be half asleep—just a figment of my imagination.*

The hallway exited into the formal dining room. A long, rectangular wooden table, able to seat twelve, was the focus of this room. In the center of the table, an elegant crystal vase containing a beautiful floral arrangement gave life to the room. The flowers oddly remained untouched by decay. A built-in hutch displayed fine crystal stemware and china, and its drawers presumably housed the family silver.

Moving onward, she entered the kitchen. Her body suddenly felt a chill as she stepped from the comfortable wood flooring onto the cold marble tile of the kitchen floor. *Wow*, she thought, *this is impressive!*

And impressive it was. The kitchen was large. Aside from the requisite refrigerator, stove, and other common appliances, it was the intricately designed island that took center stage. Sofia noticed a single item in the middle of the island. She approached and recognized the object; it was an old-fashioned, glass citrus juicer. *Everything seems to have its place*, she thought, *I wonder why this was left out?* She suddenly became inspired to push forward and find an exit to the backyard; making fresh-squeezed orange juice was her new goal for this morning.

Then her eye noticed something odd. One of the cabinet doors had a handle that was in a different position. Instead of being horizontal like all the others, this one was in a vertical position. She walked over to it and pulled on it. The door opened to a stairway that led down to a lower level. *This must be a basement or cellar*, she thought. *I'm not going down there barefoot and alone.* She returned the door to its closed position and realized that the handle could turn, thus locking the door.

Pressing on, she noticed the entrance to a large glassed-in room. *A conservatory, or maybe an orangery to protect the potted citrus plants during winter?* Whatever its purpose, it currently was the home to a multitude of rare orchids and other exotic plants, including her favorite species of carnivorous plants: *Nepenthes rajah*; one of the largest tropical pitcher plants found in Borneo.

The room was divided into two seating areas, a simple breakfast table that seated six, which she breezed by as she headed over to inspect the *Nepenthes*, and a comfortable seating arrangement set amongst the plants. She looked down at a plush chaise lounge near the south facing window and began to daydream, imagining herself sitting comfortably near her new best friend, the *Nepenthes*, and reading the latest issue of *Town & Country* as the afternoon sun warmed her body.

Her brief fantasy was suddenly disrupted as a large black raven landed near one of the panels of glass, close to where she was standing, and tapped on the window. Looking up to see what had made the noise, the raven's dark brown eyes caught hers; it began to bob its head before letting out a loud *kraa*. Startled, Sofia began to look around. She spotted a handmade besom, its worn birch bristles tightly bound around a gnarled ash-wood handle. *I am not going through this again!* Grabbing the besom, she opened the door to the backyard and rushed around to the side where the raven was, but it had flown away. *Raven 1 - Sofia 1*, she thought to herself and began to laugh at her mock scorekeeping.

Sofia leaned her weapon of choice against the side of the house and walked over to one of the orange trees. Something did not seem right. She looked down and noticed that Stinky, the garden gnome, was in a different spot; he was by her feet in front of the tree. "Oh, my God!" she cried out loud.

Awakened by Sofia's outburst, Nico jumped out of bed, opened the French doors to the garden, and darted over to Sofia.

"Sofia, what happened? Is everything OK?" Nico said as his heart raced.

"I'm sorry Nico, I didn't mean to wake you. I had come outside to pick some oranges so that I could squeeze some fresh juice for breakfast, and I noticed that Stinky had moved from his previous location. I was already on edge from a raven that had tapped on the glass while I was admiring the plants in the conservatory—it seemed like it might be the same one from last night!"

"A feral cat was probably prowling around last night and knocked Stinky over. I'll bet he then rolled over by this tree—Whoa! He isn't the only gnome that.... Look, Sofia, all of them have moved and are in a circle around this orange tree."

"Nico, I'm not sure what's going on here. Only Stinky was here when I yelled out. The others must have moved between that time and when you ran out. Either someone is playing a trick on us, or those gnomes are more than just garden statues."

Sofia, determined not to obsess over the previous events, began picking oranges.

"Would you help me pick a few oranges from the higher branches? Once I have enough, I'll bring them to the kitchen and start squeezing them while you go back inside and put some clothes on."

Nico blushed with embarrassment as the cool morning air began to chill his body. He now realized that he had run outside wearing only his boxers. He quickly grabbed a few oranges from the tree, handed them to Sofia, and walked back to his room. "I'll meet you back in the kitchen."

Using the lower half of her sweater to hold all the oranges, Sofia entered the house. As she crossed the threshold, she felt a grainy texture under her feet. She looked down and noticed a white, crystal-like substance running across the entryway. Looking closer, she thought, *that looks like salt. I mustn't have felt it on my way outside, because of the raven.*

She headed to the kitchen to unload the bounty of oranges from her makeshift sweater pouch. With her two hands, she raised the bottom edge of her sweater and watched thc oranges roll out onto the kitchen island. The oranges rolled in every direction, and some began to fall off the kitchen island and land on the floor.

Nico, now properly clothed, entered the kitchen. He rushed over to the kitchen island and tried to stop as many oranges as he could from rolling onto the floor.

"So that's what's become of my favorite sweater!" Nico said with a chuckle. "It's now a stretched-out pouch for carrying oranges."

"Well, it always seemed abandoned—just lying in the corner of your room. You never folded it or washed it. I thought you might be getting rid of it and, so one day, I took it from your room." Batting her eyes at Nico and with an innocent look on her face, she continued pleading her case. "Plus, I like the way it feels and smells—it reminds me of you. You can't be mad about my sentimentality?"

"No, I'm not mad—how could I ever be mad at you? Besides, it looks better on you."

Sofia had a sudden thought and left the kitchen.

"Where are you going? I thought we were going to squeeze the oranges," Nico said as he followed Sofia.

Sofia headed to the foyer and knelt down by the front door, passing her hand over of the floor. She felt more of what appeared to be the same grainy texture she had felt at the back entrancc. She pressed down on the grains with the index and middle fingers of her right hand and brought her fingers to her mouth. "Yep! Just as I thought."

"What *are* you doing?"

"It's salt. The back entrance had a small line of salt across the threshold, and so I wanted to check this entryway. Salt is here too! I think, between us coming in and rolling our suitcases over the threshold, we disrupted this line of salt and that's why it wasn't noticeable before."

"Why is there salt on the floor?"

"I think your nonna was trying to protect herself from something. Salt can be used as a barrier to prevent the crossing of something malevolent. And, if I am correct, that persistent aroma of garlic that exists is probably coming from…."

She abruptly stopped speaking and headed back into the kitchen. Approaching a window behind the main sink, she drew back sheer curtains to reveal two old bulbs of garlic and a porcelain figurine of a frog.

"I'll bet all the windowsills have a garlic bulb or two there."

"Come to think of it, I did smell garlic in my bedroom," Nico commented as he grabbed a knife from a drawer. He walked over to the kitchen island and began slicing the oranges in half.

Sofia reached for the glass juicer and started squeezing the juice.

"Hey Nico. When I was exploring this part of the house earlier, I noticed that *that* cabinet door over there is actually a real door that leads down to some sort of basement or cellar."

"Oh yeah, that goes to the basement. I took a tumble down those stairs once when I was a toddler—scared my mother to death. I was told that she was so hysterical that she just froze in place and my nonna had to run down to the bottom of the stairs to check on me. She found me laughing and completely unharmed by the fall—something must have protected me. After that, she installed that latch mechanism so that it would remain securely locked and prevent any future accidents."

Grabbing another orange half to squeeze, Sofia responded, "Well, it wasn't locked when I found the door. It just opened."

"Sofia that's really odd. My nonna would never leave that unlocked. Even living alone, she would have kept it locked out of habit."

"Say, is there any champagne around here? We can make mimosas. A little 'hair of the dog' to help with our hangovers."

"I'm sure there's some down in the basement. Put something on your feet and we'll go hunt down some bubbly."

Sofia went back to her bedroom. She sat on the ornate chest at the end of her bed and put on her shoes. She stood up and stretched her arms while looking out the window at the beautiful geraniums. *I wonder*, she thought. And walking over to the window, she drew the curtain all the way back. Just as she expected, in each corner of the windowsill was a bulb of garlic.

Satisfied with her findings, she returned to the kitchen, excited to further explore the mysteries of this house. "Nico, lead the way!"

Nico walked over to the cabinet door that led to the basement and turned the handle to the right ninety degrees. He pulled the door open and felt for the light switch to his left. "Ah, much better. Careful going down—the handrail is a bit wobbly."

Sofia carefully looked down and followed Nico, counting each step in her head. *One, two, three...thirteen.* As she reached the landing, she looked up and was amazed. The basement ran the full length of the house and had various rooms or storage areas.

"The room on the left is the wine cellar. Let's hope it has what we are looking for," Nico said.

He opened the iron gate to the wine cellar, and they walked into the vault-like room composed of stone walls with built-in wine racks. In the center of the room, over a small round table made of olive wood, was a chandelier covered with cobwebs. Sofia quickly found the light switch and turned it on. But, even with the lights on, the room seemed dark, except for natural light coming from the back wall. There, set into the stone near the ceiling, was a small awning window, which was barred from the outside.

Sofia approached the window. Looking through, she could see the garden at ground level; thorny rose canes grew upward toward the sun. Hoping to let some fresh air into the musty room, she opened the window. A strong gust of cool air entered the room, blowing a thick layer of dust off the table and causing the cobwebs on the chandelier to sway in the air.

Nico began to cough from all the dust in the air. As his coughing became more persistent, Sofia quickly turned to secure the open window and shrieked loudly. Outside the window was one of the garden gnomes staring at her. Closing the window, she rushed over to Nico.

"Nico—here, sit down," she said, pulling out a chair for him to sit on. "Let me go to the kitchen and get you some water."

Sofia ran upstairs and was surprised to find a drinking glass out on the counter by the sink. *This wasn't here before!* She grabbed the glass and filled it up with tap water, and quickly returned to Nico.

"Drink this," she said, rubbing his back to help calm his coughing fit.

Nico took a sip of water. "Thank you. I think I'm OK now. My lungs have never been in the best of shape. I guess that's my Achilles' heel in life. I can fall down basement stairs unharmed, but a little dust almost incapacitates me," he said, ending with a light chuckle.

He took another sip of water and turned to set the glass on the table. "Look Sofia. There are various symbols or letters painted on the table! They must've been covered before with all that dust."

"S-A-L-V-E…and on this side is written, A-D-D-I-O," Nico read.

"On my side of the table, I see, O-N and I-S," Sofia added.

"I think you are reading it upside down. From my side of the table, I see S-I and N-O."

Coming over to Nico's side of the table, Sofia agreed with Nico. "You're right. That's 'yes' and 'no' in Italian and the other words are 'hello' and 'goodbye.' I think this table is like a spirit board." Pointing to the center of the table, Sofia continued her observation. "All the letters of the alphabet are here in the center."

Nico finished his glass of water and turned the glass upside down, placing it in the center of the table. He looked at Sofia and said, "Shall we ask it a question?"

"What should we ask?" Sofia responded.

"Put two fingers on the glass—I have a question," Nico said as he put his index and middle finger onto the glass.

Sofia went to the other side of the table. She sat down on one of the dirty chairs and placed two fingers on the glass.

"How did my nonna really die?"

They sat patiently for almost a minute and then the glass began to move. It slowly scraped across the surface of the table and paused on the letter H before continuing to the next letter.

"H," Sofia whispered.

"E—He!" Nico said with a note of trepidation in his voice.

"I wonder what that could mean?" asked Sofia. "Wait, it's moving again."

Sure enough, the glass began to travel in an effort to form a second word. It stopped on the letter K, then continued.

"I-L-L-E-D," Sofia spoke. "Killed."

"I'm not sure I should've asked that question, Sofia," Nico said with regret.

The glass once again resumed movement. H-E-R.

"He killed her?" Sofia said. "If that's true, then it would explain the 'look of terror' on her face that your mother mentioned last night at dinner."

She suddenly realized how upsetting this might be for Nico. "Nico, it's just a silly game. Let's find the champagne and go make our mimosas."

"I know what you're doing Sofia. And thank you. The last thing I need to think about before the funeral tomorrow is that my nonna might have been murdered." Going over to one of the shelves, he grabbed a bottle of champagne. "Let's go back upstairs for now. We can explore the rest of the basement later. I have a suspicious feeling there is more for us to find down here."

They returned to the kitchen and Nico wiped down the dusty champagne bottle and popped the cork. He looked over toward Sofia, who was squeezing the remaining sliced oranges, and said, "Sofia, would you go into the dining room and grab two champagne flutes. I say we drink in style!"

Sofia walked into the dining room. As she turned on the light, the sound of a loud *thud* startled her. It seemed to have come from the direction of the foyer. She walked down the hallway, passing the creepy mirror, and into the foyer. *Hmm*, she thought. *Where did that sound come from? Maybe it was from outside*. She walked over to the front door and opened it. She did not see anything odd or out of place. As she was about to close the door, she looked down and noticed the morning paper: *L'Essentiale. Ah, the morning paper must have been delivered late and hit the door when it was thrown onto the porch,* she deduced. She picked up the newspaper, closed the front door, and headed back to the dining room.

Placing the newspaper on the table, she went over to the hutch and opened one of its doors. The crystal stemware began to sparkle as more light entered the space. *So many choices*, Sofia thought to herself. *Hmmm...champagne flutes or coupes? Definitely flutes for mimosas.* Reaching in for the flutes, she noticed a pewter goblet further toward the back. She decided to take that back with her as well. She started to walk to the kitchen and remembered she had forgotten the newspaper. She did a quick turnaround, picked up the newspaper, and then headed back to the kitchen.

"Here you go Nico. Start pouring!" Sofia said as she placed the flutes and goblet onto the surface of the kitchen island. "Oh, and here's the morning newspaper—looks like something major happened last night." She pointed at the frontpage headline: *Church Relic Stolen in The Dark of Night.*

Nico looked down at the paper and responded, "Wow, that's crazy that someone would even do such a thing." Then he glimpsed the goblet. "Why did you bring that out?"

"It looked interesting and oddly out of place in a hutch full of crystal stemware and bone china. I wanted to take a look at it in better lighting."

"I kind of remember it now. Whenever I stayed here and was sick or not feeling well, my nonna would make me a special drink and serve it to me in that goblet," Nico recalled.

"It looks very used and has glyphs etched into it." Sofia said as she examined the goblet closely, slowly rotating it in the light.

"Put that down and let's toast!" Nico said while handing Sofia her glass. "Now, what should we toast to? Ah yes, our new tattoos!"

"*Salute*!" said Sofia as she touched her glass to Nico's.

"OK, put your glass down and let's see how they turned out. You go first," said Nico in an excited tone.

Sofia put her glass down and removed the bandaging from her wrist. "*Voila*! What do you think?"

Nico gently gripped Sofia's arm and raised it closer to his face, so that he could see her tattoo up close. "Wow! That is some amazing work—it looks three-dimensional, almost lifelike."

"Fawn really did a nice job. When I first saw her at the tattoo shop, I was dreading the possibility of having her do my tattoo, but the more we talked, the more I realized we had a lot in common—I could actually see us being good friends. Now let's see yours, Nico!"

"You're going to have to help me remove the covering. It is hard to do with one hand."

Sofia gently rolled up the cuff of Nico's T-shirt and began to unwind the cloth from around Nico's bicep. Eventually the top half of the tattoo began to show. "From what I can see, this griffon looks to be amazing. Yes, this is awesome. Even the little red mushroom by the griffon's leg looks like it could fall right off your arm and onto the floor—such detail!"

"Cool, I am so glad to hear it turned out well—wait. What mushroom? I didn't ask for a mushroom!" Nico responded, confused and slightly irritated.

"Yeah, there's a little red mushroom with white spots," said Sofia as she looked closer. "Hmm…looks like an *Amanita muscaria*. I mean, almost like the ones you see in video games as a power-up."

Nico grabbed his mimosa and finished it quickly before leaving the kitchen to check his tattoo in the bathroom mirror. Sofia topped off both flutes and followed after Nico.

"What the fuck is this shit?" Nico exclaimed as he viewed the reflection of his tattoo in the mirror.

"Nico, here have some more mimosa." Sofia said as she handed Nico his drink. She gazed over at Nico's reflection in the mirror as he flexed his bicep in an attempt to better view his tattoo in the mirror. "It really isn't that bad. It's actually quite cute," she teased.

Nico took a big sip of his mimosa and began to feel a sense of calm wash over him. "Ha ha, it is to laugh," he said in a snarky tone, responding to her playful goading. "Well, I guess I'm stuck with it now, but why would Sterling add something that I didn't ask for?

"All right. Let's get ready and go into town for lunch and some shopping. After, we can stop by Indelible Delights and get some answers."

Chapter 8: Shopping, Questions, and Answers

Nico and Sofia finished getting ready and met in the foyer. Taking into consideration they might still be slightly inebriated from their morning libations, they decided to forgo driving into town and that walking would be more prudent.

Stepping out of the house, a slight breeze of fresh spring air carrying the scent of roses invigorated their senses, making the start of their journey back to the piazza a pleasurable one.

"Ah, smell those roses, Nico. Such a beautiful fragrance. It must be from the roses in your nonna's garden," Sofia commented as Nico locked the front door.

"Yes, it is a wonderful scent," Nico replied. "But my favorite scent comes from where we are going."

As they headed toward the piazza and neared the alley where Indelible Delights was located, the most delicious aroma wafted about in the air and caught Sofia's attention.

"Aha! I bet what I'm smelling is coming from our next destination!" Sofia said with excitement.

Grinning, Nico responded, "If you are smelling the same buttery goodness of fresh baked goods with a touch of caramelized sugar and toasted pecans, then you are spot on. The bakery has been here decades and has the best baked goods for miles around."

Then they reached their destination. On the corner of the block, just before the piazza, was Patisserie Angelique. Nico turned to Sofia and directed, "Grab a table for us so we can eat outside. I'll go in and order us some goodies and, of course, coffee!"

Sofia sat down at a table and took in the beauty of the morning. Looking around she saw a bustle of activity: runners, cyclists, parents taking a morning walk with their children; and then dread filled her soul as she watched a large raven land on a telephone wire across the street. It turned its head to meet her gaze.

Nico approached the bistro table that Sofia had secured for them and said, "Sofia, would...."

Sofia was so focused on the raven that she didn't even notice Nico's presence at the table. Startled by his words, she slightly jumped from her seat and let out a subdued scream.

"Calm down. It's just me! What has you so upset?"

"I'm not upset—I just...I was staring at that raven over there and I guess I was entranced—you surprised me," Sofia responded while composing herself.

"Ravens sure do have a thing for you, Sofia," Nico responded and then continued in a more teasing tone, "Maybe it is the same one from this morning and last night? Maybe it's a handsome prince, cursed by an evil sorceress and turned into a raven; awaiting the kiss of a virgin maiden in order to return him to his true form?"

"Hey, I'm not a virg—ehh, I mean that's not funny, Nico! I feel like that thing has been stalking me," Sofia replied and began to crack a smile.

"Well, back to important things. As I was trying to say, before you freaked out, would you like some macarons to take back to the house? We can snack on them later."

Sofia nodded her head in response. One of the many likes that she and Nico shared was their fondness for macarons.

Nico went back inside Patisserie Angelique and shortly returned with two cups of coffee and a box, presumably filled with a selection of delightful meringue-based treats. Nico handed one of the coffees to Sofia and placed the other one down on the table, along with the small pastry box. He then retrieved a small metal stand, displaying their order number, which had been tucked under his left arm. He placed it on the table and sat down with Sofia.

"Our order is in, and we've been given lucky number seven. My nonna must be watching over us," Nico said.

A few minutes passed and then a girl about the same age of Nico and Sofia approached the table with their food. Speaking in a light

French accent, she asked, “May I assume that the croque madame is for the lady, and the croque monsieur is for the gentleman?”

“That would be correct. Merci!” Nico responded.

“My name is Lisette. Looks like your coffees need topping off. I’ll be right back—we just brewed a fresh pot,” she said and left to retrieve more coffee.

“That was very observant of her. Make sure to tip her well,” Sofia said as she cut into her sandwich, breaking the yolk of the fried egg on top.

Nico watched the gooey yolk run over the toasted bread of Sofia’s sandwich and commented, “Wait until you taste it—I’ll bet it’s just like being in Paris.”

Lisette returned holding an antique silver coffee pot and began to fill Nico’s cup.

“What a gorgeous container,” Sofia commented as she scanned the detailing of the coffee pot’s design. “Seems very valuable to use at a restaurant.”

Lisette replied, “It belongs to the owner, Angelique. She insists that it adds to the quality of the coffee—could be why we are said to have the best coffee in town.” Lisette began to laugh. “Honestly, I think it’s really more of a prop to enhance the customer experience in an effort to help justify our prices.”

“Well, it’s working! Everything here is worth the slightly higher pricing. Delicious food and excellent service,” Nico complimented.

“Thank you. That’s very kind of you to say. Please excuse me—I need to check on my other tables—you two have a wonderful rest of your day,” Lisette said.

Nico and Sofia finished their meal and got up from their seats. Nico took out his wallet and pulled out a ten-dollar bill and placed it on the table as a tip. Then, grabbing the macarons, he asked Sofia, “Where would you like to go next? Oh, I know! How about Schwartzman’s, the clothing store on the corner that you were so keen on last night?”

“I’m so there. Let’s go! I can’t wait to see what styles of clothing they have,” replied Sofia in a gleeful tone.

Instead of walking around the block, they decided to take a shortcut across the piazza to get to the other side where Schwartzman's Quality Clothing was located.

As they approached the store, Sofia noticed that the blinds had been raised; her eyes immediately spotted an article of clothing suited for Nico.

"Nico, look at that blue shirt on the mannequin in the middle of the store—I can totally see you wearing it," Sofia said with enthusiasm.

Nico opened the door for Sofia, and they entered the store. The smell of fabric and cedar permeated the air. Everywhere they saw lifelike mannequins from another era, each uniquely styled with coordinated outfits and accessories, showcasing the vast variety of items that the store had to offer. The only thing similar with each mannequin was their hair; each had a similar style with bangs.

"Hello," said an elderly lady with a slight German accent in the back of the store. "Is there anything that I might help you find?"

"Hello!" Sofia replied. "I'm already so in love with your store, and I haven't even had a chance to look at everything."

"Hello, Mrs. Schwartzman," Nico said as they walked toward the proprietress.

"Nico, it's you!" Mrs. Schwartzman responded. Holding a handkerchief tightly in her right hand, she raised it to her chest and continued, "My precious boy, I am so sorry to hear about your grandmother's passing. She was such a large part of our community and a big help to many of us. She'll truly be missed."

Mrs. Schwartzman and her husband had owned the store long before Nico was born. Having no children of their own, they were always exceptionally nice to Nico and his friends when their parents brought them in to buy clothes for the new school year. To Nico, she was like a second nonna, and seeing her hand on her chest reminded him of how his nonna was found dead. Tears began to fill his eyes as his emotions took control.

"Thank you. That means a lot to me," Nico said while reaching to embrace her for comfort.

Opening her arms to welcome him, Mrs. Schwartzman gave him a brief hug and then kissed Nico on the forehead. "Well, my husband and I are always here for you. Now, introduce me to your girlfriend."

"Oh, we aren't a couple; just good friends," As soon as Nico finished his statement, the sound of something falling to the floor was heard near the middle of the store.

Startled, Nico and Sofia immediately turned around. Other than the three of them, no one else was in the store.

"This is an old building," Mrs. Schwartzman quickly said, as if trying to take their mind off the noise that had interrupted their conversation. "Probably just a mouse scurrying about."

Nico and Sofia turned back toward Mrs. Schwartzman and Nico resumed conversation. "Yes, probably the case. Well, let me introduce you to my best friend, Sofia. We met at college and have become somewhat inseparable."

Sofia extended her hand to shake Mrs. Schwartzman's and said, "It's a pleasure to meet you."

"The pleasure is all mine. I'm glad Nico has someone like you in his life. He's a very…special young man," she said with sincerity in her voice. "Now please browse our wares and let me know if you aren't able to find a size or have any questions."

Sofia turned and immediately headed toward the middle of the store. She wanted to get a better look at the blue shirt she had noticed from outside the store. As she approached the mannequin, she noticed a baseball on the floor. *Hmm, this must've been part of the display and fallen from his hands*, she thought. She picked up the baseball and put it back into the mannequin's hands.

"Thank you."

Sofia did a double-take and then noticed Nico standing behind the mannequin. He popped his head from around the mannequin and began to laugh. Approaching Sofia, he asked, "Did I scare you?"

"Yes, you did! I almost thought the mannequin was alive," Sofia said.

The baseball in the mannequin's hand then dropped onto Nico's foot.

"Ouch! That hurt." Nico exclaimed. "Obviously, this mannequin doesn't appreciate my humor." Nico picked up the ball and placed it back into the mannequin's hands. Sarcastically addressing it, he said, "My apologies, good sir."

Sofia began to laugh.

Nico walked away to search for a new pair of shorts, while Sofia remained near the mannequin, obsessed with trying to locate where more of the blue shirts were displayed.

"Sofia."

Sofia looked up. Nico was across the way with his back to her, looking at a rack of shorts. She quietly sneaked up behind him and poked the sides of his ribs with her two fingers and yelled, "Boo!"

"Eyahh!" Nico shouted. "What was that for? Trying to get me back from earlier?"

"I was going to let it go, but since you decided to continue on with the charade, I decided you deserved some payback."

"Charade? What are you talking about?" Nico replied. "I just pranked you that one time."

"You mean you didn't whisper my name?"

"No," Nico replied and then paused briefly before continuing. "Think about it. I'm way over here with my back to you; do you think that if I'd whispered your name, you would've been able to hear it from where you had been standing?"

"I guess you're right. But I did hear my name! Maybe I just need more coffee."

"Well, you'll at least be happy to know that I found some new shorts," Nico said, proud of his accomplishment. "You should pick something out for yourself."

"I like that suggestion. Besides, they didn't seem to have any more of that blue shirt I wanted to get for you," Sofia conceded.

Sofia walked toward the section of the store where the Mrs. Schwartzman was busy folding women's T-shirts. "Excuse me, Mrs. Schwartzman, do you have any more stock of that blue shirt the mannequin in the center of the store is wearing?"

"No, my dear, unfortunately that is the last one, but I can have Marvin make another. It will only take a few days. What size did you want?" replied Mrs. Schwartzman.

"It is for Nico—I think it would look stunning on him," Sofia commented. "Probably a medium…no, maybe a large—I'm not really sure now that I think of it."

Mrs. Schwartzman grabbed a measuring tape, along with a pencil and paper. "I will go take Nico's measurements. In the meantime, why don't you go into dressing room number one; I pulled some items that I think will suit your tastes."

Surprised, Sofia responded in a grateful manner, "Wow, how unexpected and thoughtful of you. I can't wait to see what you chose."

Sofia rushed off to dressing room number one to see what awaited her while Mrs. Schwartzman approached Nico.

"Sofia is such a sweet girl. She is the perfect complement to you and will be a big help to you for what's to come," Mrs. Schwartzman said as she placed her pencil and paper down on a display table and extended her measuring tape. "Now let me take your measurements. Sofia has her heart set on that blue shirt for you, so I am going to have Marvin construct one for you."

"Yes, I'm lucky to have her in my life," Nico replied and then questioned Mrs. Schwartzman, "What did you mean by 'for what's to come'?"

"My boy, pay no attention to my eccentric ramblings," she replied with a chortle. "Now raise your arms and hold them horizontally so that I can take an accurate measurement."

Mrs. Schwartzman finished taking the needed measurements. "Come. Let us check on Sofia. She's trying on some clothing. I hope she likes the items I've chosen for her."

As they neared the dressing room area, Sofia appeared wearing a completely new outfit: a crisp, white shirt, a denim skirt, and coordinating belt and shoes. She twirled in front of the mirror as she presented her new look to the two of them.

"You look amazing. It was as if the clothes were made specifically for you," Nico said as he circled her, inspecting the fit of the clothing. "Wow. You're hot!"

"Mrs. Schwartzman, I love what you chose for me. I always have trouble finding clothes that fit my body type, and the fit of your clothing is perfect—they're so comfortable, too! I can't believe that you and Marvin make all these clothes yourselves—and the shoes and belt, too! How do you have the time?"

"Well, the shoes and belt are from the cobbler down the street—we can't take credit for making them. A few years ago, Marvin and I decided to consign some of his items to help his business grow. As far as our clothing, we've found a way to make everything in-house by using traditional methods passed down through our family," Mrs. Schwartzman replied, finishing her sentence with a slight grin.

"I'd like to keep the outfit on and wear it for the rest of the day. May I give you the tags so you can ring up my purchase?"

"Dear we don't put price tags on our clothing. All shirts are the same price; all pants are another price, etc. We've found that it makes it easier for people to shop—they don't have to worry about what the price is for each style of shirt, for example—they can just focus on finding what they like. It makes it more efficient for the shopper, and us as well."

"That's a brilliant business model. Here's my credit card. You can put Nico's shorts on my purchase as well," Sofia said and then turned to Nico. "You paid for that delicious lunch and the macarons, so this is me paying you back."

"Ah, Sofia, you don't have to do that. But since I know it'll make you happy that I *finally* will be wearing a new pair of shorts...."

"Here you go, Sofia," Mrs. Schwartzman said as she put the receipt in the bag and handed it to her. "I've put your other clothes and shoes in the bag along with Nico's new shorts. Nico's blue shirt should be ready in a few days, so we'll see you again soon."

Nico gave Mrs. Schwartzman another hug, and they both thanked her for her assistance. Sofia, beaming with confidence in her new outfit, led the way to the store's exit, taking each step like a model on a runway. Nico picked up his pace so that he could reach the door before Sofia and open it for her. As Sofia neared the exit, she heard a muffled whistling sound, like a cat call. She immediately stopped and turned around. She looked around and noticed she was standing near the mannequin with the blue shirt that she'd been so enamored with. For the first time, she took more notice of the mannequin; examining its features. Blond hair, slightly messy, with bangs that covered its forehead, framing its dark brown eyebrows and sparkling blue eyes. *A rather handsome looking mannequin*, she thought to herself.

"Sofia, what's the hold up?" Nico said while holding the door open.

"Nothing. Just thought I heard something again," replied Sofia.

Exiting the store and heading right, they decided to walk down the block toward the east side of the piazza, since they hadn't explored that side of the piazza previously. Passing Trattoria Moraiolo, the smell of the wood-burning oven reminded them of the delicious meal they had with Nico's parents. Next to the restaurant was the shoe store: Lederarbeiter. Detailed, handmade shoes and other leather goods were displayed in the windows on either side of the entrance to the store.

"If I hadn't just bought these shoes, you know I'd be dragging you in there, Nico. At least his business will make some money from my purchase," Sofia said, trying to justify avoiding the temptation of going inside and possibly spending more money.

Next to Lederarbeiter, and seeming out of place, was a pet store: Beast Friends. Peering into the window, they could see various animals: birds, cats, puppies, snakes, and other creatures seemingly uncaged but remaining in their designated sections.

"I wish we could have our own pet back at Hornsby Manor, but that probably wouldn't be fair to the poor creature since we're in classes most of the day. Thankfully, all nine of Mrs. Hornsby's cats are friendly," Sofia said with a sigh.

Nico turned toward Sofia and replied, "I know what you mean, I miss having a dog around. Don't get me wrong, I love all animals, but sometimes one is enough. There are always three to four of her cats in my room at the same time. It's like I'm in *their* room."

Out of the corner of her eye, something distracted Sofia. Across the street, on the southeast corner, was another clothing store: Falena's Fine Wares.

Nico noticed Sofia turning her head and immediately responded, "I know what you're thinking. You see another clothing store."

"How do you always read me so well?" Sofia huffed. "We can go there another time. From what I can see from here, the clothing doesn't look as nice as Schwartzman's."

"The town gossip is that Malvina Falena opened her store about twenty years ago just to spite Schwartzman's. I guess something happened between them long ago that caused Malvina to harbor ill will."

"Well, I don't want to shop *there* then," Sofia interrupted. "Mrs. Schwartzman was so kind to me, and it's just the two of them making all those clothes by hand—I'm now officially loyal to the Schwartzman brand."

"Glad to hear that, lady ambassador," Nico ribbed. "Now, let's cross the street so I can show you the east side of the piazza, before we go to see Sterling."

At the beginning of this block was the Hotel Oliveto, the town's signature hotel; the doorman, dressed in formal attire, greeted them with a cheerful "*buongiorno*" as they passed by. Nico and Sofia both smiled and responded in kind to the doorman. Next to the hotel was Filippo Ascolano, Esq., Nefertiti's Fine Linens, Petali Floral Design, and ending the block with L'Essentiale, the local newspaper.

"And there you have it, Sofia. You now know the town," Nico said jokingly.

"There's more to this town than just these four sides of the piazza, I just know it."

"Of course, there's more—other stores, services, and of course, more delicious places to eat. They're just off the piazza on the side streets. I figured once you mastered the 'monopoly board' layout, as you referred to it last night, then you'll never get lost."

Crossing the street, they headed down the sidewalk toward Vicolo Fato. Nico began to pick up the pace, anxious to ask Sterling his questions. As they reached the alley, they peered down it and observed that things looked noticeably different in the daylight. The alley didn't appear to go on and on, like at night; it actually led to a dead end about ten feet from the entrance of Indelible Delights.

"Totally different perception at night," Sofia pointed out. "And look at this! I didn't see this last night. Probably because it was so dark."

Sofia was referring to a small door to the right of the tattoo shop's entrance. It was only about a foot and-a-half tall. She hunched down to better inspect her new find. The door seemed to have a decoration on it.

"Nico, come look," Sofia said while waving at Nico to come closer.

"Why it's a little door. How odd," Nico commented as he squatted down near Sofia to get a better look at its detailing. "Seems to be decorated with a spire or steeple with a cross on the top—looks just like the one at St. Anthony's."

Out of curiosity, Sofia reached for the miniature doorknob to see if the door could be opened. As her hand touched the knob, a spark emitted, giving her enough of a jolt to cause her to fall back.

"Ouch!"

Nico rose up and extended his hand to help Sofia back up off the ground, "Are you OK?"

"Yes. I wasn't expecting that to happen."

"Here, let's get you inside so you can sit down and maybe have some water or tea to drink," Nico suggested, as he waved his hands through the three little black bells to the right of the main door.

And just like the night before, a clicking sound was heard and the door to Indelible Delights was now unlocked. They entered the building and Nico called out, "Hello! Hello!"

"Hello," answered Fawn from down the hallway. Coming out from behind the curtain, her face beaming with a big smile. "Hi, you two! Long time no see."

"Hi Fawn. I was wondering if I could speak to your dad. I have a few questions for him," Nico said, trying to keep his tone polite.

"Father, can you come out? Nico and Sofia are here," Fawn yelled back toward the hallway.

"Be right there, kids," Sterling's voice sounded.

Sterling came out from the back looking a little haggard, like he had just woken up.

"Sterling, are you feeling well?" Sofia asked with concern.

"I am fine. Haven't been sleeping well. So much on my mind," Sterling replied. Looking toward Nico, he continued, "So, I hear you have questions for me?"

"That I do," Nico responded in a huff and began to roll up his sleeve. "What's this?" he said while pointing to his tattoo.

"Why it's a griffon of course," Sterling quipped.

Nico started to get irate and responded, "I know it's a griffon, but what about this added mushroom? I didn't request it."

"If I recall, you said you trusted me with the design," Sterling smiled.

"Yeah, the design of the griffon. I didn't know you were going to take liberty in adding other elements to the design," Nico said feeling defeated.

"Listen, boy. I did it for you," Sterling spoke sternly and then softened his tone. "You have no idea what is truly going on in this town."

"What do you mean? This is Oliveto, the same sleepy little burg I grew up in and that tourists now flock to because of its charm, amazing wine, olive oil, and other culinary delights." Nico responded with a tone of sarcasm.

Almost in sync, Fawn and Sofia spoke in unison, "Nico, please hear him out."

"You really don't know, do you?" Sterling said in amazement and continued in a disappointed tone. "I would've thought that your grandmother had prepared you."

Intrigued and curious, Nico asked, "Prepared me for what?"

Fawn spoke up trying to help her father explain, "Nico, do you recall ever having seen or experienced things in your youth that didn't seem natural—that some might even consider supernatural?"

Nico took a moment and thought deeply before responding. "I guess I used to when I was a kid, especially when I stayed at my nonna's house. When my mother would pick me up from visiting, I'd tell her the most amazing stories of what I had seen—or thought I had seen. My mother would just tell me that I had an 'overactive imagination' and dismissed everything that I'd tell her—she said I was being silly. She even sent me to Dr. Matto for therapy. Eventually, I started telling myself that certain experiences could be explained by science or that they were just coincidences."

"Nico, I think they were probably real," Sofia said with a compassionate tone and paused briefly. "You know this is my first time visiting Oliveto, Nico, and you know all the strange and unexplainable things I have already experienced—things *we* have experienced together. You're so quick to laugh them off—that's probably a mechanism you created while growing up to dismiss these occurrences. Think of it this way. Most children claim to see the boogeyman or a monster in the closet, or even have an imaginary friend, right? Adults then repeatedly tell them that they don't exist, and so children start to no longer see these things. They 'grow out of it,' as they say. But what if the boogeyman is real? Or the imaginary friend has actually been there the whole time until the mind starts ignoring their presence and then they become a distant memory?"

"Then that would explain so many things," Nico said with a sigh of relief as tears filled his eyes. Years of repressed emotions suddenly surfaced all at once, and it became difficult to contain himself as he continued. "So many incredible things I've seen and felt—and still do! I've put forth so much energy in repressing them, when I should've embraced them—I could've been a much happier person if I had."

Sofia reached over and gave Nico a hug while whispering into his ear, "Well, now you can."

Sterling interrupted Nico and Sofia's moment to continue his original conversation. "Nico, now that your mind is in a more accepting place, what I'm about to tell you will hopefully be more believable." Sterling's tone became more serious as he continued speaking, "You have a special role to play in protecting this town. Not just because you are from one of the four founding families, but because of the gifts that flow within you. Now, I don't want to overwhelm you with too much information—I think it's best that you learn these things at your own pace—you'll be able to process and accept them better that way. But what I will tell you, is that magic *does* exist and my kind desperately needs your help. Thankfully, Sofia is here to help you along this road of discovery."

"Magic exists?" Nico turned his head and looked around. "Wait! Am I on camera? Is this one of those hidden-camera television shows?"

He then began to smirk, and turning to Sofia, asked, "Are you in on this too?"

"Nico, my father is serious! This isn't a prank," Fawn chided. "We need your help."

"Fawn is correct. I'm being completely serious," Sterling said in a grave tone. "Your grandmother helped this town for many, many years with all its—we'll say, *supernatural* needs. Unfortunately, she's no longer here to help us, and I'm afraid a dark force is running amok in Oliveto."

"Well, if I'm to be open-minded about my previous experiences and accept that magic exists, then what are you? You said your 'kind' need my help," Nico asked Sterling.

"I am part Fey, as is Fawn," Sterling explained. "We are among the many Fey, and other magical inhabitants, that secretly coexist with the humans in and around Oliveto. We happen to be half-fairies—sharing both fairy and human blood."

Nico briefly looked Sterling up and down and commented. "So that explains your human size. I always think of fairies being small, winged beings," Nico turned to Fawn and continued, "similar to the hummingbird you tattooed on Sofia's wrist—great job, by the way."

Fawn blushed and responded, "Thank you. It's some of my finer work. You see, full-blooded fairies, like my mother and grandmother, can change their size at will—even shrinking all the way down to the size of a hummingbird, which is when humans mistake them for one." She then turned to Sofia with a smile and continued, "Like Sofia did when my mother flew into Nico's garden to check on you two, shortly after you arrived."

"So, are you telling me that the design inspiration for my tattoo is actually your mother? That's incredible. I guess with all that fast fluttering about in my face, I hadn't noticed that it could've been something other than a hummingbird. My tattoo has an even deeper meaning for me now. Imagine that Nico—inspired by a true fairy! That's something I won't be able to share with most people."

"Well, in Oliveto, things aren't always as they appear," Fawn replied. "You'd do well to remember that."

Once again Sterling took control of the conversation and turned to Nico. "Here's where we need your help Nico—and of course you too, Sofia. For the past six months, members of the fairy community have been vanishing without a trace. So far, only full-blooded fairies have been victims of what we are calling The Oliveto Abductor—I'm guessing it's because they possess more magic than us half-fairies…but I digress. The only noticeable pattern I've been able to discern is that these abductions only occur between the moon's first quarter and until it becomes full."

"Oh, that is terrible," exclaimed Sofia. "But how can we help?"

"Well, I'm hoping that Nico's grandmother left him something that might help him to help us," Sterling replied.

"She died so suddenly. I don't think she would've had time to set anything aside for me that could help," Nico said with a sigh.

"You see, a few months after the disappearances started to occur, I visited your grandmother to seek her guidance," Sterling began to explain. "I'd spoken only a few sentences when she interrupted me to say that she would help. I thought it was the desperation in my eyes that caused her to immediately offer her assistance, but it seems it was much more than that. She then explained to me that she had noticed a 'shift'—that the town was 'out of balance' and that a 'growing darkness could be felt.'

"A few weeks passed since we'd spoken, and the moon's first quarter was once again approaching. I was becoming anxious. Then, last week, she called me to give me an update. She told me that she was close to uncovering the source of the disappearances; stressing that she wanted to be absolutely certain before coming forward with her theory as to who or what was behind the nefarious activity. Sadly, she didn't live long enough to tell me what she had learned."

"Nico!" Sofia said with excitement. "Maybe she did leave you something. Remember that crumpled note that you found? What if that's a clue? Even you thought it might be a riddle of sorts."

Nico recalled the note's message: *Never give up on hope*. His mind began to wander, and he began to envision when his mother first found the note in his nonna's hand, clutched to her chest. "Got it!" he exclaimed. "I think I've figured out the riddle."

Nico turned to Sterling and continued, "When you were tattooing my arm last night, I drifted off and began to recall an experience from my past. It was from back when I was a child while staying at my nonna's house. I was with her in the front bedroom, the same bedroom that Sofia is now staying in—I was helping her make the bed. I had asked her about the antique chest at the end of the bed and as to why I was never able to open it. She told me that only a lady can open it, and that one day, when the time was right, I'd be able to see its contents."

Nico then turned to Sofia. "That note that my nonna had clutched to her chest when she was found; it said to 'never give up on hope.' A chest that only a lady would probably open would be a *hope chest*. She didn't want me to give up on trying to open it! So, she did leave me a possible clue as to how I—er, *we*, can help. The answer might lie inside that chest."

Sofia's face lit up at Nico's realization. "That totally makes sense. I wonder what's in that chest that could be so important?"

"We'll head back to the house shortly and find out," Nico replied and then turned to address Sterling. "But before I get sidetracked with this new adventure, I would like an answer to my original question. What is with this mushroom on my arm?"

"Ah yes, I suppose I do owe you an explanation. Better that I just show you its purpose before I explain the how and why. Leave your belongings here with Fawn and come with me." Sterling replied.

Sterling walked to the door and stepped outside. Nico and Sofia handed their shopping bags to Fawn and followed him outside. Before closing the door behind them, Fawn whispered words of caution, "Prepare to have your minds blown."

With their curiosity now piqued, Nico and Sofia picked up the pace to catch up to Sterling, who was already a half of a block ahead of them. How he got so far ahead in such a short time, eluded them. As Sterling reached the end of the block where the hotel was, he stopped briefly and turned back to Nico and Sofia. Reaching his hand out, he gestured for them to follow and then rounded the corner, disappearing from their sight.

"He sure has a quick stride. I've never seen someone walk so fast," Sofia panted. "It must be a fairy feat."

"Well let's hurry and catch up," Nico responded, wiping his brow with the sleeve of his sweater.

As they reached the corner, the hotel's doorman greeted them once again with a cheerful "*buongiorno*" and then pointed his gloved hand in Sterling's direction. Now a full block behind him, Nico and Sofia transitioned from a brisk walk into a light jog in order to catch up. The street, for as far as they could see, was lined on both sides with cherry trees, now in blossom. Every now and then a cool, seasonal breeze would pass through the branches of the trees and cause a light rainfall of white petals.

"Wow, what a beautiful sight, Nico. It almost reminds me of..." A blossom landed on her lip and interrupted her. She removed the blossom and continued, "...reminds me of Japan."

"Truly a beautiful time of the year. Seeing these trees reminds me of my nonno." Nico replied while catching his breath. "Every Easter, at our family dinner, he would tell us of the time he sold his first home. He said that one spring, back in the 1940's, a distinctive man of Japanese descent arrived in town. He came into the real estate office wearing a nicely tailored green wool suit, a brown felt fedora sat on his head at a slight tilt, and he carried a small well-traveled suitcase. In broken but understandable English, he introduced himself as Mr. Daiki Sakura, and asked my nonno for help with buying a home—one specific home." Nico paused once more to take in some more air as they neared Sterling. "In fact, the very house that Mr. Sakura had his heart set on is just further up this very street. Anyway, my nonno shook his hand and gave him a personal loan so that he could buy the home. In gratitude to the kindness that he had received, Mr. Sakura planted all of these cherry trees as an everlasting gift to the town. He eventually opened the town's nursery and garden center, which is still in business to this day."

"That's a wonderful story and you finished it just in time—looks like we've finally caught up to Sterling," Sofia said as she stopped jogging.

Sterling stood there staring at the two of them and asked, "What took you so long?"

Nico and Sofia looked up at the building that Sterling had led them to: Oliveto Public Library. It was an impressive two-story building with a grand stairway leading up to the main entrance. Two large Tuscan columns preceded the double door that welcomed daily visitors.

"Why are we at the library?" Nico questioned.

"Look around and tell me what you see," Sterling responded.

Sofia jumped into the conversation and asked, "Who is that woman waving from the corner window up there?"

"That is—" Sterling started to reply before Nico interrupted.

"Teresa, Teresa Libretto. Why, I haven't seen her since we were kids. My nonna would often take me with her to the library when she went to see Teresa's mother. While they would talk, Teresa and I would play hide-and-seek amongst the never-ending rows of bookshelves." Nico said.

"As I was saying," Sterling continued, somewhat irritated by the interruption, "aside from the young Ms. Libretto, who'll be a source of knowledge for you two and can help you catch up on everything you are lacking, knowledge-wise, tell me what you notice that's out of the ordinary."

Nico's eagle eyes locked onto a small door to the left of the stairs, partially obscured by the property's landscape. "There. Over there." Nico pointed to the little door and turned to Sterling. "That little door. It is similar to the one by the entrance to your business."

"Right you are," Sterling commented, and he headed over toward the door, motioning Nico and Sofia to follow him once again.

"Odd little door," Sofia said. "Hardly seems functional. Looks like it is decorated with seashells around the frame and with a single starfish on the door."

"OK, so you brought us here to see townie art?" Nico joked.

"Please don't joke Nico. This is more than just 'art.' These are fairy doors. They're portals to other locations around this town and elsewhere."

"I apologize Sterling—I didn't mean any disrespect," Nico said, slightly embarrassed by his previous comment.

"Thank you, Nico. Apology accepted. I keep forgetting, all of this is new to you. Now enough dawdling, let me show you what I promised, and then I shall explain," Sterling reached for Sofia's hand, and she extended it to him. Grabbing hold of it, he directed Nico. "Now boy, grab Sofia's other hand—hold it tightly—and then touch the door."

Nico looked toward Sofia with trepidation and grabbed her hand. Squatting down so that he could get closer to the door, he reached out and touched it.

Everything suddenly went black. Seconds later Nico felt the salty mist of ocean water spray against his face. Looking around, he saw that Sterling, Sofia and himself were now slightly offshore from the beach on an islet with a huge rock formation,

"That was incredible!" Sofia said in amazement. "How—did we just teleport?"

"Follow me. I want to get you out of the elements so that you aren't swept away by a rogue wave—it can be dangerous here," Sterling said.

Sterling took a few steps toward a large crevice and entered into a dim, dank cavern that had been worn into the rock over the centuries. A narrow path, slick with seaweed, led downward into an open area. Nico and Sofia quickly followed, holding each other's hands for safety.

Reaching into his breast pocket, Sterling pulled out a small vial and removed the stopper. Fireflies flew out and danced above their heads, lighting the cavern's damp walls.

Nico looked around, examining the new surroundings. A demarcation line along the wall, about eight feet from the floor, marked the cavern's potential water capacity. *Thankfully, it must be low tide*, he thought. Across from the entrance, he eyed a throne-like chair, carved of stone. Near its base were the remains of a single shackle, which was attached to a corroded chain, about six feet in length, its end securely staked into the rock. A multitude of sea urchins, barnacles, and starfish clung to the cold stone seat, almost as if in adornment. Above them, various bits of sea glass hung from unknown fibers, possibly as some sort of primitive decoration. When the fireflies would flutter close to the various bits of colored glass, their light would cause a kaleidoscopic display on the cavern walls.

"Now that we are in a safer location, let me answer the rest of your questions." Sterling's voice echoed slightly as he continued to speak. "First, Sofia, yes, we did teleport. That's how fairy doors work. They're all connected, and the rules are simple: only a person with fairy blood may use the doors and can also bring another without fairy blood through, by holding their hand—"

Sofia interrupted, "What if someone let go of the guest's hand?"

"The teleport is so quick that there is rarely time for that scenario to occur," Sterling answered. "But it is possible and has happened twice."

Nico chimed in, "Then what happens to the unlucky guest?"

"They end up in the fairy realm unharmed, but usually unconscious or dazed," Sterling responded. "A fairy on patrol will notice the disturbance and bring them back to their proper realm.

"Now, Nico, let me continue by answering your question in regard to the red mushroom tattooed on your arm. Last night, when I told you that I was leaving the room to get more ink, I wasn't completely honest with you. I had gone to the sink and purposely cut myself in order to collect my blood, collecting enough of it to use as the ink for the red mushroom. Since the mushroom tattoo was designed with fairy blood, it allows you to use the various fairy doors around town, and in other surrounding locations, for quick travel."

Nico stood there in silence; his mind trying to process what he had just been told. Sofia and Sterling were also quiet, looking intensely at Nico for some kind of response, but all they heard was the crashing of the waves outside the cavern.

After about a minute, Nico spoke, "Thank you. Thank you for being honest with me. I suppose under the circumstances, this method of travel will help us on our quest to help you. I'm sure my nonna would have approved of this and so I'm willing to accept it."

"Very good, my boy," Sterling said with relief. "Now, one more thing. The other rule to using the fairy doors. The fairy doors were created to work in one direction. When you arrive at a door's destination, there will be another door nearby that will lead you forward to a new destination, but never back to your previous location. Follow me—we need to go before the tide rises and starts to fill the cavern."

Sterling led them back to the entrance of the cavern and reached into his breast pocket once again to pull out the glass vial. Uncorking it, he called down to the fireflies in an unknown language. The fireflies came to him and returned to their former home; he then replaced the stopper and returned the vial to his breast pocket.

"OK," Sterling said in an authoritative tone. "This is the location that the fairy door from the library took us. Somewhere near us you should find another door that is decorated differently and will give you a clue as to where it will lead."

Nico and Sofia began to look around the rock; their shoes now wet from the sea water that had risen since their arrival.

"There it is," Sofia called out, pointing behind Nico.

Nico glanced behind him at the door against the main rock that contained the cavern. He looked closely and saw that the door was decorated with a tree that had four major limbs.

"I am fairly sure I know where it will take us. That has to be referencing the giant olive tree in the piazza!" he said with enthusiasm.

"Good job, you two. Let's take the portal before we are overcome by the sea," Sterling said.

Nico grabbed Sofia's hand and held it tightly, making sure there could be no chance of her being left behind or ending up in the fairly realm. They all lowered themselves and Nico and Sterling both touched the door.

Once again, a brief moment of darkness and then they appeared as Nico had correctly guessed in the piazza. They stood near a small utility shed about 100 feet from the great olive tree, obscured from public view by strategically placed bushes that helped camouflage the shed.

Nico looked over to make sure Sofia was still there. With a sigh of relief, he said to Sofia, "Looks like we made it! I could get used to this kind of travel."

Sofia, more curious to find the next fairy door, responded with an unenthusiastic, "Yes, uh huh." Then her eye spotted the fairy door and she perked up and said, "There it is!" This small door was decorated with vines on the door frame and the image of grapes on the door. *I wonder where this one leads to*, Sofia thought.

"OK, kids, we need to go back and check on Fawn. I know she's capable of protecting herself, but I'd feel terrible if she were the next to be abducted." In an instant Sterling turned and headed toward the alley so quickly that the Nico and Sofia had to scramble to catch up. "Nico, I suggest you wait a bit before exploring the rest of the fairy doors and their destinations—some can lead you to potentially dangerous locations, and I'd rather you be more familiar with your new gifts so that you can better protect Sofia and yourself."

"But what are these 'gifts' you speak of?" protested Nico, a little breathless. "How am I supposed to learn about them? I have no clue where to start."

"Oh, but you do, Nico," Sofia said with confidence. "I believe it has to do with your nonna's riddle that you figured out. Something in that hope chest will give us some answers—I just know it!"

Sterling nodded. "Sofia is correct. You need to follow the clues. Remember that not everything in Oliveto is as it seems, and speak with Teresa at the library. She can provide much information about the town's history. Good luck to you both and keep in touch with what you find out in regard to the abductions. Ah, here we are. Fawn? Fawn? Are you there?"

"In the kitchen!"

"Thank goodness. Nico, Sofia, there are your bags. Now remember what I've said." And he disappeared into the back rooms, leaving his guests a little overwhelmed.

"All right lady," said Nico, after catching his breath for a moment, "let's head back and figure out how to open that chest."

Chapter 9: More Answers, More Mysteries

As soon as they entered the house, they both made a beeline to the front bedroom and stood in front of the hope chest, staring at it in silence. Sofia paced about, looking at the chest from different angles, trying to find something out of place that could be a clue. Nico decided to see if he could lift the lid, now that he was older and stronger, but as with his many attempts as a child, the mysterious latched lid remained sealed.

"Sofia, my nonna had told me that only a woman could open it. Why don't you give the lid a try?" Nico said slightly frustrated. "Maybe you'll have the magic touch!"

Sofia gave it a try, and the lid remained sealed. She tried it again from the left side of the chest, and then once again from the other side, but it still would not budge.

"Phew, it's getting warm in here. I forgot how the afternoon sun really warms up this room. I'm going to get something to drink—do you want anything?" Nico said.

"Water is fine, unless there's some leftover orange juice," Sofia responded as Nico left the room. She then walked over to the window and opened it to let some air in.

Sofia sat down on the floor in front of the magnificent chest and inspected the detailed marquetry work. Different types of flowers were represented in the design. *Maybe there's a pattern amongst the flowers,* she mused to herself as she ran her hand across the top. She decided to begin identifying each flower, in the hopes that it could help her decipher the mystery of how to open the enigmatic chest. *Rose, iris, daffodil....*

Nico returned to the room and handed Sofia a glass of chilled orange juice. Sitting down on the floor, Nico felt the refreshing breeze from the open window. "Ah, that feels so good…and the smell of the geraniums…"

Geranium, Sofia thought as she identified the next flower. Almost spilling her orange juice with excitement, she said to Nico, "I bet the secret to opening this chest has to do with the geraniums designed on this chest. Help me find all the ones that look like this flower."

"Which one, they all kind of look similar."

"Like this one!" Sofia said, as she put her finger down on one of the wooden geraniums. She felt the image depress slightly from the weight of her finger. Thrilled at her possible discovery, she applied more pressure and the wood sank almost a half an inch, and then she heard the sound of a click.

"Another one over to the right," Nico said with excitement. "Sofia, you're a genius! I think you've figured this out—look here's another!"

Sofia pressed down each of the geraniums until they clicked—five more, six in total. A whirling sound then emerged from the antique chest, and whatever was previously holding the lid shut now released its grip. As she propped the lid open, a pleasant camphoraceous and woodsy smell from the cedar-lined chest filled their nostrils. They peered into the chest and found a layer of ivory linens, neatly folded.

"Ah, come on!" Nico said with disappointment. "All this anticipation just to find old bed sheets. How are they going to help us?"

Sofia reached in and took out the beautifully crafted linens, handing them to Nico. "The chest is deeper than it appears. I think there's more in here than just the sheets. Here, put these on the bed."

Beneath the linens were some old photo albums which were on top of layers of bath and hand towels. Sofia quickly handed the items to Nico, who placed them neatly on the bed. As she handed him the last set of towels, she discovered a large, leather-bound book at the bottom of the chest along with a small iron ring attached to the far-right of the chest; it lay flush with the bottom of the chest and appeared to be some sort of latch. Ignoring the ring, Sofia lifted the heavy tome out of the chest and took a good look at it. "This is odd—there's nothing on the cover or the spine." She then cracked open the book, and a wave of disappointment filled her. "And to top it off, there's nothing inside—all of the pages are blank."

Nico placed the last set of towels on the bed and walked toward Sofia. "Here let me see that. It looks vaguely familiar."

Sofia fumbled slightly as she handed the book to Nico, almost dropping it. He brought it over to the bed and lay down across the bed on his stomach.

"You must be losing your vision, Sofia. It says *Benandanti*, right here on the cover. Maybe turning on the light will help you see better?"

Sofia turned on the light and walked over. "I still don't see anything. Are you playing a trick on me?"

"Not at all," Nico responded with a light chuckle. "Maybe you're looking at it from the wrong angle. Come up here on the bed."

Sofia climbed onto the bed and looked again at the book. Still not seeing anything on the book's cover, she began to get irritated. "You *are* playing a trick on me—that's mean!" she said and elbowed Nico's side.

Then she gasped. For a brief moment, when her elbow had touched Nico, she did see something.

"I think I saw it!" she said with amazement. "But now I don't." She then had a theory and scooted her body closer to Nico so that she was touching him, and like magic, she was able to see the book's title once again. "Apparently, you can see it, but I am not able to unless I am touching you. Similar to how I am able to use the fairy door with you. But I don't think the fairy blood has anything to do with this book. It must have to do with the 'gifts' that Sterling was referring to, or maybe it's like the fairy blood, but has to do with your bloodline—your heritage!"

Now that Sofia was able to view the book with Nico, he opened it and quickly thumbed through the pages, reading tidbits out loud.

"'Binding;' 'Call Rain;' '*Corno Portafortuna*;' 'Enlargement;' 'Fairy Fire;' 'Poison Curative.' What is this stuff?" Nico asked.

"I think it is a grimoire of spells, potions, and charms," Sofia responded. "Wait, go back a few pages, I see a spell you might need to use," Sofia continued, while holding back her laughter.

Nico started flipping back the pages and then stopped when he realized Sofia was being playful. "Enlargement. Ha, ha. Very funny. I am quite happy with the size of my manhood and don't need that spell, thank you!"

Continuing forward once again, Nico reached the middle of the book. As he turned the next page, they both noticed that the following pages had their lettering upside down. Nico closed the book and turned it over. On this side of the grimoire's cover was embossed: Malandanti.

Quickly paging through contents of this side of the book, Nico read out more page titles:

"'Change Voice;' 'Mad Honey;' 'Mirror of the Dead;' 'Shrink Object;' 'Summon Darkness;' 'Tea of Forgetfulness.' This side appears to reference spells, and the like, that are of a darker origin."

As Nico neared the middle of the book again, he noticed that the remaining pages were different; there was a familiarity to them. It was the penmanship.

"Sofia, these last pages were written by my nonna. I recognize her handwriting," Nico remarked.

"Wow, check it out," Sofia said with amazement. "This page is titled: *Prophecies*. I wonder what this one means."

When the blood of the sun meets the moon,
The bound one shall be released from its tomb.

"I have no clue. Maybe it is another riddle of sorts?" Nico replied and turned to the next page.

"This looks like a note to you," Sofia pointed out and began to read the message:

My dearest Nico,

If you've found this message, then it is with regret that I've met an untimely demise. I'm sorry I didn't get the chance to say a proper goodbye. That being said, you are in good hands now that you've found the family grimoire.

Since I am not here to explain and educate you on the mysteries of our ways, it is my hope, that along with this book and the house, some of the townsfolk will assist you in understanding the many gifts you've been given, and the responsibility you now bear in keeping this town safe.

Now that the house is yours, you need to claim it and bind it to you by reciting the following words:

Haec Domus Mea Est

Once those words are spoken, the house will serve you as it once served me.

Until we speak again….

Love, Nonna

P.S. The garden gnomes come with the house.

Nico's emotions began to surface at the thought of his nonna's words. But, instead of tearing up as he had done before, he felt a sense of peace wash over him; he felt reconnected to her, as if she were still alive. The thought of tomorrow's funeral no longer felt as dreadful; he no longer felt as if he were going in order to say goodbye to her one final time.

"Nico, are you OK?" Sofia said in a soft tone.

"Never better," Nico replied with a resilient smile. "I suppose I have some Latin I should be reciting about now."

Nico looked down at the page and spoke the instructed words, "*Haec Domus Mea Est.*"

They both lay there in silence for about a minute, listening and looking around for some sign that something had occurred.

"Well, that was anticlimactic!" Nico finally said with an air of disappointment.

"I agree," Sofia said, "but at least you found *one* of the things that your nonna wanted you to find."

"What more could there possibly be, Sofia?"

"At the bottom of the chest, there's something else. It looks like a pull latch," Sofia responded.

Nico sprang up from the bed, went over to the chest, and saw the small iron ring latch Sofia was referring to. On the opposite side of the latch, he noticed a set of hinges. He reached into the chest and fished up the iron ring so that he could loop his finger though it. With a gentle tug, he was able to raise the entire bottom of the chest, revealing a set of narrow stairs that led down into the darkness.

"It must lead to the basement," Sofia guessed.

"Let me get a flashlight so we can see. Stay here, I'll be right back."

Moments later Nico returned with the old candelabra from his nonna's room.

"Why did I think I would be able to find a flashlight in this house?" he chuckled and struck a match to light the three nearly spent candles. "I'll go first—who knows what's down there."

Nico slowly crept down the narrow staircase, holding the candelabra outward to better see what was ahead. After only three steps, one of the candles suddenly went out, narrowing his field of vision. Sofia followed closely with one arm on Nico's shoulder and counted the steps in her head.

When they reached the bottom of the stairs, they heard a loud *bang* like a door slamming above them. Startled, they bumped into each other. Nico raised the candelabra and looked toward the top of the stairs; the entryway appeared to be sealed off. They then heard another quieter *bang*, followed by six *clicks*.

"Sounds like the chest locked itself back up. We're going to have to find another way out," Sofia remarked. "I gather we're in another area of the basement. We went down exactly thirteen steps—same as the main staircase—so, we should be at the same level."

Nico searched for an alternate light source as a second candle was now threatening to dim and go out. Frustrated, Nico vented openly, "Would be nice if there was some light down here!"

Within seconds an overhead light flickered on.

Sofia looked at Nico in amazement and said, "I guess the house truly *is* yours now! There's no denying that the light went on right when you requested it. That must be what your nonna meant when she mentioned that the house would 'serve' you as it did her."

"Well, I hope it can do more than just switch on a light," Nico said and then paused. He realized how ungrateful his comment sounded. If it were not for the house's action, the remaining two candles would have eventually gone out, leaving them in the dark and lessening their chances of finding an exit. He turned his head toward the ceiling and continued speaking in an effort to apologize to the house. "I mean, thank you for turning on the light—we really, really appreciate it."

With the room now properly illuminated, their need to find an exit did not seem as dire; instead, they were now distracted by the room's collection of oddities. Some of the items seemed familiar, yet others they'd never seen the likes of before. Each item was labeled and arranged on various shelves and tables that lined three of the walls in the room.

Sofia was drawn to a section of the room where she noticed three reclaimed tree branches, used as dowels, evenly spaced and hanging horizontally from the ceiling. Groupings of different herbs were bound with twine and hung upside down to dry. Below the drying racks was a long potting table with a small sink. Six rows of shelves, affixed to the back of the table, displayed an assortment of glass and ceramic apothecary jars. Under the table was a shelf slightly raised from the floor; on it was a row of gourds.

"It's like we stepped into a giant cabinet of curiosities," Nico said as he tried to take in all the interesting items displayed about the room.

"Check this out, Nico. I've never seen such a large collection of so many different herbs and seeds. Some must be from the garden, but others—maybe she got them from Mr. Sakura."

"It's possible. I remember him coming over many times when I stayed here. He would have tea with my nonna, and they would talk for hours. He'd always bring with him a gift—either a rare orchid or some odd-looking plant, like that rare *Nepenthes* you discovered the other day."

"Nico, look at this jar. It is full of beans. Fava beans—just like the one I found under the doormat when we first arrived." Sofia noticed the jar's dusty and faded handwritten label and lightly brushed off the dust with her finger so that she could read it. "Hmm…it is labeled: Fagioli Fortunati, which translates to Lucky Beans."

Nico joked, "We might need some of those to get out of this room!"

Sofia knelt down to inspect the lower shelf of gourds. All of them appeared to have something written on them. She picked one up; it was light in weight and appeared to be dried. On it was written the name *Mario M.* She put it back in its place and noticed another one at the far end of the shelf, directly under the sink. This gourd differed in color than the others; it had greenish-black spots on it, and the name written on it was starting to smear. Sofia picked it up; it felt slightly slimy and slipped from her hands. The moldy gourd hit the cement floor and broke open. "Whoops!" she exclaimed, slightly embarrassed.

"What's going on over there?" Nico asked sharply.

"I accidentally dropped one of the gourds. The sink appears to have a slow leak. Over time the water must have dripped on this gourd causing it to mold. I'll clean it up." Sofia picked up the decaying pieces, one of which had the name *Amara P.* written on it. She placed the collected pieces into the sink. *Once we find an exit to this room, I'll return later and properly dispose of this decomposing mess*, she thought to herself. Finding a small hand towel near the sink, she turned on the water in order to wet a corner of the towel. The pipes rumbled, and rust-colored water trickled out from the rarely used faucet. Eventually the water became clear, and its flow increased. Wringing out a corner of the wet towel, she knelt back down, wiped up the remaining gooey mess, and then rinsed off her hands.

Meanwhile, in the opposite corner of the room, Nico came upon a large apothecary chest that intrigued him and he'd gone over to examine it. It had at least forty little drawers and sitting on top of it was a marble bust of a young woman. He eventually recognized the figure; it was his nonna. The unblemished marble surface captured the likeness of a more youthful version of her, similar to the portrait upstairs. He looked down at the multitude of tiny drawers and scanned each label. He stopped at one and pulled the drawer's tiny handle. "Sofia, check this out: 'Hag Stones.'" Nico removed one of the stones from the drawer to get a better view of it in the light.

Sofia, now curious because of the unique name, went over to where Nico was standing. In his hand he held what appeared to be a greyish stone with multiple holes running into it, some holes actually going through to the other side.

"That is very cool. I wonder what it does or is used for?" Sofia questioned. "I'm sure the grimoire has an explanation for all of these items."

"Well now that we know how to get down here, we can always come back and explore further—providing we find a way out. Speaking of which, we should really get back to finding an exit," Nico said with some concern. And, without thinking, he placed the hag stone into his pocket and closed the drawer from which it came.

"I agree," Sofia responded while scanning the room. "Three of these walls have shelving or tables against them, which leaves this wall free for possible access."

Sofia grabbed the candelabra, its candles now extinguished, and they walked over to the unadorned wall. It was composed of narrow, vertical pine wood panels; each one running from the floor to the ceiling. After staring at the wall for about a minute, Nico finally noticed that one of panels was slightly different.

"Look here. This one appears to be the only one with a horizontal cut, and there is some darkening of the wood just below the cut," Nico said as he ran his hand over the cut portion of the panel. Pressing on it, just below the cut, he felt the panel give slightly. A rumbling, mechanical noise could be heard as a large portion of the paneling moved outward and then slid to the right, offering them an exit from the room.

Relieved at first, they were soon disappointed to find that the exit led into a rather small, empty room with a simple door; the only light came from the room behind them, which shone onto a silver door handle.

Sofia anxiously pushed the lever downward. As the door opened, they heard again the now familiar mechanical noise of whirling gears and moving pulleys hidden within the walls of the house. They turned around and watched as a portion of the wall behind them began sliding back into its closed position. Above a demilune table that was bolted to the wall, hung a painting, but the dimness of the room made it nearly impossible to see the details depicted in the artwork.

"Come on. We can always return when we have a better source of light," Nico said as he exited the room and entered the main part of the basement. Sofia put the candelabra on the demilune and followed.

Across from them was the south facing wall lined with more awning windows, as in the wine cellar, a window placed about every six feet, just a few inches from the ceiling. The light filtering in through the windows cast shadows of the security bars and garden plants onto the basement floor.

"Ah, natural light," Sofia said with relief as she scanned the room. Looking down at the cold cement floor, she noticed something was off.

"Nico, look at the shadows from the far-right window. Notice anything different?"

"That I do!" Nico remarked. "It lacks shadows from the security bars."

They immediately went to investigate and noticed that this particular window was not only missing its security bars but also had been shattered. Nico started to formulate a theory, and he decided to run it by Sofia.

"I have a thought. You said that you found that the cabinet door to the basement was unlatched when you were exploring; you also said that all the upstairs entryways and windows had some sort of protection, whether it was a line of salt or bulbs of garlic; we then received that message from beyond when we were in the wine cellar that my nonna was murdered—"

"I see where you are going with this, and I think we're on the same page," Sofia interrupted. "The killer must have entered in through this unbarred window—it's the only unprotected area of the house—and then sneaked upstairs into your nonna's room at some point."

"I bet if we check outside in the garden, we'll find that the security bars for this window were tampered with. Let's go look," Nico responded anxiously.

Sofia turned and started heading back in the direction of the wine cellar. She abruptly stopped and shrieked.

"What is it, Sofia?"

"Over there!" Sofia pointed at a stack of boxes in the corner and then turned away. Three large brown rats were huddled on top of the boxes, starring at Nico and Sofia with their beady eyes.

"They can't hurt you, Sofia. I'll protect you," Nico said in a mock chivalrous tone while holding in his need to laugh at the current situation. He then looked over at the three watchful vermin and said in an exaggerated tone, "Stop looking at us—turn away! You're frightening my friend."

Nico turned to Sofia and let out a big laugh while offering her a hug. "See, I'm here for you!"

Sofia's dismay was lightened by Nico's comedic actions. She started to laugh, but stopped short and pointed. "Nico, I think they really heard you!"

Nico turned to the pile of boxes. The three rats were still huddled together, except now they were facing the wall; they had done an about-face.

"Probably a coincidence," Nico said, slightly puzzled. "Or maybe, because they're in the house, they are also affected by my ability to control it? Either way, all is good, and you're no longer in a state of terror." Nico smiled.

Sofia knew by his expression that he was teasing her with his last exaggerated comment and poked his side. "Yes, crisis averted—let's get back upstairs and check out the garden."

They ventured forward past the wine cellar and ascended the staircase. As they entered the kitchen, Nico, closed the cabinet door and latched it while Sofia headed to the conservatory. Nico caught up to her and opened the door to the yard so that she could pass through.

The garden's air was quite a contrast to the musty basement. As they inhaled the sweet aroma of orange blossoms and filled their lungs with fresh air, two hummingbirds came to greet them.

Sofia tried to focus on the fast-moving feathered friends, to see if they might actually be fairies this time but was slightly disappointed that they were not. Inspired, she held up her tattoo and the two hummingbirds flew over to investigate. They hovered about her arm and brushed up against the inked likeness. Another hummingbird flew over to check out the activity, followed by a fourth.

"Apparently you are now the hummingbird whisperer, while I'm stuck being the rat whisperer," Nico observed.

"Perhaps. But remember the other night? The raven seemed to listen to you as well when you told it to be quiet—and it wasn't in the house like the rats! So maybe you can influence more than just one type of creature," Sofia suggested.

A fifth hummingbird arrived and landed on Nico's shoulder for a few seconds and then flew off, as they made their way down the path along the south side of the house. They viewed each basement window carefully as they passed by, checking for evidence of tampering.

As they approached the sixth window, small conical hats could be seen peeking through the partially damaged foliage; the garden gnomes had moved from their previous locations and were now congregated by the window.

Just as they had anticipated, this window's security bars had seemingly been ripped out, bolts and all, from the window's frame. A few of the bolts could be spotted in the dirt while the others remained in the welded section of bars, which was now semi-hidden on top of a large lavender bush; its weight slowly causing it to sink into the center of the bush over the passing days.

"That confirms our theory," Sofia said. "But who or what could have had the strength to remove the bars? There are no pry marks against the frame, so it definitely appears to have been pulled out with some force." Sofia paused briefly and then continued, "And who moved all of the gnomes over here?"

"I guess those are two more of the many mysteries we need to solve," Nico replied and then changed the subject. "Well, it's near five p.m. and I'm starting to get hungry. Would you like to grab some take-out food from Moraiolo's and bring it back to the house? We can watch a scary movie on TV and then have our macarons for dessert."

"Sounds good!" Sofia agreed. "I couldn't have planned a more perfect evening. After all of today's adventures, a low-key evening is probably best. Plus, we need to be up early for tomorrow's funeral."

Nico and Sofia went back inside the house. Sofia made her way to the front bedroom to freshen up before heading back down to the piazza, while Nico made a phone call to Moraiolo's.

"Hello, this is Nico Frantoio. I'd like to place an order to pick up…"

After placing the order, he yelled across the house hoping that Sofia would hear him. "Food is ordered—should be ready in thirty minutes or so. Meet me in the foyer when you are ready."

Nico headed to the foyer and saw that Sofia was already there, patiently waiting. He motioned to her, and they exited the house and headed down the stairs.

Sofia stopped halfway down the stairs and said to Nico, "You forgot to lock the door."

"Oops, you're right—my mind was so focused on getting food, that I forgot. We sure don't want any more unwanted intruders," Nico said and then turned back to the house. "Time to see what *my* house can really do. House, secure yourself."

At once they could hear a *click* as the bolt to the front door moved into the locked position. They began walking down the sidewalk and heard another sound. It was a brief squeaking noise followed by wood slamming against wood.

Sofia recognized the sound and responded in amazement. "Nice! I had forgotten that I had left the window open in my bedroom."

It was slightly after five p.m. when they reached the piazza. The hustle and bustle of people moving about gave life to the town's center. Some people were closing up their businesses for the day and going home to their families; others, like Nico and Sofia, were coming into town for dinner and other nightly activities that the town had to offer.

Sofia nudged Nico as they reached the other side of the piazza. "Hey, look over there," she said while pointing in the direction of Schwartzman's Quality Clothing. "That guy coming out of the store—he looks somewhat familiar. And he's wearing the blue shirt that I wanted to get for you—I was told they were all sold out."

"Looks like they're closing for the evening—the blinds are already drawn. Maybe he was their last customer and had gone in to pick up a custom-made shirt, just like the one you saw on the mannequin. He probably wore it out of the store—like you did with your purchase." Nico responded.

Determined to find out more, Sofia briskly crossed the street and walked up behind the stranger and tapped him on the back. "Excuse me. Sorry to bother you."

The man stopped and turned around. "Sofi…uh, yes, hello. What can I do for you?" the unknown man replied.

Nico caught up to Sofia, who appeared to be captivated and just stood there in silence.

"We are sorry to bother you. My name is Nico, and this is my friend Sofia. She appreciates your taste in clothing and wanted to ask you about your shirt."

"Nice to meet you both. My name is Solomon."

Sofia continued to stare in silence, scanning the familiar blond figure up and down, trying to make sense of what she was feeling.

"Sofia, aren't you going to say hello?" Nico chided.

"Oh yes, I apologize for my rudeness. Nice to meet you as well," Sofia said to Solomon as she extended her hand and looked into his piercing blue eyes.

Solomon reached out, lowered his head, and, taking Sofia's hand into his, kissed the back of it. She immediately blushed and smiled back politely, in an attempt to mask her conflicting feelings: she was flattered, but something had felt unnatural.

"As Nico mentioned, I was admiring your shirt. Did you buy it today?" Sofia questioned Solomon.

"No. I have had it for quite some time," Solomon replied.

"Oh, that makes sense then. Nico and I had gone into Schwartzman's earlier today and I wanted to buy that exact shirt but was told that they were out. You have great taste!"

Solomon raised his hand and swept his hair to the side. Looking directly into Sofia's eyes, he smiled and asked, "Would you two care to join me for a drink at Moraiolo's? I was just going to get a beer at the bar."

"Sure! Beer sounds great—I mean, if that's OK with Sofia."

"Of course," Sofia replied with another forced smile. "We'll meet you there in a few. I just want to show Nico something in one of the store windows."

"All righty. I'll see you shortly," Solomon said and then continued to the restaurant.

Nico faced Sofia and rolled his eyes. "What was that all about? You were acting really bizarre. I can tell there's some chemistry going on there, but instead of being giddy with excitement, you became so reserved. Normally I can read you quite well, but this behavior has me stumped. I mean, even the raven prince that is stalking you around town causes more of a reaction."

"Well, he truly is a handsome man—those captivating eyes, that ashy blond head of hair with those messy bangs. It's like he just walked off a catwalk and onto the street. He's so perfect!" Sofia paused, realizing that she was sounding a bit infatuated and refocused before continuing. "Almost too perfect. But what really caused me to freeze up, was when he touched me."

"Are you referring to the hand kiss? Rather old fashioned, but I can see where a romantic soul such as yourself might go for that sort of thing," Nico joked.

Sofia tried to do her best to elaborate. "It was charming, don't get me wrong, but…but there was something unnatural about the whole thing. His hand, his lips…there was just this strange energy—I can't put my finger on it."

"Oh, I thought you were more put off by the fact that he was wearing the exact same outfit as the store mannequin. Right down to the shoes, belt—everything!" Nico said in a playful manner.

"You know, other than the shirt, I didn't even notice the rest of his outfit," Sofia replied.

"Well, now that you've gotten that off your chest, let's have a beer with our new friend and pick up our food—it should be ready soon."

Nico and Sofia stepped into the restaurant and headed over to the bar. They immediately spotted Solomon, who was engaged in conversation with a female; her back was turned toward them. Solomon noticed the two and waved, beckoning them to come over. The unknown female turned around to see what the excitement was about; it was Fawn.

Nico whispered to Sofia from the corner of his mouth as they approached. "Looks like you might have some friendly competition."

"Sofia! Nico! So great to see you two!" Fawn said with excitement and hugged them both. "Solomon was just telling me that he invited you to join our Saturday evening ritual: beer and small-town gossip—I've already filled him in about you two."

"We just happened to be in the area to pick up some dinner to take back to the house and figured that a quick beer before dinner wouldn't hurt," Nico said.

Sofia stood there quietly, once again staring at Solomon, whose blond hair seemed to glow like a halo in the dimly lit bar. Realizing Sofia was non-responsive, Nico gently and discreetly stepped on the toe of her left shoe, snapping her out of her trance-like gaze.

"Yes…" Sofia responded, realizing that she had been deep in thought once again. And, in an effort to cover up her embarrassment, she attempted to divert attention. Speaking in a peppier tone, she continued, "Yes, where's my beer? I'd like to make a toast!"

Solomon set his beer down and looked into Sofia's eyes while saying, "Let's get you two some beer. Come with me—orders are placed at the other end of the bar."

Without a word, Sofia followed Solomon over to the bartender and requested two chilled steins of beer.

Nico leaned over to Fawn, and in a hushed tone, questioned her. "Shouldn't you be at home? It'll be getting dark soon, and you know, your father might begin to worry about your safety—you know, with all of the abductions that have been happening."

Fawn, with a note of confidence in her voice, whispered back, "Solomon will protect me. He'll make sure I get home safely."

As Sofia and Solomon headed back to the table, each carrying a beer, Nico rushed out one more question to Fawn. "Is he one of your kind?"

Fawn mouthed, "No" as Solomon handed the beer he was carrying to Nico and then reached for his stein that was awaiting him on the table.

Sofia raised her stein and, looking into Nico's eyes, began her toast. "Nico, you are like a *brother* to me." Pausing briefly, she gave a side glance in Solomon's direction and then continued, "And it is with great honor and privilege that I'm here to support you during this time in your life. As I begin to learn more and more about your nonna, I feel that I'm also learning more about you."

"To Chiara Frantoio and all she has done for this town and its people," Fawn cheered.

"Yes! To Chiara Frantoio—without her, I wouldn't be half the man that I am," Solomon followed.

After everyone clinked their steins and took a sip of their beers, Nico turned to Solomon and asked, "You knew my nonna?"

"Yes. Truly a wonderful lady. There's probably only a handful of people in this town who haven't had their lives changed by her in some amazing way," Solomon replied.

Nico returned a toast to Sofia. "Sofia, you are like a *sister* to me," Nico said and winked. "It is obvious that this new journey I'm on wouldn't have been possible had you not been by my side. I'm so grateful for your friendship. Grazie!"

At that moment Matteo, the waiter from the previous evening, appeared with Nico and Sofia's food; all nicely packed up to-go. "*Buonasera ragazzi*! Welcome back!"

"Thank you, Matteo," Nico said with gratitude. Reverting his attention back to Sofia, he said, "Bottoms up! Time to go home and eat!"

Nico and Sofia finished the last of their beer and said their goodbyes. The fresh evening air cooled their flushed faces as they left the restaurant. The moon was visible and bright, lighting their way as they walked back to the house.

Forgetting that he could command the house to unlock the front door, Nico retrieved his key and inserted it into the keyhole. As the tumblers clicked into place, the memory of his nonna unlocking the front door, after returning from Saturday evening mass, flooded his thoughts. *Tomorrow I will be with her again at church.*

Once inside, Sofia brought the food into the kitchen and began to plate it. Nico went to wash up and then joined her for their well-deserved and delicious meal. Shortly after finishing their meal, which consisted of rosemary focaccia, lasagna, and a simple *insalata mista*, Nico grabbed the box of macarons and led Sofia into the family room; a room that Sofia had not yet discovered. Sofia quickly claimed her spot on the comfy, plush couch and Nico sat down at the other end while turning on the TV with the remote control.

It was now 9:00 p.m. and a local television station's horror host was introducing tonight's feature: "Night of the Living Dead"; a classic zombie film that they had seen multiple times back at the boarding house. As the movie began, Nico opened the box of macaroons and scanned its contents. Choosing the one that might be lemon-flavored, he then passed the box to Sofia before taking a nibble.

About six minutes into the film, the famous line, "They're coming to get you, Barbara," played through the television speakers. Normally they would mimic the line together, but this time Nico was quiet, and Sofia spoke the line alone.

"Earth to Nico, where are you? You missed our favorite line," Sofia said with concern.

"Sorry, Sofia. The movie was reminding me about tomorrow's funeral and having to be at the cemetery for the burial."

"I hope you aren't worried about zombies—you know zombies aren't real, right?" Sofia responded, trying to lighten the mood and knowing that Nico was probably starting to feel down again.

"No, of course they aren't real. But then again—after all we've experienced and learned in the past two days, who knows—maybe they do exist," Nico replied with a smile. "By the way, I want to thank you again for being here with me—and for me. As I said in my toast earlier, I really don't think I'd be able to go through this alone."

"You know I'm here for you—like a *sister*," Sofia started to chuckle at her further attempt to lighten the mood; and it worked. Nico began to laugh along with her.

Focusing on the last three words of Sofia's previous response, he teased, "You really are smitten by that guy! I mean, we've been in public together many times and you've never made it that obvious that we're *just* friends and nothing more."

"I don't know what it is about Solomon. I think the fact that something isn't quite right about him is what attracts me. Other than the fact that he is drop dead gorgeous."

"Well, he's friends with Fawn, so he can't be that bad. And, when you two were getting our beer, I asked Fawn if he was Fey like her, and she said he wasn't. So maybe he's just a regular townie who happens to be exceptionally handsome."

"Either way, there's nothing I can do about it tonight, so let's watch the rest of the movie," Sofia replied.

Toward the end of the movie, Nico began to nod off, exhausted from a combination of the day's revelations and his emotions. Sofia lightly nudged him and suggested he go to bed and get some rest.

Nico said goodnight and headed off toward his bedroom. Sofia turned off the television and went to the kitchen to throw away the empty box of macarons, before heading to her bedroom.

Sofia opened the bedroom window to air out the room, which was still warm from the afternoon's setting sun. She grabbed her toiletries and went into the bathroom to get ready for bed. She was feeling somewhat anxious and not at all sleepy. She returned to her room and sat on the bed. The grimoire was still lying there where they had left it before being trapped in the basement's secret room.

She reached for the aged, leatherbound book and opened it. Once again it was blank. *There goes my late-night reading*, she sighed.

As the temperature in the room began to cool from the light breeze coming from the open window, Sofia felt a slight chill. She reached for Nico's sweatshirt and pulled it over her head and then went over to close the window. Returning to the bed, she picked up the grimoire and was about to put it away when she noticed words beginning to appear. She thumbed through the pages and was excited that she now could see the book's entire contents.

Sofia pulled back the bedcover and propped a few pillows up against the headboard. She crawled into bed and pulled up the covers while getting into a comfortable position. With the book on her lap, she began reading each page, starting from the Benandanti side. She went through each spell, charm, and potion until she reached the exact middle of the book. This last page of the Benandanti side had a spell which was partially written; it was like someone divided the paragraph vertically into two columns and removed the second column. The partial title of the spell read:

The Grand

She flipped the page and saw that the backside had similar formatting as the previous page, but was this page was missing its first column of words and appeared to be written upside-down. *This must be the end page of the Malandanti side*, she reasoned and turned the book around. The partial title of this spell read:

Reversal

She deduced that both sides were needed in order to complete the spell. *Wow this is pretty cool stuff. I guess since we didn't thoroughly go through each page, we missed it...and this!* Sofia noticed a small, folded piece of paper; it looked like it might be from the same stationery that Nico's nonna had written her note on. Sofia opened the folded paper; it was a list of Italian words, each sorted into one of three columns:

M	*B*	*V*
Lucertole	*Api*	*Pipistrelli*
Corvi	*Rane*	*Ratti*
Ragni	*Colibrì*	*Lupi*

She stared at the list for a good five minutes trying to discern any possible logic to it. Finally, she gained some clarity. *The "M" and the "B" must stand for Malandanti and Benandanti, but I have no clue about the "V"—I'll have to ask Nico.*

Sofia began to yawn. Reaching over to the nightstand, she grabbed her wristwatch to check the time; it was now 1:00 a.m. *I guess time does go by fast when you're having fun*, she thought as her eyelids continued to grow heavier and eventually closed. She soon fell asleep.

Chapter 10: Good Mourning?

Sofia, wake up," Nico said in a frantic tone, while standing in front of her bed. "We have to be at the church in less than an hour."

"I'm so sorry, Nico," Sofia replied as she jumped out of bed. "Thank you for waking me up. By the way, you look very nice."

Nico was already dressed in his suit and tie, which was quite a rare sight, since he regularly wore shorts almost every day of the year.

"Thank you, sleepyhead. Now go get ready! I'll lay out your clothes and then make us cappuccinos—no mimosas for you this morning!" He teased.

About twenty minutes later Sofia walked into the kitchen as Nico finished adding the frothed milk to their cappuccinos.

"Wow that was fast! Did you find a 'Quick Dress' spell in the grimoire last night and decide to try it out? Oh, and might I add, you look stunning!" Nico said in amazement.

Sofia laughed as she reached for her cappuccino and then brought it to the table and sat down. Nico followed and sat down opposite her.

"You know, there's some really incredible stuff in that book." Sofia said as she took a sip from her cup, which left a trace of frothed milk above her lips.

Nico smiled at the sight of her in full makeup with a milk moustache and remarked, "I'm sure it will all be useful at some point."

"I couldn't sleep, so I thought it'd make for some interesting reading material. At first it was blank, like when we first discovered it—well at least it appeared blank to me. Then I started to get cold, so I put your sweatshirt on and that's when—that's it! Your favorite sweatshirt must still have traces of your energy since you've worn it so much. It must've acted as a conduit, in the same manner like when my elbow touched you, allowing me to see the written words. I guess the book is invisible to the eyes of most people, except for those who have Benandanti or Malandanti blood in them.

"Then, when I reached the middle of the book, I found a spell that was split—half of it was on the Benandanti side and the other on the Malandanti side. But things became more intriguing when I found a folded piece of paper that was stuck in between the pages. On it was a list of nine words written in Italian and separated into three columns. Each column had a letter above it and contained three of the nine words under each—I think it was in your nonna's handwriting."

Nico interrupted her. "Sounds interesting. You'll have to show me when we get back. But for now, we need to get going—and make sure to wipe your lip."

"Right. We should go. By the way, did I tell you that you looked nice? I am not used to seeing you all dressed up. I think you're ready to join Solomon as a model on my imaginary catwalk," Sofia said as she blotted her upper lip with a napkin. "Go ahead and start the car, I need to run back to my room and grab my purse and a scarf—I'll meet you outside."

As Sofia headed off to her bedroom, Nico called out, "I'm putting the house key on the entry table. Please lock the door since the house probably won't obey you." Nico said as he left the house to go start the car up.

It was an exceptionally cold spring morning; heavy fog surrounded the small town of Oliveto and blocked the sun's warmth that had graced them the previous morning. Even Nico, who normally ran warm, felt chilled enough to turn on the car's heater.

"Brrr!" Sofia said, as she stepped into the car and shut the door. "What a cold morning!"

Nico did not respond and chose to focus on driving to the church through the misty air. As the car approached the center of town, they noticed how desolate and lifeless the piazza seemed. Not even one person could be spotted moving about.

Passing the hotel, he turned down the same street that Sterling had taken yesterday, when he led them to the library. Ahead of them on the right was the town's main church, St. Anthony's Catholic Church; its structure was rather imposing and dominated a huge portion of the city block. As Nico was looking for a parking spot, he drove past a hearse that was parked in front of the church's main entrance. A slight chill ran through his body when he noticed a raven sitting on top of the vehicle, eyeing them as they passed by.

"Nico, look!" Sofia gasped as she pointed to the raven.

"Don't even say it—I saw!" Nico continued searching for a place to park. Frustrated, he decided to drive around the block to see if a space had become available.

"So many cars! Now we know where half the town is this morning," Sofia commented.

As they made their way around the block and returned to the front of the church, they could see that another raven had joined the first, perching on top of the hearse. A third now landed and joined the duo; they all began to *kraa* in unison and stared toward Nico and Sofia.

"There's a spot! Up ahead on the right.!" Sofia exclaimed.

"Finally!" Nico said in relief and pulled into the free space.

They exited the car and headed toward the church. Sofia locked her arm through Nico's and walked closely by his side.

"Let's go this way," Nico suggested, turning away from the church's main entrance. "I want to enter the church from the side door, so that I don't have to pass by the hearse—I'm just not ready for that."

They approached the side door. Nico opened it and allowed Sofia to enter first. A light smell of incense greeted them from the hallway ahead. As they continued forward, they could see a small chapel area on the right; multiple women dressed in black could be seen kneeling there and reciting the rosary together. Ahead, light came from a slightly open door. Nico peered his head inside and noticed a priest dressed in a white alb; he was taking an elegantly embroidered black chasuble off its hanger. Nico entered the room and approached the priest as he was placing the detailed garment over his head. The priest began to turn around, and as his head popped through the hole in the garment, he was startled by Nico's presence.

"Hello, Father Michael," Nico greeted.

"Son, so good to see you—I'm just so sorry it had to be on a day like today. My condolences to you and your family."

Sofia entered the room and stood near Nico. "Father, this is my best friend, Sofia. Sofia, this is Father Michael D'Angelo."

"Nice to meet you," Sofia greeted while extending her hand. "I'm so sorry to hear about the recent break-in—I saw the headline in the newspaper yesterday."

Father Michael shook Sofia's hand. "A pleasure to meet you as well, Sofia," he replied and then continued dressing while adding, "It is such a loss to have our sacred relic taken."

"I never knew that the church had a relic. What was it?" Nico inquired.

Father Michael was adjusting his chasuble in the mirror and replied to their mirrored reflection. "All Catholic churches have a relic that is representative of that church's patron saint. Our church, for example, has—err had—a boar's tusk."

"Father," Sofia interrupted, "I find this all interesting as I am minoring in theology and religious studies. But what would a boar's tusk have to do with the life of St. Anthony of Padua?"

"That, my dear, is a common assumption by many. This church's patron saint is actually St. Anthony the Great. And, as part of your ongoing education, I will let you do the research to find out the connection, since I need to continue preparing for mass."

"Yes, of course. I realize we're keeping you from your duties," Sofia respectfully replied. "Nico, maybe we should find your mother."

"We probably should. Nice to see you again Father Michael. I'm sure we'll talk further after the service," Nico said and then followed Sofia out of the room.

Further down the hall they could see the entryway to the nave of the church. Piano music could be heard in the distance and began to increase in volume as they neared. The church seemed bigger on the inside than one would have thought if viewing it from the exterior. The ceilings were extremely high, about three stories, and slightly vaulted. In the center of the church was a raised area where a modestly adorned altar was placed directly under the church's spire; two altar boys were there lighting the candles. On either side of the altar there were numerous rows of pews for seating, all of which appeared to be filled with people. The church was at full capacity; a sight Nico had rarely seen when he served as an altar boy.

"There's my mother," Nico said turning to Sofia, who was now beginning to trail behind.

Sofia had become distracted by a series of paintings of lesser-known saints that lined one of the walls leading to the back of the church. The first painting to catch her eye was of St. Veridiana facing two large serpents. Moving to the next painting, she immediately recognized its subject, it was St. Cuthbert standing by the sea with two otters at his feet. The third painting depicted St. Roche with a dog by his side; she recalled having seen this one in her school textbook. St. Corbinian was portrayed in the next picture. She was not familiar with this saint but from his attire, she could tell he was a bishop; next to him lay a bleeding mule that had been attacked by a nearby black bear. *Interesting. When I research St. Anthony the Great, I'll have to look up Corbinian as well*, she noted. As she reached the last painting toward the back of the church, she gasped. She squinted in the dark corner of the church to read the label on the frame: St. Meinrad. In this picture, St. Meinrad is shown kneeling in prayer as two robbers ready their clubs to beat him; two ravens, hovering above, seem to be watching the scene. *I can't seem to escape being around ravens*, she thought.

Suddenly, realizing that Nico was now halfway across the church at the pew where Siena was sitting, Sofia quickly abandoned her latest distraction and made her way to him. The clacking of her heels caused many of the seated people to turn as she moved hastefully down the aisle to the front of the church.

"Sorry about that, Nico, I saw something…" she whispered to Nico and then greeted his mother and stepfather. "Hello Siena, Dr. Kynigós—I mean Pétros."

"Come you two, sit here," Siena said, as she and Pétros scooted down the pew to make room. "The mass is about to start."

Nico allowed Sofia to sit first so that he could take a seat at the end along the center aisle. The church was now quiet, and the pianist sat poised and ready to play the entrance hymn. As Nico looked toward the altar, he could see his nonna lying peacefully in the open coffin which was surrounded by at least forty unique floral arrangements. She looked just like the last time he saw her; hair perfect, skin flawless, impeccably dressed, but something was off, something was missing.

Nico tried not to obsess but found himself continuing to stare at her coffin. It was simple, understated, and black in color. The only detailing was that of the silver swing handles and a floral design at the base where they were attached. Nico recognized the design as being geranium flowers and smiled to himself. *Probably another clue purposely put in place just in case I wasn't able to figure out the secret to opening the chest*, Nico thought. *She had it all planned out in advance.*

Nico felt a poking on his right arm; it was his mother.

"Nico, would you mind being a pallbearer? We are one short. I know this is last minute and you don't have to if you don't want to, but I just thought…."

"Of course, I will," Nico whispered back.

The funeral director quickly breezed by to close the coffin lid, as the mass was about to begin. And, as soon as he completed his task, the pianist began playing the entrance hymn, prompting everyone to rise from their seats. Father Michael made his entrance with one altar boy on his left carrying incense and the other carrying the processional cross. As all three passed the coffin, Father Michael veered off to quickly greet Nico and his mother before joining the altar boys and continuing up to the altar. Deacon Santo Servitore, who must have been running late, suddenly appeared and made his way up to the altar as well.

"Today, we're here to mourn the loss of Chiara Scuro-Frantoio, beloved mother, nonna, and friend to all in our quaint little town," Father Michael began. "As a priest, it's my duty to provide pastoral care and help to all of our parishioners. But many times, it was Chiara who took the time to care and help not only me, but many of you. Her wisdom and guidance knew no bounds. And so, we say this mass for her departed soul."

Toward the end of the mass, after communion, Father Michael invited a few people up to the lectern who wanted to share how Chiara impacted their lives. Sterling was first and spoke about how grateful he was for Chiara's guidance and support of the community. Mrs. Schwartzman followed and talked about how blessed and indebted she was for all of Chiara's help. A few other people, that Nico did not recognize, spoke as well. After everyone had finished, Father Michael spoke into the microphone, "Nico, would you like to come up and say some words about your nonna?"

Caught off guard, Nico began to blush and feel warm. Public speaking was not his forte and he was not expecting this; he had nothing prepared and Sofia knew that. "You got this Nico. It'll come to you. Just take a deep breath and speak from your heart."

Nico rose from his seat and walked up to the altar and bowed before it. He looked out at the vast sea of people on both sides of the church as he approached the lectern. He cleared his throat and then was silent for about thirty seconds as he collected his thoughts and reined in his emotions.

He took a deep breath, and as Sofia had suggested, the words finally came to him. "Thank you all for coming. Your support during this time means a lot to my family and myself." Nico took another deep breath before continuing. "We're all taught to love unconditionally and my nonna was a testament to that. She loved us all no matter what.

"When I was a child, I used to spend a lot of time with her. If I wasn't spending the night at her house while my parents were away, I was at the real estate office after school, doing my homework by her desk before walking home.

"She had a keen eye for detail and took pride in doing things the proper way. She would always spot the smallest piece of lint on my school sweater and pick it off or notice that one stray hair on my head that wasn't lying down and make sure it was in place. While doing my homework, she would critique my handwriting abilities and tell me that I should loop the *L*'s like the textbook showed. As a kid I found this to be annoying, like many children might, but I always felt loved.

"As I grew older and into my late teens, I began to relate to her on a different level. I was no longer afraid to joke or be playful around her. In jest, I started picking the lint off of her sweaters and telling her when her hair was out of place, which was very, very rare. When I would do this, she would just look at me sternly and then release a big smile that she had forcibly been trying to hold back. It was as if she was proud that I had inherited her keen sense of spotting things out of place."

Nico paused for a second, trying to hold back his tears. He looked down at Sofia for strength and continued, "Making her smile was such a big joy for me—I would do anything to see her smile again. She was always committed to making sure—"

Nico was interrupted by a disheveled, older-looking woman who had just entered the church and began ranting and screaming maniacally as she ran toward the coffin. Nico rushed down to protect the coffin and secure the area where Sofia and his parents were sitting.

About a dozen men, including Nico's stepfather, immediately rose from their seats and headed toward the crazed woman to help restrain her and stop the disturbance.

"She has to help me!" The woman screamed, as tears ran down her face.

Fortunately, three of the men were able to grab hold of her and prevent her from reaching the coffin. The sound of fabric ripping from her already tattered dress could be heard throughout the hushed church as she struggled to get free.

A man rushed up. "She is a patient of mine—I'll take care of her. She's just out of her gourd." The man, Nico recognized, was Dr. Mario Matto, his childhood therapist.

Dr. Matto turned to the restrained woman and, putting his hand on her forehead, spoke calmly and quietly to her. "Amara, it's me, Dr. Matto. Everything is going to be OK." As he was speaking, he reached into his left coat pocket and pulled out a small amber bottle, and using the same hand, unscrewed the top which then fell to the floor. He placed the strange bottle under Amara's nostrils. She immediately threw back her head and seemed to come to her senses.

Sofia stepped out of the pew and went over to Nico to offer support. On her way she reached down and picked up the tiny lid that had fallen from Dr. Matto's hands. She discreetly brought the lid to her nose and took a quick smell. The lingering pungent odor from the lid seemed almost as potent as the full contents of the amber bottle and caused Sofia's eyes to water.

"Excuse me sir, I think you might need this," Sofia said and handed the lid to him.

"Thank you," He replied in a muted tone to Sofia and replaced the cap on the bottle. "Gentlemen, you can release her. I think she'll be fine for now. I'll take her back to my office."

Dr. Matto led Amara outside as the sound of everybody whispering could be heard throughout the church.

Father Michael stepped up to the lectern to speak, and the funeral attendees became quiet once more. "I apologize for the interruption. Nico would you like to continue?"

Nico shook his head no and returned to his seat with Sofia.

Siena reached across Sofia and grabbed Nico's forearm to get his attention. "Nicolino, that was a lovely eulogy; she would've been touched to hear your moving words. I just wish that crazy town gossip, Amara Pettegolo, hadn't disrupted the moment."

Sofia let out a restrained gasp when she heard the name Amara Pettegolo. *Oh, no!* She thought, *that was the same name on the gourd I dropped—and I forgot to return and dispose of the pieces that I left in the sink.*

Father Michael stepped down from the altar and approached the coffin. Deacon Servitore followed, carrying a censer of burning incense. Father Michael reached into the silver aspersorium of holy water being held by one of the altar boys and pulled out the aspergillum. As he sprinkled holy water over the coffin, he said a final blessing. He then took the censer of burning incense from the deacon and gently swung it back and forth as he circled the coffin and ended his prayer. Looking up to the people, he blessed them and let them know that he would see them shortly at the cemetery for the burial.

The pianist began to play a closing song and people began to rise from their seats and line up to pay their respects to Nico and his family. *So many people*, Nico thought.

Eventually, the crowd of people lessened and the final three people in line gave their condolences. Nico, Sofia, and his family stepped out of the pew and walked over to the coffin. The funeral director, Mr. Primo Cadaveri, came over to greet them. As he turned to begin preparing the coffin for transport, Nico noticed something fall off the shoulder of the funeral director's suit jacket. The object seemed to flutter slowly down onto the stone floor. Nico went over to pick it up and returned to where Sofia was standing.

"Sofia, look at this," Nico directed. "It looks like…"

"Almost like part of a dragonfly wing," Sofia chimed in. "It has the same type of veining and membrane structure—similar to leaded glass. Maybe it's a clue!"

Sofia opened her purse and took out a tissue. Nico handed her the mysterious object and she gently wrapped it up and placed it into her purse, next to the house key.

"Nico, we need you," Siena called out.

"Time for me to do my duties. I think this is going to be the hardest part for me." Nico said to Sofia and then slowly walked over to the coffin to take his place as a pallbearer.

No sooner had Nico touched the coffin, than he felt a mysterious hand rest on his shoulder. Immediately his body seized up and he froze in place. He could only tell that the person behind him was similar in height and gave him cause to be fearful for some reason. He took a deep breath and turned around. It was Mr. Cadaveri who had come to position Nico at the left front of the coffin, and then have the other pallbearers take up the other positions.

Nico reluctantly reached for the silver swing handle. As his clammy hand touched the cold metal, he saw his nonna. This time it was not a vision of the past; he was in the present and saw her standing near the main entrance of the church; she was smiling at him. Nico began to tear up. *That beautiful smile. I said I would do anything to see her smile again and there it is.*

Nico suddenly became lightheaded and collapsed to the ground. Tears continued running down his face.

Siena ran over and propped Nico up into her arms. "Nicolino. My precious boy. Are you OK?"

Nico looked up to his mother and replied, "Yes, mom, I'll be OK. I'm so sorry. There's so much going on…and I guess my emotions got the best of me."

"I understand. You two were very close, closer at times than I was. Your relationship was a special one," Siena replied in a comforting tone.

Nico stood up and took his place once again. He reached for the coffin's swing handle and, along with the other pallbearers, lifted the coffin off the bier. The coffin felt light; almost empty, but he could still feel his nonna's embalmed corpse rocking back and forth as they headed toward the hearse, and this disturbed him immensely.

I can do this, he thought. *Just a few more feet.*

The church doors opened, and the light of the sun shone across the threshold into the church, reflecting off the shiny black coffin lid as they approached the awaiting hearse. Nico looked away from the glare that was blinding him and noticed that all traces of the dreary morning fog had vanished; a perfect blue sky was now visible.

One of Mr. Cadaveri's sons, Dino, opened the backdoor of the hearse, while his other son, Gino, helped guide the coffin safely inside the vehicle.

Nico stepped away from the hearse as the last part of the coffin slid inside. Dino closed the shiny black door and glared at Nico, completely devoid of emotion, as he walked to the driver side door and entered the vehicle.

Nico shivered slightly, having felt uncomfortable by the silent interaction, and walked over to Sofia, who was chatting with his mother and stepfather.

"Nico, would you and Sofia like to ride with us to the cemetery?" Siena asked.

"Thank you, but we'll take the rental car. I might want to stay a little longer after the burial," Nico responded. "Come on Sofia, let's get to the car so we can line up and follow the procession to the cemetery."

Walking back to their car, Sofia stopped and turned to Nico. Putting her hands on his shoulders, she looked him in the eyes and asked, "Are you OK? I'm concerned with all that happened back there."

"Which part?" Nico chuckled, trying to lighten the moment. "A lot happened."

"I know. I know. But I really was concerned when you fainted. Your mother was frantic—she'd been calm the entire time, but seeing you faint really stirred something up within her. And the way she rushed to your side—the only person I've seen move with such speed has been Sterling."

"No, she isn't Fey if that's where you're going with this. It was probably just a mothering instinct that came to the surface, causing her to act so quickly."

"No, I wasn't thinking she was Fey. It was just an incredible sight to see—rather touching actually. But, when she was holding you as you lay there, I noticed that tears were rolling down your face."

"They were actually tears of joy. You know the strange visions that I have been having? Like the one I had during our plane flight; and then the one I mentioned I had while Sterling was tattooing my arm? Well, they've all been about events in the past and referenced my nonna in one way or another. This time, it wasn't a vision of the past—I actually saw my nonna standing across from me, near the church doors—she was smiling at me. I think the joy of seeing her smile one last time overloaded my senses with so much happiness that it caused me to faint. I didn't want to tell my mother what I'd—what I *thought* I'd seen."

"I have no doubt that you actually saw her," Sofia reassured. "Let's get to the car before everyone leaves us behind—we can continue our conversation there."

Nico started up the car. Pulling away from the curb, he made a U-turn and headed back toward the church. Sofia was already preoccupied with searching for a good song on the radio; changing stations until a familiar song was heard.

An old pickup truck at the intersection ahead had stopped and was allowing Nico to enter the procession of vehicles. Realizing it was Sterling and Fawn in the car, Nico smiled and waved in gratitude as he pulled forward.

Now began the slow drive through town to the local cemetery, which would occupy the next ten to fifteen minutes of their lives. Sofia let out a sigh as she gave up on finding a good song on the radio and switched it off.

"Nico, who was that person that took Amara away?" Sofia asked.

"That was my childhood shrink, Dr. Matto. The one I told you about yesterday," Nico replied.

"I have a confession to make. I think somehow, I was the cause of her—madness, for lack of a better word."

"What do you mean? How could you have caused it? You've never even met the lady!" Nico responded as he signaled to make a right turn.

"Remember when we were in that secret room, and I dropped one of the gourds? Well, I forgot to mention that each one was labeled with a first name and last initial. The one that slipped from my hands was labeled: Amara P. I heard Dr. Matto mention that she was 'out of her gourd' just before he escorted her out of the church. I think a part of her psyche was held in that gourd and then released upon its destruction."

"That's highly plausible," Nico said in reply to Sofia's speculation. "So, when you were reading the grimoire last night, do you recall anything that referenced gourds?"

"I only made it through the Benandanti side. Maybe there is something on the Malandanti side—I'll look tonight." Sofia became quiet for a moment and then spoke once again. "One more thing. I was able to figure out the contents of the strange bottle that Dr. Matto held up to Amara's nose."

"Yeh? What do you think it was? Smelling salts, maybe?"

"No, it lacked traces of ammonia. I believe the bottle contained Seven Thieves Vinegar. Dr. Matto had dropped the lid to the bottle when he was attending to Amara. I went over to retrieve the lid so that no one would step on it and took a whiff of it before handing it to Dr. Matto. Immediately, I recalled that strong pungent herbal smell from my childhood. We had a bottle of Seven Thieves Vinegar in our caravan—in fact, I think it was a staple item for every Romani family to have a bottle."

"I wonder how they came up with that name?" Nico asked.

"As a kid I was told that sometime during the 14th century, at the time of the Black Death, seven thieves decided to make a career of robbing the dead. To protect themselves from the plague which had already decimated a third of the population, they created a preventative concoction. Each brought a unique herb and added it to a large jug of vinegar. After the seven herbs had macerated for a period of time, it was then ready for use. The thieves would then dab the pungent liquid behind their ears, on their temples, and on each hand, thus avoiding the plague while plundering the homes of its victims—until one day when they were finally apprehended."

"Fascinating," Nico responded. "I find folklore so entertaining."

"Well, here's a more modern tale from my early childhood. One day when we were traveling, the wheel of our caravan hit a large branch lying in the road, and we almost tipped over. As the caravan rocked back and forth, books and bottles started falling from the shelves. I was so scared, and as I tried to dodge the falling objects, a bottle of the Seven Thieves Vinegar came crashing down at my feet. As the glass shattered, the acidic contents of the bottle splashed all over my dress—that smell lingered for days! And so that's how I was able to identify the contents of Dr. Matto's bottle. Sadly, nothing supernatural to report—just a story about an herbal concoction and my misfortune." Sofia finished with a brief chuckle.

Chapter 11: Burial and Fulfillment

Nico made a left turn and drove up a small hill. As the hill leveled off, they could see their destination: Olive Tree Hill Cemetery. A large, rusted gate, barely hanging from its hinges, had been opened earlier to allow access for the oncoming procession of cars.

"Talk about a scary-looking cemetery. This reminds me of the one in last night's movie!" Sofia commented.

The pavement transitioned into gravel as the car passed through the open gateway. Small stones crunched under the weight of the car as Nico drove forward; wisps of dust filled the air behind them.

"It's not so bad, actually," Nico remarked. "See that hill of olive trees ahead? Well, the area this side of the hill is referred to as the old section—it isn't very well-maintained. Once we round the hill, we enter the new section, which is like night-and-day in comparison to this side."

"What's on the hill other than the cluster of olive trees?" Sofia asked.

"That's where some of the really old graves are located. In fact, a few of my relatives, as well as some of the town founders, are buried there. A beautiful water fountain is placed in the center and adds to the tranquility of that spot—it's almost like you're in another world.

"My nonna would visit our family's mausoleum and other graves once a week to tidy things up and place fresh flowers. If I was staying with her, she would take me along. As soon as she parked the car, I would bolt out and run up to the top of the hill. A rope swing, which hung from one of the larger olive trees, would be my amusement while watching water trickle from the fountain. I would swing the entire time until my nonna came up the hill to check on one final grave before bringing me back down."

"Sounds really cool. Maybe, depending on how you are feeling after the burial, you can take me up there and show me around?" Sofia asked, trying to be sensitive to Nico's well-being.

"I think I can manage that. Plus, I'm now curious to see if the old swing is still up there, and if the fountain is still running," Nico replied.

As Nico rounded the side of hill, the new section of the cemetery became visible. The vehicles ahead of them began to slow and pull off to the side of the road to park. People were exiting their vehicles and making their way to the Frantoio family mausoleum. In the distance, Nico could see his mother and his stepfather standing by the hearse waiting for them.

Nico pulled off to the side of the road and parked the car. The long line of vehicles behind them did the same.

"Nico, can I hold your arm as we walk? I'm not used to walking on gravel while in heels, and I really don't want to fall."

"Of course. Here, grab ahold," Nico offered.

They continued up the road until they reached the mausoleum. Siena was standing near the entrance of the large, weathered marble construction speaking to Father Michael; Nico's stepfather was further away, conversing with a group of attendees.

As Nico and Sofia drew closer, they noticed Mr. Cadaveri and his two sons coming out of the mausoleum. *They must have just delivered the coffin*, Nico thought. As the solemn trio passed Nico and Sofia, Dino once again gave Nico a soulless scowl.

"What's up with him?" Sofia asked. "I caught him staring you down outside the church. Did you go to school together or know their family?"

"I don't think either of them ever went to school. In fact, outside of the mortuary and cemetery, I've never seen those two brothers anywhere else in public," Nico replied. "Now, their father I'd see occasionally around town, and I have no idea about their mother—I don't think I've even seen her before. Occasionally rumors would float around that she was a very sick woman—completely bedridden."

"Well, the whole lot of them give me the creeps!" Sofia said in a hushed tone and then joked, "We're definitely not inviting them to join us for drinks with Solomon and Fawn."

Nico began to laugh. "Lady, you're too much!"

Now that most of the attendees had parked, Father Michael cleared his throat to get everyone's attention before speaking. Once the chatter quieted, he spoke. "Since the mausoleum can only hold about six people—living people that is...." A light laughter filled the air and then faded as he resumed speaking. "…the immediate family and I will be the only ones to enter. Before I begin the Rite of Committal, I ask that you all gather closely so that you can participate in prayer. Oh, I almost forgot. Following the service, Siena and Pétros have asked me to invite everyone to their home for food and beverages."

As they headed into the mausoleum, the drop in temperature became quite apparent. The marble structure was still chilled from the cool morning air. Each time someone exhaled, their breath would condense and become visible. Sofia huddled closely to Nico for warmth.

Father Michael opened his prayer book and began the service, "Our sister Chiara has gone to her rest in the peace of Christ. May the Lord now welcome her to the table of God's children in heaven. With faith and hope…."

Nico's mind began to wander as he stared at his nonna's coffin lying in the uncovered crypt. There were no flowers, such as the ones that had surrounded it in the church, but Nico could smell a faint floral note perfuming the surrounding air. But it was not the odor of roses, or carnations, or even lilies that his senses picked up on; it was the scent of geraniums. Once again that comforting fragrance warmed his soul and gave him peace.

"Nico, are you coming?" Siena called over to him.

"What?" Nico said as he snapped out of his daze. Looking about, he realized that Father Michael had finished his prayer service, and everyone was leaving the mausoleum. "Yes, I'll be right there."

Nico touched the coffin one last time and whispered, "I love you nonna." As he turned to exit, he could see Mr. Cadaveri and his sons heading his way. As they passed each other, Nico turned back and paused to watch them place the heavy cover on the crypt.

"Ouch!" shouted someone within. Nico stepped forward a bit to see what all the commotion was about. One of Dino's fingers was trapped under the cold heavy stone lid they were trying to place. Nico rushed over and joined in the efforts to release his nemesis's crushed finger.

"On the count of three, we all lift," Mr. Cadaveri instructed. "One, two, three, lift!"

As the stone lid rose, Dino quickly pulled out his trapped finger. The grisly sight of the crushed and bloodied digit caused Nico to turn his head away.

"Thank you," Gino whispered with a slight smile.

Nico smiled back in response and quietly left, returning to where his family and Sofia had gathered. Sofia approached and asked, "I heard some yelling. Are you OK?"

"I'm fine. It was Dino—his finger was severely injured. I guess when they were placing the lid on the crypt, he didn't move his finger in time, and well—let's just say, it wasn't pretty."

"Ha! Probably karma for having been so rude to you. Or maybe it was your nonna taking revenge on your behalf?" Sofia commented and then quickly apologized. "Sorry. That last part was probably a little too soon."

"It's OK. I know you were just being playful, but I don't want to think about it anymore. In fact, I'm feeling a bit queasy. Let me say goodbye to my parents and then I can take you to the top of the hill. I think a nice walk in the fresh air will help."

Nico left Sofia and went over to where his parents were standing and mingling with the other attendees.

"Excuse me, mother," he said to Siena in a polite tone, attempting to get her attention.

"Nico, there you are. Are you going to join the rest of us at our house for some food?" Siena replied.

"No, I'm not feeling that well. I'm going to stay here for a bit with Sofia and walk around, but there is something I want to tell you."

"Very well. I'm sure we'll have plenty of extra food if you and Sofia want to pick some up later. You know how everyone brings a casserole to this sort of thing," Siena interrupted, preoccupied with getting back to her home before the guests arrived. "And, with all the people at the service, I'm sure we'll have enough food to last us till next month."

Realizing that now was not a good time for deeper conversations, he gave his mother a hug, said goodbye to his stepfather and then walked back to where Sofia stood waiting.

"OK, Sofia, follow me. There's a path over there that might make it easier for you to get to the top of the hill in your heels," Nico said pointing to a worn area in the grass alongside the hill. "Or I could carry you?"

Sofia smiled and replied, "I'm a strong woman—I can handle it."

Nico led the way, and they reached the top of the hill. Olive trees, in various states of growth, covered the hilltop. Some were only a few decades old; others, much older, had thick, gnarled trunks with wide spreading branches.

Sofia spotted the fountain that Nico previously mentioned. "That's truly a beautiful fountain. I can see why you found it so peaceful up here. So somewhere around here should be that swing you wanted to find, right?"

"Yes, if it still exits. It should be ahead on the left, closer to the fountain."

As they reached the center of the hill where the fountain trickled, they could see four incredibly old olive trees; one at each corner of the pathway around the fountain.

"Wow, after all these years, it's still here!" Nico said, amazed. "And it looks like someone has replaced the ropes—looks almost brand new. Have a seat and I'll give you a push."

Sofia dusted off the seat with her hand. She looked over at the old olive tree, whose branch was about to support her while she swung, and noticed something at the base of the tree. "Nico, look. Is that another one of those fairy doors?"

Nico went over to investigate. "Hey, I think you're right."

They both knelt down in front of the door to get a close look. The door appeared to be the same size as the other three they had seen. This one had stacks of books on either side of the door.

"I bet this one leads to the library—it has to be what those books reference." Nico observed.

"I concur, Mr. Frantoio," Sofia replied sarcastically. "Should we try it?"

"If we did, then we'd have to walk all the way back to the cemetery to get the car—are you sure you want to make that entire journey in heels?" Nico reasoned. "Now, if we knew the location of the door that leads to the cemetery, then I'd be all in."

"You have a valid point," Sofia conceded. "My feet are killing me as it is."

"Well, take a load off and have a seat on the swing. I'll push you and you can let your feet rest a bit."

"Best plan I've heard all day!" Sofia said and sat down on the swing.

Nico pushed her forward and then stepped back, readying himself to push her higher upon the swing's return. They both sighed simultaneously at the peacefulness the hilltop had brought to them; it was just them, about a hundred burial plots, and the trickling fountain. A frog, somewhere near the area of the fountain, began to croak. A second one chimed in, almost in unison: *ribbit, ribbit*. Somehow their noise was almost musical and added to the relaxing atmosphere.

"Sofia, did you know that I've always loved frogs?" Nico commented as he continued to push Sofia higher. "There used to be a lot of them in my nonna's garden, hiding near the…"

Something Nico said triggered a reminder for Sofia and she interrupted. "Frogs—that was one of the items on that list, the one I was telling you about earlier, the list I found in the grimoire! Although it was written in Italian, I knew most of the words, and it seemed to be a list of creatures categorized into three columns. I know frogs were on the list. Remind me to show it to you when we get home."

"Yes, milady. Is there anything further I may do for you?" Nico replied facetiously in his best British accent.

"Push me higher, peasant!" Sofia giggled as she replied in her version of a British accent. And as she reached a new height, she could now see further into the distance; something suddenly caught her eye. Something striking, something absolutely beautiful. "Nico, I want to stop the swing—I see something over there and I want to take a look."

Nico helped bring the swing to a halt and Sofia hopped off. She began walking toward the captivating object. Nico followed her past the fountain and to the eastern section of the hill. As he drew closer, he eyed what he believed to be the object of Sofia's fixation. Located in a sunny corner, off to itself, was a solitary grave marked with just a name: Vincenzo Luna. The cement covering of the burial vault was severely cracked and sunken in. The large fissure not only allowed for a slight glimpse into the darkness beneath, but also was an escape for a growing rose bush which had pushed through toward the light, its young spring leaves with their glossy sheen still holding on to the last of the morning dew. From the center of the bush, a large cane shot up toward the warm afternoon sun and ended with the most perfect blood-red rose that either of them had ever seen.

"Did you ever…?" Sofia gushed, so smitten by the rose's beauty that she did not bother to finish her sentence.

"I haven't," Nico responded, knowing what Sofia was trying to ask, "not even in my nonna's garden."

Nico felt drawn, or rather compelled, to moved closer. He needed to get that rose. He carefully began reaching his hand toward the center of the bush. Every inch forward was greeted with a light scrape or poke from a nearby thorn. He knew he had to go slowly and strategically. If he wasn't careful, he might risk a more serious injury. Just one deep poke might cause him to jerk his hand back quickly, like when one touches a hot stove, and cause the skin on his hand to be shredded by the multitude of thorns.

"Be careful!" Sofia exclaimed.

"I've got this. I made it through to the center—I just need to find a safe, thornless spot to grab and then I can hopefully snap off it off." Nico said confidently, as he leaned further into the bush. "Ah, I see a spot!"

Nico reached for the cane and quickly grabbed it, not aware that a large thorn was hidden on the other side.

"Son of a—mother—!" Nico shouted while trying to release his impaled hand from the sharp thorn. He knew that if he leaned any further forward, he might lose his balance and fall into the bush, and being pricked by the other thorns was something he was hoping to avoid. As his palm ached with pain, blood began to pour from the fresh wound and slowly trickle down the center cane. "I can't seem to get my hand free without possibly falling. Quick, find a branch or stick to knock the cane free."

"Let me look—just keep breathing slowly—stay calm." Sofia quickly replied as she frantically searched for an object long enough to reach the center of the rose bush. Spotting a small olive branch on the ground, she rushed over to where Nico patiently stood in pain. "Turn your head away. I'm going to have to push the cane toward you to release the thorn."

More blood continued to flow from Nico's wound, down the tall cane to the base of the plant and then further into the darkness below. Nico turned his head away and Sofia successfully released the thorn from Nico's palm with the olive branch. Nico slowly and carefully pulled his bleeding hand out from the center of the rose bush.

"Go rinse the wound in the fountain!" Sofia directed. "I saw some yarrow growing over there—I'll be right back."

Running over to the yarrow plant as fast as she could in heels on loose gravel, she picked about ten leaves and rushed back to the fountain. After tearing and bruising the leaves, she removed Nico's hand from the now pink water of the fountain and placed the leaves on the wound.

"Nico, apply pressure and hold them in place," Sofia said as she removed her scarf and wrapped it around Nico's hand and tied it securely to hold the leaves in place. "There, that should help stop the bleeding and hopefully relieve the pain."

"How did you know to do that? You're such an amazing friend. Sometimes I don't know what I'd do without you," Nico said in appreciation.

"Yarrow is a wonderful plant. It's also known as soldier's woundwort and nosebleed. I remember my mother using it often whenever Paolo or I fell and scraped our knees. It would quickly stop the bleeding and help with the pain," Sofia replied and smiled at the brief memory from her almost-forgotten past.

"Sorry I wasn't able to get the rose for you. I was hoping to retrieve it as a token of my appreciation—especially for all the support you've shown me these past few days," Nico said with a note of disappointment in his voice.

"That's OK. I know in my heart how much you care. I see it by your actions and in the thoughtful things you do for me—even in the simple things, like holding a door open for me so that I may enter a building first. Nothing goes unnoticed. Besides, maybe that most perfect rose is meant to remain so that others can appreciate its beauty as well. You know, we can always come back again to see the rose now that we know there's a fairy door close by—we just need to find the one that leads here!"

"You're right," Nico said in agreement. "Let's get back home. I'm feeling a bit faint from the blood loss and need some food."

"I'll drive. I think I can easily find the way back," Sofia suggested.

They slowly made their short journey back down the hill to the car, holding onto each other's arm for support, in case one of them should lose footing.

Nico handed the car keys to Sofia and they both got in. The warm afternoon sun, which was a pleasant reprieve from the morning's chill, had heated up the car, so they rolled down their windows before driving off.

As Sofia drove and rounded the hill, heading toward the cemetery exit, she noticed a familiar sight; a large, black raven was perched on the gate watching them as they approached.

Nico spotted the raven as well and ribbed Sofia, "Look, your buddy has been waiting for you!"

"Ha, ha!" Sofia said and sped up the car, passing through the gate and leaving the raven behind in a trail of dust.

Chapter 12: Research Time

The brief ride back to the house was a quiet one; Sofia concentrated on driving while Nico briefly nodded off, exhausted from the earlier events. As Sofia pulled up to the house, she reached over and gently nudged Nico.

"We're back home," Sofia said softly. "Why don't you go change out of your bloodied clothing and clean up—I'll see if I can find some food in the kitchen and whip us up something to eat."

"Sounds good to me," Nico replied and exited the car. Still not quite awake from his brief nap in the car, he trudged up the steps to the front door and casually called out, "House, unlock the door…and help Sofia with anything she needs."

Nico went directly to his bedroom with the intention of cleaning up and changing his clothes but ended up lying on his bed and falling back asleep. Sofia had gone to her bedroom and quickly changed into something more casual and less restricting. As she headed into the kitchen, she noticed two of the many cabinet doors were open. One of them clearly displayed a variety of boxed pasta: fusilli, rigatoni, spaghetti, bucatini; almost every shape and size she had ever seen. *Clearly, I am making a pasta dish*, she thought. *Spaghetti sounds like a winner*, and she grabbed a box. *I wonder what else the house might suggest*, she mused as she wandered over to the other opened cabinet. This cabinet predominantly stored various types of oils; the majority being olive oil. *Aha! I know what to make. One of Nico's favorites and simplest of pasta dishes: spaghetti aglio e olio.*

"Now to get some parsley from the garden, and all I'll need is some good parmesan cheese to grate," she said out loud, curious to see if the house would respond in some sort of manner.

And the house did just that. She watched as the refrigerator door opened on its own and a wrapped wedge of parmesan cheese fell to the floor. The refrigerator door then closed and a small cabinet door beneath some drawers opened. Sofia immediately spotted a large cheese grater.

"House, you are too kind to me!" she said in glee as she picked up the parmesan cheese and walked over for the grater.

She placed all the items on the counter near the sink and took a bulb of garlic from the windowsill to add to the collection of ingredients.

Finding a pot, she filled it with water and placed it on the stove. She turned on the burner and reached into a nearby salt cellar, grabbing a small quantity to salt the water. While waiting for the water to boil, she headed to the back door of the house in order to go outside and pick some parsley. As she opened the back door, she was astonished by what she found: On the steps stood three of the garden gnomes; in front of them was a bouquet of picked parsley wrapped in twine.

She bent down to pick up the surprise gift and looked at the gnomes with gratitude. "Quite the gentlemen you three are! Thank you for your assistance."

Amazed by the experience, she smiled to herself as she closed the door. Returning to the kitchen, she rinsed off the parsley and chopped it. She then peeled the garlic, and after thinly slicing each clove, added it to a pan with some olive oil.

As the fragrance of fresh-cut garlic warming in olive oil began to fill the air and overtake the already present odor of it from the windowsills, Nico groggily walked into the kitchen; his hair sticking up in various directions from having taken a nap.

"Something smells delicious!" He said with delight.

"I'm making—" While stirring the ingredients with an old wooden spoon, Sofia looked up at Nico. "Did you fall asleep? You're still wearing your bloodied suit!"

"Yeah. As soon as I got to my bedroom, I just had to lie down. I know I must've slept for only ten minutes, but it seemed like two hours. I think the morning took more out of me than I—hey, are you making *spaghetti aglio e olio*? Aren't you the master chef!"

"Well, to be honest, I had some help. But we can talk more about that after you go wash up. Lunch should be ready in about five minutes," Sofia advised.

Nico left the kitchen and went back to his bedroom. He removed his suit, throwing each article of clothing into a pile in the corner of the room. He then slipped into some gym shorts and quickly pulled a sweatshirt over his head while walking to the bathroom to wash up. As he removed Sofia's scarf from his hand, he noticed that the bleeding had stopped, and the wound had entirely closed up. He gently washed his hands and then carefully blotted them dry to avoid re-opening his wound. He looked once more at his hand, and there was no longer any trace of the previous injury—no pain either.

Making a quick return to his bedroom, he grabbed a baseball cap and covered his out-of-control hair before heading back to the kitchen. The smell of food was making his stomach growl in anticipation of Sofia's cooking.

"Here's your plate—grab a couple of forks and a few napkins," Sofia said as she handed him his meal.

"Thank you. What would you like to drink?" Nico replied while opening a nearby drawer with his free hand and grabbing two forks and two cloth napkins. Hands now full, he used his hip to close the drawer.

"A nice Chianti would be great—do you have any?" Sofia replied.

"My nonna used to keep some wine here in the kitchen so that she wouldn't have to go down to the wine cellar if guests came over. If I recall, I think it's over here in this cabinet," Nico said as he set his plate and the other items on the kitchen island and then walked over to a cabinet in the corner. "Yes, this cabinet. She used to call it *the cooler* since there are screens at the bottom and top that allow for cool air to rise up from the basement and then out through the roof—kind of like a chimney."

Nico opened the cabinet and found what Sofia desired. He placed the twine-wrapped bottle of Chianti near their food and went to get a corkscrew.

"Wow, this is definitely an older bottle," Sofia commented. "You don't see these older wrapped bottles around much anymore."

Nico uncorked the bottle and handed the cork to Sofia to smell. "There you go madame."

"Mademoiselle," Sofia interrupted to correct him.

"Yes, mademoiselle; my apologies," Nico continued in a French accent, while trying to hold back his laughter. "While the wine is having a chance to breathe, I'll fetch you a glass."

Nico grabbed two wine glasses and promptly returned to the kitchen island, where Sofia was already seated. "*Voila*!" he said and poured the wine for Sofia to taste.

Sofia swirled the wine around in her glass and smelled its bouquet. "Ah, full bodied, with notes of cherry. Yes, this will do. *Merci, garçon.*"

Nico sat down next to Sofia, and raised his glass. "To my wonderful friend, thank you for helping me through this day; for this wonderful meal that I'm about to eat, and for healing my wound."

Sofia clinked her glass against his. "Well, that's what friends are for—wait, how could your wound have healed already. The yarrow might have helped control the bleeding so that the wound could begin sealing, but it wouldn't heal it completely."

Nico quickly finished chewing his mouthful of Sofia's delicious pasta so that he could respond. "Well, see for yourself!" Nico said and held out his hand for her to inspect.

"That's nearly impossible. The thorn pierced your hand deeply—you were bleeding profusely. How—how could there be no trace of your injury?" Sofia said in disbelief while thoroughly searching his hand.

"I really don't know. I just assumed it was your quick use of that herb, along with the makeshift bandage's compression. And there's no residual pain either!" Nico remarked. "Oh, and sorry about your scarf. Maybe tomorrow when we go to Schwartzman's and pick up my shirt, I can buy you a replacement."

"You're too kind!" Sofia said and kissed him on the cheek with her olive-oil-coated lips.

Nico quickly wiped off the garlicky remnants of Sofia's kiss with his napkin. "Eww! I feel like half your plate is now on my cheek."

They both laughed and then continued eating the rest of their meal. Nico finished off the last of his glass and asked Sofia if she would like more wine, but she declined.

"One is enough for me, at least this early in the day," Sofia replied.

"So, what would you like to do for the rest of the afternoon?" Nico asked.

"I do want to show you that note I found in the grimoire. Also, I think we should figure out how to get into the secret room from the basement—that way we don't always have to get there from the chest in my bedroom."

"That'll certainly keep us busy!" Nico noted. "Oh, by the way, what did you mean about having help making this meal?"

"Well, before you went to your bedroom, you had told the house to help me. I was trying to figure out what to make us for lunch, and when I entered the kitchen, two of the cabinet doors were open—one contained various boxes of pasta and the other had different types of oil, mostly olive oil. I figured it was a hint to make some kind of pasta, and that's when I got the idea for your favorite dish. I didn't know if the house had really assisted, so I put it to the test. I spoke, slightly above a whisper, that all I needed was some parsley and parmesan cheese. I watched as the refrigerator door opened and a wedge of cheese fell to the floor. I then headed to the garden to cut some fresh parsley, and when I opened the door, three of the gnomes were on the porch with a fresh bunch of parsley before them. It was actually quite an incredible experience. I think I now know how your nonna kept this house clean and the garden so well-tended."

"Sounds like the gnomes are finally warming up to you," Nico said, ending with a slight grin. He then had a thought, "Wait. If the gnomes are outside and the house can basically open, close, lock and unlock doors, then who or what is tidying up the house? Come to think of it, I didn't make my bed this morning before we left and when I went to my room to lay down, I noticed it had been made."

"Maybe the house can animate anything within its confines? That would negate the need for a physical being or entity to do certain activities," Sofia said.

"I think we have much to learn. And probably the sooner the better, since we have my nonna's murderer somewhere out there to contend with, along with helping Sterling find out who the Oliveto Abductor is *and* putting a stop to these abductions—I haven't even tried casting a spell yet!" Nico said, sounding overwhelmed.

"Don't worry Nico, I'm here to help you," Sofia comforted. "Besides, you know how much I enjoy this supernatural stuff—it's going to be fun!"

"Thank you. Now if you could help me with my carb coma. I'm starting to get drowsy from the pasta—or maybe it was the wine. I could definitely use an espresso."

"I'll make you one—" Sofia started to offer and abruptly stopped.

They watched as a cabinet door creaked opened and two demitasse cups and their saucers floated over to the counter by the espresso maker, which had already turned itself on and was heating up.

"You just saw that, right?" Nico asked Sofia.

"Yes!" Sofia replied as they remained transfixed with the house's performance.

"Is this similar to what you experienced earlier?" Nico asked.

"Yes. Well, no. I didn't see anything float about, and the two cabinet doors were already open when I entered the room. But I did see the refrigerator door open and the cheese falling to the floor. I guess the house can do it all by itself!"

They continued to watch as the top of the coffee grinder removed itself and a bag of espresso beans was poured into the grinder. Once the lid returned and locked into place, a whirling sound was heard as the coffee beans were ground. The lid once more removed itself and a measuring spoon added two scoops of the freshly ground beans to the portafilter. An espresso tamper rose up from the counter and compacted the grounds before the portafilter reaffixed itself to the espresso machine. A demitasse moved and aligned itself underneath the spigot of the portafilter and the handle of the machine moved downward as if guided by a ghostly barista. The filled demitasse returned to its matching saucer and then floated over to Nico, gently landing before him.

"House, I hate to be a difficult customer, but I would like a twist of lemon rind with mine." Nico said jokingly.

"You are really pushing your luck here!" Sofia laughed as she watched a lemon rise from a fruit bowl on the counter and land near Nico's espresso. "It looks like the house wants you to do the rest of the work yourself. Must be because it's uncommon in Italy to use the lemon peel with espresso, unless you are sick or something."

Nico chuckled. "I think you're correct—I shouldn't have pushed my luck. But I wasn't feeling well earlier, and you know how much I like lemons."

Suddenly they noticed a paring knife remove itself from the knife block on the kitchen counter and slowly head in their direction.

"Shit, it's pissed now..." Sofia said with concern.

The knife hovered eye level to Nico as the nearby lemon rose into the air. The paring knife removed a thin strip of rind, which then dropped into Nico's espresso.

"Or the house had a change of mind when it heard that I hadn't been feeling well and how much I like lemons," Nico said and smiled smugly. "Better order your espresso before the kitchen closes for the afternoon."

"You are too much!" Sofia giggled. "OK. House, may I please have a regular espresso? Nothing fancy like the prince over here."

They both looked over toward the espresso machine and saw it repeat the same routine as it had done for Nico's espresso, but without Nico's slice of lemon rind.

As Sofia's finished espresso floated over to her, Nico asked, "I wonder if the house has a name. It sounds so impersonal when I address it as just *House*. What do you think?"

"I didn't see anything in the grimoire, but I think I might know a way to find out." Sofia said with a glimmer of hope. "When I was exploring the house, the morning after we arrived, I had an experience that I hadn't shared with you—mostly because I thought it was just my mind playing tricks on me or that I was still half asleep."

"What happened?" Nico asked.

"Umm, you know that short hallway between the foyer and the dining room? Well, I was looking into the mirror there and messing with my hair. That's when I noticed in the reflection, behind me, the bust of your nonno, Benito. It seemed to blink its eyes. I know that sounds crazy, but after everything we've experienced so far, I think what I thought I'd seen, actually did occur."

"That's entirely possible! I remember when we first skimmed through the grimoire, there was one spell on the Malandanti side. I think it was titled: *Mirror of the Dead*." Nico recalled before Sofia interrupted his line of thinking.

"And maybe your nonna used that spell to enchant the mirror so that she could communicate with her late husband?" Sofia finished.

"Only one way to find out! Let's see if I'm able to introduce you to my nonno," Nico laughed.

They finished off their espresso and made their way through the dining room to the short hallway and stood before the mirror.

"I guess we'll need to step apart so we can see the bust's reflection in the mirror," Nico suggested.

Nico and Sofia each took a small step away from each other so that the reflection of Benito could now be seen.

"Nonno, can you hear me?" Nico asked.

"See!" Sofia shrieked as she watched the milky white marble eyelids open. "This is what happened before!"

"Nonno, it's Nico." He took a deep breath before continuing, "And this is my friend Sofia."

"Nico, you've grown much. It's been so long," the bust of Benito groaned.

"Yes, it's been almost ten years since you passed. I think about you often and wish you were still here—I have so many questions." Nico replied, slightly emotional at the unconventional reunion.

"And your friend, Sofia, we exchanged glances the other day. Lovely girl. Now, what questions do you have for me?"

"Well right now, just one; it's about this house. Does it have a name?" Nico asked.

Benito began to chuckle. "My dear boy. I gather by your question that you've found the family grimoire. You must be piecing things together about our family, and the others. Your nonna did her best to keep your mind open, open to a world of possibilities and prepare you, but she wasn't able to tell you much—because of your mother. I wanted to protect her—but that is another story. As to this house…it was your nonna who woke it from its slumber, shortly after I died. You'll need to ask her."

After finishing his last sentence, the bust of Benito closed its eyes and became silent.

"I think he's gone for now," Sofia said. "It takes a lot of spiritual energy for a manifestation such as that to occur—it'll probably be a while before we can try again."

"Well, nonetheless, I would've never imagined it possible to speak with him again. That was pretty incredible, but sadly I squandered the opportunity with such a trivial question, which wasn't even answerable," Nico replied and shrugged his shoulders.

"Well, there'll be other opportunities. Now have to find a way to ask your nonna! We can stick a pin in that for now. Come, let me show you the note in the grimoire."

Nico followed Sofia to her bedroom. She reached for the book that was lying on the top of hope chest. Opening it to the middle, she retrieved the mysterious note.

"Here," she said while handing the note to Nico.

M	*B*	*V*
Lucertole	*Api*	*Pipistrelli*
Corvi	*Rane*	*Ratti*
Ragni	*Colibrì*	*Lupi*

"Hmm, very interesting," Nico pondered. "It does look like they are all various types of creatures written in Italian and that's definitely my nonna's penmanship—a perfect match to the note she was found clutching. The first column looks like it would translate to: Lizards, Ravens, and Spiders...."

Sofia excitedly interrupted. "And the second column is: Bees, Frogs, and Hummingbirds. The third is: Bats, Rats, and Wolves. Like I said at the cemetery, I believe the first two column headers represent Malandanti and Benandanti, respectively. I just don't know what the 'V' stands for."

"Well, now that we've finished translating the list, we need to find out what it means." Nico responded. "When we go into town tomorrow to pick up my shirt, I think we should make a stop at the library and talk to Teresa. She might be able to help us sort out what Malandanti and Benandanti represent—then the list might make more sense. Plus, we need to show Sterling that wing-like object that fell from the funeral director's suit. You still have it, right?

"Yes. It's still wrapped up securely and in my purse," Sofia replied. "Sounds like we have a busy day planned tomorrow!"

"For now, let's explore the rest of the basement and find a way into that secret room!" Nico said with enthusiasm.

With that, they headed to the other side of the house and into the kitchen. Nico searched a few of the drawers until he found a small box of matches and an unused candle. "Here you take these. We'll need it for that dark room," Nico said as he handed the items to Sofia. He then unlatched the cabinet door leading to the basement and reached for the light switch to illuminate the stairway.

"Go on down—I'll meet you at the bottom. I want to get some paper towels and a garbage bag so I can clean up that rotting gourd in the secret room—it must smell something awful by now!"

Nico stopped at the landing and waited for Sofia. She quickly appeared and began her descent. As she drew closer, Nico commented, "So, we've already been to the wine cellar, and to the right is just the laundry room—nothing exciting about that. But there are still two other storage rooms, one on either side of the secret room—we have yet to check those out."

"I'm game. Lead the way!" Sofia said, tightly clutching the unlit candle and her cleaning supplies as she followed Nico.

"OK, this is the first storage room. Why don't you put your items down over by the entrance to the secret room and we'll explore this room first. There should be a light switch for the room somewhere around here." Nico said as he searched. "Oh, the heck with it—House, please light this room."

The low-wattage bulb of a nearby pendant light immediately flickered on at Nico's request. The room, now dimly illuminated, was filled with various steamer trunks, each covered in dust and connected by a series of cobwebs; the air in the room was slightly moist.

"I'll bet these trunks could tell some tales! I'm guessing, by the age of them, that they probably belonged to your relatives from when they first came over to America—what a long boat ride that must've been!" Sofia mused.

"If that's the case, then they're probably from the late 1880s." Nico said as he continued looking around. "Hey, Sofia, come here for a second. The dust pattern beneath this trunk shows that it was moved recently."

Sofia walked over to where Nico was standing and looked down at the dusty outline on the floor. "Whoever moved the chest didn't move it back to the exact spot. Maybe it is covering something?"

"Let's find out. Help me slide it away." Nico replied.

With much effort, they were slowly able to move the heavy trunk. As it neared being almost halfway out of its original spot, they noticed a metal grate that was secured by a heavy iron padlock.

"I wonder where it leads to?" Sofia said.

"Well, if we could unlock the padlock, we might be able to find out," Nico replied and then thought for a moment. "House, unlock the padlock."

Nothing happened.

"Guess we will have to find another way," Sofia replied.

"Maybe there's a spell that can help? I'll go check the grimoire—you light the candle and see if you can get a visual as to what's down there. I'll be right back."

They exited the storage room and Sofia went to get the candle and matchbox she had left by the secret room. Nico made haste up the stairs, skipping every other step on his way up, and then to Sofia's bedroom.

Nico went over to the grimoire and began thumbing through it. *Aha!* Nico thought as he stopped on a page with a promising spell.

Enchant Lock – secures a lock without the use of a key. Touch lock and say: ***Sero****.*

Shoot! That won't do. I need to unlock something, not lock it back up! Nico continued thinking as he reached the end of the Benandanti side of the grimoire. Flipping the book over, he started thumbing through the Malandanti side.

Here's what I need!

Pick Lock – unlocks most mechanisms without use of a key. Touch lock and say: ***Resero****.*

Repeating the magic word in his head so that he would not forget, he closed the book and placed it back on the bed. Nico decided to take the shortcut back to Sofia and went over to the hope chest. He pressed all six images of geraniums on the chest and heard the anticipated click of the chest unlocking. As he lifted the lid of the chest, he could smell the faint scent of the rotting gourd wafting up from below. He reached in for the metal ring and opened the trapdoor. As he descended the stairs to the secret room, the putrid smell coming from the darkness was overwhelming. He quickly called out, "House, please turn on the light." Now that he could see, he pressed the wood panel to open the hidden door so he could escape.

Sofia could hear Nico speaking from the other side of the wall. "Lazy—taking the easy way back I see!" she joked.

As the door slid open, Sofia was standing there to greet him with her lit candle and a smile.

"I was just being…efficient," Nico replied as he darted past Sofia toward one of the garden windows lining the basement wall. Opening the closest one, he took a deep breath of fresh air to help quell his nausea.

"Wow, that's one rank smell! I should have cleaned up the mess much sooner," Sofia apologized. She reached for the candelabra they had left from their previous visit to the room and removed one of the three spent candles to make room for her lit one. Setting the candelabra back on the demilune, she went over to where Nico was and opened another window. "By the way, I think I found a clue that might help us find the way in. It's in the painting."

"Well, let's allow the smell to dissipate before going back in there," Nico suggested as they could hear the sound of the secret door sliding back to its closed position. "In the meantime, I found a spell that should open the lock. Were you able to see what's down there?"

"Unfortunately, the candle wasn't bright enough to pierce the darkness. Whatever lies beneath the grate must be a long way down," Sofia replied.

"Grab the candle and let's take a look. Once I open the lock and lift the grate, then I can lower the candle and see if that helps to light the area."

Nico and Sofia entered the storage room and walked over to the mysterious grate.

"The grimoire said to touch the lock and then say: *Resero*," Nico explained. He reached for the iron padlock and spoke meekly, "*Resero*."

"Well, that was anti-climactic. Nothing happened!" Sofia said with a tone of disappointment in her voice. "Try saying it with more confidence, in a more commanding tone. I mean, if I were that lock, even I wouldn't open for you."

"*Resero*!" Nico enunciated loudly and with a forceful tone.

The padlock released its shackle and Sofia expressed her approval. "Bravo! You know, Nico, I think spell casting is going to help boost your self-confidence. I'm actually impressed."

Nico just smiled as he removed the padlock. He gripped the bars on the grate and with some effort was able to lift the old rusty grate. Sofia handed the lit candle to Nico, who then slowly lowered it into the darkness. As they peered further into the depths, they could see the ground about twelve feet below.

"Hey look," Sofia said as she pointed to a wooden ladder leading downward.

"Let me go first to make sure the ladder is safe to use," Nico advised and began his descent into the unknown space. As he stepped off the last rung of the ladder, his feet splashed in a puddle. He looked up at Sofia and called to her. "Seems safe. I'll come halfway back up with the candle—I want to make sure you can see you way coming down. And watch for the puddle of water at the bottom. My shoes are totally soaked."

Sofia agreed and carefully climbed down and, at the last rung, jumped off to the left and avoided the puddle. Nico extended his arm to illuminate the way ahead. Within the dank space, they noticed the walls surrounding them were wet and covered with slime. The passage ahead was narrow, and something ahead could be seen blocking the way. Holding onto each other for stability, they continued forward down the slippery path. The sound of trickling water could be heard throughout the cavern and an occasional drip of water would startle them when it hit one of their heads. As they neared the blockage, they recognized it as roots of some sort.

"It looks like the lateral roots of huge tree," Sofia observed.

Nico held the candle out further. About six feet above them, large roots branched off into smaller feeder roots, which created a net-like structure extending further down and into the ground.

"Well, it looks like the way is blocked and we can't proceed any further," Nico sighed.

"That's OK. I'm getting cold anyway—it's so chilly down here!" Sofia responded and drew closer to Nico for warmth. "What do you think this area is?"

"I'm guessing we're in the sewer tunnels which run beneath the entire town." Nico replied. "When I was young, I was told stories about kids coming down here to explore and becoming lost; the ones who wandered too far in were never found. The town eventually sealed off the majority of entrances to prevent such perils. And I even remember this one time, during a Boy Scout campout, we were all sitting around the campfire and our scoutmaster told us a chilling tale about these tunnels. Apparently, they are unmappable and are constantly changing their direction so that wanderers are always routed to the same location—the underworld, where Orcus rules and feeds on the souls of the unfortunate."

"Stop that! You're making that last part up!" Sofia responded, irritated not only from being cold, but now a bit spooked from Nico's story.

"Scout's honor!" Nico said while chuckling. "That's what I was told. Anyway, I hope we never have to find out if that's true! Come on, let's go back up—I'll even help you clean up the mess you left in the other room."

They headed back to the wooden ladder and climbed up to the surface. Nico blew out the candle and placed it on the floor. He lowered the grate and secured it with the padlock. Sofia assisted him with moving the trunk back over the grate.

Nico took the candle with him as they left the storage room. Suddenly, Nico stopped and turned to Sofia. "You know, there are so many spells in the grimoire, that I'm going to need your help learning them all—I have a feeling we're going to need to use some of them at one point or another. So, maybe we can make flash cards and you can quiz me—like we do when we have to study for one of Professor Cerveau's tests. What do you think?"

"I think it's a brilliant way to learn them. It'll be fun! We can open a bottle of wine, sit in front of the fireplace, and study through the night," Sofia said with enthusiasm.

"Sounds perfect! I'm sure there is a stash of index cards somewhere in the house. My nonna was always using them to write down recipes. Sorry, I'm getting sidetracked—let's go clean that smelly gourd."

They walked back into the small room where the secret door was located. Nico placed the candle in the candelabra and Sofia re-lit it.

"So, you were saying earlier that you might have figured out how to open the secret door from this side?" Nico asked.

"Well, I was staring at the painting, and then I recalled having seen it before. When I was in high school, art history was offered as an elective, so I took it. During the month of October, our teacher embraced the season of Halloween by having us study works of art that were a little darker in nature. This painting, entitled *The Search for the Alchemical Formula* by Charles Meer Webb, was one of those paintings. The man, who is sitting and reading through a large tome, is turned, and looking toward a skull on the table. That *memento mori*, I figured, must be a clue. That was as far as I got."

"OK, so if your hunch is right, we should be looking for a skull somewhere," Nico reasoned as he moved closer to examine the painting. Then he suddenly noticed something. "Look at the frame, Sofia!"

"Wow!" she replied in amazement as she noticed that within the frame's woodwork, various detailed images were carved into the wood. "From far away, it'd be hard to notice because of the gilding."

"Here's a bird; and there's a frog; and a shamrock. They're so detailed. I think the frame is probably more valuable than the actual painting!" Nico joked.

"You continue searching the right side and top of the frame and I will scan the left side and bottom," Sofia directed. "Cute! Here's a ladybug; and a rose."

"A bat; aha, a skull!" Nico exclaimed victoriously.

"Ha! I let you have this win," Sofia teased. "Well, don't just stare at it, try pushing or turning it."

Nico placed his finger on the skull and applied pressure. The skull retracted into the frame and the wall began to rumble before sliding open.

Sofia raised her hand and Nico high-fived her back. "We do make an awesome team," Nico praised. "I'm so glad you—whoa! I totally forgot about that horrid smell."

Nico opened the trash bag they had brought from upstairs and went over to the sink. Sofia followed but then stopped to reach for one of the apothecary jars on a nearby shelf; the jar was labeled: White Sage. She removed the lid, reached inside, and withdrew a sage smudge. Striking a match, she lit the leaves that were tightly bound with twine.

"This should help," she said while waving the smudge near the sink. Its thick, herbaceous smoke slowly cleansed the air of the remaining putrid odor.

"OK, you smudge away. I'll finish cleaning up this mess you left," Nico said while lifting the slimy pieces of gourd out of the sink and plopping them into the open trash bag.

Nico tied up the garbage bag and then cleaned out the sink. Sofia continued moving about the room, smudging every nook and cranny she could find and then stopped abruptly in front of the large apothecary chest.

"Nico! I know how we can communicate with your nonna—isn't this a bust of her?" She asked while pointing to the marble effigy on top of the chest.

Nico turned to look. "Yes! I completely forgot about having seen that the last time we were down here. That should do the trick—let's head back upstairs. Why don't you extinguish the smudge and grab the bust? I'm done cleaning up and will take the trash and candelabra."

Nico turned off the light and Sofia went over to close the basement windows they had left open. The secret door slid closed once more, and they headed back upstairs to the kitchen.

"I should really return this candelabra to my nonna's room where it belongs. Will you come with me?" Nico asked.

Sofia placed the bust of Chiara down on the kitchen island. "Of course, I will."

As they began the short walk down the hallway to the *stanza naturale*, Nico paused briefly. "You know, when we first walked down this hall together, before we knew about any of this magic and Fey stuff, I thought my eyes were playing tricks on me when I looked at these walls. Now I know it wasn't an illusion—those painted vines *are* actually moving!"

"It's almost as if they could wriggle free from the plaster and—hey, what if they can do that?" Sofia asked excitedly.

"I doubt it," Nico replied. "If they could've, I'm sure they would have latched onto my nonna's killer and prevented them from entering, detained them from leaving, or something worse."

Nico reached for the silver doorknob and opened the door. As Sofia stood in the threshold, he placed the candelabra back onto the nightstand. Before exiting the room, he noticed the closet door was ever so slightly ajar.

Walking over to the door, he called out to Sofia, "Come over here for a second. Do you recall this door being open?"

"I'm pretty sure it was closed," Sofia replied. "Maybe it wasn't closed tightly and opened because of a draft or the house shifting."

Nico opened the door all the way, and Sofia peeked inside only to see darkness.

"It'd be nice if this room had electricity. The sun is starting to set and even if we drew back the curtains, there wouldn't be enough natural light to see what's in there. Do you still have the matches? We can always use candlelight."

"Yep," Sofia replied and went over to the candelabra to light the lone candle. She walked back to Nico and handed the candelabra to him. "Here. Let me know what you can see."

"Looks like her dresses and other clothing items. It seems like a bigger space than would be possible."

Nico stepped in further, and Sofia entered the space behind him and commented, "You're right. Technically this wall should not be as deep as it is. Actually, this closet is huge! I would love to have a closet like this—although, I'd need some proper lighting."

"I'm sure there must be a spell we can find to help with our ever-present lighting issues—let's make sure to include it in our flash cards!" Nico joked.

"Hey, what's that ahead? Is that another door?" Sofia asked as the candlelight reflected off what looked like another silver doorknob.

Nico slowly approached what was now clearly another door. "I never knew this existed."

A chill ran through him as he gripped the cold metal. He turned the doorknob, but the door would not budge. Lowering the candle, he noticed that the door had a keyhole.

"It seems like a warded lock, and since I don't have a skeleton key handy—*Resero*!" Nico commanded, and the door quickly unbolted.

Sofia's curiosity was now piqued. Reaching in front of Nico, she opened the door, almost singeing her hair on one of the candles.

"Stairs," Sofia said puzzled. "I can only guess it leads to the attic, although from the outside of the house, it doesn't appear that it has the height for an upper level."

"This closet didn't appear to have the space either, but as Sterling said, 'not everything in Oliveto is as it seems,'" Nico commented back. "Looks dark up there, and I don't think this single candle will provide us with the lighting we need. Let's wait until we find a spell or more candles."

"Good point, Nico. Plus, you've had an exhausting day and should rest up," Sofia said in a caring manner. "We can do something low-key like studying the spells and having some wine."

"I am in complete agreement with you. Why don't you go open a bottle so it can breathe; I'll meet you in the kitchen—give me a few minutes," Nico replied.

Sofia headed off to the kitchen and Nico closed the door leading to the unexplored upper level. He took a brief moment, enjoying the peacefulness of the quiet candlelit closet, and thought of his nonna. So many great memories came flooding back. And, looking down at the lock, he smiled and quietly said the magic word: *Sero*; and the door bolted at his command. He no longer needed to sound confident when saying the magic words; his confidence now came from within.

Stepping out of the closet, he blew out the candle and placed the candelabra back onto the nightstand and left the room.

As Nico entered the kitchen, he could see an open bottle of wine on the counter near Sofia, who was struggling to reach for something from the top shelf of one of the many kitchen cabinets.

"Here, let me help you with that," Nico offered.

Sofia jumped slightly. "You startled me. I didn't see you coming—the cabinet door was obstructing my peripheral vision."

It was an easy reach for Nico since he was a good six inches taller than Sofia.

"Here. Is this what you were trying to take down?" He asked while pulling down two wine glasses.

"Yes genius. How did you ever guess?" Sofia said sarcastically. "Oh, I found some cheese that was still good, and I cheated. I asked the house if there were any crackers and it graciously showed me the location by opening the correct cabinet."

"Perfect! Nothing better than cheese, crackers, and some good wine," Nico replied. "I just need to figure out where my nonna kept her index cards."

"House, please show Nico where the index cards are kept," Sofia spoke.

With that, the sound of a drawer sliding open on the opposite side of the kitchen island was heard.

"You know, a girl could get used to this," Sofia joked.

"Well, don't get too used to it—we'll be back at the boarding house in a week and our rent doesn't include that nifty perk," Nico said as he walked over to retrieve the index cards from the open drawer.

Sofia rummaged around for a plate and then carried everything over to the kitchen island. Grabbing a knife from the knife block, she began slicing the cheese and arranging it on the plate alongside the crackers.

"Wow that looks nice—if you fail in college, maybe you can get a job as a caterer," Nico ribbed.

"And from the look of your grades, I'll be able to hire you as one of my servers." She joked back.

Nico put the index cards in his pocket and brought the glasses and bottle of wine with him to the living room. Sofia grabbed a few napkins and followed Nico with her plate of cheese and crackers but stopped. She looked over at the lonely marble bust of Chiara Frantoio.

I should at least put this bust next to Benito's—it only seems right, Sofia thought.

She then picked up the effigy and carried it to the small hallway where the other bust was kept. After placing the bust of Chiara next to Benito, she turned and looked into the mirror. In the reflection, she could see Chiara's face smile as their eyes met. The sculpture began speaking.

"Grazie! Now go help Nico learn his spells. They'll be needed in the coming days and prove quite useful—to you both! You're a good friend to my Nico. I knew that you would be, and I've left you something special...."

"Are you coming Sofia?" Nico shouted from the living room, interrupting her focus. "The fireplace is lit, and I'm about to pour the wine."

"Yes. Be right there. Just had to do something," Sofia called out and then looked back into the mirror at Chiara, but the moment had passed, and the bust was no longer animated. She quickly went back into the kitchen to grab the items she had left behind and then rushed to the living room where Nico was impatiently awaiting.

"There you are. Come sit down," Nico said and handed Sofia a glass of wine.

Sofia placed her plate of morsels onto the ottoman, which was in front of the fireplace. She sat down on the Flokati rug beneath her and began to enjoy the warmth of the crackling fire.

"This rug is to die for—it's so soft!" Sofia commented. "Where did your nonna get it?"

"My dad had it shipped from Greece one year as a Christmas present," Nico recalled. "Or maybe it was an anniversary gift. Either way, it's a wonderful rug."

"Oh, darn. I forgot to get the grimoire from my room," Sofia said, irritated that she had to get up now that she was so comfortable.

"Can you grab a couple of writing utensils from your purse as well?" Nico asked. "I totally forgot—we'll need them to write out our flash cards."

"Just like at school, always forgetting something," Sofia laughed and teased while walking to her bedroom. "I firmly believe you're destined to be my cater-waiter."

Sofia retrieved two pens from her purse, and before taking the grimoire with her, she put on Nico's sweater so that she would see the writing in the book. She then returned to the living room and sat back down on the plush rug.

"OK. A quick toast, some nibbles, and then let's get down to business and make you a wizard."

Nico held up his glass to toast. "To our friendship—where the real magic exists. May it never end."

"*Cin cin*!" Sofia responded as she clinked her glass against Nico's.

They finished their first glass of wine and decided to start creating their study cards. Thoroughly going through each spell on both sides of the book, from *Avert Disaster* to *Zeal*, they carefully wrote the name of spell on one side of the index card and the incantation and/or ingredients needed, on the opposite side; with the limited number of index cards available, they carefully chose the spells that they hoped would be the most useful.

After they exhausted their supply of index cards, Nico poured both of them another glass of Merlot and Sofia started quizzing him. They decided to turn it into a drinking game; if Nico correctly identified the spell's magic words and/or components, then they each could take a sip.

"This is definitely one college drinking game that most of our peers won't be playing," Sofia joked. "Are you ready Nico?"

"Yeah, let's make magic happen!" Nico replied enthusiastically, his face flushed from his first glass of wine and the warmth of the fireplace.

For the next three hours Sofia quizzed Nico. It was a slow start, but eventually Nico picked up the pace and began answering correctly. Eventually they finished the entire bottle of wine and their snacks.

"I think this method of studying was most helpful," Nico said to Sofia in the middle of a yawn. "Thanks for staying up—it's getting late."

"Well, who knows, one of your spells might save me from impending danger someday. And, if I'm going to be on this adventure with you, it makes sense that I should do all that I can to make sure we're both protected," Sofia acknowledged.

With that, they both said good night and headed off in opposite directions. Nico took the empty bottle of wine and other items to the kitchen before retiring to his bedroom, while Sofia picked up the grimoire and brought it back with her to her bedroom.

Chapter 13: Educational Outing, Part 1

Sofia awoke the next morning to a delicious aroma wafting into her bedroom from the kitchen. Her stomach began to grumble from hunger since her last meal had only been the cheese and crackers from the night before. Sitting up in her bed, she reached for Nico's oversized sweater and pulled it over her head. Then, pulling her hair back out of her face, she grabbed a scrunchie from the nightstand and tied her hair back into a high ponytail. Swinging her body out of bed, she stepped into her gym shorts and then tied its drawstring while walking to the kitchen.

"Good morning, sleepyhead," Nico said to her as she entered the kitchen.

"What are you making? It smells so good, and I'm starving!" Sofia replied.

"My nonna's famous lemon ricotta pancakes, which will be served with homemade lemon curd—and yes, I woke up early for this," Nico said with a chuckle. "It's the one recipe that I actually know how to make and not screw up. I wanted to surprise you by showing my appreciation for having stayed by my side yesterday. It was a rough day for me, as you know, but now I somehow feel different."

"I'm glad I was able be there for you—you're like another brother to me—one that I actually enjoy being around. And I know you'd do the same for me if the situation was reversed," Sofia responded.

"*Mademoiselle, assieds-toi, s'il te plaît*. Breakfast is served," Nico said in his best French accent as he put her plate down on the counter.

"Luckily, I know what you mean," Sofia replied as she sat down, "but you're never going to get that French accent down. I suggest you give that one up and stick to Italian or the invocation of spells—those I know you can do convincingly."

"Well, hopefully, at the very least, I will win you over with my cooking skills!" Nico responded, slightly defeated.

Sofia took a generous helping of the freshly made lemon curd and spread it across the top of her pancakes, smearing the decorative dusting of powdered sugar as her knife glided over. Her stomach grumbled once more as she reached for her fork and cut into the stack of pancakes. She took her first bite and looked at Nico; her face emoting bliss as she chewed her breakfast.

"I'm guessing they are pleasing to you?" Nico asked.

"Don't interrupt me," Sofia responded while chewing. "I'm savoring this moment. Total foodgasm happening right now."

Nico smiled, content that his meal was a success, and began eating his breakfast. For the next few minutes, silence enveloped the room and only the slightly audible sounds of masticating could be heard.

"That was the best breakfast I've ever had," Sofia gushed. "I'm going to make a cappuccino. Would you like one too?"

"Sure, that sounds perfect. I'll start cleaning up while you make those, and then we can plan our day," Nico replied.

With the kitchen nearly cleaned and the cappuccinos ready, they went back to the kitchen island and took their seats.

"So, I think we have at least three things to do today: pick up my shirt at Schwartzman's; talk to Sterling about what we found at the funeral; and go to the library to see if Teresa can provide us with any useful information about my family's origin and magic."

"That should keep us busy for a bit. We can leave the car here and walk off our breakfast—I'm so full!" Sofia replied.

"Those pancakes are quite filling," Nico said before taking a sip of his cappuccino. "Ah, delicious—you're a true barista, Sofia!"

"Why, thank you, sir," she replied while rising to bring her cup to the sink. "So, meet in the foyer in about an hour?"

"Sounds like a plan—see you then."

***

And, almost like clockwork, they met precisely one hour later in the foyer, dressed and ready to begin their excursion.

"I think I'll take you a different way into town," Nico said. "We can walk down Oliveto Avenue. It's the town's main street and is quite nice—it'll be a good change of scenery."

"Sounds lovely," Sofia replied as they exited the foyer and began walking down the front steps. "Wait. We forgot to lock up."

"I'll let you do it," Nico said with a smile. "I know how much you enjoy giving the house its commands."

"House, please lock up," Sofia said smugly, and they heard the door bolt.

The air was a little warmer than the previous days, yet the fog still persisted in its attempt to block the warmth of the morning sun.

After walking for about two blocks, Sofia spoke out, "Is that your mom and stepdad ahead?"

"It sure looks like them from behind," Nico replied and then shouted out, "Mom! Dad!"

The couple, about a half block ahead of them, stopped walking and turned around.

"Nicolino!" Siena called out and waved.

As they approached each other, they exchanged greetings and hugs.

"What a nice surprise running into you. Glad to see you both still take your morning walks," Nico commented.

"Yes. Every day unless it is too chilly out," Pétros responded. "You know how your mother detests being cold."

"I don't like being cold either," Sofia added.

Nico realized that his brother wasn't with his parents and asked, "Is Remus still staying with his friend?"

"No, we picked him up last night," Pétros said. "Today he is with his cub scout troop—they're working on a community project while school is out for spring break."

"That sounds like fun—I remember being in cub scouts and having a blast," Nico said. "Well, we're walking into town to do some errands. Do you mind if we walk with you for a few blocks?" Nico asked.

"Sure. The more the merrier," Siena said and smiled with joy at being able to spend some time with her son.

"You two go ahead. We'll catch up," Nico said, motioning to Sofia and his stepfather. "I want to ask my mother something."

"What is it Nico? What did you want to ask me?" Siena said to her son.

"It's about nonna. I don't believe she died of SCD, or a heart attack, or whatever the funeral director told you."

"Oh, really?" Siena replied, shocked by Nico's comment.

"I think she was murdered!" Nico explained. "She was clutching her chest as a clue, a clue for me to decipher. That, and Sofia and I found evidence of a break-in."

"That's nonsense. I think you've been watching too many episodes of *Murder She Wrote* or something," Siena snapped in reply. "The coroner, who reported the results to Mr. Cadaveri, has a degree and you…you're not even out of college. So, what would you know?"

"Look, mother, I don't want to argue with you, so let's just agree to disagree and catch up to dad and Sofia," Nico said, defeated.

After a moment of silence, Siena gave Nico a hug. "I know this has been hard for you. Let's try not to think about it and have happy thoughts."

Nico smiled, surprised at her response, but continued to maintain his own beliefs as to what really happened to Chiara Frantoio. With that they continued walking and eventually caught up to the other two.

"We're going to get some coffee and a treat at Patisserie Angelique. Would you like to join us?" Pétros asked as they reached the end of the block, facing the piazza.

"Thank you, but we've already had breakfast," Sofia replied to Pétros and then turned to Siena. "Did you know that your son is quite talented in the kitchen? He surprised me this morning by making me lemon ricotta pancakes—they were to die for!"

"I didn't know my son could cook," Siena responded, slightly in shock. "Regretfully, I never really let him in my kitchen."

"To be fair, mom, it's probably the only recipe I actually know, aside from the lemon curd that goes with it," Nico confessed. "I carefully watched nonna prepare them for me whenever I stayed over—the process is visually ingrained in my mind."

"Very well then," Pétros replied, "you two kids have a great day and stay out of trouble."

Once again, they each exchanged hugs, and this time said their goodbyes. Nico and Sofia headed toward their first stop of the day: Schwartzman's Quality Clothing.

As they entered the store, they stopped and stood there awestruck.

"It looks like a completely different store," Sofia remarked. "All thirty-plus mannequins have been changed out. How do two senior adults do all that work *and* make all this clothing?"

"Well, I think we now know there are a lot of magical things happening in this town—this is probably another instance of that," Nico surmised.

"Good morning, kids," Mrs. Schwartzman greeted from across the room. "Such a beautiful memorial service for your grandmother yesterday—Nico your eulogy was quite touching. I'm guessing you're here to pick up Nico's new shirt? Let me get that for you."

As Mrs. Schwartzman left the room to retrieve the shirt, they began walking to the back of the store toward the register.

"Sofia."

Sofia stopped abruptly. "Did you call my name, Nico?"

"No. Haven't we been through this line of questioning before?" Nico chuckled in disbelief. "Odd though, this is the same area of the store where you claimed you heard your name being called during our last visit. Right here by this mannequin—the one that wore a shirt similar to the one we are picking up today."

Sofia turned around and commented, "You're right!" She then looked up at the mannequin. "You know, Nico, something about this mannequin looks strangely familiar."

"It does. Reminds me a little of that guy Solomon—your new crush," Nico laughed.

"That's the connection! Right down to the same hair style and dazzling blue eyes. Sadly, this version is only wood with an exceptionally detailed paint job," Sofia added before being interrupted.

"Here's Nico's shirt. Made to order and sewn to perfection," Mrs. Schwartzman called out as she re-entered the room and headed toward them with the shirt.

"Absolute quality—top notch! I can tell from the stitch detailing," Nico praised as he held the shirt up for inspection.

"How much do I owe you?" Sofia asked. "And, by the way, I noticed on the receipt from my last purchase that you did not include Nico's shorts, so I still owe you for that."

"Both are on the house. With all his family has done for ours—I mean, for Marvin and myself—well, it's the least we can do," Mrs. Schwartzman responded. She then looked directly at Nico and asked, "So, how is it staying in the family home? Experience anything unusual?"

"Well, now that you mention it…" Nico paused, not wanting to say too much.

"Oh, good! It's all happening then as your grandmother had hoped. I didn't want to say too much when you were in the other day," Mrs. Schwartzman said with a note of relief in her voice.

"What exactly are you referring to, Mrs. Schwartzman?" Sofia chimed in.

The shopkeeper looked around the store briefly, as if to make sure no one else was in the store before speaking. "As I had mentioned during your last visit, your grandmother has done a lot for many of the townspeople, and, by now, I'm sure you're aware of her *gifts*; those which you have inherited, along with a lot more. Sterling mentioned he had spoken to you, so I feel that I can speak more freely now, and hopefully you will believe what I am about to tell you."

"So, are you like her? I mean, do you have similar *gifts*?" Nico asked.

"Oh, no—not even close. Maybe I should start by going back in history a bit—I'm not keeping you two from anything, am I?" Mrs. Schwartzman said with concern.

"We have nothing planned, so please go on. You have our complete attention," Nico replied.

"Yes, please do. I love hearing about the lives of people and their journeys," Sofia added.

Chapter 14: Mrs. Schwartzman's Story, Part 1

Back in December of 1938, when Marvin and I were teenagers, we fled Nazi Germany. I remember that very night—almost like it was yesterday. Our families lived next door to each other and had begun to plan for the worst. Each household had created a secret hiding space in their homes. Ours was a carved-out space in the wall covered by a heavy tapestry. My mother kept some money and other valuables hidden there, along with some rations. We were instructed to go to our designated hiding spots whenever there was a knock on the door and to not make a sound, no matter what happened. Thankfully, all of the knocks had been from neighbors calling to exchange gossip or update us on the latest worries concerning the regime.

"Then one night an unfamiliar knock came at the door—more like an aggressive pounding. My mother quickly ushered me to my hiding spot and handed me a piece of paper, instructing me to read it only if something bad happened. Those were her last words to me. Within minutes I could hear the struggling of my parents as they were dragged out of our home.

"I remained frozen in fear for hours, and it wasn't until the next day that Marvin cautiously left his house and sneaked into mine. My childhood friend suddenly became my hero as he drew back the tapestry and extended his hand to me. As my eyes adjusted to the light, I looked up at his tear-stained face and rose to greet him. I felt his strength permeate my soul and it gave me hope.

"He told me, in detail, what had occurred at his home, and I relayed my similar experience to him. Then I remembered the note my mother had given me, and I reached into my pocket to retrieve it. As I unfolded the wrinkled paper, I noticed that Marvin was doing the same; he had received a note as well. Both our pieces of paper had the same message:

hier lassen und nicht zurückkehren—leave here and do not return. Our parents had known their fates and gave up their lives in order to spare ours.

"Marvin and I gathered the money that had been left for us, along with a few articles of clothing, some cans of tinned meat, and one special item to remember our families by. Marvin took his father's leatherbound journal; I took my mother's prized silver hatpin which was topped with a heart-shaped ruby, framed by small diamonds.

"And so, we left our hometown and traveled northwest by foot during the day and in the evening sought shelter to escape the freezing winter temperatures. Most nights we were fortunate to find a barn or stable to sneak into and sleep on the hay amongst the horses and other farm animals that shared our company.

"One day, late in the afternoon, we decided to take a break from walking and rested on the side of the road. Marvin pulled out his pocketknife and started whittling a piece of wood he had found, while I rested my head on his shoulder and began to nap. Suddenly, a strong breeze blew in our direction. Amongst the dust, leaves and other debris carried by the wind, a single page from an old newspaper came flying toward us. And as mysteriously as the wind had started, it suddenly dissipated, causing the airborne newspaper page to drop to the ground at Marvin's feet. Putting down his knife and the piece of wood he was working on, he picked up the dusty piece of yellowed paper. He glanced down at it and then quickly turned it over. His eyes widened and he pointed to an advertisement in the lower-left corner. I lifted my head off his shoulder to view what had him so intrigued; it was a picture of an ocean liner, referred to in English as *The Largest Liner in the World*, and it was sailing to the United States.

"He looked at me and I at him. And in that very instant, we knew where our destiny was to lead us. If we could just locate that ship and sneak onto it, we could travel to the U.S. and start a new life. We figured it must be docked in Hamburg, which was about a day's travel from where we currently were. Filled with hope and excitement, we barely slept that evening and awoke early the next day to begin our journey to the Port of Hamburg.

"Traveling all morning and late into the evening, we finally reached our destination. We wearily made our way through the desolate, fog-filled wharf searching for the ocean liner pictured in the newspaper. An occasional stray cat would dart across our path in pursuit of a tasty rat, startling us both. Each darkened pier had a vessel of one type or another, but nothing stood out as being worthy of the title, *The Largest Liner in the World*.

"As exhaustion started to consume me, I began trailing behind Marvin by a couple meters. Nonetheless, we pushed forward with a spirit of determination and the light of the full moon to guide us. And, as we approached Pier 13, we saw our hope. Ahead, the moonlight's reflection on the water illuminated the side of the large vessel before us: *SS Leviathan*.

"Consumed by emotions at our find, I ran up to Marvin and kissed him on the lips—it was the first time that either of us had expressed our budding love for each other. And, as a woman during that era, it was very bold of me to have made the first move, but I think he would have made one a lot sooner had we not been fleeing for our safety, while still processing the loss of our parents.

"After the minor distraction I had created, we refocused our efforts on finding a way to board the *SS Leviathan*. To our good fortune the gangway was still accessible, and no one seemed to be on watch, so we were able to sneak across it and board the ship.

"All seemed eerily quiet onboard. Not a soul could be seen as we scanned the deck trying to decide which direction to go. Eventually we found a set of stairs leading downward and decided to take them, not only to get out of the elements but to find a safe place to rest as well. As we headed below deck, a sign read: A Deck. We continued further down the stairwell to the next level. It was then we heard the sound of voices drawing nearer and began to panic. Marvin grabbed my hand and we quickly headed down to the C Deck. We found a recessed area along the hallway and huddled there, eventually falling asleep.

"It was the first night, since I'd left home, that I had finally felt warm and was able to sleep comfortably, given the circumstances. But that didn't last long, as we were awakened a few hours later by one of the room stewards making his rounds. He began yelling at us in a language that we didn't fully understand. I'm guessing that from the garments we were wearing he realized that we didn't belong on a first-class deck and probably should be somewhere on the H Deck or lower.

"All of the commotion had awakened the occupants of a nearby stateroom. As the door to the room opened, a distinguished gentleman stepped out, dressed in black satin pajamas, and wearing a stylish silk smoking jacket. The room steward became silent and turned a deep shade of red out of embarrassment from having awakened such a distinguished passenger.

"Frantically, he began speaking to the gentleman. He appeared to be apologizing profusely for having disturbed him—at least that's what we thought he was doing.

"The man's wife, having overheard the loud conversation in the hallway, stepped out of the stateroom. She looked over at us and motioned for us to come stand by her. She put her pale, white hands on our shoulders and, speaking in perfect German, told us to go into the room and not to say a word.

"Doing as we were told, we entered their large and luxurious stateroom. In awe of the room's size, which was almost as large as one of our meager homes, we just stood there taking it all in, until we heard the door slam shut behind us. We rushed over to the door and pressed our ears against it, trying to hear what was being said out in the hallway. We could barely make sense of the conversation since we only knew a few basic English words and phrases, but we could tell from the caring tone of the woman's voice, that she was covering for us. Her husband seemed to continue to berate the room steward until there was a sudden silence—they must have come to an agreement we thought.

"We quickly backed away from the door and watched as it opened. The affluent English couple entered and shut the door quietly behind them. The gentleman, speaking in German to us, told us not to be afraid. He let us know that we had been accused of breaking into rooms and stealing, and that his wife had reassured the room steward that this was not the case.

"Together, they had quickly crafted a story, telling him that we were their niece and nephew, whom they had brought with them on holiday. And that at some point in the evening, after the couple retired, we must have sneaked out of their stateroom to explore.

"The lady continued, letting us know she had told the room steward that we were probably bored, since no one on the C Deck was our age, and so we must have gone below to explore the lower decks in hopes of finding others in our age group to associate with.

"She further embellished the story by telling him that we must have found some common clothing to change into so that we could better blend in with the other classes on board. And that after our adventure, we returned to the room but realized that we had not taken our key with us and could not get in. So, we chose to sleep outside the stateroom.

"We were thankful for their rescue, and sensing that we were weary and hungry, they presented us with their fruit basket and told us to eat. I had never seen a more beautiful red apple, than the one I reached for. Many of the other items were fruits that Marvin and I had never seen before at our age.

"Suddenly, a knock came at the door and our 'uncle' went to open it. The captain of the ship stood there, along with the room steward who was nervously shaking. A further conversation ensued—we were later told that the captain had come to personally apologize for the terrible mishap and treatment of us. He mentioned that since we weren't listed on the ship's manifest, that it must have confused the room steward, whose job was to know all the passengers on his assigned deck.

"Because of their social status, our saviors were able to reassure the captain that we were their niece and nephew and implied that it must have been a crewmember's error that we were not listed on the ship's manifest. The captain, embarrassed by the accusation, said that he would make sure that all of the ship's staff would be made aware of our presence, so that we would be treated as well as the other first-class passengers.

"As the captain left, the gentleman shut the door behind him and turned to us with a serious look on his face. A smile began to emerge followed by a loud and hearty guffaw. His wife, now praising her husband's performance, erupted in laughter.

"Apparently partaking in our little mishap, by rescuing us with some clever dialogue, added some spice to their life. This didn't seem like their first time doing something like this. Eventually, as the excitement died down, exhaustion returned and we were shown to the stateroom's second bedroom, which became ours for the entire transatlantic crossing—I barely recall my head touching the fluffy down pillow before I was sound asleep.

"The next morning, a gentle rapping at our door woke us up, and we feasted on a delicious in-room breakfast. As we indulged in our first experience with fine cuisine, we spoke of our recent journey and all that had led up to it. As our benefactors listened intently, tears ran down their faces—I think that's when we all bonded.

"They truly seemed to care for us. During the rest of the voyage, they made sure we were properly fed, educated on proper etiquette, and taught a crash course on how to speak proper English. Each morning, new outfits for us to wear would mysteriously appear from one of their steamer trunks—I think we experienced and learned more in those two weeks than we had in the previous years.

"We never knew the true identities of our mysterious benefactors, other than their possible surname: Hornsby, which Marvin had noticed imprinted on all the luggage. Nonetheless, we were so grateful for the couple who had shown us pity and protection, that we eventually began to call them *onkel* and *tante*—which is uncle and auntie in German. Of course, this also helped with the ruse of us being family members.

"Eventually the ship made it to the United States and docked in New York. After disembarking with our temporary family, they wished us well, and before parting ways, our new 'uncle' reached into his breast pocket and pulled out a sealed envelope, which he handed to Marvin. In it was a large sum of money accompanied by an elegantly written note telling us to make our way to California and seek the small town named Oliveto—that we would be safe there.

"A few minutes after we walked away from *The Largest Liner in the World*, I turned back for one last memory of our voyage. To my surprise, the vessel was gone—it had completely vanished. Our benefactors, who still should've only been a few meters away, were gone as well. I tugged on Marvin's newly tailored jacket to get his attention and to verify that what I was seeing was true. He turned around and immediately noticed my pallor. With a tone of concern in his voice, he asked what was wrong and if I was OK. I turned and pointed back toward where we had disembarked, and I saw his face turn almost as pale as mine as he looked up in shock. How could a ship so large in scale disappear in a matter of minutes and leave no trace of its existence. And more importantly, where had our benefactors gone as well?

"There were no plausible answers that we could come up with to explain what we had witnessed, and so we did as the note directed and made our way to Oliveto."

Chapter 15: Mrs. Schwartzman's Story, Part 2

We traveled frugally, only spending money for food and basic necessities—nothing more. And when we finally reached the town, we were gobsmacked by its beauty. We must have circled the piazza three or four times just to take it all in and enjoy the serenity that now surrounded us. Eventually we stopped walking and took a seat on a nearby bench. Marvin turned to me—I will never forget his exact words—he looked into my eyes and said, 'My dearest, we are finally home.' Tears welled up in our eyes and we embraced for what seemed like an eternity.

"Shortly thereafter, our sentimental moment was interrupted as a man approached us. He greeted us saying, 'So you are the new ones to our beloved town. *Willkómmen*! *Benvenuti*!' He introduced himself as Supremo Frantoio—your great-grandfather—and invited us over to your family's real estate office. We picked up our luggage and followed him across the piazza and into the building. As we entered his private office in the back, we placed our suitcases near the door, and took seats in the comfortable leather-tufted chairs which faced his desk.

"He let us know that he had received a telegram in regard to our pending arrival and had been expecting us. He further elaborated that he was asked to help us secure a place to live and find work.

"We told him of our journey and everything that we had gone through leading up to our arrival in town. And after listening to our long and emotional story, he walked us over to the Hotel Oliveto and put us up in a nice suite. We were instructed to rest up and return to his office the next day at 9:00 a.m., at which time he would reveal a plan to help us put down our roots here in Oliveto.

"We woke up early the following morning, filled with anticipation of the unknown plan Supremo had in store for us, and made our way down to the hotel's café for an enjoyable continental breakfast. As Marvin and I sat there eating, we discussed how blessed we were—it seemed like not long ago we were fleeing in fear, and now we were safe and had a sense of hope.

"In the moment, Marvin seized the opportunity, and got out of his chair. He walked over to me and got on his knee. He then reached into his pocket and pulled out a small robin-egg blue box. In it was the most beautiful engagement ring I had ever seen. This moment was a long time coming, so I barely let him finish proposing before blurting out 'Yes!'

"The patrons around us began to clap and congratulate us. I was giddy with excitement, but in the back of my mind, I wondered how he obtained the ring. Marvin later told me that he had been given the ring by Mr. Hornsby, while on the *SS Leviathan*. Mr. Hornsby had told him that we were destined to be together, and that he wanted to make sure Marvin had a ring, so that he could propose to me when the time felt right.

"Shortly after our meal, we met Supremo at his office, precisely at 9:00 a.m.—punctuality was one of the many rules of etiquette that we learned from our benefactors, while at sea. We all sat down in his office, and he told us that he had spoken to his wife Margherita the previous evening and told her of our story. That is when she came up with the perfect solution to help us get started.

"Supremo rose from his chair and asked us to follow him to the other side of the piazza. He said it would be easier to explain the plan with some visuals. We anxiously got up and went with him. He ended up bringing us to this very building we are now standing in. He showed Marvin and me inside, and aside from this prime retail space, there was an upstairs with a livable flat, which has been our home ever since. But even more promising was when he led us downstairs to the basement level. There, he envisioned, we would manufacture garments, which we could then sell in the retail space for income.

"I could see the wheels turning in Marvin's head as he began to get excited by Supremo's suggestion. Since Marvin's father had been an expert tailor, it only made sense for him to continue on with his father's craft to honor his memory. And the journal that Marvin had taken with him had everything we needed to know about his father's trade. It was filled with a variety of designs and methods for constructing every imaginable article of apparel—and something else, which I discovered later.

"Supremo and his wife had complete faith in us. He said that he would allow us to live and work here rent-free for a year or until we could make the business profitable. We put the majority of our money into buying fabric and sewing equipment, so that we could begin our adventure in retail.

"Marvin would spend up to eighteen hours a day, designing and constructing garments for us to display. I would then finish the product by sewing on the buttons, removing any errant threads, and then pressing them to iron out any wrinkles. Since I wanted to be able to better assist Marvin in the production of our garments, I began reading his father's journal, usually, while I ironed. One day as I was pressing a shirt, I was distracted by a spider that was crawling across the floor and moved the iron too close to the journal. Much to my surprise, I didn't burn any of the pages, but strangely, the heat from the iron revealed a hidden section written in some form of invisible ink. I gasped and beckoned Marvin over to see what I had discovered.

"Marvin, thinking that I might have burned myself, rushed over to make sure that I was unharmed. I pointed down to the cryptic text, and he didn't seem surprised at all. For written there were the instructions for animating an inanimate object—more specifically how to create a golem.

"As children we were told tales of how a mighty golem was once created to protect our people from persecution, but we always dismissed them as folklore. We looked at each other and wondered if the stories were true. There was only one way to find out. So, we set out to create our own version of a golem. Since we lacked a source of clay, which was used in the childhood story and also mentioned in Marvin's father's journal, we improvised and used wood, which was locally abundant.

"Marvin spent days in the basement carving and sanding down pieces of wood to create a complex and jointed human-like figure. He paid careful attention to detail and designed everything to scale. He even painted realistic looking features and repurposed an old wig in order to insert individual hairs into the wooden scalp. Once completed, we followed the last step of his father's instructions and carved the mystical words on the golem's forehead, bringing it to life.

"Once animated, the golem would then assist us in manufacturing of apparel. As our business grew, we created more golems, dressing them as store mannequins to display our clothing during the day and, in the evening after we closed, we would lower the blinds and lead them downstairs, where they would help us by sewing and restocking the sales floor.

"Our business continued to flourish, and within the year, we were married at St. Anthony's. Your great-grandfather, instead of moving forward with collecting rent, signed over the deed to the building as a wedding present to us—his only request was that his family would never be without clothing. And that's why there was no charge for Nico's clothing.

"A few years had passed, and we decided to try to start a family. Unfortunately, after multiple attempts, I was told by the local doctor that I was unable to conceive. I was heartbroken that I could not provide Marvin with a child and fell into a deep depression. Marvin did everything he could to raise my spirits—he even fashioned a golem that resembled some of our best features: my blonde hair and his sparkling blue eyes.

"Bless his heart for trying, but Marvin's creation, like the others, lacked emotion. It was just another zombie-like creature that shuffled about the store doing menial tasks—that is until the day I met your grandmother, Chiara.

"Shortly after settling in Oliveto, we met your grandfather Benito. He was around eighteen and worked at the real estate office, helping with various things, and preparing to take his real estate exam. Your great-grandfather had been mentoring him for about two years, teaching him all he knew about real estate. Benito was destined to become a realtor like his father and help grow the family business.

"During that time, your grandfather had become enamored of a raven-haired girl named Chiara Scuro, who recently arrived in town. She started working at Doc's Drugstore & Soda Shop as a waitress and lived at one of the local boarding houses. No one knew much about her, other than she came from Italy and her parents were deceased.

"It was a short courtship before they decided to marry, and we were commissioned to create a wedding dress for her—one unlike the town had ever seen. As I got to know her during fabric selections and fittings, she quickly picked up on my inner sadness. Chiara instinctively knew my life was lacking something—she was very intuitive about such things and what people desired.

"During the second fitting, after Marvin had left the room, Chiara casually mentioned to me that she knew the secret about the store mannequins—that they were more than just figures displaying our wares. She then pointed over to the special one that Marvin had created for me and told me that she wanted to repay us for the kindness we had shown to her as a newcomer to Oliveto.

"She requested that I obtain a small but extremely sentimental article from my possessions—something that I would be heartbroken if I ever lost it. Then, shortly before midnight, I was to let her back into the store and provide her that object.

"That very night she returned as promised. I almost didn't see her outside, waiting for me to open the door, because of how she was dressed. A black, hooded cloak covering her petite frame caused her to blend in with the shadows. Had the moon not peeked from the cloudy sky and illuminated her figure, I would've thought she'd forgotten to return.

"I unlocked the door and beckoned her inside from the cold night air. She quickly reached for an antique pendant watch that she wore around her neck and checked the time: 11:55 p.m. 'Come. We must work quickly,' she said as she rushed toward the basement stairs and descended.

"All the golems were busy doing their various tasks: sewing, pressing, folding, and organizing garments. She quickly singled out Marvin's special creation, which halted its movement at her approach. She turned to me and asked, 'Do you have the item I requested?'

"I acknowledged by nodding my head and handing her my mother's silver hatpin. 'How uncanny that you chose this item—it is beyond perfect!' She then instructed me to remove the golem's shirt and to stand next to it. 'Be strong,' she advised, 'this is going to hurt a little.'

"Once again, she checked the time: 11:59 p.m. Immediately she grabbed my hand, and taking the hatpin, jabbed it into a visibly raised vein. I yelped at the intense pain and winced as blood began to flow from the fresh wound, encircling the pin's sharp tip.

"The church bells at St. Anthony's began their count up to twelve and Chiara removed the bloody hatpin from my arm, then started to chant:

Blood from a mother,
Taken from her vein,
You without emotions,
Shall have feelings and know pain.

"And as she spoke the last line of the incantation, the golem's hard wooden chest became almost flesh-like. She quickly plunged the hatpin deep into it and the heart-shaped ruby began to glow and pulse. I watched the golem's painted complexion flush with a more humanlike realness, its eyes blink, and its lips part. A restrained sound escaped from the golem's mouth, as if it were trying to express how it was feeling.

"A surge of emotions overcame me, and I began to feel a mothering instinct to protect and comfort a child—my child. I took the golem's hand, which now felt warm and alive, and held it to my racing heart. I looked into his blue eyes and saw tears had formed. As he looked down at me, a tear released from the corner of his eye and ran down his cheek. I reached up and blotted his ruddy cheek with my handkerchief, and to my astonishment, he spoke: 'Muh…muh…mother.'"

Chapter 16: Educational Outing, Part 2

"And so that's my story," Mrs. Schwartzman finished with an accomplished smile on her face.

"Amazing!" Sofia commented and then asked, "Did you ever find out more about the mysterious ship that brought you to the U.S.?"

"Funny you mention that. A few years ago, Marvin and I were having a quaint little dinner to celebrate our anniversary, and we began reminiscing about everything we had been through," Mrs. Schwartzman replied. "We both began to question and wonder about our experience on the *SS Leviathan*—something neither of us had thought about for decades. The next day I decided to close the store for an hour and take a stroll over to the library. I was hoping that Teresa, the librarian, would be able to shed some light about the *SS Leviathan* and our voyage from the Port of Hamburg.

"She was eager to help and went down to the library's basement level, where she said all the historic records were kept. After a good ten minutes, she returned with a puzzled look on her face. She brought me over to a seating area. We sat down and she began to relay the most fascinating information.

"Teresa said that the *SS Leviathan* had been dismantled months prior to our voyage and sold for scrap. Even more remarkable was that Pier 13, where we originally boarded the vessel, never existed. Apparently, we might have boarded some type of ghost ship or phantom vessel."

"Wow, that's kind of cool—but also kind of creepy," Nico responded. After a brief pause, something clicked in his mind, and he decided to share. "I just thought of something—a piece of interesting information that might hold a clue. Those two mysterious benefactors that you and Mr. Schwartzman traveled with. You said you believed their surname to be Hornsby, correct?"

"Yes," Mrs. Schwartzman replied. "That's the name that Marvin saw on their luggage."

"I see where you are going with this Nico," Sofia jumped in. "Mrs. Schwartzman, the boarding house where we reside in Connecticut, happens to be named Hornsby Manor. The owner is a Mrs. Agnes Hornsby, but she seems to be in her forties and couldn't possibly be the same person. Maybe she's a relative of the people you met during your transatlantic journey?"

"A very interesting connection that would be," Mrs. Schwartzman responded with interest.

"If you'd like, when we return next week, we'll ask her if she might be related," Nico offered.

"That would be a wonderful gesture. I'd love to be able to tell our son more about how we came to Oliveto."

Curious, Sofia then asked, "About your son, is he working downstairs today with Mr. Schwartzman? It would be nice to meet him."

"Oh yes, my son. He's taken quite a fancy to you, Sofia," Mrs. Schwartzman replied and turned her gaze toward the mannequin behind Sofia and continued. "Haven't you, Solomon?"

Sofia abruptly turned around, slightly shocked at what she now imagined to be true. She had barely gained sight of the figure stepping down from the display before she felt lightheaded and lost consciousness. Fortunately, Solomon was there to catch her as she fell forward into his arms.

Solomon lowered Sofia's limp body to the floor. He gently turned her over and cradled her head in his arms. Mrs. Schwartzman rushed off and returned with a cool wet towel, which she placed on Sofia's forehead.

"Sofia. Wake up, Sofia," Nico called out while holding his best friend's hand and trying to help revive her.

Sofia's eyes began to open and first focused in on Nico. "What happened?" She asked.

"My dear, you became faint and started to fall to the ground, but my son caught you in time, and likely prevented you from having a nasty bump on your head," Mrs. Schwartzman replied.

"Solomon?"

"Yes, Sofia. It is I," The living mannequin replied. "I would never let any harm come to you."

Sofia tilted her head back and looked up into Solomon's calming blue eyes. His strong arms, supporting her collapsed body, felt warm and comforting. Her mind began to accept the magical reality that Solomon was actually alive.

"Thank you," Sofia said softly, embarrassed by her previous reaction. "I'm so sorry. I didn't mean to—"

"That's OK, dear," Mrs. Schwartzman said in an effort to comfort Sofia. "Most people would not be able to accept what you've just experienced. You and Nico are still new to the ways of this town and the magic that abounds."

Solomon helped Sofia back to her feet and, taking her hand, kissed it.

Yep, those are the same soft lips that touched my hand when we first met, Sofia recalled to herself.

Nico could tell that Sofia was slightly embarrassed and still needed some time to make sense of it all, so he turned to Mrs. Schwartzman and Solomon and said, "I'm going to take her outside—I think she just needs some fresh air."

Still feeling a little shaky, Sofia put her hand on Nico's shoulder as he walked her out of the store and back onto the piazza.

Always knowing the right words to get a reaction from Sofia, Nico joked, "So, you did fall for that dummy. Literally and figuratively!"

Sofia couldn't hold back from Nico's comment and let out a boisterous laugh in response. As she regained her composure, she asked him, "Do you think it is OK to have feelings for him? I felt a connection early on, even when I thought he was just a mannequin, but now that I know he's a magical being, does that make it wrong?"

"Sofia, love is love. A person's heart will naturally yearn for its complement, and once it's found a match, whether the individual is the same sex, opposite sex—or in this case wood— then it will cease searching and enjoy feeling complete." Nico replied in a comforting tone. "I can't say whether it's right or wrong—that's something only you have the right to answer. What I do know is that in just a few days' time, we've learned that fairies and golems exist; that talking to the dead is actually possible; and that I can cast spells! Who knows what else exists or is even possible here in Oliveto?"

"You're right," Sofia agreed. "I guess I need to be open to possibilities—I don't want to miss out on 'the one.'"

"Why don't you stay out here for a bit and collect your thoughts. I'll go back in and get my new shirt," Nico suggested.

Sofia sat down on a nearby bench in front of the store window while Nico went back inside the store.

Once inside, Nico said to Mrs. Schwartzman and Solomon, "Sofia apologizes for her reaction—she's a little embarrassed. I think she, like myself…well, we're just trying to comprehend everything that is happening. Things that we never imagined possible are actually a reality. And, at times it's just been a bit overwhelming for us."

"I'm sure it has been, especially for you, Nico. Between mourning the loss of your grandmother and finding out that you have a legacy of magical talents to boot!" Mrs. Schwartzman replied.

"Yes, it's been a lot to wrap my head around. I still have so many questions, many of which I'm sure will be answered soon. Speaking of which, the library is our next stop, so I'd better rejoin Sofia before she thinks I've abandoned her."

"Well, my dear, here's your shirt. You left it behind when you took Sofia outside. Would you like a shopping bag for it?" Mrs. Schwartzman asked.

"No thank you. I'll save a tree and carry it with me," Nico responded and then turned to Solomon with a smile and asked, "Would you like to meet Sofia and me for a drink tonight?"

"Really?" Solomon answered with a tinge of delight in his voice.

"Absolutely. I think it'll be good for Sofia, and despite her earlier reaction, she actually does like you and feels a connection. And, maybe Fawn can join us as well. After the library, Sofia and I will be going to Indelible Delights to talk to Sterling—I'll invite her then!"

"Very good. Same place, and around the same time as our last encounter?" Solomon asked.

"We'll be there. See you then," Nico said and then turned to Mrs. Schwartzman to thank her. "Please extend my gratitude to Mr. Schwartzman—I'll always remember today every time I'm wearing this shirt."

Nico took his shirt which Mrs. Schwartzman had refolded ever so nicely and waved goodbye.

Sofia heard the door to the store opening and looked at Nico. "Wow, that took you a while. I hope you didn't spend all that time making excuses for my behavior."

Nico chuckled. "No, not at all. I was actually doing you a favor. But we can talk about that later—we need to head to the library."

"Wait, you didn't get a bag? You're just going to walk around town carrying a folded shirt with you all day?"

"No. You're going to carry it. In your purse," Nico responded with a grin.

"My purse? There's no room in there," Sofia said, confused by Nico's suggestion.

"Ye of little faith," Nico joked and then turned his back toward the street so no one would see what he was about to do. Placing his hands on the purse, he recited, "*Fac Spatium*. There. The Secret Space incantation should have fixed that dilemma—you should have plenty of room now."

Nico rolled up his new shirt like a newspaper and handed it to Sofia. She opened her purse and looked inside. It appeared to be more spacious than before. Her comb and other various cosmetic articles no longer seemed to be crowded together and competing for space. She inserted the shirt, whose dimensions would have normally extended past that of the purse, and was amazed that it fit.

"Oh no! It's got my hand!" Sofia jokingly exclaimed as she thrust her hand deeper into the purse as if it were being consumed.

Startled at first, Nico caught on to Sofia's prank and began to laugh. "Clever girl. You almost got me!"

"Looks like our late-night study session paid off after all—bravo!" Sofia commended and then rambled enthusiastically, "I've always loved this little purse, and now I don't have to trade up for something larger to carry everything. In fact, now I can carry my tarot cards with me wherever I go! And I can carry around any necessary spell components we might need—I could probably even fit the candelabra with the matches—you know, in case we need light."

"Slow down there. I know this is all exciting to you," Nico said. "But there's a lot we still need to learn and better understand. For all we know, there could be consequences to all of this! Hopefully, the library will provide us with more answers. Let's get moving."

Chapter 17: A Wealth of Knowledge

After walking for a few blocks, they arrived at the town library. And, instead of walking up the stairs to the second-floor main entrance, Nico motioned to Sofia to follow him around the corner to a ground-level side entrance.

Nico opened the door and Sofia entered first, as was their routine. The smell of musty books mixed with the scent of lemon oil from rows of recently polished wooden bookcases filled the air.

"Nico! The rows of books seem to go on forever—this place appears almost bigger than the Sterling Memorial Library on campus," Sofia remarked rather loudly. "And everything is so neatly organized!"

Suddenly a low *shhh* could be heard, followed by another coming from a different direction. They looked around for the sources of the shushing sounds, but not a soul could be seen.

Nico whispered, "Maybe the books are enchanted to remind people to keep their voices down."

Sofia whispered back, "As often as I frequent the campus library, I should've known to keep it down."

Nico closed the door behind them, and they continued onward. One of the floorboards suddenly let out a loud creak under the weight of Nico's foot.

"Nico, is that you over in the Periodicals Section?" A voice from the next room ahead quietly called out.

"Yes," Nico responded somewhat surprised. "Teresa, is that you?"

"Yes. I'm in the main room, returning books to their proper locations," Teresa spoke softly and then continued in a more melodic tone, "Just follow my voice."

Nico and Sofia headed further inside, toward the heart of the library, drawn to the location where Teresa's captivating voice was coming from. As they passed numerous shelves of magazines and newspapers on display, to their right they noticed a roped-off staircase leading downward. Nico had always wondered what was kept below. A sign affixed to the rope read: *Employees Only!* As they passed by the staircase, a light breeze caressed their faces and a salty tang, reminiscent of ocean air, filled their nostrils.

"Do you smell that, Nico?" Sofia asked.

"I sure do. It reminds me of the first time we used a fairy door with Sterling and went to that cavernous rock out in the ocean," Nico replied seriously and then joked, "Maybe someone left the door open?"

Sofia laughed. "Funny. But at this point, I'd believe almost anything was possible," she replied, as a floorboard creaked once again.

"Stop dawdling by the stairs," Teresa spoke out in a low volume. "Put some pep in your step and come visit. I can give you a tour later if you wish."

Now slightly embarrassed, Nico and Sofia made haste and entered the expansive center of the library and spotted Teresa over in a corner aisle with a cart of books.

"I must say, I am quite intimidated by her already. She's stunningly beautiful. I almost can't keep my eyes off her," Sofia remarked after first seeing Teresa.

Teresa Libretto had always been beautiful. Ever since Nico had first met her when they were kids, he was captivated by her visage each time he was in her presence. She was blessed with a flawless complexion and naturally ash blonde hair that had an oddly greenish hue to it. She now stood five feet ten inches, and even without shoes she seemed to tower over most of the library visitors. Today was no exception; she did look stunning. Her hair was pulled back into a high ponytail, and she wore a cream-colored silk blouse with a brooch of a small cephalopod pinned to it; a tight fitting, black pencil skirt and high heels completed her look.

They approached Teresa, who was in the midst of using a step stool to reach a high shelf.

"Nico, would you please hand me that last book there on the cart? And introduce me to your lovely friend," Teresa asked.

Nico reached for the book, a first edition of *The Birds of America* by John James Audubon, and handed it to her.

"Here you go," Nico said. "Teresa, this is my best friend, Sofia Saggio; Sofia, this is Teresa Libretto."

"Nice to meet you, Teresa," Sofia said. "By the way, how did you know it was Nico who entered the building? And how did you know where we were located each time?"

Teresa pushed the last book back snug into its place and started to descend the step stool. Turning to Sofia, she said, "A pleasure to meet you as well. As to how I knew your locations, it's no secret that I know this place like the back of my hand; each floorboard in this building gives off its own unique creaking sound. Now, as for how I knew it was Nico, it was your calling him by name that was a quick tell."

"I do apologize. When we first walked in, I was quite impressed by the spaciousness of the interior and the quantity of books—I guess I was a bit overly expressive," Sofia explained. "I spend a lot of time at our campus library—so much time, that it almost feels like a second home to me. I guess I was comparing homes."

"Home. Yes, I dare say, I do know the feeling." Teresa mused a bit and then asked, "So, what is it I can help you with? Sterling said you might be stopping by to do some research."

"Yes, Teresa. I was wondering if you knew anything about what Benandanti and Malandanti are?" Nico inquired.

"Not *what*, but *who* they are," Teresa responded quietly. "Come with me and let's sit down and I will tell you all I know."

Theresa escorted them over to a comfortable seating area near a lit fireplace. Four leather reading chairs faced the corners of a square coffee table, which was covered with various books needing to be returned to their proper shelves.

"Please have a seat," Teresa directed, pointing out the two chairs nearest the fireplace. As she herself began to sit down, she noticed the pile of books on the table and stood back up. "Drat! More books to return!" she exclaimed and then continued jokingly, "It's like my never-ending hell. Sometimes I won't have a single visitor all day and yet, I'll still find books here on the table."

Sofia offered, "I can help you put them away after we are done chatting."

"Thank you, but you are both my guests, and I don't wish to burden you with my responsibilities. Let me quickly take care of these books before my OCD takes over," Teresa said. She then became silent, listening carefully. After a few seconds, she continued speaking. "Good, we're the only ones in the library. Now, by Sterling's account, you are already aware of the goings-on in this town, so what you're about to see should be of no surprise."

Teresa looked over at the table of books and began humming melodically. The enchanting sound she emitted caused the books to start to rumble on the table before standing upright. The books then lined up like members of a marching band and began to levitate from the table, dispersing in different directions within the library, presumably returning to their proper locations.

"There. Now that that's taken care of, let me give you a brief history of who the Benandanti and Malandanti are.

"Back in Italy, many centuries ago, there was a sudden increase in caul births—"

"Wait," Nico interrupted. "What's a caul?"

Sofia spoke up to clarify, "It's the amniotic sac. Now, please go on, Teresa."

"As I was saying," Teresa continued, "an unusual number of caul births were suddenly occurring. Most of those births though were regular caul births, where only a piece of the amniotic sac is covering the head or face of the newborn. This normally occurs in about one out of every eighty thousand births. But rarer still is an en caul birth where the newborn comes out of the womb inside an intact amniotic sac—almost like being born in a see-through egg. These children were regarded as special and said to have powerful mystical gifts. Those raised with goodness and morals were called Benandanti or Good Walkers, whereas those who followed a darker path in life were called Malandanti or Bad Walkers and sought to challenge Benandanti whenever possible.

"During the 16th and 17th centuries, both Benandanti and Malandanti were considered heretics of the church and were persecuted. This led to families having births in secret, whenever possible, so that if the child were born en caul, no one else in the village would know and the baby could be kept safe.

"Eventually the persecutions ended and the occurrence of en caul and caul births became almost unheard of. But as with most things in life, they tend to go in a cycle, and once again, in the late 1800's, an area of Northern Italy began to report a larger than normal number of this type of birth.

"As gossip about these rare births spread from village to village, superstitious people began to blame everything, from crop failures to illnesses, on the birth of these children. A few fanatical priests saw an opportunity to make money for the church and took it upon themselves to rid the land of this new 'evil'—for a price.

"Parents feared for their children's lives. Would this turn into another witch hunt like it was two centuries prior? Would children born without a caul be falsely accused as before? Well, four families did not want to take that chance, since their children had secretly been born en caul years prior. And so they gathered their children, three boys and one girl, and hid them until they could sneak them on board a cargo ship bound for the United States, where they would be free of persecution. Those four teenagers eventually made it safely to America and traveled across the states where they finally settled in an area where the land reminded them of home."

"Let me guess," Nico said. "They settled here and became the town founders?"

"Exactly!" Teresa responded passionately.

"That must have been a rough go for the four young kids," Sofia sighed. "To leave your family and start over in a foreign place."

"Oddly, my family never told me this story," Nico commented.

"Well, should you ever wish to know the true story, let me—" Teresa was interrupted by a book falling off a nearby shelf.

Nico and Sofia both jumped slightly from their seat as the book hit the planked flooring with a loud thud.

"How did that happen? You said there was no one here other than us!" Sofia said nervously.

Teresa walked over to the lone book lying on the floor and held something up to her eye.

Nico and Sofia, curious to see what she was doing, rose from the comfortable leather chairs and went over to where Teresa was standing. They observed her holding a familiar looking hole-ridden stone; a chain ran through one of the holes of the blue-gray stone which Teresa wore around her neck.

"Is that a hag stone?" Sofia asked.

"Why, yes," Teresa responded. "I'm using it to examine the book—just as I expected: book worms! They all must've traveled to this bookcase, since it's the only one that I haven't polished yet. They absolutely detest the scent of lemon oil, so I'm constantly keeping the bookcases polished to deter them."

Nico reached into the right pocket of his shorts and retrieved the hag stone which he had been carrying with him for the past few days. Holding it up to his eye, he looked through the largest of the many holes at the book. "I don't see anything," he said with dismay.

Teresa turned away from the worm-filled book to address Nico's comment. "Ah, let me see your stone."

Nico handed his trinket to her so she could examine it.

Teresa fumbled with the stone a bit. "Ah, I recognize this stone." She then looked through one of its holes at the book. "This is one of the many stones I collected from the ocean and gave to your nonna—it was one of the ways I tried to return the favor for all that she had done for me." Teresa paused for a bit, seemingly reminiscing about a past event, and then continued. "This hag stone has not been charged—that's why you are not able to see anything. Here, take a look through mine."

Teresa removed the chained stone from around her neck and handed it to Nico.

Nico looked at the object. It was smaller than his hag stone and had only one hole that went completely through it. He held it up to his eye and looked through it. Amazed and somewhat shocked at what he was now able to see, he quickly handed the stone to Sofia.

"Here, take a look, Sofia—and be glad we didn't just eat. It's not a pretty site."

"Eww, gross!" Sofia exclaimed as she looked down at the mass of tiny wriggling worms covering the pages of the open book. "So, is a hag stone's only purpose for seeing book worms?"

"Not only book worms, but any unseen magical beings and spirits that may be wandering about," Teresa explained. "As I mentioned, Nico's stone did not work because it hasn't been charged yet."

"How do we go about charging it?" Nico asked.

"You need to bathe it in saltwater under the light of the full moon." Teresa answered. "In a few more days, the moon will be full, and you can do it then."

"Good to know," Nico responded. Turning toward Sofia, he whispered, "I don't think we saw mention of the hag stones in the grimoire."

"We can always add it! There are a few blank pages in the center of the book."

Teresa's ears perked up at the mention of the grimoire. "So, you found it? That's wonderful! Your nonna would be so happy to know that."

"Oh, she knows!" Sofia chuckled.

"How do you know that Sofia?" Nico asked, somewhat confused.

"After we had brought her bust upstairs from the basement, I placed hers next to Benito's, and she spoke to me through the mirror," Sofia confessed.

"Did you at least ask her the house's name? That was our original purpose for communicating with her," Nico replied, slightly perturbed.

"No, I didn't," Sofia snapped. "We were about to go study the grimoire and I felt bad about leaving her in the kitchen. My intent was to place her by Benito and then go study with you, but she caught me off guard by speaking to me."

"I'm sorry." Nico apologized. "I didn't mean to sound cross. I guess in the moment I was a little jealous that you got to speak with her."

"Don't worry about it. I know you miss her, and I understand," Sofia replied calmly.

"Now that you two lovebirds have made up—" Teresa teased before being interrupted.

"Oh, we are just friends," Nico laughed. "Besides, she's already found her soul-mate here in town."

"That must be Solomon, the town's best kept secret bachelor," Teresa responded.

"I barely know him," Sofia commented. "I just felt drawn to him, even before I knew he was real."

"That is some of Chiara's best work." Teresa said and her eyes started to tear up. "To have given the Schwartzman's the gift of a son—that has made all the difference in their lives."

Nico and Sofia watched as the tears in Teresa's eyes hardened into small nacre orbs and fell to the floor.

Sofia knelt down and picked up the two iridescent spheres. While holding them in the palm of her hand for Nico to see, she asked Theresa, "Are these pearls?"

"Yes," Teresa admitted. "I'm so embarrassed. I try my best not to cry in front of others."

"So, you don't just know magic, you are a magical being too?" Nico questioned. "All of these years growing up, and I never knew."

Sofia spoke up with excitement. "Tears of the sea…so, that would make you a mermaid?"

"Close," Teresa answered. "I am actually a siren—third in a line of sirens to be exact. But we can save my tale for another day. Come with me. There's something I want to show you that can help answer all your questions."

"If it isn't too inappropriate to ask, may I keep the pearls?" Sofia asked cautiously, not wanting to upset Teresa.

"Of course, you can—maybe you can fashion them into a pair of nice earrings. I think they'd look nice on you," Teresa replied as she led them out of the main room, back toward the periodical section, and stopping by the roped-off stairs.

"Ah! Finally, after all these years, am I going to get to see what lies below?" Nico said with excitement.

"Yes, that's where we're headed," Teresa replied while unfastening the rope so they could proceed further. "Wait. I should probably lock the doors, since I'll be leaving the library unattended. There are too many valuable first editions and historical documents kept here."

"You sound very protective," Sofia commented.

"That I am," Teresa sighed. "Long ago, a family member of mine made a deal with the four town founders. In exchange for protection, we

Libretto women were bound to this building; serving and protecting it, never able to leave."

"Well, that would explain why I never saw you at school when we were children. Now that I think of it, the only time I ever saw you, was here in the library—totally makes sense now," Nico reasoned.

"So, you're trapped here within the confines of this building?" Sofia asked.

"Not entirely. Thanks to Chiara, I became the first Libretto woman to be able to leave the building, but only for short periods of time. As long as I wear this enchanted brooch that she created for me," Teresa answered and pointed to the object pinned to her blouse.

Sofia moved closer to examine the small brooch of a nautilus shell pinned to Teresa's blouse. As she studied it, she could see small tentacles writhing about within the shell. Amazed that the shell contained a living sea creature, she moved even closer. A slimy tentacle immediately lashed out from within the shell and slapped her on the nose.

"The little guy is feisty—guess he thought I was invading your personal space," Sofia said with a laugh as she wiped the tip of her wet nose.

"That he is," Teresa said with a smirk. "Now let me lock the doors and we can head downstairs."

Nico and Sofia watched as Teresa closed her eyes and clapped her hands twice. Immediately, the sound of multiple steel bolts sliding into place were heard echoing throughout the building as it secured itself.

"There, now I feel better. OK, follow me and hold onto the banister—I spilled some polish on the stairs the other day, and they may still be a little slick."

Nico and Sofia heeded Teresa's advice and carefully followed her down to the mysterious lower level. As they reached the landing, they noticed they were in a small room containing one rather oversized door which was fashioned out of various pieces of reclaimed driftwood; the wood was moist and appeared to be sweating droplets of what smelled like sea water, which pooled near the threshold. Various maritime glyphs were carved into the wood and seemed to glow with increased intensity as they drew closer.

"Stand back," Teresa warned. "The door is magically warded and packs a nasty surprise to those who try to enter without my knowledge."

As Teresa approached the door, her heels splashed in the puddle of seawater collecting at its base. Raising her hands, she began touching the warded glyphs in a specific pattern: Unicorn fish; Narwhal; Lamprey; Octopus; Conch shell, Kelp. The seawater at the base of the door began ebbing back into the door as if it were a small outgoing tide. Moisture from the door began to evaporate, and as it became dry and unswollen, a space between the door and its frame could now be seen; the door was now unsealed.

"Just when I thought I couldn't be any more amazed, I see this incredible feat of magic!" Sofia responded with excitement.

"Even after all these years, I'm still impressed by this particular enchantment that a foremother of mine created almost century ago," Teresa commented.

"Impressive indeed!" Nico added. "So far all I can do is lock and unlock doors and objects."

"Nico, you've just started learning," Sofia responded supportively. "Don't forget that you tried a new spell a few hours ago and were successful with it—totally surprised me!"

Teresa added her own words of encouragement. "Your nonna prepared you for this moment in your life, even knowing that much of your knowledge of magical things would be locked away in the recesses of your mind by Dr. Matto's therapy sessions. Trust me, it will all come back to you and soon magic will feel like second nature to you. You are one of the strongest living members of the four founding families, having both Benandanti and Maladanti blood flowing through your veins—you're destined to do great things for the people of this town."

"Thank you. Thank you both for your kind words of support," Nico said gratefully. "At times, it's still very overwhelming. I feel like I'm having to process so much in such a short period of time."

"You are!" Teresa agreed. "This is why Sterling and I, as well as others who knew your nonna, are slowly revealing things to you—we don't want to shock you."

"Yes, that was probably for the best," Sofia added. "Nico, can you imagine if Mrs. Schwartzman told us her story when we first visited her, before we had any knowledge of the secrets this town holds?"

"You're right. Between grieving and the other rollercoaster of emotions I deal with on a daily basis, it would've been an overload. I'm thankful there are so many wonderful people looking out for me."

Teresa tugged on the door handle a few times. Eventually the door released, sounding as if it had been hermetically sealed. A light aquatic breeze blew past them as they stood at the threshold. The room before them was completed flooded, about three feet deep; a small set of stone stairs led downward into the dark pool of seawater.

The walls of the expansive room were lined with seaweed as if it were wallpaper, and pendant lights, created from sea glass, hung from the ceiling by long strands of kelp. As they stepped onto the stairway landing, the lights nearest to them began to illuminate as the fireflies contained within were alerted to their presence. With each step inward the seawater would recede toward the back of the room and into the basin of a large fountain. An intimidating statue of Poseidon's hippocampus, placed in the center of the basin, seemed to be protecting its contents.

Scattered about the room were four platforms; each raised high above the original waterline to protect their contents from damage. On them were various antiquities: familiar works of art, chests overflowing with gold and silver coins, various cut gemstones, and articles of jewelry, as well as other unknown but seemingly valuable trinkets. In the center of the room was a circular dais with three pedestals, and on each one was a thick, leatherbound book.

"Here is what I wanted to show you," Teresa said while pointing to the books. "These are the Books of Knowledge, and they have the answers to any questions you may have—ones that I or anyone else may not be able to answer."

Nico and Sofia were so amazed with the mysterious room and all of its contents that they barely paid attention to what Teresa had said.

"Wait, I'm still trying to take this all in. What is this room?" Sofia asked.

"This is the founders' treasure room. This is the main reason that I, and my foremothers, were tasked to guard this building. Only one living person from each of the founding families is allowed to know about this room, and it's my duty as the current guardian to choose said person. Since your nonna was the last representative for your family—and sadly no longer with us—I choose you, Nico Alessandro Frantoio, as her replacement.

"Now for the rules. Each platform contains one of the four families' collection of valuables, which has been accumulated over time—your family's section is the platform in the back right corner of the room."

"So, I'm basically rich now?" Nico said, his eyes lighting up as he looked at his family's designated platform.

"Theoretically, yes, but you can't just take things without a purpose," Teresa answered. "I'm not only the guardian, but I'm also like a trustee for each family's possessions. If someone wishes to take an item, there has to be a valid reason before I will allow it to be removed.

"This room and its rules were created by the founders so that future family members would never have to experience the many struggles and hardships that were endured after being forced to leave Italy—to start out with nothing in a foreign country."

Sofia chimed in, "That's a pretty thoughtful and caring thing to do. They really planned ahead for the possible future needs of their family members."

"I guess when you put it that way, I should feel very fortunate," Nico sighed.

"Now, as I was saying about these books here, these are the Books of Knowledge," Teresa said.

Now more focused, Nico and Sofia peered at the titles of each book: *Persons*; *Places*; *Things*.

"So, it's a trilogy about nouns?" Nico joked.

"You could actually refer to it as such," Teresa replied with a straight face. "Each book can be used only once per day to retrieve accurate and detailed information regarding a specific person, a place, or a thing."

Sofia asked, "The books don't seem large enough to contain much information."

Theresa opened the book titled "Persons." It appeared to be filled with blank pages.

"Each book starts out blank and will write itself once a question is asked. After the information is retrieved and the book is closed, it will erase itself and become a blank canvas once more, awaiting the next question," Teresa explained. "Nico, I'm sure you'd like to know how your family, and the other founders, came to America and built this town?"

"I kind of pieced together some of the details from what you told us earlier about children born en caul," Nico replied.

"Yes, but that's general historical knowledge," Teresa commented. "The true story of how this town was founded, even I barely know."

"I'd love to know the history Nico," Sofia said with excitement. "So, Teresa, how do we go about using the book?"

"Nico come over to this book and place your hands on it," Teresa directed.

Nico nervously walked over to the pedestal with the book titled "Places" and put his clammy hands on its damp leather cover.

"Now command the book to tell you about the founding of this town and then remove your hands after you're finished speaking," Teresa instructed.

Nico thought for a moment, composing a sentence in his mind, and then commanded, "Book, tell me the history of how the town of Oliveto was founded." After speaking, he removed his hands from the book, as Teresa had advised.

The book began to rock lightly back and forth before slightly rising off its pedestal and then falling back down and opening up to reveal pages of text.

Sofia and Teresa gathered around Nico, and they began reading the information provided.

Chapter 18: The Founding of Oliveto

Northern Italy, 1887—Four neighboring families, surnames: Ascolano, Frantoio, Moraiolo, and Pendolino, each having a child born en caul, were desperate to save their now adolescent children from being persecuted as Benandanti. Each family packed a steamer trunk full of valuable family heirlooms and special items, as well as a single suitcase for their child, and gathered together during the dark of night. As a group, they traveled throughout the night, and just before sunrise, they reached their destination, the seaport of Genoa.

Carlo Ascolano had arranged to meet the captain of the *SS Werra*, who was standing outside his vessel waiting to greet them. He directed his crew to begin bringing the children's belongings on board. Before the children were escorted onto the ship, they hugged their parents one last time and, with tears in their eyes, reluctantly boarded the ship. Carlo handed Captain Schrecklich a sack of gold coins as payment in advance for the safe passage of the children to America.

The greedy captain took the money with no intent of guaranteeing their safety and directed his crew to take the children and their belongings down to the lowest part of the ship where they would remain hidden during their passage.

The cold, damp, rat-infested steerage area of the ship, which contained the ship's cargo, was now their new home. Stained and torn mildewy mattresses with a single wool blanket were their beds. Slight variations on porridge were provided twice a day for meals.

The children, each from different villages, had only known each other from having partaken in regional festivals, but had never been close friends. Since they were forced to be in such unsavory conditions, a bond quickly formed amongst the four of them.

During the evenings, after lights out, they would wait patiently in the dark for about an hour. Once they were certain that most of the crew were asleep, they would relight their candles and begin searching through the numerous cargo crates, in hope of finding items to help make their stay more pleasant. Viola Moraiolo was the first to find something useful. She opened a crate of sweet and savory spices, which she used to transform their porridge into something quite tasty.

When members of the ship's crew would come down to check on them, Enzo Ascolano would take the opportunity to negotiate with them. He convinced them of the unfairness of their treatment and slowly gained their favor.

Lorenzo Pendolino had befriended some of the crew and found an opportunity to make some money using a deck of cards found in one of the crates. He began playing nightly rounds of Gioco delle Tre Carte, where he would take the bets of the greedier crew members in exchange for the chance to win one of his gold coins. All they had to do was guess where the queen of hearts was amongst the three face-down cards. Lorenzo eventually accumulated a large sum of coins and valuables from the foolish players. Every so often Viola would come over to play a round. She was in on the con and was allowed to win. This enticed the crew to keep playing, after seeing that a young female was able to win.

Supremo Frantoio spent much of his first few days aboard the *SS Werra* moving around various cargo crates to create small room-like structures; he even went as far as to repurpose old pieces of wood and create bed frames for each of them, so that their mattresses would be raised off the cold deck.

The crew eventually warmed up to the young group in steerage and would sneak down extra food and treats from the kitchen for them, which Viola would rework into a new or better meals, and then share with the crew upon their return.

After a little over a week at sea, the *SS Werra* arrived in New York. Captain Schrecklich, whom they hadn't seen since they first boarded, went below deck to tell the young adults that they were to leave his ship. He was astonished at the change. Together, the four hidden passengers had not only cleaned and organized the entire cargo hold area, but somehow managed to create individual living spaces, which were almost better than those offered to immigrants on the level above them.

The crew they had befriended during the voyage kindly volunteered to carry their steamer trunks off the boat. Anxious to leave the ship, the four quickly followed behind with their individual suitcases. When they finally reached the top deck, they were momentarily blinded and had to wait until their eyes adjusted to the natural lighting of the sun; a sight they had been deprived of for over a week.

Being the last of the passengers to disembark from the *SS Werra*, they walked down the gangplank and said their goodbyes to the crew members who had taken a liking to them.

The four now stood together on the docks in silence, relishing the sun's warmth as it penetrated their chilled bodies. They looked around, observing this new world of modern buildings with terracotta-free roofs. Further down the pier, they could see two people approaching them, waving their hands.

As the strangers neared, the four could make out it was a well-dressed man and woman. The gentleman, speaking in near-perfect Italian, asked the four if they were the children sent by Carlo Ascolano.

The four nodded in reply. The woman, who also was able to speak in their native tongue, let them know that Carlo had asked her and her husband to make sure they had arrived safely. She happily added that she would being sending telegrams to each of their parents, so they would all know of their safety.

Two additional figures began to approach from the distance. The gentleman turned to the two men, whom he employed, and directed them to retrieve the four steamer trunks. With extraordinary strength, each servant took two trunks, one in each arm, and carried them off.

The generous couple asked the four to follow them down the pier to a large, parked vehicle which was waiting for them.

The lady instructed them to get into the car with her and her husband. She informed them that they would not be staying in New York but instead would soon be on their way to California to start their new lives. Shortly after the car drove away from the pier, the lady turned to them and extended her gloved hand. In it were four train tickets, which showed their destination to be San Francisco. She then opened her purse and pulled out four small dark green books with green-edged pages. They were pocket-sized Italian/English dictionaries, which she instructed them to study during their travel by railway. She further suggested they keep the dictionaries under their pillows at night as they slept.

The gentleman opened up a map of California so that they could all see, and using his sausage-like finger, traced the route they would take from San Francisco. He tapped at a spot which was about seventy miles north of the city. He instructed them to make their way to that general area, and to not stop until they came to a place where the scenery reminded them of home. That location would be where they should settle and create new lives for themselves.

After a short, pleasant drive, during which the four dozed off in their seats, the car pulled up to the train station. The four were jolted from their brief slumber. The manservants gathered their luggage and trunks, and they all followed the mysterious couple, who still had not mentioned their names, to the train terminal.

The couple took turns hugging the four and providing them with words of encouragement. As the lady finished hugging Viola, she opened her purse and retrieved a silver monogramed makeup compact, and powdered Viola's face. Then taking out a tube of lipstick, she applied it to Viola's lips, leaving them a bright, carmine shade, and accentuating the natural cupid's bow of her lips. She then gave a quick brush of Viola's long, wavy chestnut-colored hair to remove any tangles and revive its shine. Viola retrieved from her pocket a stunning rhinestone spider hairclip, which she had taken from one of the ship's cargo boxes. The lady pulled back Viola's hair, styled it into a loose bun, and secured it with the hairclip, leaving wispy tendrils of hair to frame her face.

Viola turned and faced the gentleman and her three young companions. They looked at her in awe, amazed at the quick transformation that commanded attention and immediately added a sense of refinement to her.

As their luggage and trunks were being loaded, the gentleman walked over to one of the train's porters and instructed him to look after the four and make sure they were treated properly. He then opened his billfold and discreetly handed a fifty-dollar bill to the porter.

The porter took the money and nodded with a smile of gratitude. He then walked over to escort the four onto the luxurious train. The four turned to wave goodbye one last time before following the porter to their private car which was labeled: Hornsby.

Exhausted from their previous nautical travels, they decided to take naps. But before their heads touched the awaiting plush down pillows, Viola reminded them of the gracious lady's advice, and they each retrieved their little Italian/English dictionaries and placed them under their pillows. Soon they fell into a deep sleep; sleeping well into the early evening until a rapping on their door awoke them from their slumber.

Startled, the three males jumped up, slightly confused, thinking they were still aboard the ship and prepared to protect Viola at all costs. Supremo collected himself and answered the door. The porter greeted him and told them that dinner would be served soon and to freshen up; he would return in ten minutes to escort them to the dining car. Supremo nodded in response and closed the door.

Perhaps still in a dream-like state, they were almost unaware that they had understood nearly everything the porter had said—in English. After a moment, they looked at each other with the same realization and as they began to converse amongst themselves, almost every other word they spoke was now in English.

After a delicious dinner, they were escorted back to their cabin and prepared for bed. They checked to make sure that their dictionaries were still under their pillows and said their nightly prayers. Soon after they had crawled under the covers, they were fast asleep.

To their amazement, the next morning when they went to the dining car for breakfast and were spoken to in English, they were able to respond in broken, but intelligible English. Throughout the coming days, they would continue to put their magical green books under their pillows whenever they slept and practiced speaking English to the passengers and each other.

After eighty-three hours and thirty-five minutes, the Transcontinental Express arrived in San Francisco. Before they detrained, Enzo showed the conductor their map and asked him which method of travel would take them further north. Somehow anticipating the question, the conductor, with a smile, immediately pointed to another platform across the tracks. He told them that the next train, arriving in twenty minutes, would take them further toward their desired destination.

The four thanked the conductor and waved goodbye as they began transferring their belongings to the other platform. Lorenzo went inside the station building to purchase four tickets, after which he rejoined the others, who were sitting on a worn wooden bench enjoying the warmth of the morning sun.

Soon the whistle of an oncoming train alerted them that the final phase of their journey was about to begin. The train rolled up to the platform, brakes squeaking as it came to a stop. The four gathered their belongings and boarded the train. The interior was plain and unadorned. The luxuries of their previous travel car were replaced with worn seats whose cushions provided no comfort from the hard wood planks beneath them.

The four sat patiently during their travel, watching the scenery change through the large windows, as they headed further north. The train made brief stops along the away and then a much longer stop in a town named Santa Rosa, where many people transferred to and from other trains.

The journey resumed and as they traveled onward, the four looked in amazement and began pointing at various parts of the landscape which were reminiscent of Italy's Tuscany region. They began to feel almost as if they were returning home and remembered the gentleman's advice: to not stop until they came to a place where the scenery reminded them of home.

The four concurred that they were nearing the end of their journey, the place where they would start their new lives. Agreeing to disembark at the next stop, they readied their items.

No station building greeted them at the next stop, just a small, unmaintained platform with weeds growing out of the cracks in the cement.

As they stepped down onto the platform with their belongings, the train whistled and then took off, slowly fading into the distance. The four looked in every direction for a sign of what to do next. Supremo noticed something in the distance and alerted the others. He pointed to the east where there was a small mountain, but before it, alone in a field of mustard flowers, was a large, majestic, wild olive tree that almost seemed to glow in the warm afternoon sun.

They all agreed completely: This was to be the location where their new lives would begin. In the days to come they created a primitive shelter for themselves underneath the large olive tree, used a forked willow branch to locate a freshwater spring, and explored their trunks to sort through the unique items their families had each packed for them. The one thing they found that they each had in common were jarred olives from each family's grove.

They decided to plant the stones of their namesake olives and create four separate groves further north near a local river, which would eventually provide irrigation. Every other day or so, two of them would take the train back to Santa Rosa to buy needed supplies and equipment to improve their living situation.

One late morning, while the train made one of its daily stops near their encampment, a mysterious man disembarked and walked toward them. He was short in stature and dressed in a green, double-breasted business suit. A fedora covered most of his bright red hair and protected his fair skin from the harsh rays of the sun.

As he came within a close distance, he greeted them in a thick Irish accent, "*Maidin mhaith*—good morning to ye!"

The three young men rose, as if to protect Viola from the oncoming stranger, but she brushed by them unafraid and welcomed the visitor as if he were a known guest. She removed the scarf from around her head, releasing her beautiful, wavy locks of hair, and laid it across the nearby log they used for seating. Gesturing for the man to sit down, she walked over to the campfire and poured a cup of strong coffee from a unique-looking pot that was kept warm near the fire. She then reached into a nearby basket of freshly baked dark chocolate and dried cherry biscotti and retrieved two. Effortlessly she balanced the biscotti on the coffee cup's saucer and carried it over to their first guest.

The man nodded in appreciation and, famished from his train ride, quickly took the biscotti and dipped it into his coffee before taking a bite. Apparently, Viola's biscotti were not only a hit with him, but also with the attendees of Santa Rosa's farmers market where she would sell them to make extra money. How she was able to bake such perfection on a campfire is unknown to this very day.

The mysterious guest finished his delicious treat and then explained to the four the reason for his arrival. He told them that word had spread for miles about the four who had settled here, and that his clients, who owned the land, wished to sign over the deed to them; a total of over 2,000 acres.

Taking their names down, the man said he would process the change of ownership and return soon with the new deed.

That night, the four sat around the campfire, excited about the pending ownership. They spent the entire evening brainstorming ideas on how to make the most of the vast expanse of fertile land. They all agreed that in addition to the four olive groves, vegetables, fruits, and herbs of all kinds would be grown to sell at the farmers market for income. Proper housing was also needed, a priority, in fact.

The next morning, they began tilling the soil with a mixture of the primitive tools they had created and the newer tools they had purchased during their trips to Santa Rosa.

As the three men tilled, Viola followed behind, dropping seeds into the ground, and covering them with the moist turned soil. The repetitive motion began creating a meditative state amongst the four and Viola, unknowingly, began to chant softly:

Germino...Amplifico...Maturesco

The others stopped their tilling and drew closer so they could hear what she was saying. After hearing the words a few times, they began to join in and continued through the day and into the evening, planting all the seeds they had acquired from vendors at the farmers market.

After having dined on a delicious meal prepared by Viola, the exhausted four quickly fell into a deep and peaceful sleep. The hours passed and, as the morning sun began to warm their faces, they awoke fully rested and ready for another exciting day.

As Lorenzo stood up and stretched, his eye caught sight of something spectacular. He suddenly darted from the campsite in the direction of yesterday's plantings. The other three instinctively followed. To their amazement, all of their seeds had not only germinated but were near maturity and beginning to produce fruit. Even the olive stones they had put into the ground had miraculously grown into six-foot-tall trees with full branches.

The four returned to their campfire and discussed what they had witnessed and decided it must have to do with them being Benandanti, and that perhaps Viola's impromptu chant was some type of spell that affected the growth of the plants. Enzo took out his leatherbound journal and a pen. He asked Viola to repeat the words she had originally chanted so that he could document them for future use. This became the first spell entry in the Founders' Grimoire.

Later that morning, after the train made its local stop, the familiar face of the young Irish gentleman could be seen as he walked down the dirt trail toward them. They all went to greet him, excited with the prospect of being owners of land reminiscent of home.

As they anticipated, they were given the deed to the land they had settled on. They made an oath to each other to always do what was best for the land, and so they each cut a branch from their namesake olive tree and grafted it onto the ancient olive tree that had once been a source of shelter.

From that day, the vision of creating Oliveto began. The little village slowly began to take shape and a piazza was created to highlight the majestic olive tree. More and more the four developed their magical abilities and carefully documented their spells into their own family grimoires. As the overwhelming presence of positive magic grew, mythical creatures and other beings were drawn to the mystical haven; a place where all could live in harmony together.

Unfortunately, that harmony was short-lived, and soon the excessive amount of positive magic drew the attention of the Malandanti, whose dark magic would bring unknown strife to the growing village of Oliveto.

It didn't take long for the town founders to catch on to the nefarious activities of the Malandanti. But, instead of banishing them from

Oliveto, they came to an agreement in which the Malandanti could remain and take residence, as long as they kept their battles solely with the Benandanti, and to never harm any of the other inhabitants in Oliveto. But even though the Malandanti agreed to those terms, the presence of their dark magic slowly drew creatures and beings of a darker nature.

Chapter 19: An Unexpected Series of Events

And as Nico read the last words from the Book of Knowledge, the book snapped shut. Sofia, worried that they could have missed some important information, quickly reached to open the book back up, only to be disappointed by the blank pages before her.

"As I said earlier," Teresa said, "you can only use each book once per day. After information is asked and retrieved, the books wipe themselves of all text."

"Well, I'm grateful you told us about these books," Nico said. "Without them I would've never been able to find out more about the Benandanti and Malandanti, as well as about the founding of Oliveto."

"Yes, what a wealth of information! Truly incredible," added Sofia. "But I'm curious about one thing. What ever happened to the Founders' Grimoire?"

"Good question. Unfortunately, no one really knows for sure," Teresa answered. "Some say it was lost, and others claim it was stolen by the Malandanti."

Nico continued, "Well it's a good thing then that you keep these books hidden. I'd hate for them to ever be lost or stolen."

"Well, anytime you need to access the books, just stop by for a visit—you know I'll be here." Teresa said, ending with a sigh which reminded Nico and Sofia that she was unable to leave the building.

"Thank you, Teresa. Next time we're in town, we'll make it a point to stop by," Nico said with a cheerful smile before turning to Sofia. "We still have to stop by Sterling's. We should get going."

As they went to exit the founders' treasure room, Sofia noticed that water from the fountain in the back of the room began to pour out onto the floor. It followed at a distance, slowly filling up the room behind them. Once they were all out of the room, the water crested, level to the threshold of the door, but it did not leave the room. Teresa closed the heavy wooden door, while Nico and Sofia watched it absorb sea water and swell up, sealing tightly into place.

“Amazing!” Sofia said with astonishment. “Well, it was nice to meet you, Teresa, and thank you for allowing me to keep the pearls—I’ll always treasure them.”

They headed back upstairs, and Teresa unlocked the library door. She waved goodbye as Nico and Sofia left to head back toward the piazza. The midday sun had won its battle against the damp mist of the morning fog and now the clear blue sky could be seen in all its glory.

As they neared the piazza, Sofia noticed something to the right of *S. Frantoio & Company Real Estate* and excitedly alerted Nico. “Look! What do you think is going on next to your family’s real estate office? It looks like they’re opening that boarded-up building.”

“Let’s take a closer look!” Nico said, walking faster toward their new destination.

Now standing in front of the building, they noticed seven shorter than average construction workers hastily removing boards and refinishing the building’s facade. The sign that was originally obscured, could now be seen.

“The Griffon’s Claw,” Sofia read out. “Well, now we know the name of the place.”

“And you’re right! I now see what you saw that first night when I had lifted you up so you could look through the knothole. It *is* a bar, and everything has remained untouched and impeccably maintained, as if it had been open all this time. Incredible!” Nico remarked.

“Maybe they’ll open for business while we’re still here in town,” Sofia said, hinting her desire for a future visit.

“We’re definitely going to check it out! Hopefully, they can make a good Negroni—I’ve been craving one lately,” Nico responded.

“Mmm! I love Negronis—I know that’s your favorite cocktail. Too bad Moraiolo’s only serves beer and wine, or we could have one tonight with Fawn and Solomon,” Sofia said.

“Yeah, too bad. Well, let’s go talk to Sterling and invite Fawn to join us tonight.”

They rounded the corner and headed toward the alley. As they turned down Vicolo Fato, they noticed the front door to Indelible Delights was open, which caused them to become slightly concerned, as it had been securely closed on their previous visits.

Nico peeked his head inside and called out, "Sterling. Fawn. Are you there? Is everything OK?"

They heard Fawn's voice in the distance replying, "Yes, come on in."

Nico and Sofia entered and almost gagged at the faint, indescribable stench of something in the air; something worse than the rotting gourd from Nico's basement.

Fawn walked into the waiting area to greet them. "Hello, you two! What a nice surprise."

"What *is* that smell?" Sofia asked.

"Oh, you can still smell it? I guess I've gotten used to it now. I was trying to make a new incense blend and grabbed the wrong herb—bad combination."

"Bad indeed!" Nico said jokingly. "I saw the door open and thought something might be amiss."

"Other than my failed fragrance attempt, all is good."

"Glad to hear that," Sofia said in relief. "By the way, we wanted to see if you were up for joining us and Solomon tonight at Moraiolo's for a beer?"

"That'd be totally awesome! What time were you thinking?" Fawn replied as her father walked into the room to see whom she was talking to.

"Good afternoon, Sterling," Nico said, before answering Fawn's question. "Say around seven o'clock?"

"I'll be there!" Fawn answered with excitement in her voice. "I'm sure Solomon is looking forward to it, too!"

"Are you here for a social visit?" Sterling asked Nico and Sofia.

"That, and we have some information we'd like to share with you," Nico replied.

"We think it may have to do with the recent abductions," Sofia added as she opened her purse and removed the tissue-wrapped item that she had retrieved from the church floor.

“What do you have there?” Sterling asked as Sofia revealed the tissue’s contents and handed it to Sterling.

Nico quickly replied, “We found this at my nonna’s funeral. It had fallen off the shoulder of the funeral director’s suit jacket. What do you think it is?”

“Kind of looks like part of a dragonfly’s wing,” Sofia added.

“Well, it isn’t from a dragonfly—the veining is different. This is definitely part of a fairy’s wing!” Sterling said. “Whose suit, again, did you say it fell from?”

“The funeral director’s—Mr. Cadaveri,” Nico answered.

Sterling’s face began to turn red with rage as he raised his fists and said, “He must be the culprit. Dammit! How could I have not noticed—he’s a Malandanti, after all.”

“But father, what could possibly be his motive?” Fawn asked calmly, hoping to pacify her father. “Without knowing the reason for the abductions, it’d be hard for anyone to assume who the perpetrator could be.”

“True,” Sterling responded with less tension. “How did I get so lucky to have such an insightful daughter as you? I don’t know what I would do without you.”

“So, I guess the next step is to find a way to sneak into the mortuary and see if there’s any evidence of wrongdoing,” Nico surmised.

“But how would we get in?” Sofia asked. “Mr. Cadaveri, or one of his sons, would surely catch us.”

Sterling thought for a moment before responding. “Most of the Malandanti men meet on Wednesday nights, allegedly for beer and poker, but now I’m imagining it’s for something far less innocent.”

Fawn interrupted, “Father, they aren’t all that bad. Remember how kind Chiara was? And Nico is also part Malandanti—look how he’s stepped up to help us. Besides, the town’s agreement, set by the founders, says that as long as the Malandanti keep their mischief between themselves and the Benandanti, and harm no other factions in Oliveto, then they can remain. Most wouldn’t risk being banished from this wonderful town.”

“Once again, you bring up a valid point. I shouldn’t have allowed my anger to cause me to assume that all Malandanti behave in the same manner. Now, that being said, I do have a plan. Nico and Sofia, go see Geoffrey Barbieri, the town barber. His shop is just a few doors down. First, make sure he isn't with a customer, then tell him that I sent you. He'll come up with the perfect solution as to how you can gain entrance to the mortuary undetected. Return to me afterwards."

Nico turned to Sofia and said, "I guess we've got our marching orders—let's go!"

And with that, Nico and Sofia left Indelible Delights for their next destination. As they left the alley, they could see the familiar swirling red, white, and blue stripes of a barber's pole off in the distance.

"That must be the place," Sofia commented.

As they approached the small barber shop, they could see through its large window that Geoffrey was currently with a customer, who was reclined in the barber's chair with a towel wrapped around his face.

"Let's wait out here until his customer leaves," Nico advised.

Sofia carefully watched Geoffrey as he removed the towel from his customer's face. He then reached over to the counter behind him and grabbed a bottle containing a strange, greenish liquid. Opening it, he splashed some into his hands and gently began to pat it onto the customer's clean-shaven face.

"So, what do you think his deal is? Do you think he is human or Fey?" Sofia teased.

"He could be neither! Maybe he's some other type of magical creature," Nico responded, causing Sofia to ponder.

She was quiet for almost a minute, deep in thought, before she spoke out, "You're right—one shouldn't assume too much in Oliveto—hey, it looks like the customer is paying and about to leave."

The door opened and the customer hurried past them. Nico quickly grabbed the door before it could close and held it open for Sofia.

"Welcome!" The barber exclaimed as he turned toward them. "Are you here to have some of that length taken off? Oh, wait, tilt your head down."

Puzzled but curious, Nico obliged and allowed the barber to see the crown of his head.

"Ah yes," he replied and then asked. "You're Nico Frantoio, correct?"

Before replying, Nico keenly eyed the youthful appearing barber, who was dressed in black pants, a white shirt with a rather stylish tie, and a white lab coat. Geoffrey looked vaguely familiar.

"Yes, I am," Nico politely replied. "And this is my friend Sofia Saggio. You know, I feel as if we've met before?"

"Yes, we did—a long time ago, when you were just an infant," the barber replied. "Your mother had brought you in for your first haircut! Faces changes as we get older, but I never forget the pattern of a person's hair," Geoffrey said with pride.

"Sterling said that we should come see you. He said that you'd be able to help us with—" Nico paused briefly; something seemed off. "Wait, how could you have cut my hair when I was an infant? You look as if you might be no more than ten years older than me."

"I'm sure by now you and your friend have discovered that this town is different from most typical towns—"

"Yes! We've learned so much in such a short period of time," Sofia said, jumping into the conversation. "We're still trying to wrap our heads around it. So, are you a type of fairy like Sterling and Fawn?"

"No, we're not fairies—and by we, I mean my daughter Stevie and myself. We're a type of Fey called shapeshifters. Unfortunately, our natural abilities to transform on demand were stripped from us long ago, but we've learned to adapt and create our own type of magic which still allows us to change, but on a limited level. Since a great number of Oliveto's inhabitants are now human, I have to change my appearance every fifteen to twenty years so that people don't question why I haven't aged—I just reintroduce myself as my son who has taken over the family business.

"Stevie, on the other hand, uses this magic to her advantage, preserving her youth as a form of self-promotion. You see, she's an aesthetician, and her age-defying facials are nothing short of that! She's created quite a following among the town's elite—she's even developed a diluted version of her special youth elixir that I use on some of my special clients.

"But enough of that. Nico, you were saying that Sterling sent you to me for assistance. Tell me how I can be of help."

"Sofia and I have discovered who we think might be behind the fairy abductions. We just need a way to sneak into P. Cadaveri & Sons Mortuary Wednesday night to see if we can find evidence to support our claims."

"Ah, I see. Well, Sterling did send you to the right place for assistance. I just gave Primo Cadaveri a shave the day before Chiara's funeral—just between us, he's a squirrely one, so be careful when dealing with him and his two sons," Geoffrey said as he went to lock the door. He then flipped the sign to display: *Out to Lunch*. "Follow me to the back of the shop, and I'll get you exactly what you'll need."

The barber opened a narrow door along the back wall of his shop. It led to a large and rather damp storage room; a room much bigger than the front space, and filled with shelves of various glass jars, each labeled.

Sofia closed the door behind them, and they watched as Geoffrey slid a library ladder along the shelves to the leftmost one and then climbed up to the second shelf to retrieve one of the liquid-filled jars that had something white floating in it.

Geoffrey placed the jar labeled: *P. Cadaveri*, on a table near them. "Here you go. This is the solution to your dilemma."

Upon further inspection of the jar, Nico began laughing. "So, a jar, with what appears to contain a common hand towel, is going to allow us undetected access into the mortuary?"

"Yes. I guarantee it!"

"I'm with Nico," Sofia asserted. "What can a wet towel do for us?"

"You kids really are green and lack faith," Geoffrey said, slightly disappointed. "That's not any ordinary towel. In fact, all of these jars here contain towels that have been used on my many clients. After I give each client a shave, I wrap a hot towel around their face. Each towel keeps a magical imprint of their face, which I then store in a jar. When Nico is ready to access the mortuary, all he has to do is wrap his face with Primo Cadaveri's towel and his face will take on the exact likeness of the mortician—even his two sons won't be able to tell. You will even sound like him, but beware, the effects only last for one hour. So be efficient with your time!"

"I apologize Geoffrey. We both should've known better than to doubt you."

"No need to apologize Nico. I know you've been through a lot this week and are probably still in mourning. I shouldn't have assumed as much," Geoffrey said in a more polite tone. "Now you two kids need to get going. I have my next client coming in a few minutes—I don't want them seeing you taking one of my jars."

"Not to worry," Sofia said as she opened up her purse on the table. "I'll put the jar in my purse, and no one will see it."

"And how are you going to fit that jar into such a small purse, young lady?" Geoffrey asked curiously.

"Now who's the green one?" Nico joked as Sofia placed the entire jar into her purse with ease.

"Touché! I need to give you credit for your resourcefulness. I'm guessing you've been studying your family's grimoire?" Geoffrey enthusiastically commented.

"Yes, sir!" Nico smiled. "Now let us get out of your hair. We'll return the jar and its contents after we've completed our mission."

"Thank you, and good luck!" The barber said as Nico and Sofia went to unlock the front door, so that they could exit. "Would you do me a favor and flip my sign back to *Open*?"

Nico flipped the sign as requested. The two walked back to Indelible Delights so that they could update Sterling and finish formulating their plan to search the mortuary.

"That was quick!" Fawn called out to Nico and Sofia as they entered the tattoo shop.

"Yes, and Geoffrey gave us a means for one of us to enter the mortuary tomorrow night," Sofia responded.

"Your dad said you were going to help with the plan?" Nico asked.

"Yes," Fawn replied and ran past the curtains to the back of the shop, returning shortly with a small vial of liquid which she handed to Sofia. "You'll need this."

"What is it?" Nico asked. "Do we drink it?"

"No! It's not for you—it's for Dino and Gino. They'll be at the mortuary in the evening while their father is out," Fawn advised. "I'm guessing Geoffrey gave you the means to temporarily shapeshift into Mr. Cadaveri?"

"Yes," Nico and Sofia replied in unison.

"Good," Fawn said. "OK, here's the plan. Mr. Cadaveri should be leaving for poker night a little before seven p.m. Sofia, you will order a pizza from Moraiolo's about a half hour before and bring it directly to Schwartzman's. Since the store will be closed by then with the blinds drawn, it'll become our makeshift headquarters—it has the perfect view of the mortuary so that we can keep watch in case Mr. Cadaveri returns unexpectedly. Oh, and make sure to pour the vial I gave you onto the pizza. It is a safe but potent narcotic, and will put anyone who consumes even a drop of it, into a deep sleep for up to two hours.

"Nico, you will transform into Mr. Cadaveri according to Geoffrey's instructions and bring the pizza over to the mortuary for Dino and Gino to eat. Since they'll think you're their father, make up some excuse as to why you returned—like that you wanted to surprise them with a pizza for doing such good work. After a few bites, they'll be out cold, and you should then have enough time to explore the entire building.

"I called Teresa while you were at Geoffrey's, and she reviewed the mortuary's floor plans with me. The main level is the public area with an arrangement room, three viewing rooms, and a chapel area; upstairs are the living quarters where Dino and Gino will likely bring their pizza to eat; downstairs is the cremation room, morgue, and embalming room.

"There! I think that's a well-rounded plan! Any questions?" Fawn finished.

"I'm totally impressed—you've thought of everything!" Sofia said.

"I should be a bit nervous since I'm going in alone, but I can't think of anything that could go wrong," Nico mumbled.

"Well, we can go over the plan again tonight with Solomon while at Moraiolo's. I'm so looking forward to having drinks with you two again."

"Yes, I can't wait!" Sofia said with a smile. "And it looks like there'll be a new place for all of us to try soon—they seem to be cleaning up that previously boarded-up building."

"Ah, I noticed that today on my way to work," Fawn acknowledged. "The odd thing is that there's been no official word, or even gossip about town, in regard to that location opening back up. It's like one day someone woke up and decided to open up a bar."

"Something to look forward to, I say," Nico said as he opened the door to leave.

"See you tonight!" Fawn said as she waved goodbye.

As they stepped out into the alleyway, Sofia stopped Nico. "It's still early in the afternoon and we have about five hours before we have to meet Fawn and Solomon. How about we try that fairy door there and see where it leads?" Sofia said to Nico with a note of temptation in her voice, while pointing to the small door to the right of Indelible Delight's entrance.

Nico hunched down near the fairy door that was decorated with a steeple and a cross at its top. "I'm guessing this will take to the church—at least it's not a long walk back from there, so I'm game. Hold onto my hand."

Sofia grabbed hold of Nico's hand as he touched the tiny door, and they were immediately transported to their destination.

"Hmm, I don't really know where we are. This doesn't look the least bit familiar to me. Maybe the church wasn't that door's correct destination." Nico said with a puzzled look.

They looked around their unknown location. Walls of stone and earth-lined pathways led in all directions from where they stood. Niches carved out in certain walls either contained sarcophagi or various types of religious items.

"This looks like some type of catacomb. It reminds me of the Vatican Necropolis, where many of the saints are buried, but a lot less creepy," Sofia suggested. "I gather that we must be under St. Anthony's, and this is where they store their relics!"

"I never knew this area existed," Nico replied as he knelt down to survey the ground, hoping for a clue as to which direction to take. "Well, that way there seems to be the most traveled. I see multiple footprints in the dirt," Nico said as he pointed to the northmost passageway.

Deciding to go with Nico's hunch, they cautiously started walking down the north passage. It gradually began to slope upward, arriving at a set of stairs carved into the stone. As they ascended, a light breeze touched their faces, and the familiar scent of church incense alerted their senses. At the top of the stairs, a short corridor rounded the corner and led to a locked wrought iron gate.

As they looked through the gate into the main part of the church, Nico commented, “I recall this gate from when I was an altar boy and always wondered where it led—I just thought it went behind the altar and around to the other side of the church. I had no idea it actually descended beneath the church!”

“Look, there’s someone in the church,” Sofia whispered.

“Where?” Nico said as he scanned the pews. “Ah, I see him. In the sixth row.”

“I think I saw him sitting in the same spot during the funeral.”

“I saw him then, too. I don’t know who he is, but he’s always in that seat saying the rosary. In fact, I used to see him when I was an altar boy, and he looked the same then—he hasn’t aged a bit!”

“Interesting! Anyway, we should get going. Would you like to do the honors and unlock the gate so we can get out?” Sofia asked with a smile.

“It would be my pleasure,” Nico replied and then invoked the magic words he was now all too familiar with. “*Resero*.”

Sofia reached for the gate to push it open, but it did not budge, “I think you didn’t say it with enough pizzazz—try it again.”

“*Resero!*” Nico said in a more commanding tone.

Sofia tried again and still the iron gate would not budge. “Maybe it is protected against magic? Or maybe because the incantation is from the Malandanti side of the book, it’s considered dark magic and unusable here.”

“That must be the case,” Nico said with a tone of defeat. “I guess our only option out of here is to go back and find the fairy door and see where it leads to.”

Making their way back down the short corridor, they descended back down into St. Anthony’s catacombs and located the fairy door. They closely examined it for clues as to where it might lead. This fairy door was adorned with what appeared to be a scythe and an hourglass with its lower chamber filled with sand.

"Any guesses on where this will take us?" Nico queried.

"Let me think. The hourglass having run its course probably references the end of something. The scythe might be a symbol for the grim reaper, so I am guessing it would have to do with death," Sofia answered.

After a moment of silence, they turned to each other and, at the same time, exclaimed, "The cemetery!"

Sofia grabbed Nico's forearm as he reached to touch the door. Within seconds they were transported to the large olive tree at Olive Tree Hill Cemetery. The familiar rope swing next to them began swaying in the light breeze.

"We got that right. From what I recall the last time we were here, this fairy door should lead us back to the library," Sofia said with relief.

"While we're here, let's take a moment to relax and enjoy the tranquility," Nico suggested. "Have a seat on the swing and I'll push you."

Sofia obliged and sat down on the swing, and Nico gave her a light push. As she swung back toward him, he pushed again with a little more force so that Sofia would swing higher into the air.

"Oh, my god!" Sofia shouted.

"What?" Nico said, slightly panicked.

"The rosebush I liked—it's gone!" Sofia said. "Push me higher so I can see more."

Nico pushed with more effort, causing Sofia to rise higher, so that she could see further ahead.

"Can you see anything else?" Nico asked.

"I see the rosebush now. It looks destroyed—and something's happened to the grave as well!" Sofia reported back.

"Let me help you stop swinging so we can go over and take a look," Nico suggested as he grabbed Sofia on her return.

Sofia rose from the swing's wooden seat, and they set off toward the location where the once beautiful rosebush had mysteriously grown from a sunken grave. As they rushed past the trickling fountain, a chorus of frogs began croaking loudly, almost as if they were warning the two not to proceed any further.

The scent of recently turned earth filled the air as they approached the site of where the beautiful rosebush once grew; it had been uprooted and now lay a good four feet from an open grave; broken pieces of the granite slab, which once covered the grave, now lay strewn about the surrounding area atop various mounds of moist dirt.

A passing cloud started to block the mid-afternoon sun; the sky suddenly darkened the already-shaded area. A chill ran down their spines as they slowly approached the grave's edge. Sofia grabbed Nico's hand and they both looked down into the open grave. To their surprise, and relief, they found that it was empty. No coffin, no rotting corpse or skeletal remains, just an empty six-foot hole.

"What do you think happened here?" Sofia asked.

"Your guess is as good as mine," Nico replied puzzled. "Maybe the caretaker relocated the contents of the grave since the slab cover had that crack in it?"

Sofia turned around and looked closely at the ground. "Aside from the footprints we left leading up to here, there are no others. The earth is freshly dug, so this most likely happened in the last twelve to twenty-four hours."

Nico scanned the area and noticed something. "There's another set of prints; you missed these, detective," Nico joked while pointing to a set of animal tracks.

"Those look like they might be paw prints from a large dog," Sofia mused. "Those don't count."

"Then let's close the case on this mystery, or at least mark it as unsolved for now, and head back. I don't think what's happened here relates to my nonna's death or the missing fairies, especially since this grave's disturbance happened after both initial occurrences," Nico replied.

"Perhaps. But, I feel like this spot somehow does have a connection to your nonna."

"How do you figure?" Nico asked.

"Hear me out," Sofia said. "So, when we were here last time, didn't you mention that she would 'check on one final grave' up here on the hill? What if this was the one?" Sofia pointed out.

Nico stood there silence, trying to recall memories of when he visited the cemetery with his nonna. “You know, I think she did head in this direction, but I'm not completely sure if this is the exact grave that she visited—she always told me to wait behind and swing a bit longer.”

“See, I knew it!” Sofia said.

“It’s still pure speculation. My gut feeling says this occurrence is unrelated to the other two,” Nico responded with conviction.

“You’re probably right,” Sofia sighed. “There’s just so much about Oliveto we don’t about; everything seems suspicious to me right now.”

“Careful, or people might mistake you for a conspiracy theorist,” Nico teased as he led the way back to the fairy door by the swing. “There must be an empty gourd back home in the basement with your name on it.”

Nico suddenly realized that Sofia wasn’t following him. He turned around to see what the cause might be and saw her heading back to the open grave.

“Hey, I was just kidding!” Nico shouted to Sofia. “Don’t be mad at me!”

Sofia was just steps from the grave and turned her head slightly to yell back, “I’m not mad, I just wanted to—” And before she could finish her sentence, she found herself slipping at the edge of the grave and falling forward into the deep hole. “Oh, no—” she cried out.

Nico ran to check on Sofia. Once at the grave, he looked down and found her rising up from a prone position, her face and the front of her clothing completely covered with moist soil.

“Are you OK, Sofia—are you hurt?” Nico asked with concern.

“Surprisingly, I’m OK. I think the loose dirt acted as a cushion and eased my fall.”

Nico knelt at the edge and extended his hand. “Here. Grab hold, and I will pull you up!”

Sofia took a few steps forward across the loose soil and reached out toward Nico. She grabbed hold of his wrist and he took hold of hers and began to pull. Sofia, still slightly stunned from her fall, tried her best to assist Nico by using the soles of her shoes to create traction in the dirt walls of the grave. She was making great progress and was almost halfway up when the earth gave way beneath her feet.

Nico, caught by surprise, did not have time to brace himself for Sofia's sudden pull. "Whoa!" Nico exclaimed as he flew forward into the grave and landed alongside Sofia.

"Are you OK, Nico?" Sofia asked, laughing slightly at their current predicament.

Nico lifted himself up, his face and clothing now covered in dirt just like Sofia's, and turned to her. "Puh!" He said as he spat out particles of dirt. "At least the landing was soft."

"Thankfully, I moved to the side just in time, or you'd have landed right on me," Sofia said.

"Now, what's going to be the best way for us to get out of this hole?" Nico pondered.

"Well, if you boost me up, I doubt I could pull you up," Sofia said. "And if I try to give you a boost, chances are that you still might not be able to pull me up, and we'll end up at square one again. Maybe a spell?"

"Hmm," Nico mumbled while trying to remember which of the many spells from Sofia's flash cards might be the solution.

In the distance, the frogs by the fountain began to croak as if they were calling out to Nico and Sofia.

"Do you think the frogs want to help us?" Sofia laughed, slightly joking. "They're listed in the grimoire under the Benandanti column, so maybe you can control them? Just call out to them like you did to the rats in the basement—after all, they listened to you."

"Definitely worth a try," Nico replied and then thought deeply about what he would say to the croaking amphibians. "OK, got it. Frogs from the fountain, I call out to thee; come to our rescue and help us be free."

"I see what you did there. Nice rhyming action." Sofia praised in a slightly mocking tone.

Nico stood there in silence and listened. The croaking of the frogs now sounded closer and louder. Looking up toward the edge of the grave, they began to glimpse an occasional frog hopping near the edge of the plot. Nico and Sofia now were no longer the only ones being silent; the frogs had now stopped croaking.

"What do you think is happening?" Sofia questioned. "I don't see any sign of them. Did they just bail on us?"

Within a few seconds of Sofia's comment, Nico pointed to the side of the dirt wall which they faced. "Look!" Nico exclaimed with excitement.

At various levels in the earthen wall, the dirt began to move as six frogs burrowed through and dropped down into the grave.

"I think they've made little pockets in the earth for us to use like hand-and-footholds," Nico said.

Excited at the prospect of leaving, Sofia responded, "That's genius! I totally have a newfound respect for our little green friends!"

"Ah, now I remember," Nico muttered.

"What did you say?" Sofia asked.

"I remembered a spell that might help," Nico said. "I'm not sure if the holes in the wall will be enough to get us out."

"I'm all about the spells. Go for it!" Sofia said supportively.

"I hope I recall the words correctly," Nico said and then called out, "*Vinea Auxilio*!"

A rustling could be heard in the leaves and a brownish green serpentine shape began to descend into the grave.

Sofia immediately jumped back. "Oh my God—you know I hate snakes. Why did you cast that spell?"

"Yes, I know. You detest snake and rats, but that isn't a snake—look closer," Nico said.

Sofia stepped forward and realized, much to her relief, that it wasn't some dreaded serpent coming toward her, but a thick vine from the nearby vegetation.

"I figure we can use the vine as a rope to pull ourselves up while using the frog holes as footholds to make our climb easier," Nico reasoned.

"Ah yes—I'm surprised that I didn't think of having you cast the Enchant Vegetation spell!" Sofia said, slightly defeated as she grabbed hold of the vine and began her ascent. "Drinks are on me tonight!" She called out as she climbed out of the hole.

Before Nico began his climb, he looked down at the frogs and picked one of them up. Holding it up to eye level, he spoke to it, "Thanks to you and your buddies for hearing me and coming to our aid. I appreciate you all."

Nico gently put the frog down and made his way out of the hole by use of the rope-like vegetation. At the top of the grave, he began to dust himself off. As he was brushing the dirt off his knees, a thought came to him, and he looked up at Sofia who was in the middle of finger combing dirt out of her thick head of hair.

"So, what was your reason for coming back here? You were about to tell me before you took a plunge," Nico asked.

"Oh, right. I wanted to get the rose bush and take it back to the house so that we can replant it in the backyard. I think by the basement window, where the break-in had occurred, would be perfect—after all, the current plant was trampled, and I doubt it can be revived," Sofia replied.

"Excellent idea! Almost makes this misadventure worth it." Nico laughed and walked over to the uprooted rose bush and carefully grabbed hold.

Sofia opened up her purse so that Nico could put it in. "Careful now!"

"I know. I'm trying my best to not get another gash from a thorn."

"No. I mean watch out for my purse. It has a narrow opening, and I don't want the leather shredded by the thorns."

"Oh, how nice! You're not the least bit concerned about me," Nico chuckled as he reached for a length of the vine he had summoned earlier. He began winding it around the rose bush, constricting it so that it would better fit into the opening of Sofia's purse. "Do you think your purse will ever run out of room?"

"I sure hope not," Sofia replied while guiding the bound rosebush into her purse. "Looks like it was a perfect fit! Now we should head back and get cleaned up before meeting Fawn and Solomon for drinks."

In the distance the bells at St. Anthony's could be heard chiming. Nico looked down at his watch to verify the time. "Yep, it's already five o'clock—let's get a move on!"

Once again, they made their way back to the fairy door, but this time with haste. They used it to travel to their next location, which happened to be the library as they had anticipated. From there, they continued by foot back to the Frantoio home to clean up for their next outing.

Chapter 20: A Sobering Realization

"Nico, are you ready?" Sofia called out from the foyer of the Frantoio family home. "We need to get going or we're going to be late."

"Coming!" Nico replied. He entered the foyer half hobbling, trying to slip his right foot into his already-tied shoe while buttoning up his shirt.

"I'll bet you were styling your hair the entire time!" Sofia teased and then noticed that Nico was wearing the new shirt from Schwartzman's, but it was buttoned wrong. "Nice shirt! Too bad you can't even button it properly!" Sofia began laughing as Nico looked down at the front of his new shirt.

"Yeah, too much time on my hair," Nico said with a sigh. "I need to create a 'Styling' spell or find out how to enchant a comb; then I'll never run short of time again."

"Well, when it comes to your hair, time is definitely your enemy," Sofia replied as she began rebuttoning Nico's shirt. "But your hair does look great, and now that your shirt is buttoned properly, you look even better!"

Nico appreciated the boost to his ego and smiled warmly at Sofia. He opened the front door for Sofia and allowed her to exit first, following after her. As they walked down the front steps, Nico turned back to the house and commanded, "House, please secure yourself." They barely noticed the now all-too-familiar sounds of the house locking itself up as they made their way to the sidewalk and begin their jaunt back into town.

As they neared the piazza, Nico looked at his watch to check the time and was surprised that they were early and had a half hour to kill before meeting Fawn and Solomon.

"We should probably eat something if we plan to have a few drinks—after all, we never ate lunch," Nico suggested. "How about some fries or onion rings at Doc's?"

"Now that you mention it, onion rings sound really good, along with a milkshake—let's be bad and enjoy those calories," Sofia replied.

"Perfect, let's cross here," Nico said.

As they stepped into the street, Sofia suddenly screeched at the sight of a raven perched on a streetlight opposite them. "Wait, it's coming toward us!"

Sofia grabbed Nico's arm and quickly retreated back to the curb, pulling him with her. The raven was in flight and more than halfway across the street when, to their horror, a bus zoomed by, hitting the raven, and knocking it onto the sidewalk a few feet from them.

"Poor creature," Nico said, while shaking his head.

"It was coming right for us, probably to attack me," Sofia said frantically.

Nico walked over to the contorted raven, whose wing flapped against the ground a few times before it expired.

"Sofia, I don't think this bird was trying to attack you; in fact, I don't think it ever meant you any harm," Nico suggested.

Sofia paused briefly before responding, as her mind began to vividly recall her previous avian encounters; she noticed something familiar from each. "That's that same one from the mortuary—the same one that scared me back at the house! I know because of that gold band around its leg!"

"Hmm…." Nico thought for a second. "In the grimoire, it lists ravens under the Malandanti column, so I doubt it was flying toward us in an effort to harm us—at least not to harm me. I think it was trying to save us from the oncoming bus that we weren't aware of. Had we not hurried back to the curb, the bus probably would've hit us, too!"

"I think you're right on this one," Sofia said, slightly defeated. "Now I feel bad. All this time I should've been kinder to it and not let it invoke fear in me."

Nico knelt near the lifeless raven and picked it up. "Come on, let's cross the street."

Sofia followed Nico to the other side, and instead of going toward Doc's, he made his way toward the mortuary. Looking both ways this time, they crossed the street once more, and stood near the mortuary's sign, where they had first encountered their now deceased feathered friend. He knelt down once again and placed the limp carcass on the ground, near the base of the sign. He then whispered to it, "Thank you for your bravery."

Sofia had an idea. "Nico, check the band around its leg. Looks like there may be writing on it."

Nico read the gold band. "Looks like it says: M-O-N-E-S-I.'"

Sofia laughed. "Start with the 'S' first!"

Nico, slightly embarrassed that he had not noticed, joked back, "I knew it read Simone—I was just seeing if you were paying attention."

"At least we now know the name of our savior," Sofia said. "Unfortunately, there's not much more we can do now, so maybe we should go eat while we still have time."

"Agreed. *Ciao,* Simone," Nico said with a tinge of sadness in his heart.

Ahead, as a customer of Doc's was leaving, the smell of delicious fried food escaped from the open door and became a welcoming distraction from the upsetting event they had just witnessed. Upon entering the diner, they immediately spied an empty window booth off to the left and chose to sit there instead of at the counter.

They only spoke to order and were quiet for the remainder of the time, sipping on their milkshakes until their food arrived. Once the large plate of crispy onion rings arrived, they each took one and dipped into the house-made ketchup. As they took their first bites, they looked up at each other with a grin.

"Wow! These are outstanding!" Sofia exclaimed.

Nico reached for another onion ring. "Definitely satisfying my need for something calorically sinful," Nico responded.

After their mini food binge, Nico went to the counter and paid the tab. They left Doc's and made their way across the piazza to Moraiolo's, excited to hang out with Fawn and Solomon again. Nico, as usual, held the door open for Sofia and they entered the dimly lit restaurant. They briefly stopped in the entryway, as the heavy door closed behind them, and allowed their eyes to adjust to the dim lighting. Sofia spotted Solomon near the bar, as well as someone familiar off in the corner.

"Nico, isn't that Gino over there in the corner drinking alone?" Sofia asked.

"Yeah, that's him. Poor guy, I don't think he as any friends—in fact, even his brother Dino doesn't treat him very well," Nico added.

As they approached Solomon's table, Sofia caught his eye and he stood up to greet them.

"So glad to see you again…" Solomon said while gazing into Sofia's eyes. "I mean to see *both* of you again—oh, nice shirt by the way!"

Sofia became quiet once again while in the presence of Solomon, so Nico spoke up to help keep the conversation flowing. "Yes, this shirt was a great find. Thanks to Sofia and her impeccable taste in fashion."

"The shirt looks great on both of you," Sofia blurted out and immediately felt a little embarrassed. Changing the topic, she asked, "I take it Fawn isn't here yet?"

"No," Solomon replied. "She's usually quite punctual. I'm not sure why she's not already here."

"Maybe she's working on a client and in the middle of a detailed tattoo?" Nico suggested.

"Probably the case—she does enjoy doing the more intricate ones, and is always up for a challenge," Solomon added as he flagged down the bartender to bring them a pitcher of beer.

Nico and Sofia took their seats at the high-top table, and Sofia smiled at Solomon.

"We should probably bring you up to speed. We need your help with a plan that Fawn helped us put together earlier today," Nico said.

"What kind of plan?" Solomon inquired.

Sofia whispered, "Wait. Do you think Gino can hear us?"

"Nah. But, if he were elven or a vampire, he'd be able to. Fortunately for us, he's just a Malandanti human," Solomon responded.

"Vampires? They don't really exist, do they?" Sofia asked. "I mean, I can get onboard that elves might be real, now that I have met a fairy or two, but…"

Solomon huddled in and quietly whispered, “I’ve never met one, but I do believe they exist. I’m told that, in addition to having excellent hearing, they also can control various creatures like bats and rats—and some other creature, but I forget which one.”

”Wolves?" asked Nico in great excitement. "Sofia, that must be the 'V' mentioned in the grimoire!"

“Yes, wolves. That’s the other one,” Solomon answered. “Anyway, as I was saying, a vampire has the power to command those three creatures to spy and report back with information.”

“Well, thankfully Gino is neither—just another lonely person drinking in a bar,” Nico said, expressing his sympathy for the mortician’s son.

Solomon raised his glass and said, “Cheers!” After taking a big gulp of cold beer, he continued, “So, tell me about this plan.”

Sofia took a sip of her beer and then began to explain to Solomon their suspicions; that the funeral director, Mr. Cadaveri, might somehow be involved with the recent fairy abductions. She further continued in detail the plan that Fawn had created to help Nico gain access into the mortuary. “And since Schwartzman’s is across the street, we thought that Fawn and I would stay there with you. Together, we could watch the mortuary, in case Mr. Cadaveri returns early.”

“I’m in!” said Solomon enthusiastically. “It’s not often that I have the opportunity to assist two lovely ladies.”

“Well, you’d better take good care of them!” Nico advised, and then turned to Sofia and smiled as he continued. “Especially this one here.”

Sofia let out a big laugh in response, which caught the attention of most of the patrons in the bar, including Gino. The guys joined in with the laughter, and they felt the eyes of everyone in the room looking at them. Nico looked around the room and noticed that Gino was still looking over in their direction and raised his hand to offer a polite wave to Nico and his party. Nico presented a polite smile in return and waved back.

Nico turned back to Sofia and Solomon. “I wonder what’s keeping Fawn. It’s been a good twenty minutes now. Solomon, do you have a way to contact her?”

Solomon stood up from his seat. "I'll see if they'll let me use the phone at the bar to give Indelible Delights a call."

After Solomon left the table, Sofia said to Nico, "I think I really like him. I still don't know what it is, but I've never felt like this before…and in such a short time!"

"Well, I wouldn't get too attached. Soon we'll be back at school, all the way over on the East Coast. How would you plan to continue things?" Nico reasoned.

"It will give us a reason to return often. I'm sure your parents would enjoy seeing you more, and we could also stay at your nonna's home—I mean your home." Sofia said and then held back laughter while teasing Nico, "Plus, it looks like you have an admirer of your own to give you a reason to return."

"Who?" Nico replied and turned his head to see who Sofia might be referring to. He was slightly startled as he saw Gino standing there next to him.

"Good evening, Nico," Gino greeted with a warm smile. "I wanted to thank you again for helping my father and me lift that heavy stone cover to free my brother's finger."

"Oh, yeah, of course." Nico replied, feeling a bit awkward. "Uh, I'm sure you'd have done the same for me if I were in that situation."

"I certainly would—hey, the next round is on me. I hope you all have a pleasant evening and enjoy the beer," Gino said and then headed over to the bartender before leaving.

"See," Sofia said. "I think he likes you!"

Nico began to blush and then chuckled. "You're too much! He was just being polite—grateful that I was able to help him and his father. There was no way the two of them could've lifted that heavy stone covering my nonna's sarcophagus by themselves."

"I know. I'm a little buzzed from this beer and am just giving you a bad time," Sofia replied and then turned toward Solomon who was heading back to their table.

"Well?" Nico asked.

"Her father said she left about a half hour ago. Maybe she went home to change?" Solomon raised his hands and shrugged his shoulders.

"Oh, you'll never guess what happened while you were making your call?" Sofia teased.

Slightly concerned, Solomon asked, "I saw Gino walk over. Is everything OK?"

Nico spoke up before Sofia could start with her teasing again. "Oh yeah. All is good. He just wanted to thank me for helping him the other day. And he bought us another round of beer before he left."

"That is a bit of a surprise!" Solomon responded with disbelief. "Somewhat out of character for him. Do you think he came over to spy, or try to get a better idea of what we were talking about?"

"Nico thinks he was being genuine," Sofia said. "I'm kind of feeling that might've been the case."

The bartender approached their table and quietly placed the three chilled glasses of beer on the table and discreetly slipped a folded piece of paper to Nico, which he discreetly placed in his pocket before the others could notice.

"I'm guessing Fawn bailed on us—probably tired. At least she already knows the plan, so we can still move forward with things tomorrow night," Sofia said and then had an idea. "You guys up for a little contest?"

"Sure!" Nico and Solomon replied simultaneously.

"Since we should be heading home soon, due to the reading of Nico's nonna's will tomorrow morning, let's have a chugging contest and see which of the three of us can finish their glass first!"

"OK, on three," Nico replied and began the countdown. "One, two, three!"

The three of them quickly raised their glasses and chugged down their beers. Solomon was the first to finish and he forcibly slammed down his glass, asserting that he was the winner of the contest.

Within a few seconds, both Nico and Sofia had finished their beers and slammed down their glasses in unison.

"Well done, Solomon!" Sofia said and quickly stood up from her barstool, slightly losing her balance and falling into Solomon's waiting arms. She looked up into her rescuer's eyes and said, "And on that happy note, we should take our leave."

"What? No prize for winning your contest?" Solomon asked as he lifted Sofia to her feet.

Flushed in the face and mildly intoxicated, she turned to Solomon and kissed him on the cheek. "There's your prize, my prince."

"I shall never wash that side of my face, milady," Solomon teased back.

"Good to see you again, Solomon. We'll meet up tomorrow," Nico said as he rose from his seat. "I need to get this one home before she causes any more trouble." He laughed as he picked up Sofia's purse from the floor and handed it to her.

Sofia smiled and waved goodbye to Solomon, and then followed Nico out of the restaurant.

"You're a naughty girl. I've never seen you so flirty," Nico joked as they stood outside in the fresh evening air. "It's true that alcohol lowers your inhibitions!"

Sofia smiled back with a devilish grin, and they crossed the street. Cutting through the piazza, they noticed that The Griffon's Claw appeared to be open.

"Look! How strange that they're open already," Sofia said in amazement. "Weren't they just removing the boards from the building earlier today? Maybe they opened just for you!"

"That's bizarre. I'm not sure how they pulled that off so quickly. But this is Oliveto, after all. I'm sure magic must've been involved," Nico responded, acknowledging Sofia's surprise. "Do you want to go inside and check it out?"

"Let's!" Sofia answered enthusiastically.

As they approached, they noticed the door to The Griffon's Claw was open and they could see a multitude of patrons inside. They were about to enter the bar, when a surly bouncer appeared, blocking the doorway. He stood about six and-a-half feet in height and had a solid, muscular build. He looked them both in the eye and then grunted, "IDs?"

Nico and Sofia, intimidated by the bouncer's demeanor, quickly began to retrieve their IDs in order to present them. And, just as they were about to hand them to the bouncer for inspection, an unknown voice from within the bar called out to the bouncer in a commanding tone, "Baron, let them through."

The brawny figure immediately moved aside, allowing them entrance to the crowded bar.

"Apparently word got out about their opening!" Nico said with a raised voice so that Sofia could hear his comment over the sound of loud music and people's voices in the room.

"Like you said earlier, magic had to be involved. How else could they have cleaned and stocked a place so quickly, let alone drawn such a huge crowd, after having been shuttered for decades," Sofia yelled back.

"We made it in at least! Maybe we should have one quick drink—what do you say? The walk back home should help sober us back up and we should be fine by morning."

Sofia smiled deviously and then nodded in reply. Grabbing Nico's hand, she pulled him through the crowd toward the main bar, but then suddenly stopped midway.

"Nico," she asked, "do you see that guy headed toward the back door, marked private? Isn't that the deacon from the church? I remember him from the funeral service."

Nico turned his head to look, but was only able to capture a glimpse of the mysterious person's back as he passed through the doorway, which appeared to lead to some sort of storage room or office area.

"Darn—missed him," Nico said with disappointment. "It would be odd if it were Deacon Servitore—I mean, what would he be doing at a place like this? And, if that was him, why would he be entering into an area clearly reserved for staff only?"

"Maybe he'll come back out—I'll point him out to you if I see him again. For now, let's get our drinks!" Sofia said.

Weaving through the crowd of people, they soon made their way to the center station of the bar. While they waited patiently for one of the bartenders to take notice of them, they recognized the song playing through the speakers; it was one of their favorite Duran Duran songs.

Sofia started bopping her head and mouthing the lyrics to "Hungry Like the Wolf," eventually letting the words audibly escape.

A few seconds later, a slightly inebriated Nico, and the rest of the bar patrons, joined in singing the all-to-familiar chorus.

A female bartender popped up from behind the bar and surprised them. She was dressed in a white ribbed tank top, a faded denim skirt with a thick black belt, and a slew of fluorescent jelly bracelets lining her arms. A scrunchie gathered her long bleached hair and held it off to the side. She placed two cocktail napkins on the counter and greeted them, "You two should come back next week when we start karaoke night—you two would be a hit!"

Now embarrassed, the two stopped singing and turned to the bartender and smiled. "Hello," they responded in unison.

The bartender was just about to ask what they would like to drink when a man approached from behind the bar and spoke. "I'll take care of these two—go take your break." She immediately headed to the mysterious door at the back of the room.

Nico and Sofia could feel the commanding presence of the man that now stood in the bartender's place. With his hands resting on the edge of the bar, he leaned forward and looked deeply into Nico's eyes.

Nico felt paralyzed, unable to avert his eyes, yet he felt no fear. The man turned his gaze toward Sofia and then spoke, "Welcome Nico and guest. I've been expecting you."

Sofia immediately recognized the man's voice and spoke out. "Hello. And the guest's name is Sofia. You were the one who called off the bouncer, so that we could enter, right?"

"A pleasure," the man said in a gentle tone as he reached for Sofia's hand. Sofia felt almost a compulsion to extend her hand toward him. His cold hand grasped hers and held it up to his lips to give it a gentle kiss. As he released her hand, he continued to speak, "And yes, I was the one who asked Baron to let you enter. Let me introduce myself. My name is Vincenzo. Welcome to The Griffon's Claw."

"Sofia and I were amazed at how quickly you opened your doors. It's been boarded up ever since I can recall. When I was a kid, I remember walking by it after school when going to my family's real estate office next door." Nico paused briefly and then continued as he recalled another memory. "I would always pause at the front of the building, trying to find a crack between the wooden planks that would allow me a view of what was inside—It was my childhood goal to find out."

"And here you are, almost as if it were kismet," Vincenzo commented. "Now what are you two kids having? Might I suggest tonight's house special?"

"Kids?" Sofia responded in laughter. "You look no more than maybe a few years older than Nico and me."

"Don't be rude Sofia," Nico blurted as he gently elbowed her side. "Take it as a compliment—after all, we'd all like to remain youthful looking, if we could."

Sofia apologized to Vincenzo, "Sorry, I didn't mean it to come out that way. So, what's tonight's drink?"

"It is a mix of Campari, blood orange juice, a dash of maraschino cherry juice, and a splash of tonic water—we are calling it The Bloodletter." Vincenzo responded.

"Not quite the Negroni I previously had my heart set on, but at least it satisfies my Campari craving *and* love of blood oranges—I'll definitely take one," Nico said with excitement.

"And for you Sofia?" Vincenzo asked. "Would you like one as well or is your palate desiring something different?"

"I'm going to join Nico on this adventure and have one as well," Sofia replied.

"Very good then. Two Bloodletters coming right up!" Vincenzo announced and then turned away to mix the drinks.

Nico and Sofia turned away from the bar and scanned the crowd.

"Other than your sighting of the deacon, there doesn't seem to be anyone local here—at least no one that I recognize," Nico commented.

"Perhaps they're all college tourists—choosing the same destination for spring break as we did," Sofia added.

"Hey," Nico said in a lowered tone to Sofia, "there's something about the owner—I just can't put my finger—"

The sound of two old-fashioned glasses hitting the wooden counter behind them interrupted Nico's comment and they quickly turned around.

"Wow, that was super-fast!" Sofia said, trying to distract the bartender in case he had heard any part of Nico's comment. "You certainly have some wicked bar skills."

"I'll let you two enjoy your cocktails. Drink up! They're on the house." Vincenzo said as the female bartender returned, as if on cue. "If you need anything further, Payton is now back from her break and can get you whatever you desire."

With that, Vincenzo headed toward the closed door in the back of the room.

"So, Payton. What is behind that door in the back?" Sofia asked.

Caught off guard, Payton replied nervously, "Oh, uh, that is just the back-office area—nothing but supplies and the break room back there."

"Yes, of course. What else would be there, Sofia?" Nico added with some laughter to cut the tension. "Sofia, let's toast so we can take a sip of our cocktails—I'm anxious to see how it tastes."

Sofia raised her glass. "To your nonna—may she always watch over you!"

"I'll drink to that!" Nico responded and touched his glass to Sofia's. He then held the sanguine colored cocktail up to the light and remarked, "It is quite beautiful."

They each took a sip and were quite enamored with its taste.

"This could be my new favorite drink—it's absolutely delicious," Sofia said and took a second sip.

"Bloody good, I'll say!" Nico said with an intoxicated smile.

Payton interrupted, "How are your drinks? What did he end up making you?"

"Delicious!" Nico answered. "According to your boss, it's tonight's special drink, a Bloodletter, he called it."

"Hmm. Never heard of that drink before," Payton replied, a bit confused. "I didn't even know we had a 'special drink.' Opening night, I guess, and well, maybe no one told me."

The two finished their drinks and left a tip on the counter before stumbling out of the bar to head home. As they walked down Oliveto's main street, Sofia abruptly stopped at one of the store windows along the way. Something had caught her attention. The brightness of the nearly full moon was illuminating one of the window displays at Midnight's Treasures – Fine Antiques & Curiosities.

"What is it you see, Sofia?" Nico asked.

"What is this place?" Sofia replied, ignoring Nico's question.

"It's just an old antique store—been here for years." Nico answered while recalling a childhood memory. "I remember my nonna would deliberately cross the street to avoid walking anywhere near this place. She never told me why, but I'm sure she had her reasons. So, what is it that has you so captivated?"

Sofia pointed to the odd window display which seemed to be an assortment of various antique mannequin and doll arms and hands. "Look closely amongst the items. Two of the items are quite unique and extremely rare."

Nico looked intently through the glass at the array of artificial limbs displayed, and eventually spotted the two items Sofia was fixated on, opposite each other near the edges of the display.

"One looks like the hand of some small furry animal and the other, well, it appears to be an old, desiccated hand—with wicks coming out of the fingertips," Nico replied with a tinge of confusion.

"Back in the old country, I had seen the Hand of Glory before—that's the one whose fingertips can be lit like a candle." Sofia paused and then suddenly continued in astonishment, "I think—I think the other one is the legendary Monkey's Paw. When Paolo and I were kids, we would gather around the campfire—the elders would tell terrifying tales about the misfortune of those who had been in the possession of the Monkey's Paw and dared to make its three wishes."

"Seems like the oddities are purposely placed to be somewhat hidden from the common eye—only someone with such knowledge, like yourself, would've known of their significance, let alone given them any notice," Nico said. "Perhaps items such as these are what caused my nonna to steer clear of this place."

"That's probably the case," Sofia agreed. "Items like those, along with how many others this store might contain, can only lead to no good. They're dark items—some would venture to refer to them as cursed."

"You're creeping me out now," Nico shuddered just as a cloud passed in front of the moon, darkening the window display. "Let's get home. It's starting to get chilly."

Sofia began walking, leading the way back home, and Nico followed. Both were quiet and said nothing further along the way.

As they approached the front door of the home, it unlocked on its own and opened, seemingly inviting Nico and Sofia to enter.

"Apparently, I have found favor with the house!" Nico joked as he stepped across the threshold. "I'll no longer have to worry about losing a key."

Sofia stopped before entering the house and turned to look across the street.

"Did you hear that Nico?" Sofia said, slightly panicked.

"No, I didn't hear anything, except for a frog croaking somewhere in the yard," Nico responded. "What do you think you heard?"

"Sounded like something rustling in the bushes across the street," Sofia replied. "It's stopped now."

"Probably a stray cat or opossum," Nico said, trying to lighten the mood.

Sofia stepped inside to join Nico in the foyer, and suddenly the front door slammed shut, causing them to jump; then a *click* was heard as the door bolted itself.

"Now, I know a large truck didn't just drive by causing the door to slam," Sofia said, her nerves slightly shaken.

"I have no answer, other than it's late and we should probably head to bed before we start over-analyzing the situation and freaking out," Nico replied calmly and headed toward the hallway that led to his room. From the corner of his eye, he noticed Sofia heading in the direction of the kitchen, instead of toward her bedroom. "Where are you going?"

"I'm going to take the rose bush and put it on the back porch so we can plant it tomorrow. It's still in my purse and I really don't want a thing of such beauty to dry up and die," Sofia answered.

Nico turned back and walked up to her. "Good thinking—you know, you're going to make an excellent mother one day. You're always thinking about people and things, whether animate or inanimate, and making sure that all is well. You're truly a treasure, and I'm glad you are my best friend." Nico then gave her a goodnight kiss on her forehead and headed off to his bedroom.

Sofia, touched by Nico's sincere words, smiled as she made her way to the back of the house. As she passed through the kitchen, she noticed the frog figurine sitting on the windowsill. It usually faced the kitchen, but it was now slowly turning toward the window. Paying no further attention to the porcelain amphibian, she continued toward the back door. Another frog figurine, near the *Nepenthes* plant, which she hadn't noticed before, also began to turn on its own. Sofia felt a slight chill run down her spine.

Sofia quickly opened the door to the backyard. She carefully removed the rose bush from her purse and placed it on the moonlit patio. From the nearby French doors of Nico's bedroom, his silhouette was moving about; the sight of this gave her a momentary feeling of safety.

Nico is right there. I've nothing to be afraid of, she thought. She took a deep breath to calm her nerves and went back inside.

Sofia shut the door behind her and made sure it was locked before heading back to her bedroom. She stopped as she neared the kitchen. Trying not to move a muscle, she stood still and listened carefully. From the direction of the kitchen windowsill, she could hear the faint sound of a frog croaking. She cautiously continued onward and approached the porcelain frog, which had moved even more since she last saw it; it was now pointing toward the northeast corner of the front yard. Sofia put her fingers between the slats of the Venetian blinds and spread them apart so that she could look in the direction the frog was facing. Something shadowy and misshapen appeared to be approaching from across the street. The frequency of the frog's croaking increased, becoming louder and more intense, almost in sync with the rapid palpitations of Sofia's heart. She quickly withdrew her hand from the blinds so that she would not be seen and rushed toward the other side of the house, where her bedroom was. She kicked off her shoes and jumped into bed, remaining under the covers until morning.

Chapter 21: If There's a Way, There's a Will

The next morning at 7:30 a.m., Nico was awakened by the ringing of the telephone. He lay there in bed, slightly hungover and not wishing to get out of bed. *Ring*. By the third ring, Nico gave up on any ideas of sleeping in and got out of bed. "I'm coming!" Nico shouted, slightly annoyed, as he made haste to the only phone in the house, which was located in the kitchen.

Halfway through the dining room, Nico took a running start and slid the remaining distance to the kitchen in his socks. Once again half naked, wearing only his boxers and socks, hair sticking up in multiple directions, he stopped at the threshold of the kitchen. Sofia had already answered the phone and was now in the process of saying goodbye to the caller.

"We have to stop meeting this way," Sofia teased before relaying the caller's message. "It was your mother. She wanted to make sure you arrive on time to the lawyer's office today. The reading of the will is at 10 a.m. sharp."

Nico, slightly embarrassed by his nearly nude entrance, grabbed a nearby flour sack towel hanging from the kitchen island and wrapped it around his waist like a loincloth.

"Oops! Sorry about that!" Nico apologized. "Anyway, thank you for answering the phone."

"You're definitely more comfortable here than when we're at Hornsby Manor. But this is your home after all, so who am I to judge?" Sofia replied. "By the way, before you run off to get ready, how did you sleep last night? Did you hear anything out of the ordinary?"

"I passed out soon shortly after crawling into bed—the only thing I heard was the ringing of the phone, which woke me up," Nico answered. "Why? Did something happen?"

"Well, sort of…" Sofia paused to decide if she wanted to bring up the night's events or just forget about them; she decided on the former. "Come with me so I can walk you through what happened."

As Nico followed Sofia through the kitchen he called out, "House, *due cappuccini, per favore*!" Within seconds the espresso machine turned on and a cabinet opened, allowing levitating cups and saucers to leave their shelves and float over toward the espresso machine.

"Nico! Duck!" Sofia shouted in warning as a saucer almost hit his head.

"Thanks! I guess I should have waited until we were out of the way," Nico replied with gratitude.

Sofia was about to continue with her recollection of the evening's events, but waited for an oncoming carton of milk to arrive at its destination before beginning. "OK, I think I can start now. So, I was walking right about here, near the kitchen sink, when I noticed that frog figurine on the windowsill start to move."

"Oh, yeah, there are frog figurines all throughout the house—at least one in each room. My nonna collected them," Nico said. "I guess instead of displaying them in a curio cabinet, she placed them in various locations, so that she could always enjoy seeing a part of her collection, no matter which room she was in—I think that's what influenced my love of frogs."

"Well, this frog and the pewter one in the next room are more than just figurines from a vast collection. Both of them moved last night—I would gather that they are enchanted for some purpose," Sofia explained as she walked to the backdoor and opened it. "So, then I opened this door like this and took the rosebush from my purse and put it right—wait, where did it go? Nico, I swear I put it right here!"

Nico looked out the door and, seeing nothing on the ground, stepped outside to investigate. "You say you put it right here?" he asked.

"I'm certain. Between the moonlight and the light coming from your room, I clearly was able to see where I put the bush," Sofia said in frustration. "Look, there's a faint trace of dirt from where it was."

"Yeah, and it looks like there's a light trail of earth going around the corner to the southside of the house—come on, let's follow it," Nico said, excited to get to the bottom of this minor mystery. "First let me find a robe or something from my room—it's a bit chilly out."

Nico opened the French doors to his room and went to the closet. A single item of clothing was hanging there, and fortunately for him, it happened to be an old and rather large black smoking jacket, which he recalled his nonno always wearing when doing crossword puzzles in his leather recliner. He grabbed hold of its velvet collar and yanked it off its wooden hanger, which fell to the ground with a thud. He put it on and took a brief moment to appreciate its detailed brocade design. As he went to tie the belt around his waist, he could feel the material of the jacket shrink to a size more fitting to his body.

Wow, super cool! Nico thought to himself before he stepped back outside to join Sofia.

"Ooh, very sharp, Mr. Frantoio!" Sofia said, somewhat amazed. "That looks really good on you—it's a perfect fit!"

"Thank you." Nico said with his usual grin. "My nonno's smoking jacket was the only item hanging in the closet. It must have been a sentimental item that was kept after his passing. I could tell it was oversized when on the hanger, but after I put it on, it seemed to shrink to a perfect fit. I'll bet this type of magic would greatly impress the Schwartzman's!"

"I'm sure it would." Sofia agreed. "While you were inside, I was able to find the missing rosebush. Looks like it was planted during the night, near the basement window where the break-in occurred."

"I'll bet the gnomes must have done some moonlight gardening while we were sleeping," Nico said. "Maybe it was their activity that caused the frogs to move?"

"I'll agree that the gnomes are the ones who replanted the rosebush, but I don't think they were the cause of the frogs' activity. Those figurines were moving before I had gone outside," Sofia said. "Let's go back inside."

"Sure," Nico agreed as he entered the back of the house. "Our cappuccinos should be ready by now."

Sofia followed behind and continued speaking. "So, as I headed back to the kitchen, something felt terribly wrong. I immediately stood still and listened for any type of movement, and that's when I heard the frog begin to croak. As I approached it, I noticed it had rotated and was now facing a northeast direction. And that's when things got freaky. I looked through the blinds to see if something was out there, and I saw something across the street—it was slowly approaching the house."

"What was it? What did you see?" Nico inquired, now totally absorbed in Sofia's re-telling of the previous night's events.

"I am not sure what I saw." Sofia responded with slight confusion. "It was like a shadowy figure, but without a recognizable form. As it neared, the frog began to croak louder and faster. I was so scared—I ran straight to my bed and hid under the covers until I fell asleep."

"Well, that explains why you're still fully clothed in yesterday's attire," Nico said jokingly.

"Yeah, well, without the walk of shame that would normally go along with it," Sofia snapped back and then laughed.

Nico took the two recently prepared cappuccinos and brought them over to the kitchen island so that they could sit down and continue their conversation.

"I trust you, Sofia," Nico said. "If you felt there was some type of danger or possible evil outside the house last night, then that could only mean that the frog figurines are some type of early warning system."

"Yes," Sofia took a sip of her cappuccino and continued, "and we know that the house can do various things relating to the physicality of itself and the many contents within it—like when it unlocked the door for us and then locked the door after we were inside—it must have known that something was outside and wanted to protect us."

"Perhaps, but I don't think the house controlled the frogs. Maybe they alerted the house so that it could try and protect us?" Nico suggested before taking a sip of his cappuccino.

"That sounds plausible, in a magical sort of way," Sofia replied and then wiped off the frothy milk 'stache from Nico's upper lip.

"Like I said last night, you're going to make a wonderful mother one day," Nico said with a smile before finishing off the last of his morning drink. "And on that note, we should get ready. If I'm late, I'll never hear the end of it from my mother."

***

Nico rushed out of his room and headed to the foyer to meet Sofia, who was already there waiting impatiently. She looked down at her watch and tapped its face while looking at Nico.

"I know, I know! Too much time spent on my hair again," Nico huffed. "We can still make it—just need to drive quickly."

"Here's the car key," Sofia said as she handed it to Nico. "It is times like these when you wish there were more fairy doors around for quick travel!"

Sofia opened the door and Nico darted toward the car to start it up. "House, please lock up," she said as she walked down the steps toward the idling car.

Nico quickly sped off toward the center of town and was there within two minutes of their appointment time. Thankfully, a nearby parking spot was available; he pulled in and then turned off the ignition.

Before Nico opened the car door, he turned to Sofia and once again expressed his gratitude. "Thanks again for coming with me. I know this probably isn't the spring break you expected or deserve—having you here gives me much strength."

"I'll always be there for you, my friend," Sofia replied with a slight tremble in her voice, touched by Nico's appreciation.

They exited the car and crossed the street. Nico reached for the door to the offices of Filippo Ascolano, Esq., and held it open for Sofia. Just as they entered, an antique grandfather clock in the reception area began to chime. They had made it on time.

Nico caught his mother's eye from the nearby conference room. Siena waved her hand and beckoned them to hurry on in. Nico took a seat next to his mother around a sturdy mahogany conference table that took up much of the room. His stepfather sat opposite them. Sofia went over to a spare chair that was off to the side and began to sit down.

"No, no," Siena called out to Sofia. "You're like a sister to my dear Nico; you're family. Please come sit with us."

Sofia quietly rose and joined them at the table, sitting next to Pétros.

Mr. Ascolano entered the room, impeccably dressed as usual, carrying a black leather briefcase. He placed it on the table, popped opened the two clasps that secured it, and drew out an oversized manilla envelope, its opening sealed with wax and marked with the Frantoio family insignia.

"Wanda," he called out. "Would you please bring me the letter opener?"

His dutiful secretary quickly appeared with a larger-than-average silver implement with black lacquered handle. "Here you go, Mr. Ascolano," Wanda said as she placed her hand on his shoulder in a rather seductive way and leaned forward to set the letter opener down on the table. "Would anyone like something to drink before you begin? Coffee, tea, water?"

Everyone at the table was silent and just shook their head to signify that they would pass on the beverage offer.

"Very well," Wanda acknowledged and then directed a comment to Mr. Ascolano. "If you need anything, I'll be at my desk—just call out."

As she left, she closed the sliding pocket doors so that they would have some privacy.

"Well, let us begin," Mr. Ascolano announced as he inserted the sharp silver blade of the letter opener under the envelope's flap, breaking the will's wax seal. Broken pieces of green wax fell onto the conference room table's polished surface and then bounced toward Nico, reassembling themselves before him.

Nico looked at Sofia to see if she had also seen what had just happened. Sofia shrugged her shoulders, not knowing what to make of the experience.

Mr. Ascolano pulled the will out of the envelope and glanced at it. He started thumbing through the stack of papers. The rest of them at the table could see that each page that he flipped over appeared to be blank. "This is odd!" he remarked. "Chiara stopped by last week to have me make some updates. After reviewing everything, she insisted that she seal the envelope with wax, using Benito's insignia ring to mark the wax."

"What is this?" Siena blurted as she stood up from the table, slightly aggravated. "Is the entire will a blank document? Let me see it."

The perplexed lawyer handed the papers to Siena so that she could examine them for herself. Nico rose from the table to try to calm his mother, who now seemed to be on the verge of crying.

"All these years they'd been telling me how important the estate was, how much it was a part of our family's legacy, how it needed to be preserved. They never explained any of it to me—they just kept it a mystery," Siena said with a shaky voice.

Nico spoke gently, "Mother, I'm sure there is an explanation. Here, let me take a look at those papers."

As soon as the papers touched Nico's hands, letters began to appear and darken on the ecru-colored linen paper. Siena gasped and collapsed into her chair.

"Wanda!" Mr. Ascolano called out. "Quick! Bring a glass of water for Mrs. Kynigós."

Uncannily, within seconds of the request, Wanda entered the room as if she had anticipated Siena fainting, glass of water in hand. Nico took the glass from Wanda and put his hand on Siena's back. "Here, mom. Please take a sip of water. I think the funeral and everything else has affected you more than you realized."

Siena opened her eyes at the sound of her son's voice and took a sip of water. Composing herself, she then turned to Nico and said, "Thank you, my Nicolino."

Comforted that his mother was now calm and alert, he turned to the lawyer and said, "Mr. Ascolano, here's the will back, I think we can continue now."

Sofia looked over at Nico and gave him a slight smile while shaking her head back and forth, amazed, yet not surprised, at this small display of magic. Chiara must have implemented it to ensure that Nico had to be present at the reading of the will or nothing would be seen.

"Mrs. Kynigós, am I OK to continue?" Mr. Ascolano asked.

"Yes, I am fine now," Siena replied. "Please continue."

"This revised will reads as follows:

I, Chiara Scuro-Frantoio, being of sound mind and body...

...to my beloved figlia, Siena Frantoio-Kynigós, I bequeath all of our rental properties, commercial and residential, as well as vineyards, olive groves, and other vacant parcels of land. Whether said properties are kept and rent is collected, or they are sold for profit, 20% of all monies must be set aside and divided as follows: 10% going to St. Anthony's as a tithe of gratitude for having helped me through life's

many trials; 5% to be put into a trust for Remus Frantoio, which is to be transferred over to him at the age of eighteen; and finally, the remaining 5% going to Nico Frantoio; may this help him with any monetary needs during his soon-to-be busy life. I also leave to Siena the real estate office known as S. Frantoio & Co. Real Estate, which includes ownership of the building, the business, as well as its other assets, to do with however you see fit.

To my remarkable nipote, Nico Frantoio, I leave the Frantoio family home and all of its contents. May it always be a reminder of the love your nonno and I have for you, the many memories that were created there, and those that are yet to come; may the Frantoio family home always be a place of love, goodness, and security for you. I also bequeath to you this key, which Mr. Ascolano will turn over to you momentarily. I know that you will know what to do with it.

Mr. Ascolano reached into the envelope and pulled out a key, which he handed to Nico. "Here you go."

Nico stood up and held out his hand. Mr. Ascolano placed the odd-looking key onto his palm. The key was slightly longer than a standard key and relatively flat. On the key's head, Nico noticed a worn engraving which read: *P S & L*. He placed his nonna's odd gift into his pocket and sat back down.

"And that concludes the reading of the will," Mr. Ascolano announced. "Siena, I'll draw up all the necessary legal papers for you to sign and have them brought to you in the next few days. Nico, since you'll be leaving tomorrow, I'll mail yours out to you—just sign and mail them back. Are there any questions?"

"No, Filippo," Siena replied. "Thank you for meeting with us and taking care of everything, as usual."

Nico rose from his seat and walked over to a beaming Sofia. He knew they had a lot to talk about. "Shall we head back to *my* house?" Nico said with a bit of pride.

"Ah, you knew it was being left to you. Your mom already blew that surprise, but at least now it's now official," Sofia commented and smiled. "Now the key; that was a surprise—I didn't see that coming! Do you have any idea what it goes to?

Siena walked over to the two and asked, "Did you two want to have breakfast with us at Angelique's?"

"Thank you, but we'll make something back at my house," Nico replied with a smile.

"Suit yourselves," Siena said, slightly disappointed in Nico's decline of her offer. "Sofia, good to see you again. I hope you two have a wonderful day."

"Thank you, Siena," Sofia replied and then waved goodbye to Dr. Kynigós, who was patiently waiting at the door for Siena.

Nico waved to his stepfather as well and then resumed his conversation with Sofia. "I noticed an engraving on the key." Taking the key out of his pocket, he handed it to Sofia. "Here, take a look."

Sofia examined the key. "I'll bet my tarot cards that the engraved initials stand for: Pendolino Savings & Loan. It looks like it might be a safe deposit box key—my mother has one similar to this."

"I guess at some point we'll need to drop by the bank and see what my nonna had stored there," Nico suggested.

"You know me, always up for a good mystery," Sofia responded with a chuckle. "I mean, how many mysteries are we solving now?"

"Too many!" Nico said while laughing in return. "I'm trying not to get distracted and stay focused on tonight's mission. I hope I don't get caught sneaking into the mortuary. I can just imagine what would happen if my mother found out—I'd never hear the end of it!"

"Nico, you worry too much," Sofia said. "We've got a solid plan and all the best intentions of finding out who the Oliveto Abductor is."

"You're right, as usual," Nico sighed. "Maybe a distraction *is* what I need!"

"So, we're headed to the bank then?" Sofia asked with enthusiasm.

"First, let's get a cup of coffee," Nico said with a slight yawn. "I still have a slight hangover headache and could use a little pick-me-up. We can stop by Doc's on the way."

Nico and Sofia cut through the piazza to the other side where Doc's was located and purchased two cups of coffee to go. As they headed toward Pendolino Savings & Loan, Sofia felt the sudden brush of wind against her hair. Looking up, she noticed a large black bird which must have gently grazed her as it flew toward the mortuary.

"Nico!" Sofia exclaimed, startling Nico, and causing him to spill some of his coffee while taking a sip. "That can't be the same raven that was hit by the bus yesterday, could it?"

"I very much doubt it—that bird was toast," Nico replied while wiping coffee from his chin.

"I could have sworn I saw the gleam of a gold band around its ankle," Sofia continued.

"Maybe conservationists are tagging birds to keep track of them—probably just one of many that inhabit this area," Nico reasoned.

"Yeah, you're probably right," Sofia said with a smile as they resumed their walk to the bank.

Chapter 22: Banks a Million

Pendolino Savings & Loan was different from most modern banks; it was a very stately building that retained the glamour of a bygone era. Clients were greeted by large, fluted Corinthian columns that held up the archways of the bank's impressive brick and stone façade. This created a sheltered area before the main entrance and protected customers from the elements.

A security guard, dressed more like a formal doorman, stood motionless near the main doors. As Nico and Sofia approached, he gripped the shiny brass door handle with his gloved hand and opened the door for them.

"I loved coming here as a kid," Nico recalled.

"I can just imagine you running and sliding across these slick polished marble floors—must have driven your mother crazy!" Sofia said.

"Yeah, good times!" Nico replied with a devilish grin. "This way, I believe. I think we need to talk to the bank manager in order to be escorted to the safe deposit boxes."

As Sofia followed Nico toward the manager's desk, she slowed her pace in order to admire the building's timeless architecture. She reached her hand out to gently caress one of the cool marble columns as she passed by it. Each of the interior columns, similar to those outside, held up the twenty-five-foot-high ceiling, whose center section contained an impressive stained-glass skylight. Natural light beamed down through the various lead-lined colored shapes, illuminating the area beneath. Sofia stopped walking and tilted her head back to view the skylight's design. The border depicted various types of vines, reminiscent of those she had seen painted in the hallway leading to Chiara's bedroom—except these did not appear to writhe about. Further inward was a milky white glass section, where most of the light was coming through; this separated the border from the center design, which consisted of four olive trees. *One for each of the founding family members*, she surmised.

"Sofia, are you coming?" Nico tried to call quietly over to her, but his voice still carried, and multiple people turned around to see what all the noise was about. Slightly embarrassed, Nico spoke out to the bank's patrons, "Oh, excuse me—just trying to get my friend's attention."

Sofia delighted in Nico's gaff and did her best to not laugh too loudly at the situation. "Coming!" she responded.

Nico was standing by a large wooden desk that was neatly organized. A placard displayed the name: Rocco Pendolino, President. Sofia caught up and now stood at his side.

In the distance, a man passed through a heavy iron security gate and locked it behind him before heading toward the desk where Nico and Sofia stood waiting.

"*Ciao*, Nico!" the man greeted as he neared them. "I haven't seen you since you were a young lad."

"*Ciao*, Mr. Pendolino," Nico replied. "Yes, it has been a while."

"So sorry to hear about Chiara—such a wonderful woman! And to think, I'd just seen her here a few days prior to her passing," Mr. Pendolino said, shaking his head with disbelief. "By the way, that was a wonderful eulogy you gave for her at the funeral."

"Oh, thank you—kind of you to say," Nico responded and then something clicked in his head. "Did I hear you right? You said you saw my nonna a few days before she died?"

"Why, yes," The banker responded. "She came in to access her safe deposit box in the vault below."

Sofia lightly elbowed Nico and whispered, "Imagine that coincidence."

Almost forgetting his manners, Nico quickly spoke up. "Mr. Pendolino, this is my best friend, Sofia. She decided to keep me company during my brief stay in Oliveto."

Mr. Pendolino extended his hand toward Sofia. "Welcome to our quaint little town. I'm sorry your visit was during such a somber occasion. I take it you both are on your spring break?"

"Yes, we are," Sofia said with a smile. "I figured that the duty of a best friend is to be there for the bad times as well as the good."

"I'm glad to have her with me," Nico said as he put his arm around Sofia, giving her a side hug. "So, you mentioned that my nonna made a visit to her safe deposit box? I'm actually here to do the same." Nico pulled out the key he had received at the reading of the will. "I believe this is the key to her box?"

"Yes, that looks like one of her two keys," he said as he examined it. "Goes to safe deposit box 711, which belonged to her. If you'd follow me, I'll take you down to the vault."

Mr. Pendolino stepped off the carpeted area, where his desk was located, and onto the marble floor. The wooden heels of his handmade leather shoes, which boosted his less-than-average stature, clacked against the floor as he walked off.

Nico and Sofia were trailing behind until Mr. Pendolino stopped at the top of a marble spiral stairway so that they could catch up. The steps led down to a landing a good twenty-five feet below the bank's main floor.

"Hold onto the railings," He cautioned. "It's a long way down and the worn stone steps have become smooth and slick over the years."

Taking his recommendation, they both held onto the railing and made their descent to the lower level where the vault's huge steel door, a little over a foot thick, was already open. Beyond the door, a narrow red carpet created a pathway down an excessively long hallway. Other than the room's cold, bare stone walls, a large gold door at the end of the walkway was all that was immediately noticeable. This door would soon lead them to a secured area, where the safe deposit boxes were kept.

"Follow me this way," Mr. Pendolino instructed. "And don't touch anything! Remain on the carpeted area at all times."

Obeying his instructions, they entered the chilly vault. The temperature seemed to have dropped a good twenty degrees.

"Brrr. It's cold in here," Sofia said.

"It's just one of the many safety and security measures we have put in place," Mr. Pendolino remarked. "Not only does it help preserve the various valuables of our clients, but the low temperature also helps prevent certain intruders from entering and slows down the actions of others."

Nico whispered to Sofia, "Clearly this area is enchanted, as I am not seeing any visible form of security, unless cameras are hidden in those small ceiling vents."

Sofia looked up and noticed the various linear vents in the ceiling that Nico was referring to. She whispered in reply, "Did you notice they only seem to be on either side of this carpeted walkway, but not directly above it?"

Nico's curiosity was about to get the best of him. He reached into his pocket and casually tossed a penny off to the right of the carpeted pathway. As soon as the penny hit the floor with a faint clink, what seemed like a thousand or more spiders of various sizes and species, descended down upon the lone penny, and quickly covered it in spider webs before ascending back up into the vents.

Mr. Pendolino, having heard the sound of the fallen coin, quickly turned around with a perturbed look which then eased into a smile.

"Ever the mischief maker, Mr. Frantoio!" Mr. Pendolino joked. "And I'll bet you're happy that you remained on the carpeted area as I advised?"

Slightly embarrassed, Nico replied, "Yes, sir. It didn't appear that there was any real security here—I thought you might have been just saying that for effect."

"Well, now you know," Mr. Pendolino replied. "That is actually one of the security additions that your nonna helped create. Since spiders are one of the three creatures Malandanti are able to control, Chiara decided this would be a humane way to trap intruders—well, at least most of the non-Malandanti ones."

"That's right, spiders were mentioned in the grimoire, along with ravens and lizards," Sofia said quietly to Nico.

"OK, enough with the dallying," Mr. Pendolino continued. "Let's open that safe deposit box for you."

A few feet further, they arrived at the golden door; it appeared to be made of actual gold. It shimmered in the low light, displaying swirling hypnotic patterns. Unlike the steel one at the entrance which was already opened, this one was secured and prevented further passage.

"Kids, don't stare at the door too long or you'll find yourselves mesmerized and unable to move further," Mr. Pendolino warned. "Just another one of our ingenious security measures."

He then reached into his suit's inner breast pocket and pulled out a black fountain pen. Waving it in the air like a magic wand, he mumbled some words which then caused the door to open, swinging outward.

Nico and Sofia were slightly dizzy from having looked almost too long at the door. They staggered behind the banker and together entered the vault within a vault. Thousands of safe deposit boxes, some small and others rather large in size, lined every inch of the walls before them. In the center of the room, three large tables, each surrounded with comfortable, red velvet tufted chairs, were provided for clients to sit at.

"Let's see. Straight ahead, on the back wall should be where box 711 is located," Mr. Pendolino said. As he located the correct box, he withdrew the guard key from his pants pocket. It was attached to a retractable silver chain which extended in length as the key was inserted. He turned his key and then said, "Nico, time to do your part."

"Oh, right," Nico replied and retrieved his key, inserting it alongside the guard key. "There. Now, just turn it?"

"Duh!" Sofia sarcastically commented and then whispered. "I think you know you probably could've opened it without a key."

Mr. Pendolino overheard Sofia's comment and chimed in, "If you meant unlocking the safe deposit box by magic, that wouldn't work. All the locks at Pendolino Savings & Loan are magically warded—even those most proficient in magic wouldn't be able to break the enchantments."

Nico turned his key and finished unlocking the safe deposit box. Mr. Pendolino reached in front of Nico to open the door. He pulled out the long metal drawer and carried it over to one of the tables in the center of the room.

"I'll let you two have some privacy," Mr. Pendolino said. "Normally I remain with customers until they are finished, but since you're a member of a founding family—and I trust you—I've removed the guard key from my chain and left it in the lock. So, when you've finished, please return the drawer to its location, and make sure to use *both* keys to lock it back up. Then find me upstairs and return my key. We can then see if there's anything else I can assist you with."

"Thank you, Mr. Pendolino," Sofia responded. "We'll be up in a bit."

The banker headed out of the vault, and eventually the clacking of his heels could be heard once again as he left the carpeted area and made his way upstairs.

Nico and Sofia each took a seat in the comfortable chairs and stared intently at the metal drawer before them.

"What do you suppose is in it?" Sofia asked.

"At this point in our adventure, I have no clue what to expect!" Nico chuckled and shook his head while lifting the drawer's lid.

At first glance, the mysterious contents seemed to be nothing more than an assortment of various property deeds and legal documents. As they sorted through each and organized them on the table, a purple satin sack with a gold cord drawstring and a ruby ring were all that remained at the bottom of the drawer.

"Ah, the plot thickens!" Sofia said with a tinge of excitement in her voice before focusing on the ring. "Wow, did you ever see a more perfect looking ring!"

"Odd." Nico said slightly puzzled. "My nonna always wore that ring. Why she would take it off and put it here doesn't make any sense. I remember looking at her body before the funeral service started and thinking something was missing but I couldn't place my finger on it—now it makes sense!" Nico exclaimed.

"Mind if I try it on?" Sofia asked while batting her eyes.

"Please do—I doubt it would fit me anyway," Nico responded. "Now to see what's in this sack!"

Nico loosened the golden drawstring and emptied the purple sack. About thirteen clattering coins hit the table. Sofia picked up one of them and noticed the image of a flame was embossed on one side and an anvil on the other. "What an odd-looking coin," she said and then bit into it. "It is definitely made of gold, so there's value to it."

"If it was kept here, we know it has value," Nico replied sarcastically. "I think finding its purpose or use is what we need to figure out. I'm going to take one with us and we will leave the rest here in the safe deposit box."

Nico put the remaining coins back into the sack, pulled the drawstring, and then casually tossed it into the open drawer. Sofia reluctantly removed Chiara's ruby ring and placed it and the organized stacks of legal papers back into the drawer, and then replaced its cover.

Nico picked up the drawer from the table and they walked over to its slot. He slid the drawer in and locked the safe deposit box back up as instructed. He retrieved both keys and placed his key in his pocket while keeping the guard key in his hand, so that he wouldn't confuse the two.

Side by side they made their way back, following the red carpeted pathway. Halfway along the way, Nico felt as if Sofia wasn't near him and immediately thought, *did she go back for that penny*?

Nico immediately turned around and yelled, "No!"

As Nico had guessed, Sofia had stepped off the carpet and was in the midst of picking up the webbed penny.

Startled, Sofia looked toward Nico. "What?"

With a frustrated look on his face, Nico didn't say a word and just pointed upward.

"Oh my God!" Sofia gasped as she looked upward at a multitude of spiders stopped mid-descent above her. "I totally forgot about them! Thankfully they listened to you."

"Hmm, let's test that theory," Nico responded and then looked up to the spiders and commanded, "Return to your posts!"

The spiders immediately obeyed Nico and climbed back up into the ceiling vents.

"Not bad!" Sofia said and then handed the web-covered coin to Nico and jokingly laughed, "A penny for your thoughts?"

Nico shook his head at Sofia's bad joke but still found enough humor in it to laugh.

By the time they made it to the top of the stairs, they were slightly out of breath. Mr. Pendolino was within sight, and they headed over to his desk.

"Here's your key back," Nico paused to take a breath. "Thank you."

"The stairs got you, eh?" Mr. Pendolino teased. "Part of our *non-magical* security system—one needs to be in tip-top shape to carry a good haul up those stairs!"

"Yes, they definitely slowed us down," Sofia commented. "Say, are you familiar with this coin and its purpose? Nico, show him the coin."

Nico fished the coin out of his pocket and tossed it onto Mr. Pendolino's desk.

The banker pulled his glasses out from his breast pocket and put them on. His eyes lit up and he quickly reached for the coin to examine it closer. "Hmm. I haven't seen one of these in a long time! These are very rare—and extremely valuable."

"My nonna had a bunch of them stored in her safe deposit box. I figured if anyone would know of their relevance, it would be you," Nico responded.

"Well, this coin is one of thirteen coins, known as The Coins of Favor. They were created by our families as a solution to a problem which arose shortly after Oliveto was founded.

"When I was a kid, my nonno Lorenzo told me that various magical beings, drawn to Oliveto because of the mystical ley lines here, began to settle in our peaceful village. Our families had to come up with a way to encourage all beings, even ones who were sworn enemies like the Benandanti and Malandanti, to find common ground and co-exist as peacefully as possible. So, the four founders met and came up with the idea of an enchanted universal currency which could be used to repay a debt or be given in exchange for a favor done. In addition, both parties would also receive a boon of protection and good luck to their household for seven days. This would encourage the townspeople to continuously circulate the coins amongst themselves.

"The coins could never leave Oliveto, or they would magically return to Pendolino Savings & Loan, where my family would randomly distribute them back into circulation amongst the inhabitants."

Sofia's curiosity got the best of her, and she blurted out, "So where did they get the gold, and how did they even make the enchanted coins?"

"Ah, yes, that's the part of the story that even I have a hard time believing. My nonno told me that he and the other three founders were taking a walk along the river one hot summer day, trying to stay cool while discussing how to better integrate the townspeople when they came upon a large willow tree near a bend in the river and sat down beneath it. As they continued speaking amongst themselves, a river nymph popped her head out of the water and startled them. She had been secretly listening to their entire conversation and suggested that she might have a solution to their problem if they would do her a small favor. Naturally, they were open to her proposition, as nymphs were normally known to be harmless.

"The nymph introduced herself as Calypso and told them that about 300 feet further up the river, a gold necklace with the most beautiful crystal medallion she had ever seen, had been caught on a branch and unknowingly left behind by a passerby. She said she must have it for her collection, but that it was too hot for her to safely leave the water to retrieve it.

"The four obliged and walked upriver to search for the item. One of them soon spotted the rainbow colors emitting from the crystal as the sun passed through it, and ran up to untangle the chain from the tree branch. They returned to the river's bend with the necklace and presented it to Calypso. Her eyes lit up with gratitude as she gratefully thanked them.

"Keeping to her promise, she told them to join hands and step into the water. She took hold of my nonno's hand, since he was in front, and warned them that they must *never* break the chain. Anyone who lost a connection to her would lose their ability to breathe underwater and surely perish. She explained that the answer they were seeking would be found inside the nearby mountain, but that the only entrance, other than the hole at its very top, was a secret underwater cavern. Reaching this area required them to swim down deep to the opening of a warm mineral spring; from there they could follow that channel to the opening of the cavern.

"Calypso let them know that the efreet, whose domain was within the mountain, would be able to help them with their current dilemma. She also warned that he was a terrible trickster and never to look directly into his eyes…."

Nico interrupted. "What the heck is an efreet?"

"It is like a djinn—you know, a genie. It's a being from the realm of fire, and since the mountain behind the town is allegedly a dormant volcano, it's plausible that there's some fire source there for it to inhabit," Sofia said.

"And that's pretty much all I was told," Mr. Pendolino said. "He always seemed to be less detailed toward the end of the story and would just say that he received the coins from the efreet and passed them out amongst the villagers."

"It *does* seem like the best part of the story is missing," Sofia sighed.

"I guess we'll never really know," Nico added. "Thank you for your time, Mr. Pendolino. It was great to see you again."

"A pleasure," The banker replied. "If you two need further assistance with anything or have any other questions, please let me know. I'm here daily."

Nico retrieved the coin from Mr. Pendolino's desk and put it in his pocket. They waved goodbye and headed for the doors, exiting outside into the warm afternoon air.

As they were walking down the street, something puzzled Sofia. She stopped in the middle of the sidewalk and turned to Nico. "So, Nico, if the coins are supposed to bring all of the townspeople together, et cetera, and are to be in circulation, then if my count was correct, why did your nonna have all thirteen in her possession?"

"You're right!" Nico replied as he moved off to the side to prevent pedestrians from walking into them. "I don't know. I think that's a question to be answered at another time. Shall we go back to the house and have some lunch? I think I'd also like to take a nap before tonight's big adventure—I'm a bit nervous about breaking into the funeral parlor since I am going about it alone."

"You'll be fine," Sofia assured. "And since you're going to be glamoured, Dino and Gino won't suspect a thing. Besides, as soon as you drug their pizza with Fawn's potion, they'll be out of the way for an hour or two, which will give you plenty of time to search the place."

"I guess you're right," Nico nervously replied. "I just have one of those feelings…."

Chapter 23: Pizza Night

A knock came at Nico's bedroom door.

"Nico, wake up," Sofia gently called out.

"Thanks, I'm awake. Be right there," Nico responded and quickly sat up in his bed, looking over at the clock: 5:10 p.m.

Nico stepped into his shorts and put his shirt back on. Slightly groggy from his afternoon nap, he opened his bedroom door and walked barefoot to the kitchen, where he gathered Sofia would be waiting. As his feet met the kitchen's cool marble flooring, it was an immediate awakening of his senses; so was the delightful smell of the espresso that Sofia had just prepared for him, complete with a thin strip of lemon peel, just the way he liked it.

"Ah, there you are!" Sofia said. "I thought you'd like one of these to pick you up." She skillfully slid his demitasse of espresso across the island countertop toward him, as he took a seat.

"*Perfetto*!" Nico responded and raised his cup as a toast to her. "I'm glad you get me."

"We should leave soon," Sofia suggested. "I'd like to go over the plan once more with Fawn and Solomon at the store, plus I need to call in the pizza order so that it will be ready for you when you go over to the mortuary."

"Well, just don't forget Fawn's potion, so that I can pour it over Dino and Gino's pizza and knock them out—it's still in your purse, right?" Nico asked before downing his espresso in one gulp.

"I think so," Sofia said trying to keep a straight face. "Hopefully it didn't get lost with all that additional space you created."

A look of panic washed over Nico's face, and he returned the demitasse to its saucer with a loud clink.

"Just kidding, Nico! It's there, I promise!" Sofia said, realizing that her joke was poorly timed.

"Ah, good," Nico said with a sigh of relief and relaxed his shoulders. "Let's walk to town, instead of taking the car. I think the fresh air will do me good and perk me up."

"We have plenty of time, so that sounds like a great plan," Sofia concurred. "Let's meet back in the foyer in ten minutes and then we can head out."

***

Nico and Sofia met back in the foyer at the agreed-upon time and left the Frantoio home. At this point, they no longer needed to tell the house to secure itself. It seemed to have learned to anticipate their needs and bolted the door immediately upon their exit.

The late afternoon sky was still clear, due to unexpected winds that had increased throughout the day. As the sun continued its journey west, its remaining rays beamed upon their cheeks and warmed their skin as they made their way to the piazza.

"Sofia, do you really think I can pull this off?" Nico asked, breaking through the silence.

"I have total confidence in you, Nico," Sofia assured. "Look at all you've been through in the past few days and how far you've come since we've been here. You've been strong through the death of your nonna; you've discovered so many secrets about Oliveto—who knows how many more exist—and you can cast spells!"

"Well, I guess…."

"I remember your first spell and how many times you tried to cast it. And now, you barely have to concentrate—you get it on the first try. That's a sign of confidence and growth! The Nico I first met back at school, was a shy, introverted guy, who lacked confidence and self-esteem. And now, in such a short time, you've completely changed! Evolved is maybe a better word?"

"Thank you for sharing your observations. I guess I've been accustomed to repressing so much all my life, and not believing in things or having hope, that it's chipped away at any self-confidence that I may have. I feel like I'm now just starting to live my life, free of limitations, for the first time." Nico said, stopping in place to give Sofia a hug, once again grateful to have such a supportive friend in his life.

"You're welcome. And don't think you haven't been there for me," Sofia added as she embraced him back with tears welling up in her eyes. "You mean so much to me and have added much value to my life."

"You'd think we were saying our goodbyes to each other," Nico joked, trying to lighten the mood. "Let's not get too emotional. We've got to stay focused."

"You're right," Sofia responded and looked ahead toward their destination. "Ah, there's Solomon standing outside his parents' store. He must be waiting for us."

They rushed over to greet Solomon, who then unlocked the door to Schwartzman's so that they could all enter.

Once inside, Sofia gave Solomon a big hug.

"Oh!" Solomon remarked. "To what do I owe this pleasant surprise?"

Slightly embarrassed, Sofia quickly responded, "Uh, well I guess I'm still a little emotional from my previous conversation with Nico…and I just…well…I guess I crossed a line and should apologize."

"Not at all," Solomon said, smiling and slightly blushing. "I've envisioned this moment many a time, and hope there will be more opportunities in the future."

"OK, lovebirds, save it for later. We should go over the plan," Nico interrupted. "Where's Fawn?"

"I don't know," Solomon answered with a concerned tone. "Since she didn't show up for drinks last night, I went to visit Sterling this morning, and he said she never came home—he's really worried."

"Oh, no!" Sofia exclaimed. "And tonight's a full moon—she must have been the next to be abducted!"

"Well, if Mr. Cadaveri is the culprit, then I'll bet she's somewhere across the street at the mortuary—I'll be on the lookout for her!" Nico said, mentally adding that task to his mission.

"I'd better call in the pizza order—it's six-thirty now," Sofia thought out loud and then turned to Solomon. "Where's your telephone?"

"This way," Solomon replied and escorted her back to the register area so that she could make her call.

Nico stood there alone and began to look around the store. He noticed Sofia had left her purse lying on the nearby display table. He opened it and began to rummage through it, looking for Fawn's potion. He easily found it, along with the flash cards they had made so that Nico could learn all the spells.

Guess this would be a great time for a spell refresher while I am waiting, he thought and began shuffling the index cards. Once finished, he pulled the first one from the top of the pile and read it:

> *To unlock any unwarded lock without the use of a key, touch the lock and say this word: XXXXXX*

I can do this basic Malandanti spell in my sleep; Resero, he said to himself and flipped the index card over to verify that he was correct.

Noticing that Sofia was still using the telephone, he took another index card from the pile and read it:

> *To create dancing lights to follow you and light the way, hold this ingredient and say these words: XXX XXXXXXXX*

Dancing light…hmm…OK that must be a will-o'-wisp type spell which would need what ingredient? Oh yeah, decaying plant matter. But what is the incantation! Lux…Lux Saltatio, he guessed and then flipped the index card over to reveal the answer.

"Awesome!" Nico announced loudly at having answered correctly.

"Thank you, I'll be over to pick up the pizza in fifteen minutes," Sofia said and hung up the phone. Now curious, she marched over to see what had excited Nico. "Keeping yourself entertained, I see?"

"I went to get Fawn's potion out of your purse and found the flash cards. So, I thought I'd practice in case I needed a spell or two," Nico replied. "So far, I'm two for two!"

Sofia reached into her purse with both hands, extending her arms deeper and deeper, until they disappeared beyond the natural twelve-inch depth of the purse. "Ah, there it is!" She said with relief as she retracted them, holding Geoffrey's glass jar containing Mr. Cadaveri's towel. "You'll need this too!"

"Most definitely!" Nico agreed. "That's the key element needed to fool Dino and Gino into believing I'm their father."

Solomon walked away and then returned shortly with a shirt, a pair of pants, and a cardigan sweater. He handed them to Nico. "Here, change into these. Fortunately, I was able to catch a glimpse, from the store window, of what Mr. Cadaveri is wearing today. Since he shops at our store, I was able to pull the exact same outfit for you to wear."

"Good thinking Solomon—we hadn't planned for that." Sofia commented and then whispered into Solomon's ear, "By the way, I find intelligence in a man really sexy."

Nico took the articles of clothing from Solomon and went into one of the dressing rooms to change. Slowly he unbuttoned his shirt and removed it, letting it fall down onto the carpeted floor. He nervously looked up at his reflection in the floor length mirror and glanced at his tattoo. He turned to his side and flexed his bicep in the mirror, providing a better view of Sterling's indelible interpretation of Nico's griffon. He gently ran his hand over the fully healed image and said to himself, *wise like an eagle and strong like a lion—both qualities that I possess on some level. I can do this!*

After his little solo pep talk, he finished changing into his disguise and exited the dressing room, bringing his clothing to give to Sofia.

"Sofia, can you please store my clothing in your purse?" Nico asked. "My wallet and stuff are all in my shorts pockets—if you need anything, just take it."

"Sure. No problem. In fact, I might as well take some money now for the pizza; I don't have any cash on me," Sofia replied. She withdrew Nico's wallet and took out a twenty-dollar bill, before putting all of his belongings into her purse. "OK, I'm going to get the pizza—it should be ready by now. Solomon, you help Nico apply the towel to his face so that he can transform into Mr. Cadaveri."

As Sofia left the store, Solomon opened Geoffrey's glass apothecary jar containing Mr. Cadaveri's towel. "Nico, why don't you sit down," Solomon suggested.

Nico pulled up a chair and Solomon came around from behind and placed the middle of the towel at Nico's chin, and then applied the length of each end across the sides of Nico's face. With Solomon's strong hands, he pressed the towel onto Nico's face, molding it into the contours of Nico's face, making sure all areas were well covered.

"I don't know how long it needs to stay on," Solomon commented while holding the towel firmly in place. "I guess we can wait until Sofia comes back—shouldn't be long."

And thankfully, Sofia returned shortly thereafter. After having his face covered for the past five minutes, along with the weight of Solomon's hands pressing down on his face, Nico was feeling claustrophobic.

"I'm back! Doesn't this pizza smell delicious?" Sofia announced. "Guessing Nico is missing out on the aroma—hey, why is the towel still on his face?"

"I didn't know how long to leave it on," Solomon replied, now slightly worried.

Nico reached up and pushed away Solomon's hands so that he could remove the towel.

Sofia shrieked when she saw what was behind the towel and began to faint. Solomon rushed over quickly, catching her with one hand and saving the falling pizza box with the other.

Nico marched over to the dressing room to look in the mirror. To his amazement, he looked eerily like Mr. Cadaveri. Every facial detail down to chalky pallor of his skin was exact; even his receding hairline of black, stringy hair seemed to be matched strand for strand.

Nico returned to check on Sofia. "Sofia, are you OK?" He asked in the vocal tone of Mr. Cadaveri. Even his voice now matched perfectly.

Sofia almost fainted again but Solomon comforted her. "It's Nico, remember?"

"I'm still not used to such powerful magic—it's so shocking that this is even a possibility!" Sofia responded. "Nico, this is going to work out well—you look exactly like him! Dino and Gino will never know it is you. Now let's pour Fawn's potion on the pizza and send you over."

Solomon opened the pizza box while Sofia opened Fawn's potion bottle. She dripped little drops of the syrupy concoction onto each slice and then closed the lid of the pizza box.

"OK. So, here's the plan. Sofia and I will keep guard and watch from the windows. If Mr. Cadaveri should come back early, for some reason, or something else happens, one of us will come ring the doorbell three times to notify you—that will be your signal to get out—to abort the mission." Solomon explained.

"Got it!" Nico confirmed. "Boy that pizza does smell good—I should bring it over to Dino and Gino before it gets cold. Wish me luck!"

Together, they walked over to the door. Sofia gave Nico a quick hug and a peck on the cheek, and then slipped a folded piece of paper into his breast pocket. "You'll need this," she whispered and then carefully inspected Nico, wiping off any trace of lipstick on his cheek, before sending him on his way.

Nico exited Schwartzman's and Sofia locked the door behind him. Solomon went over to the windows at the side of the store, and Sofia followed. They began peering out of the Venetian blinds, carefully watching and waiting, to make sure Nico made it into the mortuary successfully.

Chapter 24: Journey into the Unknown

Nico anxiously waited for the traffic light to turn green. He didn't want to meet the same fate as that poor raven and made sure to look both ways before crossing over to the mortuary.

All throughout his youth, the corner lot of the mortuary never brought a sense of foreboding or dread, until now. This moonlit evening, as Nico stepped off the security of the sidewalk and onto the short pathway leading to the entrance of P. Cadaveri & Sons Mortuary, he shivered; not from the strong winds which began to howl, but from fear.

Nico reached for the door, and discovered it was locked. He quickly muttered "*Resero*," and opened the door, surprised to find Dino and Gino standing there to greet him.

"Father, what are you doing home?" Gino asked.

"He brought us pizza you moron—duh!" Dino responded, grabbing the pizza box from Nico's hands and then making his way upstairs to the kitchen. "Are you coming?" He called out to Gino once he reached the landing.

"Yes, I'll be there in a bit," Gino yelled back and then turned toward Nico. "That's unlike you to bring us pizza. What's the special occasion?"

"Well, you boys have been working extra hard lately and I know I don't always show my appreciation. So, I was getting pizzas for the group and thought I'd get an extra for my boys and surprise you," Nico responded, trying to sound confident with his answer. "Now you better go get a slice or two before your brother devours it all!"

"I will. Thank you, father," Gino said as his eyes gazed down toward Nico's feet. "Weren't you wearing penny loafers when you left the house earlier?"

Nico's heart began to race. *Stay calm, I've got this*, he thought. "I keep these tennis shoes in the car. Sometimes I change into them for less formal occasions because they're more comfortable," Nico bluffed. "Now enjoy your pizza and I'll see you boys later."

Gino turned away and went off to join his brother upstairs in the kitchen. Nico pretended to leave by opening and closing the door so that it would be heard upstairs.

He decided he might as well scope out the main, public floor of the building, in order to allow enough time for Fawn's potion to take effect. He pulled out the piece of paper that Sofia had given him and unfolded it. It happened to be a brief description of each floor of the funeral home, based on Fawn's last conversation with them:

> *The main level—public area with an arrangement room, three viewing rooms, and a chapel area.*
>
> *Upstairs—living quarters: kitchen, two bedrooms, bathroom, and living room.*
>
> *Downstairs—cremation room, morgue, and embalming room.*

Nico took in his surroundings. He had been here before and recalled a time from his childhood when he had accompanied his mother and nonna to make funeral arrangements after his nonno Benito's passing. He remembered being fascinated by the grand, floating staircase, toward the back of the entryway, which led to the upper level, and fearing the stairway leading downward. This staircase was tucked underneath the ascending stairs, almost hidden, and seemed to lead down to a pool of darkness.

He decided to make a quick loop of the first floor, starting to his left and passing through the arrangement room, where Mr. Cadaveri's office and massive desk were located; samples of various urns were displayed about the room along with a few casket samples.

Sliding apart a pair of wooden pocket doors toward the back of the room, he entered one of the viewing rooms. This room was currently vacant and had a few rows of chairs set up for visitors to sit when waiting their turn to view the deceased. A door to the right led to a hallway near the main staircase, and another set of pocket doors ahead, which he quickly opened, gained entry to the chapel.

The chapel seemed smaller than Nico remembered and was ornately decorated with various religious iconography. Staged outside lighting illuminated a series of stained-glass windows that lined the back wall, casting eerie shadows upon the floor. Nico stared down at the shadows and had to blink a few times to focus as he thought he noticed the shadows beginning to move toward him. As a sense of dread filled him, he decided to exit the chapel through another set of pocket doors down to his right. On his way, he passed a small door, which he now assumed led to the main hallway, granting access to all the rooms.

He reached for the handles of the pocket doors and pulled them apart so that he could escape the chapel area. He made a quick about face and slid the doors shut. He was now in the second viewing room, which seemed identical to the previous one. A small door on his right and more pocket doors ahead were his two options. As he went for the pocket doors, a loud, heavy thud from above and the faint sound of silverware falling to the floor, startled him. He stood still for a moment and listened. The sound of feet shuffling about in a panic could be heard. He slowly slid one of the pocket doors open and peeked into the room ahead; it was the third viewing room, and he could see it opened back into the main entryway. He quietly entered the room, which was decorated a little more than the other viewing rooms, and closed the pocket door behind him. As he crept forward, he heard a second, lighter thud as something from above hit the floor. *Ah, that must have been Dino and Gino passing out; they must have fallen to the floor!*

Now back at the main entrance, he headed toward the staircase to so that he could venture upward and investigate the upstairs area. He placed his hand on the smooth worn wood of the handrail and made his way up. With each step Nico took, the stairs let out a noisy creak, almost as if trying to warn the inhabitants of an intruder approaching.

At the top of the stairs, Nico decided once again to start to his left. A brief hallway opened up with a room to the left, which looked like the living room. *Seems rather common; and I doubt anything of note would be found there,* Nico thought as he skipped entering the room. Ahead was the dining room, which he also decided to ignore for now. But it was the room to the right that caught his interest and caused him almost to burst out in laughter; it was the kitchen. Dino and Gino lay sprawled out on the floor fast asleep. He could tell Dino was a messy eater. He had drippings of tomato sauce on his shirt as well as bits around his mouth and on his greasy fingers. Gino, on the other hand, looked to have been eating his pizza on a plate with a fork and knife; the utensils must have been knocked to the floor at some point when Dino first fell. A cloth napkin remained tucked into the collar of Gino's shirt to protect it from possible tomato sauce splatter. Nico couldn't help but admire Gino's neatness, which heavily contrasted with his brother's eating habits. Nico also noticed a smile on Gino's face as he lay there sleeping. *Is he dreaming? Or was the pizza that good?* Nico spied a remaining slice of the intoxicatingly fragrant pizza on the table but knew that succumbing to its temptation would lead to failure of his mission. He had to press onward, and the potion would only keep them incapacitated for so long.

He left the kitchen and went back to the staircase landing, stopping to listen for any movement coming from downstairs before heading to explore the other side of the upper level. Just as he thought he was in the clear, he heard the sound of a bell tinkle and then abruptly stop. Nico discerned the sound hadn't come from below, but from somewhere down the yet-to-be-explored hallway ahead.

The darkened hallway was dreary and uninviting, but he found a light switch to his right as he entered. The passageway was narrow and three closed doors could be seen: one on either side of him and a solitary door at the end of the hallway.

Reaching for the ornate brass knob of the door on his left, he slowly opened it. Nico peeked his head in, and the combined scents of cologne and funk hit his nostrils. *This must be Dino and Gino's room*, he mused. An invisible line seemed to delineate whose side was whose. On the left was a neatly made bed, a tidy desk, and a dresser with a collection of designer colognes on top, while on the right, the entire area looked like it was hit by a cyclone; the bed was unmade, clothes lay strewn about the floor, dresser drawers half pulled out, and a desk with random magazines, scattered paperwork, and two used coffee mugs.

Nico closed the door and turned to the one opposite him. It opened into the bathroom. He walked in to take a peek. He turned and faced the medicine cabinet mirror. Forgetting that his face had been glamoured, he was startled to see Mr. Cadaveri staring back at him. He quickly jumped back in response; his left arm knocking over a half-dead fern in a brass pot, which made a loud clanging noise as it hit the porcelain tiled floor. Nico bent down to retrieve the container, leaving behind a trail of dead leaves as he returned it to is proper location. While he was doing so, he heard a groan, which seemed to come from behind the door at the end of the hallway.

What was that? Maybe it's Fawn! Nico thought with a sense of hope.

He came to the final door and tried to open it; it was locked. *I've got this!* "*Resero*!" The door released its latch and Nico slowly pushed the door inward. The room was pitch black and even the light from the hallway wasn't enough to make anything visible. Nico reached for a light switch but could not find one. He then remembered a spell from one of the flash cards. *Shoot, what was the spell? Ah yes, the 'Fairy Fire' spell.* "*Lux Saltatio!*" he spoke, but nothing happened. *Hmmm. Ah, this is one that needs an ingredient...decaying plant matter...* He immediately went back to the bathroom to retrieve some of the dead fern leaves from the bathroom floor and put them in his pocket.

He returned to the entranceway of the darkened room and pulled a leaf from his pocket. Crumpling it, he threw the pieces into the air while saying "*Lux Saltatio.*" The falling pieces of leaf began to light up and dance about in the air like fireflies, illuminating the room.

As Nico's eyes adjusted, he realized there were no windows in this rather large bedroom; they had been sealed off. The room was filled with the scent of lavender which attempted to cover an underlying scent of decay coming from the back of the room, where a lone bed and nightstand were situated.

He heard another groan. "Fawn is that you?" Nico called out as he approached a king-sized bed which appeared to be inhabited. To the right of the bed, Nico saw a pale female hand dangling out from the covers and a small summoning bell lying on its side on the hardwood floor. *That must be what I heard earlier— she must have knocked it off the nightstand trying to get my attention.*

Nico walked over to the bell and the dancing lights followed him, floating above his new location. He picked up the bell and put it back on the nightstand and turned to the figure on the bed that was now slowly beginning to writhe about under the blankets.

As Nico drew closer to pull back the bed cover, a smell worse than the rotting gourd in his basement caused him to gag. He immediately covered his nose and mouth with his right hand as he gripped the top of the bed cover with his left hand and pulled it back to reveal what was underneath.

What Nico discovered wasn't Fawn. It was horrible. He stood there motionless, paralyzed with fear as the being that Nico had hoped was Fawn was now reaching out and trying to grab at him, while groaning, "Help…me…" The zombie-like being looked familiar to Nico, but years of layering mortician's makeup, in an effort to preserve her looks and hide decay, resulted in a mottled and even disfigured appearance. A blonde wig, to mimic her hair from years gone by, was now matted and slightly askew from her having been in bed for so long.

Then it all made sense to Nico. *This must be Mrs. Cadaveri! She was bedridden for so many years and must have died at some point. I'll bet Mr. Cadaveri preserved her body and eventually found a way to reanimate her. She must think I am him. Dear God, I need to get out of here!*

Nico turned and left the room, shutting the door behind him and calling out "*Sero*," locking the door so that Mrs. Cadaveri could not escape. He checked his watch and noted that forty minutes had already gone by, and he'd only have a little over an hour left before the sleeping potion wore off. He hastily shuffled down the stairs to the main level and then made a left to the take the stairs leading down to the lower level.

He paused and once again pulled out the paper Sofia had given him to check what was awaiting him on the lower level. *OK, cremation room, morgue, and embalming room—got it*. He folded the paper up and put it back into his breast pocket.

Grabbing the cold metal handrail, Nico slowly descended the staircase until he reached the place he was dreading. A heavy mustiness in the air mixed with the faint chemical smell of formaldehyde assaulted his senses as he stepped off the final stair into the dim area; the only lighting came from Nico's dancing light spell, which thankfully followed him from the second floor. This area felt damp, which caused it to be much cooler than the other floors of the mortuary; the ideal place for storing the bodies of the recently deceased.

Nico looked around. Behind him was a long dark hallway with doors on either side that led to a closed door at its end. He was about to assume that the floor plan matched that of the level above, until he noticed that opposite the hallway, there was only one door to the right of the landing and not one on his left, like upstairs.

The hallway must connect to the rooms, so I guess I will make a loop like I did upstairs. And with that he entered the doorway on his right.

This was the cremation room. Across from him, three original brick ovens, framed in iron, lined the long wall of the room, their doors open and ready. Curiosity grabbed hold of Nico as he passed by the ovens, and he peered his head into the last one. A backdraft, caused by the heavy winds outside, blew some remaining cremains onto Nico's face. He immediately pulled his head back and coughed while rapidly wiping his face off with his hands. *Eww! I guess this would explain the three chimneys along the side of the building! I always wondered what they were for.*

Other than a lonely gurney and two large tables, this room didn't seem to have much more to it. Nico pressed onward and opened the door at the end of the room.

This room was large and seemed to mimic the size and space of the chapel above it. What appeared to be a large chute across the room faced him. *I must be in the morgue, and this is where they slide the bodies down from the back parking lot.* To the right and left of the body chute were antique cold lockers framed in wood; three on each side. A light humming noise emitted from them and became louder as Nico approached.

"Hello. Fawn, are you in here?" Nico called out in a light voice.

He heard no response. He decided to investigate this room further and began to open the locker doors. The three on the left that he opened, were empty. *That's a good sign.* He continued to the other set, and as he unlatched the sixth locker door, he found it decidedly not empty. He slowly slid the stainless-steel tray out into the dim light. The body was covered with a white cloth that had soaked up blood in various locations. A faint scent of decay emitted from the chilled body as Nico pull down its shroud.

Nico immediately pushed the tray back into the locker, slammed the door closed, and backed away from the horror he had just seen, a sight which he would not soon forget. *How horrible!* He tried to clear his mind of the image of a petite female body which had been dissected. It was missing various parts; wings, having been torn from its back, were placed haphazardly on her chest. Nico deduced that it was one of the missing Fey girls, from possibly a month or two ago.

Tears of sadness began to well up in his eyes as he turned away from the wall of refrigerated lockers. "There's nothing I can do for her—I have to move on," he spoke quietly, trying to reassure himself. He looked around and spotted two closed doors, left of the one he used to enter the morgue. *The center door must lead to the hallway, which means the door in the left corner should lead to the final room, the embalming room.*

Nico walked up to the door, reluctantly turned the handle, and pulled the door open. As he entered the room, he first noticed two porcelain embalming tables in the middle of the room. Pendant lights hung over both tables. The tiled floor had a slight slant from each side, which led to a drainage grate in the center of the room.

Four windowed supply cabinets lined the walls on either side of him, each flanking a long counter with a deep sink in the center. Both sides of the room seemed to be mirror images of each other. As he passed by the cabinets, he noticed that some of them were filled with jugs and glass jars of various chemicals, mostly formaldehyde. Other cabinets contained linens, towels, and gloves. But it was the far wall that caught his eye. It was made of stone and two bookshelves were bolted onto it. On display were a selection of antique embalming tools, each labeled and enclosed in its own glass frame. To Nico these items looked more like medieval torture devices.

But something did not sit right with Nico. *This room seems smaller than the cremation room*, he reasoned. *There must be more to it*. He approached the stone wall and noticed a small, framed picture tucked in amongst the other items. He hadn't noticed it earlier. *Wow, that must be*

Mrs. Cadaveri when she was young and still alive. She was quite a looker in her day—a far cry from what now remains of her upstairs. As he reached for the frame to take a closer look, his arm hit the corner of one of the larger displayed instruments and sent it crashing to the floor with a loud clanging sound. *Crap, I hope no one heard that.* But maybe someone or something did: he thought he heard the muffled sound of someone moaning.

Nico assumed it must have been his imagination, coupled with the lingering experience from the other room, that caused him to hear things. Once again he reached for the framed picture of Mrs. Cadaveri, but it seemed attached to the shelf. Using both hands he tried to lift it up but failed to do so. In his efforts, he noticed that the frame did appear to be able to swivel, and so he turned the frame to the left as far as it would go, which was about ninety degrees. He heard a rumbling sound as the middle section of shelves began to open into another room.

"I knew it! A false wall—that explains everything!" He said with excitement. "Obviously this section was hidden for a reason—now to find out why."

The disembodied sound of muffled moaning returned once again as Nico stepped into the secret room. It was Fawn. She was gagged and bound to one of two stainless-steel embalming tables. Nico ran up to her and removed the dirty rag that had been secured over her mouth.

A look of terror could be seen in her eyes. Nico realized that she thought he was Mr. Cadaveri.

"Fawn it is me, Nico!" he said trying to alleviate her fear.

"You found me!" Fawn shouted with joy. Nico began untying the ropes which had held her to the table for the past twenty-four hours. "I didn't think anyone would find me in time! He's…."

Freed from her bonds, she stopped speaking and wrapped her arms tightly around Nico.

"You need to get out of here," Nico demanded. "The potion you made worked like a charm but is going to wear off soon. Quickly, go to your father, he is worried sick about you. I'll follow shortly. I still need to search this area for clues about my nonna's death—I have a feeling everything is somehow connected."

Without delay, Fawn bolted out of the room; Nico stood quietly, listening to make sure that she was able to leave the building safely. After hearing the sound of the front door slam shut, he felt better knowing that she was now free.

Nico looked around the room for the first time. He hadn't paid much attention earlier to his surroundings since he was intently focused on releasing Fawn. The room appeared to be a laboratory of sorts; it reminded him of the painting of the alchemist from his basement.

A wall of glass-paned cabinets lined the leftmost wall, and each filled with an assortment of herbs and other mystical ingredients. Near the cabinetry was a worktable with numerous beakers and test tubes, each filled with different colorful liquids; Bunsen burners heated a few of them, causing them to bubble. Along the back wall, a large bookcase contained rows and rows of dusty leather-bound tomes; some side by side, others stacked. A beautifully carved mahogany work desk was along the wall to the right; an ebony framed mirror hung on the wall behind it. On the desk, three open scroll cases lay on their sides near a large, open book. To the right of the book was small golden cage whose bars glimmered in the low lighting.

Nico walked over to the desk and was about to examine the open book, when he noticed movement from within the cage. He knelt to view it at eye level and was amazed as to what it contained.

This must be some kind of dark magic, he thought. *If I'm right, this is a homunculus.* And that it was. A small, winged construct made of human flesh, a little over a foot tall, gripping the bars of its gilded prison. Nico reached his finger out toward its tiny hand, unsure of how it would react. Surprisingly, instead of doing something violent, like biting Nico, it gently held onto Nico's finger, like a baby might do. Feeling empathy for the caged being, Nico unlatched the lid of the cage and opened it. The homunculus peered its head out and looked up at Nico. A smile appeared on its distorted face, as if to show appreciation for being released. It quickly exited the cage, and ran across the desk, jumping off toward a dark corner of the room.

Nico directed his attention to the open book. The page was titled: *Chapter 13—Beyond Resurrection: Restoring the Dead.* Nico lifted the book's left side and partially closed it so that he could view its cover, which read: *Necromancy & Other Dark Arts*.

Of course! This explains how that raven came back to life after being killed—Mr. Cadaveri must've used this type of dark magic to resurrect it, Nico thought.

His curiosity now piqued, Nico sat down and began perusing the tome's dark contents. He was suddenly interrupted by a spider, about the diameter of a half-dollar, that skittered across his arm, darted across the empty scroll cases, and climbed onto the mirror's frame. Nico noticed that the spider immediately began stringing webs back and forth across the frame.

Knowing that his time was running short, Nico tried to return his focus to the book, but another spider unexpectedly ran across his arm and joined the other. They worked in tandem to construct a beautiful web that reflected in the mirror.

Nico lowered his head and began reading out excerpts of the book's current chapter as he skimmed through it.

"Decomposition of a resurrected corpse may be stopped, and even reversed, if one is fortunate enough to obtain four rare ingredients and combine them with a previously prepared pine resin and aloe vera-based embalming ointment. All ingredients must be combined under the light of a full moon while at its highest point. This resulting, crimson-colored ointment needs to be applied to the corpse in question during darkness of the following new moon.

Ingredients Needed:
1 of Charon's Obols
1 Ever-burning ember stolen from an efreet.
4 Tears collected from a terrified child.
1 Vial of blood from a freshly killed fairy."

The sound of a door slamming shut from somewhere upstairs jarred Nico from his reading, and he froze in place. He quietly listened, holding his breath, to see if he could tell which area of the large home the sound had come from. After a few minutes of stillness and no further sounds, he turned his head and scanned the room. Seeing nothing out of sorts, he chalked off the event as having been a product of the evening's high winds. *It must have been a strong draft that caused a door to slam—yeah that must be it*, he thought, trying to reassure himself.

He turned back to his reading material, but not before he noticed the two active spiders and the web that they had created. He stood up to view the intricate silken masterpiece. As Nico peered closer, he began to make out words written throughout the web. And just as he read the words, "*He's coming,*" he felt a sharp blow to the back of his head and fell forward onto the desk.

***

"Stop it!" Sofia said, half giggling as Solomon was poking her back. "We're supposed to be at the window watching for Mr. Cadaveri."

"I know, but I can't seem to resist your beauty and charm," Solomon replied and flashed his perfect smile at her.

Tap tap.

"What was that?" Sofia asked.

"I'm not sure," Solomon answered.

Tap tap.

"It's getting louder and seems to be coming from one of the windows."

Sofia ran toward the location of the noise and pulled up the blinds. She shrieked upon seeing the milky white eyes of Simone, the large, now undead, raven, staring at her. It frantically continued tapping faster.

"Look Sofia! Mr. Cadaveri's car is back—he must've come back early!"

"Oh, no! Nico is still there and has no idea that he's returned," Sofia replied in a panic. "OK, you try to contact Sterling; he'll know what to do. I need to get over there and try to warn Nico before he's found."

Sofia quickly ran out of the store and hurried to the corner. As she stood there anxiously waiting for the traffic light to change, the raven, which she now realized had been trying to befriend her all this time, hovered by her, and guided her across the street when it was safe to do so.

The wind began to pick up as she approached the mortuary's front door, and its cold air penetrated her sweater, chilling her to the bone. Without giving it a thought, she barged right in. The guardian raven flew ahead of her, landing on the banister of the stairs leading down.

Clever! The bird obviously knows something and is trying to help, she concluded while following its lead. The raven slowly glided down the stairway to the darkened landing and then to the right, where a roaring sound could be heard. Sofia quietly followed and entered the cremation room, where the light had been turned on and one of the ovens had been ignited. As she passed by it, its warmth did nothing to lessen the chill Sofia felt; her intuition told her it had been lit for some nefarious purpose.

The raven took off, flying further onward. Sofia hastened her step to catch up to it. As she entered the mortuary area, she barely paid attention to the rows of cold storage before her. Knowing that time was of the essence, she followed the raven around the corner and into the embalming room.

Upon entering the room, she noticed that the raven had landed on some bookshelves located at the opposite end of the dimly lit room. *I must be getting close*, she thought. *There can't be many more places down here to explore.* Standing there motionless, she listened for any signs of movement that might reveal Nico's whereabouts—but heard nothing. She ventured forward to where the raven had perched and noticed that the bookshelves opened into a hidden room. She looked up at the raven who was now bobbing its head up and down, as if to acknowledge that that was the direction to go.

Stepping into the new area, Sofia was surprised to find Mr. Cadaveri strapped down to one of the two stainless-steel embalming tables in the room. "Nico, where are you?" She called out as she approached the body lying motionless on the table. As she drew closer, the form blurred and became nondescript before changing into Nico. The glamour spell had just worn off, and she realized Nico was the one lying there before her. He was gagged and unconscious, his arms partially dangling down from each side of the table.

"Oh, Nico, I should've never let you go in here alone—I'm so sorry!" As she desperately tried to untie his restraints, a hand came from behind her and forcefully held a moist cloth over her nose and mouth. The more she struggled to free herself, the more she found herself inhaling the toxic fumes from the cloth. Within a short time, she found herself losing consciousness.

***

Sofia regained consciousness sometime later when she felt something tapping the side of her head. She slowly opened her eyes and recognized the shiny black feathers of Simone, who was sitting near her head; it had been gently nudging her, attempting to wake her from her sleep. She looked around and realized she was strapped to one of the cold metal tables like Nico, who was still unconscious and close beside her.

The raven, realizing that Sofia was now awake, hopped down the table and began unbuckling her wrist straps with its beak.

Unable to sit up, Sofia scanned the room, trying to assess the situation. She saw what she assumed was Mr. Cadaveri in a dark corner. He was holding a gold cage in his left hand and reaching into the shadows aggressively trying to grab at something with his right hand.

She turned and whispered to Nico, "Psst! Nico. Nico, wake up."

Just as she finished speaking her last word, the figure in the corner turned around, prompting the raven to make a deep, rasping, warning noise before flying off and landing atop a nearby bookcase.

"Ah, my dear, you are awake," The figure spoke as it approached from the shadows. It was Mr. Cadaveri.

"Why are you doing this? What do you want from us?" Sofia asked fearlessly.

"You nosy kids," Mr. Cadaveri responded. "Had you just minded your own business, you could have expected to live a much longer life. But now you know too much, and I must dispose of you."

"But we don't know anything," Sofia bluffed. "Honestly!"

"The fact that you are here leads me to believe you know something, and therefore that makes the two of you an extreme liability." Mr. Cadaveri snapped back. "I can't have any more disruptions to my work when I am so close to finding an answer. Chiara Frantoio figured out early on what I was up to and was going to report me to the town council. But I put a stop to her before she could reveal my secrets—just as I will do to the two of you!"

Sofia heard Nico let out a moan before going silent again. She tried to stall further while scanning the room for something that might help them out of their current situation.

"What are you going to do to us?" she asked and then noticed something moving about in the corner of the room. *Mr. Cadaveri must have been trying to capture it earlier. But how can something so small be of help? I must think of something, fast!*

"Let's just say, where the two of you are going next, you'll never be cold again!" he said, ending with a devilish laugh.

Sofia found herself focusing on the homunculus, which was slowly coming out from the safety of the shadows, when an idea popped into her head. She recalled one of the Malandanti spells from their study cards and reached out and grabbed Nico's hand. With her other hand, she reached back to Mr. Cadaveri, who was at the head of Sofia's table and about to wheel her to the cremation room, and gripped his wrist. With hope and determination in her voice, she cried out, "*Adtenuo*!"

"What have you done!" Mr. Cadaveri cried out as his hand slipped free from Sofia's grip. Sofia tried to turn her head back to view her target but could only see from her periphery. The 'Shrink Object' spell was working, and Mr. Cadaveri was now growing smaller and smaller in size.

Seeing an opportunity to continue helping, the raven returned to Sofia, landing on her chest. It gave a brief look into her eyes and nodded its head before turning around. Using its beak, it unbuckled the chest strap, allowing Sofia the freedom to unbuckle the rest of the straps, freeing herself.

Sofia jumped off the table, almost stepping on Mr. Cadaveri, who was now about a foot tall and cowering on the ground. Afraid of being almost stepped on again, he ran off toward his desk where his spell books were located.

Sofia began unbuckling Nico, who was now regaining consciousness and began to speak. "Sofia, is that you?" He asked, his vision blurred from the previous blow to his head.

"Yes, it's me, Nico. You're safe. We're safe," she replied. "But we need to get out of here before my spell wears off."

"Your spell?" Nico replied with confusion.

"I'll explain later. We must hurry," Sofia replied, slightly frantic.

Nico sat up and Sofia helped him off the table to make sure he didn't fall.

"OK, I think I've got my bearings," Nico said and then stumbled a bit.

"Here…" Sofia said, and she grabbed Nico's arm. "Put your arm around me and I'll help you keep your balance."

As they began to leave the secret room, a diminutive sound of agony could be heard. Nico and Sofia quickly turned around toward the location of the sound; it was the darkened corner of the room. They slowly approached the area.

Nico reached into his pocket and pulled out another piece of the dead fern. He crumbled it and threw the pieces into the air while calling out, "*Lux Saltatio*!" Sofia watched as the pieces of dead plant matter ignited and danced about the air.

To their horror, Mr. Cadaveri's arm had just been ripped off by the vengeful homunculus. As a tiny pool of blood began to form around its victim's feet, the winged construct continued its mission of destruction and pulled off Mr. Cadaveri's remaining arm.

"It must have learned from watching all of the terrible things that were done here to the abducted Fey. It pulled the arms right off as if they were wings," Nico explained.

"We should stop it, shouldn't we?" Sofia asked.

"No! He killed my nonna!" Nico snapped back. "I was drifting in and out of consciousness and I heard him tell you. He is deserving of this and more, but there's something I can do to end his deserved suffering." And with that, Nico called out to the homunculus, "Hey, little buddy."

The creature stopped and looked up at Nico with its oversized eyes and appeared to be listening. Nico pointed to his own head and then turned to Sofia and warned her, "You may want to turn away—this isn't going to be pleasant."

The homunculus thought for a second and then comprehended what his rescuer had requested. It grabbed Mr. Cadaveri by the head and snapped his neck, putting an end to the ongoing agony and suffering.

Nico and Sofia turned to leave. They could hear a faint chomping sound and assumed that the famished creature was making a much-needed meal out of its previous captor. They moved as quickly as they could to the upper level and out of the building into the cold night air.

The full moon shone brightly this evening. The previous high winds had blown away any trace of clouds that could pass in front of it. It seemed to light a perfect pathway leading back to the store where Solomon was anxiously awaiting by the door.

As Solomon noticed them approaching, he rushed out and helped Sofia bring Nico inside and over to a chair where he could sit down.

"I was so worried about you two. What happened?" Solomon asked.

"It's a long story, but I found Fawn—and she's OK. She got out," Nico replied.

"Fawn was there?" Sofia asked.

"Yes. Mr. Cadaveri, as we thought, was the one abducting all the Fey. He was performing experiments on them, using their blood for necromantic rituals, which had to be performed during certain cycles of the moon," Nico explained.

"I am so glad she's OK," Sofia and Solomon said in unison.

"Me too." Nico agreed. "Sofia, remember when I mentioned about Dino and Gino's mother and how she was a very sick woman—completely bedridden. And how I had never seen her?"

"Yeah," Sofia responded.

"Well, I finally met her!" Nico said and then paused before continuing. "Met what's left of her, I should say."

"What do you mean?" Solomon asked.

"She was a resurrected corpse! Mr. Cadaveri had used necromancy at some point to revive her but wasn't able to stop the decaying process. No amount of makeup could return her to her former, youthful self. He must have begun to find a method of slowing things down, since her brain was somewhat functional."

"That must be what he was talking about before he was about to wheel me off to be cremated. He said he was 'so close to finding the answer.'"

"Yes," Nico responded. "Wait—did you say *cremate* you?"

"Yep!" Sofia said assuredly. "He was going to burn us alive in the furnace, so there'd be no trace of us for anyone to find."

"Wow! I really owe you a debt of gratitude for saving us with your quick thinking," Nico said.

"What did you do, Sofia?" Solomon asked, his curiosity eating at him.

"It just came to me when I saw that creature which was roaming about—the homunculus. I was staring at it, and I thought, how could something so small, be a threat. Then I remembered the 'Shrink Object' spell from our study cards—I also remembered the time we first looked at the grimoire and I was able to see the writing when my elbow touched you. I figured if I could see magic when I touched you, then maybe I could cast it as well. And thankfully it worked, or we'd be ashes by now," Sofia explained.

"Amazing job!" Nico said. He turned to Solomon with a smile. "She's one smart girl, so watch out!"

"That I am!" Sofia said, blushing. "We should get back to the house—I think we need to rest up, and besides, we're supposed to fly back tomorrow!"

"I totally forgot!" Nico sighed. "Kind of a bummer. I was just getting the hang of all this magical stuff."

"Solomon, do you mind giving us a ride to Nico's home?" Sofia asked.

Nico walked back to the dressing room to change back into his clothes. As he removed his disguise garments, he once again admired his griffon tattoo in the mirror and noticed some bruising on his inner arm. Upon further inspection, he saw a drop of dried blood and realized there was a puncture mark in the center of the bruise. *Did Mr. Cadaveri take some of my blood while I was unconscious? No need to worry now, I guess, since that horrible man is gone for good.*

Nico put the rest of his garments back on and gathered up the clothing he had worn. He returned to Sofia and Solomon who were in the middle of having a moment.

"Ahem!" Nico blurted as he approached, causing the two lovebirds to pull apart from their mini make-out session.

Solomon turned to Nico. "Sorry about that." And he took the clothing from Nico.

"Ah, no biggie," Nico replied and looked over at Sofia. "I'm happy for her—she deserves all the happiness in the world, and more!"

Still a bit embarrassed that Nico caught her in the middle of kissing Solomon, she suggested, "We should get going—oh, Solomon, would you please do us a favor and return Geoffrey's glamour towel to him? Although I'm not sure if he'd have any use for it now that Mr. Cadaveri is dead."

"Sure thing," Solomon replied.

Nico and Sofia waited outside the store while Solomon turned off the lights and locked the door.

"Come with me, my car is just over there."

When they arrived at the Frantoio house, Nico, completely exhausted, exited the car immediately. He mumbled a quick goodbye to Solomon and headed toward the front door, which unlocked and opened for him as he approached. Sofia, on the other hand, remained in the car to offer a more personal goodbye, knowing that she might not see Solomon again for a while.

By the time Sofia entered the house, Nico had already gone to his bedroom and passed out from exhaustion. Sofia went to take a quick peek into his room to say goodnight and make sure he was OK, but decided not to disturb him. The lamp on his nightstand had been left on and next to it was a folded piece of paper with the Coin of Favor that Nico had taken with him from the bank, placed on top. Nico was lying sideways on his bed all banged up and disheveled, but somehow his face displayed a sense of peace. She was truly grateful that her best friend was still alive.

Sofia suddenly smelled the apple-like fragrance of chamomile tea coming from another room in the house. She followed the scent into the kitchen where the house had prepared a steaming pot of tea for her, along with a jar of honey, her favorite nighttime duo. She was amazed that the house actually seemed to have gotten to know her during her stay and knew just what she needed to take the edge off so she could sleep.

Sofia put a drizzle of honey into her tea and stirred it gently until it was fully dissolved. She took a sip; *just right*, she thought. She brought the remainder to her bedroom, and shortly after finishing her tea, she was sound asleep.

Chapter 25: Break Over, Back to School

The next morning Nico was awakened not only by the bright sun illuminating his room, but by the sound of hammering in the backyard. Still half asleep, he made his way to Sofia's room.

"Sofia, are you awake?" Nico whispered from the doorway.

"Yes, thanks to that noise," Sofia answered, slightly irritated at being disturbed at such an early hour. "Is that hammering I hear?"

"I think it is. It's coming from outside my room, but I wanted to check on you before I checked on *it*," Nico replied.

"Don't tell me that after last night, you're afraid?" She joked.

"Uh, no! Of course not. But if something happens, I might need you there to rescue me again," Nico said, smiling back at her.

They both ran off to Nico's room and carefully opened the French doors to see what was going on outside.

Nico was surprised to see two familiar faces looking back at him. "Sterling. Fawn. What are you two doing here?"

"Sorry to disturb you so early, but we wanted to surprise you and needed the gnomes' help—they only like working in the early morning hours when people are not about," Sterling answered. "Now come outside, you two!"

Nico and Sofia stepped outside and saw Sterling, Fawn, and the gnomes standing together in front of one of the old orange trees. Even Simone, the undead raven, was in attendance and made himself known by letting out a loud *kraa-kraa* from where he was perched.

"Hey Sofia," Fawn called out. "Long time, no see."

Sofia ran up to Fawn and gave her a big hug. "I'm glad you're OK. We were so worried about you!"

"Well, thanks to you two, my daughter and the rest of the Fey are safe—we no longer have to live in fear of the Oliveto Abductor," Sterling said.

"Yes, thank you both!" Fawn added. "I saw Solomon earlier this morning and he told me everything—what a nightmare!"

"But what about Dino and Gino? And Mrs. Cadaveri?" Nico asked, somewhat compassionately.

"After I told my father all that I knew from my abduction, along with what I had learned from Solomon—well let's just say that my father and the families of the other missing Fey had an intervention with those three."

"Surely they weren't all involved," Nico said with concern. "I doubt Gino would hurt anyone, and Mrs. Cadaveri was an unwilling participant in all this."

"Interesting that you didn't mention Dino in your statement." Sterling said to Nico. "I think in your subconscious you know that he was involved, but thankfully he did not play a major role."

Nico's desire to know more welled up inside him. "What do you mean?"

"When my father and the others visited the mortuary, they came prepared," Fawn said. "The two boys were each taken into a separate room and truth dust was blown on them. Gino, as you gathered, was innocent of all crimes—he only knew that his dear mother was somehow still alive after all these years but conceded that she was nothing more than a dying husk and should have never been forced to suffer this long.

"Dino, on the other hand, knew that his father was up to something, but he never put it together that Mr. Cadaveri was the Oliveto Abductor all this time. His part in all this was that he helped his father gain access into your nonna's home. He used his great strength to pull the security bars out from the rotting frame of the basement window. Thankfully, he had nothing to do with Chiara's murder—he remained outside the house the entire time."

"And what did you do about Mrs. Cadaveri?" Sofia asked.

"With the assistance of Geoffrey, and his daughter Stevie, we were able to briefly glamour her into a more youthful state so that her two sons could remember her as she once was and say their goodbyes. She died shortly thereafter and was cremated—her soul is now finally free," Sterling explained.

"Enough doom and gloom! Let's get back to why we're here, so that we can show you our appreciation," Fawn interjected.

"Yes," Sterling chimed in and then turned to Nico and looked him directly in the eyes. "My boy, you've done well—you've brought great honor to your family name. You and Sofia have proven yourselves a great asset to the safety and well-being of this community. That being said, we, with the help and participation of your nonna's garden gnomes, would like to offer you these two gifts."

The row of gnomes standing in front of Sterling and Fawn parted; with one group moving to the right and the other to the left, leaving room for Sterling and Fawn to step forward and reveal what was hiding behind them.

Nico and Sofia approached the large orange tree and noticed something new attached to the base of its wide trunk; it was a new fairy door. They squatted down to get a closer view. It wasn't as intricately designed as the others they had seen around town; this one only had a simple monogram carved on it: **NFA**.

"Look, those are your initials," Sofia pointed out. "Nico Alessandro Frantoio!"

"Very nice!" Nico stood up and took a few steps back so that he could look at everyone. "Thank you so much. One question: where does it lead to?"

"Ah my boy, I knew you'd ask," Sterling quickly responded. "It will take you to part two of our gift." And with that, Sterling held out a second small fairy door that he had been hiding behind his back the entire time.

Nico took the gift into his hands and examined it. It was carved from orangewood and had the image of the fountain from the yard and the two orange trees, one on each side.

"The detailing is so realistic—it's almost like a postcard picture from home," Nico said.

Curiosity once again prodded at Sofia. "I thought fairy doors were stationary and could not be moved?"

"This particular one is extra special—it's one of a kind and took additional magic to fashion it," Sterling explained. "Fawn should take most of the credit...."

Fawn immediately jumped into the conversation. "Well, you saved my life, and I'll be forever thankful to you both. I also consider you both two of my dearest new friends. Last night I was already missing you, knowing that you'd be returning to the East Coast today, so I had an idea of making a special fairy door that, wherever you had it with you, you could use to return to your home in Oliveto. You would never have to fly back and forth again! You could use the door to visit us on the weekends. I'm sure Solomon would enjoy that."

Sofia, excited at the thought of possibly returning to see Solomon again, expressed her enthusiasm. "It'd be so nice to return to your lovely town and see you all again—I can't wait!"

"Thank you for these wonderful gifts. I must say, I do miss it here. And now that we have our own place to stay, we can use the two fairy doors to take a break from college life whenever we want," Nico said and then turned to Sofia. "We should really start packing—we still need to stop by my parent's house and say goodbye before heading to the airport."

Sterling and Fawn said their goodbyes and Nico and Sofia went back inside to begin packing their luggage. As Sofia passed through the foyer on the way to her bedroom, she heard the morning paper hit the front door. She decided to retrieve it and immediately noticed the headline: *Missing Girl Found.* She began reading the article to herself and abruptly stopped and let out a loud sigh of frustration.

Nico came running into the room. "Are you all right?" He asked frantically, before noticing she was OK.

"I'm so confused." Sofia snapped. "Look at this!"

Nico took the paper from her hands and immediately said, "It's an article about our heroic deeds. What's not to like about that?"

"Read it, smarty," Sofia replied.

Nico began to skim through the article. A puzzled look washed over his face. "Wait. This isn't what happened. This just says an unnamed girl was found safe after being missing for a period of time; that she had gone for a bicycle ride on a path near the river and lost control, spilling over the embankment and hitting her head on a rock."

"Maybe the local newspaper purposely covers up magical events so as not to stoke fear amongst the non-magical residents?" Sofia reasoned.

"That would make sense." Nico agreed. "At least *we* know the truth and have the satisfaction of knowing that Mr. Cadaveri will never be able to hurt anyone again."

***

Nico and Sofia returned to Hornsby Manor Boarding House later that evening. Their flight had been a pleasant one, most of which was spent dozing in their seats, still exhausted from recent events.

After they both finished unpacking, Sofia joined Nico in his room. She noticed the new fairy door lying on his bed and asked, "So where are you going to put it?"

"I'm not sure yet. I figured I would put it in the back of the closet, so that no one will see or disturb it," Nico answered. "Think that's a good spot?"

"I think so. It'll add an extra layer of protection so that if we're using it and someone happens to be in your room for any reason, we won't just appear in front of them."

***

Nico and Sofia devoted the next two months finishing up the semester and taking their final exams. They were so busy with their studies that they never found the time to return to Oliveto, like they had hoped to. Sofia did keep in touch with Solomon though, and their evening phone calls to each other would sometimes last late into the night.

One late afternoon after taking her last test of the semester, Sofia came into Nico's room and plopped down on his bed beside him. Nico had been listening to music through his headphones and didn't notice her enter the room, until she was on the bed. Startled, he jumped up.

"You scared me!" Nico said.

"Wow, why are you so jumpy?" Sofia asked. "Too much caffeine?"

"No. I've been having this eerie feeling, like something is off," Nico said in a low voice.

Knock, knock.

"Is that someone at your door?" Sofia asked. "Does anyone, other than me, even visit your room?"

"No, never. Would you please see who it is?" Nico asked.

Sofia got up and walked over to the door. She slowly turned the handle and then opened it quickly. No one was there. She peered out into the hallway and looked both ways, but no one was to be seen.

"That's odd...." Sofia remarked. Then they heard the sound again.

Knock, knock.

"It must be coming from inside the room—maybe the plumbing in the walls," Nico said.

"No, it sounds like it's coming from inside the closet!" Sofia said.

Nico bolted from the bed to check it out. Sofia ran over to Nico's nightstand and took a dead leaf from an ivy plant she had given him. Running over to the dark closet, she put her left hand on Nico's shoulder and then crumpled the dead leaf in her right hand. She threw its pieces forward while invoking the magic words, "*Lux Saltatio*!"

The dancing lights illuminated the area and hovered over the source of the knocking noise; it was the small orangewood fairy door, which was propped against the back of the closet and lightly covered in dust.

"Apparently something is calling upon us to return," Sofia reasoned.

"Indeed, my friend," Nico replied. "Are you ready to see what new adventure awaits?"

Printed in Great Britain
by Amazon

35140188R00169